Whoever it was, he pas.... and shoulders without touching; sne 1e... tween his hands and her skin. Without wanting to, she began crying....

A humid hand grazed the edge of her cheeks, catching the tears. Then she realized it was not a hand at all. *He's licking my face.* She tried to think of it as a hand, a warm, moist, rough hand, not a tongue, not a tongue, because she was going to throw up if it was a tongue, and if she pressed down on her missing eye hard enough she could make it into a hand in her mind, not a tongue. The man said, "You're the one. You're like the deformed one, ain'tcha? Only your deformity's on the inside. I can smell it." And then, even closer to her, near her right ear, the breath of some animal, and Monkey's voice, "I want to play with her...."

She felt his rough finger dip beneath the rag that covered her eyes, and then a pressure as he pushed her glass eye, and it was like a millipede crawling along the eyelid, trying to insinuate itself between her skin and the glass eye. "You promised we could play with her, you promised."

Books by Douglas Clegg

Breeder
Dark of the Eye
Goat Dance
Neverland

Published by POCKET BOOKS

dark of the eye

DOUGLAS CLEGG

POCKET **STAR** BOOKS

New York   London   Toronto   Sydney   Tokyo   Singapore

This book is a work of fiction. Names, characters, places and incidents are products of the author's imagination or are used fictitiously. Any resemblance to actual events or locales or persons, living or dead, is entirely coincidental.

An *Original* Publication of POCKET BOOKS

A Pocket Star Book published by
POCKET BOOKS, a division of Simon & Schuster Inc.
1230 Avenue of the Americas, New York, NY 10020

ISBN: 0-671-73539-X

First Pocket Books printing August 1994

10 9 8 7 6 5 4 3 2 1

POCKET STAR BOOKS and colophon are registered trademarks of Simon & Schuster Inc.

Cover art and design by David Stevenson

Printed in the U.S.A.

For Raul Silva and Charlotte Clegg

Acknowledgments

With thanks to Dean Koontz, Jude Devereaux, Julie Garwood, Richard Laymon, Harlan Ellison, Elizabeth Engstrom, Chelsea Quinn Yarbro, Nancy Holder, Poppy Brite, Claudia O'Keefe, Robert Masello, Ellen Datlow, Stefan D., Chris Curry, Alan Rodgers, Jim Paine, Dan Pollock, Rick Hautala, and Rick McCammon for being the best advisers in the world. Thanks to the Stonington Literary Grant for the place to write, and to the Charleston Writer's Award Membership for the means. Thanks also to Pocket Books for the six years together, and to Linda Marrow and Meg Ruley, who saw me through it and put out a lot of fires on my behalf.

One final thank-you to Tracy Farrell, who set me on this wonderful and accursed sea.

Who knows what evil lurks in the hearts of men?

—from the radio show *The Shadow*

But oh, the den of wild things in
The darkness of her eyes!

—from "The Gypsy Girl," by Ralph Hodgson

PROLOGUE

The First Death

1

November 2
2:15 P.M.

HE HAD NEVER KILLED A CHILD BEFORE.

Picture her dead. Already dead. Her face crushed. Life gone. No life. No live grenade. Put out of her misery. Picture death. Peace.

The man named Stephen Grace could smell death here in the room. It was a small bedroom, and something about the wallpaper reminded him of a prison. Only stripes, and candy stripes at that. He had been in a cage once, and he had been in prison many years before. But something about this room—perhaps the knowledge of what he must do—colored his perception, made everything in it seem ominous. The baby doll on the shelf; the brass lamp shaped like a horse; the child-sized French Provincial dressing table. Stuffed full of toys and games—the mother was a pack rat, that's what he'd been told. A pack rat and a manic-depressive, a pill-popper and a slob. So she had stuffed her daughter's room with childhood things. Wall-to-wall family photographs—Madonna and child, baby's first steps, first Christmas, baptism, first day of school, third grade picture. Only a few of the pictures had Daddy in them.

Only one photo of Daddy with child that was even in focus. Daddy had his horn-rims on and his dark hair slicked back and to the side, quite rakish and yuppie-looking, with that upper-class East Coast smirk like photographs were a joke. The girl—pretty, dark hair, squinty eyes from a smile too big for her face. But even with the smile, the girl looked

3

uncomfortable, like she was forcing the look of happiness. *Jesus, what some kids have got to live through.*

But no more misery for this one.

The dry desert smell of death coming through the cracks beneath the window ledge. Coming with him, in his clothes, on his skin. Carried to him.

It was his mind, he knew. It got ahead of him. He rarely visualized success so thoroughly. He could picture her dead. He could picture this place covered with dustcloths. Picture the photographs coming down, the blinds being drawn, the relatives and friends milling around downstairs during the wake, while her mother came up the stairs slowly, remembering when her girl was alive. Coming into this room, listening to the echo of her own footsteps. To the foot of the bed, now a bare mattress, sheets neatly folded at its base. He could picture her mother weeping, holding the doll as if it were her daughter.

He looked over at the girl's face and flinched.

Gauze was taped across the bridge of her nose.

How the hell could he do it? Killing was one thing. But torture. Experiments. Christ.

The mutilation bothered him.

He found the circumstances repulsive. But he had trained himself long ago to suspend judgment in favor of outcome. Outcome was the thing.

Outcome was all.

He did not look at her face again until he had steeled himself.

She was not dead. Not the girl. Not yet. But she would be. He would see to that.

He would visualize her as dead. He would look upon her as a dead girl, and then he could do his job.

"Hope," he said, too loud. But it didn't matter. No one else would come.

He saw the flat merciless sunlight through the window, and wondered what godforsaken act had brought him to this place of death. He had smelled it before, in jungles, in men, sometimes in women, but never in girls. None this young. None this innocent-looking. But, he told himself, she smelled now of death.

She looked up and he hoped she couldn't see him. She

wasn't supposed to see him. She was supposed to be out. Completely out. She could hear him, but it would be some kind of fantasy, some half-dream she was having. Hell, she'd probably O.D. on whatever she'd been injected with. She didn't know him, so she wouldn't be able to identify him. It was hard for him to trust this scenario; it seemed so out of control. He had never enjoyed the kinds of assignments he got. They made him feel like a Mafia hit man, and he was anything but. There'd been only four since he'd come back from Southeast Asia. Only four, and this would be the fifth. He wanted out soon. They promised it. Of those he had done before, all were deserved. All were threats in greater ways than anyone could ever realize. He could smell death around them. They were contagious with it. They were spreading. They were Hitlers in the making, they were monsters who would send darkness across the land, they would infect others with their madness. The harbingers of Armageddon, of human putrefaction.

Like this girl.

Long dark hair, sunburned skin, lips half curled in a sphinx smile. Her face almost triangular, her chin willful in its jutting. Like a challenge. At another time he would see a girl like this and wonder why he never settled down to have children of his own, why that part of life had escaped him. But this girl was different. She was beyond human difference.

Not a girl, he told himself, but a live grenade. Whoever pulled the pin on this one should be given a dose of what she carried.

Live grenade.

"Hello," she murmured, drugged up and giggling softly.

A beautiful child like this, pumped up with the kind of shit he'd seen only street addicts do. Where was her mother? Jesus, it made him sick, and he thought he would get the hell out of there while he still had a shadow of conscience.

But it was his conscience that did him in. The old Jiminy Cricket. Animal and man separated by that one thing that man so often put aside to do the unnatural thing. Conscience.

She must die.

All because she was a live grenade.

He smiled at her. He prayed it would be quick. He prayed that she would feel little or no pain. He hated himself for this and knew he was destined for hell, if there was one. If not, at least hell on earth until he too smelled like death.

"Hello," he replied, thinking she looked like a damned angel and the world was filth if an innocent life could come to this, this death smell.

"Are we going somewhere? With the butterflies?" Her voice was sleepy, and he knew that she was still in some dream. He hoped it was a good one.

"Sure," he said. "You want to go for a ride?"

2:30 P.M.

Hope Stewart could not remember exactly why she felt so happy and sick, all at the same time, although she found, as she slid into the passenger seat of the Mercedes, that the man she thought was her father seemed a little sick too. She knew, on some level, that this was her father taking her to do some errands, but when she glanced at his face it didn't quite seem right. Her friend Missy Hafner at school bragged that she had gotten drunk once, and told of how the world spun and how no one looked the same. She never before believed that Missy was ever really drunk, but now she was beginning to see that it was possible. She watched her father's face shiver into a mask of another man, and then back into the form of her father.

"Daddy?" she asked. "Dad?" She was aware that even that simple word seemed to expand and stretch into an indistinct slurring.

Her father, who was still trying to fasten his seat belt—the ones in the front seat of the Mercedes never worked right, she knew—didn't smile at her the way she expected. She thought he was almost about to cry, so she said something, like "Don't cry," or "It'll be all right, don't worry."

He looked away from her, out the windshield. "I'm sorry," he said.

She didn't know what he was sorry about, and for a moment she thought she was going to throw up. Then she said, "It's okay."

"It's better like this."

"Yeah," she said. Something like a train seemed to hit the back of her head, and she couldn't even take a breath. A memory came at her full force as she tried to inhale: *Denny in his crib, crying, his small pink hands stretched out to her. Above his head, the mobile with the clouds and seagulls turned and twisted. Hope leaned over, into the crib, to tickle his stomach, to try to get him to stop crying. "You're my little brother," she told him. "I'll protect you, don't worry. Mommy's gonna be all right. Don't cry, baby, don't cry."*

And then, as she watched, the baby's skin began to crumple in on itself like rotten fruit, tearing at invisible seams, and beneath it something emerged, like a moth from a cocoon.

Like a worm from an apple.

It was the baby's spinal cord, wriggling like a live electrical wire doused in water, spitting sparks across her vision.

The whip of cord shot out from the sputtering flesh as it fell, and wrapped itself around her neck, digging into her skin.

Hope caught her breath. She tried to lean forward in the front seat, but her shoulder harness chafed against her neck. Her stomach felt weird, like she was going to throw up any second. The man driving the car was beginning to look less and less like her father.

She tried to focus on his face, but something was wrong with the way she was seeing. If she closed one eye, she couldn't see at all. And when she kept the other eye open, she thought the man was crying, even though he didn't seem to be doing anything other than driving her someplace.

"Where are we going?" she asked.

The man said, "Someplace safe."

"Why?"

"Because."

"Are you my daddy?"

The man said nothing.

"I want my daddy."

The man looked across at her for a second. He was definitely not crying, even though his eyes crinkled at the corners like he was about to cry. He whispered, "No, you don't."

And then she dreamed, without closing her eyes, that she

was in a small dark room, like a closet, and something was beating at the door.

She moved to open the door, and as she did, all kinds of light and colors swirled around her.

"Butterflies," she said as the dream faded and the man gripped the steering wheel more tightly.

The man said, "What the hell kind of world. Christ."

She thought he was reaching into his pocket for gum, which was what her father always did when he drove. She glanced up at his face. Maybe he was her father, after all. When she looked down at his hand again, she saw a small box. It looked like the remote control of their VCR. Why would Daddy bring that in the car with them? She giggled, wondering if he had forgotten to leave the remote at home on top of the TV where it usually went.

"Close your eyes," he said. His voice sounded strange, but this was what her father said whenever he was going to give her a surprise or a gift.

She shut her eyes.

And then her father said, "Goddammit, shit."

And she tried to open her eyes, but the butterflies were beating at the door in the small room, and she was flying out into the air with them, and the Mercedes flew, too, and her father, all of them sprouting wings along their shoulders like angels, like butterflies, all colors and shapes, beating their swirling wings against her skin as they carried her up, up, and up into a brilliant darkness.

And then something cold scraped its fingernails across her face, across her eyes, like slivers of razors burrowing beneath her flesh to dig her bones out.

She saw its eyes.

2

November 3
11:30 A.M.

Letter, postmarked Salinas, California, addressed to Kayt Stuwurt

Dear K,
did u know about him and me? i was his furst. i think maybee your liddel girl is won too. get hur away cuz he gonna make her a spearmint.
Sinseerly,
  Poppy

November 4
10:00 A.M.

DR. ROBERT STEWART LEANED OVER THE HOSPITAL BED; HE looked very tired, and Hope expected him to grab one of the pillows and just conk out. He wore a light gray suit, but the jacket was off, and his shirtsleeves were rolled up. This meant he was working hard—maybe too hard. Her mother had called him a workaholic, but Hope was sure that this was wrong. Her father was just dedicated. He had the right sort of face for a doctor, she thought: it looked kind on the outside, and he had a smile almost like a movie star, only he was losing some of the hair from the front, so he looked more human to her than someone like Mel Gibson ever could. On the inside, his face was serious, and often so smart it scared her. He believed in his work and his science the way that some people believed in Jesus. Her father had been known to contribute to the discovery of cures and vaccines. When he did something, he did it all the way, one hundred percent. But now, with his pen poised and ready to take notes, and a small tape recorder switched on to record, he looked like he was about to keel over. Ever since the car accident, the one that landed her in Saint Vincent's, he had been working feverishly on some project and coming in to talk with her at all hours. Hope thought he might need a nap. She was aware that he had been up all night doing what he called his ramblings. But he had a clipboard in his hands, and she knew that he had one of his silly tests for her to take again. Once she came to, after the car accident two days back, he had asked her so many questions that her head hurt. But she knew that it was his job to ask them.

His eyes looked shiny and black in the harsh light of the bedside lamp, but his voice was gentle. "Do you remember the accident?" He combed the hair back from her face. She felt uncomfortable with him touching so close to her eyes.

Eye, she thought, remembering that she'd lost one in the accident.

She stared at the microcassette recorder and wondered what her voice sounded like on tape. When she thought of the accident, all she remembered were butterflies, rainbow-colored butterflies, but this seemed inexpressible, the beauty of the butterflies, and anyway, whenever she'd tried to tell him in the past forty-eight hours, he had ignored her and kept asking about the specifics of the accident and if she was seeing anything special besides butterflies.

The tape turned around and around, and he asked his question again.

"Pigeon?" He called her by the nickname he'd christened her with back when she was only four and feeding birds on their big trip to New York City. "Can you remember for me again?"

The tape

"Pigeon? Can you remember for me again?"

"Mmm . . ."

"Yes?"

"No. I remember getting in the car. We were going to the store. You told me to buckle my seat belt."

"That's right. What else?"

"The butterflies. All over the place. In my hands. On the glass. My hand hurt. Waking up here."

"Do you know where you are, pigeon?"

"Hospital?"

"Yes. You're mostly fine, you know. You don't even need to be here, not really. They said you flew, like the pigeon you are, and that saved you. Only one place got hurt. The drugs are going to wear off."

"Like Mommy's pills?"

"A little. Feel up here. With your hand. Touch it."

"Hurts."

"Bad?"

"Sore, kinda."

"Do you understand why you can't open it?"

"Mmm . . ."

"You're still beautiful, pigeon. Daddy and Mommy love you very much, and we're happy you're alive. You were very lucky. We're all very lucky. Do you understand?"

"I guess. I thought I was gonna go where Denny went. I thought I was gonna get to play with Denny. 'Member Denny?"

"Yes. I miss him, too."

"Daddy?"

"Yeah, pidge?"

"Where'd my eye go?"

"It's just gone. But it's only an eye. You have another one, so you still can see. It'll just be different. I'll help you, you know that. I'll make sure you learn how to see with only one. And we have some more tests to do, okay? Not like in school. These will be easy for you. It's about what you did with that nice boy who was sick. How you made him better. This morning? Remember? Is that okay?"

"Okay. But I can almost see with it. You know? I almost think I can see with it. The one that got lost."

"Really, pigeon? What kinds of things do you see?"

"Just dark things, like shadows and stuff, and light. Like I'm underground and there's like a little light coming from somewhere. Isn't that weird?"

"Hope Stewart, I have always said you have the wildest imagination in the West. Gonna sleep now?"

"I guess. Is Mommy coming?"

"She said she was. After you sleep. But not yet. I need you to see something. Something that isn't nice, but it's real. I need to know if you see this, in that dark place. . . . Pigeon? Look at this picture they took, and don't be scared. . . . Did it look like this?"

The girl screams softly, as if she has forgotten how to breathe.

PART ONE

Stealing Hope

November 5–7

And what rough beast, its hour come round at last,
Slouches towards Bethlehem to be born?

—William Butler Yeats,
"The Second Coming"

3

Blood Ties

A WOMAN WAS DREAMING THE DREAM OF CALIFORNIA, AS IF it were not a state at all but a memory of brief but intense happiness that existed only for her. She remembered the coastline and a small cottage on the rocks overlooking the Pacific, an ocean like shimmering liquid sapphire, a brilliant sunburst across the green, fragrant hills, and a girl of twenty and a boy of twenty-two in each other's arms. Riding bicycles, making love, exploring tidal pools, holding hands. Youth. Gone, and so early. Youth, and the dream-memory of California.

Not like the desert. Not like this living death on a hot plate. Not like this sterile hospital, this sterile world. The laboratory of Life.

The memory sometimes came to her, overpoweringly, painfully, like a lost battle with the past.

She remembered why she was here.

Today.

This woman with her eyes fixed straight ahead as if she had one thing to accomplish in her life that would matter.

In the grand scheme of things.

This woman with the smooth blond hair, wearing sunglasses and a white blouse tucked into jeans, held on to the small yellow sweater tightly as she walked through the automatic glass doors of the hospital. An orderly passed her and smiled briefly as if he recognized her. But he didn't. *Only flirting,* she thought. One reason she kept such a tight

15

grip on the sweater beneath her right arm was because she was nervous, and all her anxiety seemed to manifest itself in a constant shaking, like the jitters when she went to her psychiatrist for medication. She was able to concentrate on her right arm, and all the shaking went from her body into the right shoulder, traveling down along the elbow to her hand. She would be nervous in her right hand. *Just for now.* The sun was burning up the world outside Saint Vincent's, but inside, here, it was cool, and even the light itself was cool and relaxed. There were chairs in the waiting area, across from the nurses' station. She walked carefully over to the waiting area, telling herself: *pretend you're here just to see your daughter, pretend you're here to wait for someone, pretend you're not going to shoot up the whole damn hospital.*

The other reason that this woman named Kate Stewart hugged the sweater between her nervous right arm and her side was because it was wrapped around a Smith & Wesson.

She had spent the previous night sweating, planning, worrying about the gun. How she would use it. She'd slept—or at least had tried to sleep—in the guest bedroom of the house she and her husband shared. When he looked in on her, as he had this morning, he watched while she took her medication. Kate had not been able to bring herself to look at him, so she turned away, in bed, toward the wall with its blue wallpaper—sailing ships carried about by waves, and dolphins, for a pattern. It had been Denny's room, briefly, and although she could throw out the crib eventually, she could not bring herself to take the wallpaper down. She had faked taking the pills—it had been easy enough to drop them from her hand while still going through the motions of putting the green and red and yellow pills on her tongue and then swallowing dry, followed by a Dixie cup of water. Robert had said nothing while he stood in the doorway.

"All done," she told him, holding up her empty hand for him to see. That morning he had come over to take her pulse and her temperature. He sat on the edge of the bed, and she instinctively pulled away from him.

"It's a terrible shock, Kate," he said, brushing her hair from her face. She still couldn't look at him—just the sight of him made her sick. "You've always been very ... delicate

... your feelings. I understand. I know all the things you've been saying have come out of great pain."

She whispered, "I'm tired, Robert. Tired."

"Sleep'll do you good. I'll have Dr. Jardin come out this afternoon. I'm really no good with this, am I? It hurt me too, baby, what happened to Hope. I love her more than my life."

When he'd said this, she had wanted to lash out and strike him again and again until he was dead. How could he tell her this, gloating over his evil deeds? Like her father. So much like home. *Obscene.*

But she had gotten good at pretending things, ever since the accident. She knew that she didn't have much time.

All she knew was she had to protect Hope.

Whatever the cost.

"It may be hard to believe, sweetheart," her husband said, "but I love both of you very much. I don't want this divorce you keep talking about. I think, with some rest and time, we can reconsider our troubles. Our differences. If we think about what's best for Hope, too. She needs a mother and a father...."

Kate waited until he had left the house that morning. She got up out of bed and went to the front hallway, peering around the edges of the drapes until she had seen him in his Jeep—the Mercedes was still in the shop—driving up the road, out of sight.

Then she went back into the guest bedroom for her overnight bag, already packed. After she took just one Prozac, more for confidence than anything, she opened the door to Robert's downstairs study.

This was where he kept the gun.

He had bought it when some of the neighbors' houses had been broken into, but he had never used it. She doubted that he knew how to use it.

Robert liked the slow kill.

Kate Stewart knew how to use the gun.

Her father had taught her that one useful thing in all her upbringing. Hours of target practice, shooting tin cans, Coca-Cola bottles, clay pigeons. She had never wanted to kill any living thing, in spite of the fact her father had urged her to kill a crow once, and she had refused. Then, later, he made her kill something bigger. A dog: *Don't make me, Daddy, don't make me, I don't want to.*

A human being seemed a much less problematic target than just any living thing.

Especially when it came to protecting her daughter, she thought as she sat in the waiting room at Saint Vincent's.

The nurse at the desk was eating a bologna sandwich, writing in her logbook, and barely paying attention to what Kate was doing. Keeping her face very close to the books. The nurse's name was Lauren Childes. Kate knew a few things about her because she had talked with the nurse when Hope was first admitted to the hospital. Lauren Childes was out of nursing school three years; she'd been at Georgetown, worked at GW Hospital in Washington, D.C., and then moved to Nevada because her husband was transferred, and landed the job at Saint Vincent's eight months before. Lauren Childes had trouble seeing, too, but Lauren had heard about Kate Stewart, probably from the devil himself. Robert no doubt would be interested in seducing this girl. *You think I'm crazy, Lauren? You heard stories about Kate Stewart?* It was not Kate's main concern, not at the moment. She knew she was pale, feverish, even shivering, but she was trying to calm herself without drugs, without chewing her fingernails down. But Lauren Childes, day nurse, would not notice.

Nor would she notice the gun.

Kate watched the nurse, and for a second, the nurse looked up from her logbook and stared straight at her. The nurse didn't recognize her but smiled anyway as if she did, then looked down at her book again, picked up some potato chips from her brown paper bag.

But you'll forget I was here, won't you, Lauren? You've seen me so much in the last couple of days that when anyone asks you, you won't be sure if I was here at exactly noon or if it was two. Or if it was even me. Because you told me something about yourself in the last couple of days. About your glasses, how you hated them and how contacts hurt your eyes. But to do your job sometimes you must wear your glasses. But not when you're just sitting there, around noon, with not much to do other than make sure your log-ins and log-outs jibe. You'll remember that someone was sitting here during lunchtime, but because you nibble throughout the day, you can't say for sure what time when the police question you, or when Robert questions you. You'll know someone was here, but you will wonder about the time, and the time is important. And this someone was just waiting for someone. You didn't need to log her in. She was just waiting. For someone.

Kate had planned it this way, to come in at noon, planned for Lauren Childes, the day nurse in reception, to see her, because Lauren had trouble seeing. And Lauren was too vain to wear the glasses all the time so she could see more than four feet away.

And because Hope had promised yesterday that she would come out to the reception area by 12:15.

If she had to, Kate Stewart was ready to shoot this nurse, Lauren Childes, because as far as she was concerned, they were all on *his* side.

She would do it for Hope.

If she had to.

"Mrs. Stewart," Lauren said.

Kate looked up, feeling as if she'd had the wind knocked out of her.

Lauren Childes had put her glasses on. "I thought it was you. You don't need to sit here. Go on down and see her. She's usually up and running about by this time."

Kate said, barely breathing while she spoke, "Oh, yes, of course. I just thought I'd sit for a second—on my feet all morning."

"Your husband might even be in there already," she said, removing her glasses and scanning down a page. "He was in at eleven—he wanted to check with Dr. Falmouth on Hope's progress. Are you expected?"

Expected? Kate wanted to laugh, wanted to say, "Look, Ms. Childes, I've got a gun here and I'm feeling kind of psycho today, so just fucking get me my daughter. Today I feel like doing the unexpected."

All of her life Kate Stewart had been expected. She had been expected to be a good wife, a good mother, a good daughter, a good student, even a good lay when her husband had requested as much. Under psychoanalysis she'd been a good patient. She had rarely, if ever, done the unexpected. When she met Robert, her husband—soon to be ex, if she had her way—she had done what she could do to live up to his expectations.

"You're crying," he had said, twelve years before, and she could still remember the heat from the palm of his hand against her cheek, catching the tears. They were in a kind of nightclub, what they called, back then, an "underground party." It was dark and fairly quiet, although she could hear music coming from one of the back rooms. She had been waiting for her boyfriend, waiting, really, to break up with him, but he hadn't shown up. So she'd had a drink, not really meaning to, and spent half the night crying to another friend, who wandered off into the smoky crowd, abandoning her. The people, for the most part, seemed to be your garden variety underground-type crowd. Except the man she was talking to. He was dressed conservatively in a dark suit and said that he was in the medical profession somehow, although she couldn't really remember what he told her that he did. He repeated himself: "I said, you're crying."

"I've got a lot to cry about." She had tried to smile then, and put aside her craziness for a good five minutes.

He had eyes that were full of fire and fascination. He listened to her then. He told her that he knew all about her fears. "You're in love with someone," he said, as if reading her mind, "only you don't think it's going anywhere. You think you might just ruin his life."

"Maybe," she'd replied, then, "Yes. Yes. All right."

"Life is full of choices. Door number one or number two. You can't always get what you want."

"What I want isn't so important," she'd told him as fatalistically as she knew how. "I'm not—well, not exactly, anyway—somebody who matters in the scheme of things."

"Ah, the grand scheme of things," he sighed.

"I don't mean it that pitifully. I just don't have that much to contribute in life. Jesus, I'm an English major. All I do is read and talk about it. It's not like I'm a doctor or a writer or anything. I'll probably be one of those secretaries with a B.A. who writes third-rate poetry for college journals and has a couple of kids and gets drunk on Baileys Irish

Cream by the time I'm forty, and then ... I don't know. You can stop me from babbling anytime you want. You know what I mean."

"I think you are," he said.

"What?"

"Important in the scheme of things. Even the grand scheme of things."

"You're just saying that so I'll feel better. Well, it won't work."

"What will?"

"I should go. I came to find a friend."

"You found one," he said, and took her hand, applying a light pressure to her fingertips until she felt warm throughout her body. Music played in another part of the nightclub, but she barely heard it, as he held her close and she cried against his shoulder, and then she forgot what she was crying about.

Later she told him, "I have to get going. It's late."

"I'll see you again."

She should've known then that this was the wrong man for her, because it wasn't a question, but a thinly disguised command. If she could've gone back in time, she would've erased that night and all nights that followed, and perhaps, with her pills and medicines that was exactly what she was, very feebly, trying to accomplish: to erase all memory. But then, when she was only twenty-one, she had lived up to other people's expectations far too successfully.

"Yes," she told her future husband, "maybe."

If only she could've gone back and screamed at that young woman to run the other way, to start running then, not twelve years later in a hospital in Nevada where the stakes were higher, where the expectations were more extreme.

When her daughter might pay for all her mother's years of bad judgment with her life.

What's past is past. The thirty-two-year-old Kate bit her lower lip, remembering all the bad decisions of her life, the false starts and stops and fumbles. The hospital smelled like rubbing alcohol and, oddly, decaying gardenias. *Change the flowers now and then, Ms. Childes.* She walked down the hallway to the right, tried not to wobble, but she was getting that clutching feeling in her stomach. *No Prozac to get me through this.* Two orderlies passed; one actually looked at her as if she were attractive. *You must be a very desperate man to find this spineless jellyfish going through withdrawal appealing.* She felt for the gun and wrapped it tighter in the yellow sweater. This hall was freshly painted, and that smell, of a new coat of pale green paint mixed with Robert's rubbing alcohol cologne, was nauseating.

I am not losing it. I am here for Hope. It doesn't matter what happens to me. It doesn't matter what happens to anyone. If I have to shoot Robert. If I have to kill him. It doesn't matter. All that matters is Hope. I am not losing it.

"Oh, damn," she muttered, leaning against the cold tile, her hands shaking, clutching the sweater. Cold sweat along her face, and that clammy feeling.

A man dressed in white, perhaps a doctor, came out of one of the rooms. He looked at her, smiled briefly, then asked, "You okay?"

"Yeah," she said, curtly, annoyed. "I'm fine, all right?"

Shit, now everybody's going to remember me. Nice going.

The man held his hands up in a "don't shoot" gesture and walked past her, back toward the nurses' station.

She could not worry now. They would never get her daughter. *Who cares if they see me as long as Hope is safe?* She looked at the room number nearest her: 117.

Five more down to Hope's room.

Just a hop, skip, and a jump.

Easy as pie.

And then something equal parts unexpected and horrifying happened. Looking back, as she knew even then she would, perhaps in jail or in a mental institution, she might wonder how it could've happened, since she knew how guns worked and how you squeezed the trigger to get the bullet to come out. She knew about guns. From childhood. From ages ten to fifteen. How to load, how to aim, how to shoot, how to clean. It was like riding a bike.

But the gun, wrapped in the sweater, the gun she was holding with one hand around it beneath the sweater and the other on the outside, it went off. She was *sure* it went off, all by itself.

The bullet went into the wall, she assumed, hearing the

shattering tile, and the noise echoed up and down the corridor like a bomb going off.

She closed her eyes for a second, wishing away this nightmare that unfolded before her.

Kate's father stood behind her, and she realized she was twelve years old again, holding the pistol in both hands. She could not bring herself to squeeze the trigger.

She felt his hands coming around her shoulders, down across her blouse, along her arms.

Like a snake.

He pressed his fingers over hers.

"You got it in your sight, now kill it," he said, his voice like fingernails on a blackboard, causing her to wince. She felt that ugly feeling inside again, like she always did whenever he touched her, and she wished her grandmother was still around to protect her. But Granny was dead.

In front of her lay the dog that her father had hit with his truck. It was skinned on one side where the wheel and front fender had torn into it, and it lay there panting, foam along its muzzle. Foam and blood.

"You got to put it out of its misery," her father said. "Damn it, Katy, shoot the damn thing or so help me God I will make you watch it die slow and painful."

Kate Stewart, twelve years old, squeezed the trigger hard, but could not watch as it tore into the dog's skull.

Kate opened her eyes a moment later, after her Smith & Wesson had gone off accidentally, breaking tiles along the wall. She was in the hall of Saint Vincent's hospital, not a little girl anymore. She felt hungry and cold and frightened, but she put all this aside.

More than anything, she felt completely alone. Terror accompanied this feeling, because she had always managed to attach herself to other people before, to be part of someone else.

But now. *Alone.*

Only a few seconds, she thought, and raced for the door, hanging on to the gun and the sweater, knowing there was no chance but also knowing that she had to do this, she had to get Hope out of here. Away from these people. Away from illness.

Away from Robert.

Somewhere, far away down the hall on either side, doors opened and alarms sounded. Maybe it was just in her mind—Robert was so good at convincing her that 90 percent of her paranoia was in her mind. But there was that 10 percent . . . Men and women awoke from the tedium of their day, and she was sure an orderly would tackle her as if in a football scrimmage, but she was there at the door of room 122. She was opening it. . . .

I'm actually doing this, I'm opening this door, no one is making me, no one is holding me back, I am opening this door, and no matter what happens, Kate Stewart will go in and take her daughter out of this place, out of this nightmare, away from all this disease. If Robert is here, I'll stop him with my bare hands, whatever I have to do. . . .

On the other side of the door, as if waiting for her, Hope stood there, her mouth dropped open.

Such a sight to greet her with, you with your crazy look, and orderlies no doubt leaping for your ankles.

She grabbed Hope's hand and tugged her through the door.

Am I dragging her? Jesus, is my daughter the football and I'm the receiver and I'm running for the goal with the other team trying to keep me from it, from those double doors, from my car, from my life—

Someone tugged at her arm, but she wrenched it free, and Hope ran with her—*good girl*—and she wondered where Robert was and why he wasn't there to stop her from doing this thing that terrified her, this thing that she wasn't sure she really wanted to do at all—*but I have to, for Hope, for Hope, it doesn't matter what happens to me*—why weren't any of these people stopping her, tripping her, they all seemed to reach for her, but she was the star receiver, holding the ball, running for the goal line, down the field, so fast she could have wings on her heels—*why am I doing this now? why didn't I plan this better? where the hell is my mind?*—and she slammed her way through the double doors, out into the sunlight, to her Volvo with its engine running—*have to ditch the Volvo soon, change cars, maybe at Aileen's*—opening the door for Hope, tossing her in, running around to the other side—*why couldn't they stop me? I*

screwed up, I fumbled, why the hell didn't they catch me?—
but two men in white were running for her, and she was in
the Volvo, foot on the accelerator, and she was driving fast
off the hospital grounds, and the road ran black and shiny
beneath her tires.

She tried to block the image from her mind, the image
and the thought, but she could not. The image was probably
a benign one. When she sped out of the hospital driveway,
she'd passed a truck, parked near the curb. A yellow truck.
A man stood beside it, tall and gaunt, wearing a straw farmer's hat. He seemed out of place in Devon, and the thought
that formed was that he was there, in that place, with that
truck, because he was waiting for her. She imagined he
smiled as she drove past—a big toothy smile, with gums
showing and lips pulled back. She knew she imagined this,
because she couldn't possibly have seen him smile, not as
fast as she was driving, not as fast as her heart was beating.
It was like seeing a nightmare, but in the middle of the day,
at noon, when the sun's light flattened the desert landscape,
when nothing should terrify, nothing should bring back the
childhood memory of madness.

A man in a farmer's hat, standing beside a truck, grinning
like he knew where she was headed, and he would be there
waiting for her.

Witness.

His eyes like burning coals.

4

*Letter arriving after Kate Stewart left her house that
morning, postmark, Salinas, California*

Deer K,
cops r axing kwestshuns & i get nurvus. thay wunta no
bout hom. I scayrd, mor for yor liddel gurl, cuz he wunts
to play wth hur lyk he playd wth me. i dunt kare if i
get hurt, i just dunt wunt hur to. i stop thum if i ken.
u tayk hur owt tu sumplase sayf. pleez. i go hom & try
und stop thum. no mor spearmints.
Poppy

5

WITHIN FIFTEEN MINUTES HOPE'S FATHER, ROBERT STEWART,
got the call about his daughter being taken at gunpoint from
Saint Vincent's. He was in his Jeep, driving the craggy road
through Taquitz Canyon, just beyond the city limits. The
police had been called, and no one was injured. *"History of
emotional disturbances,"* Robert remembered the psychiatrist

*saying. "A random scattering of abuse as a child, and no
clear sense of trusting her own judgment. Delusions. Hallucinations. Yet intelligent, and aware of how confused she is.
Like an animal in pain. No wonder the suicide attempt, no
wonder the depression, no wonder the lack of conscience or
responsibility over an act that would send most women
screaming. It's like she's divided right down the middle."*

"So this is where it leads," he said into the phone.

After he hung up the car phone, he waited for the second
call he thought would come, and was pleasantly surprised
when it did not. Authorities would descend soon. If he didn't
act quickly, it would be out of his hands. He could never
help Kate or Hope if something happened to them. And
Kate was a loose cannon. All her medication.

He pulled over at an overlook, popped the tab from a
can of Pepsi, and took a sip. There was some hard candy
on the dashboard, and he popped a piece of Jolly Rancher
watermelon into his mouth. He had never quite outgrown
his sweet tooth, even though Kate had tried to wean him
off sugar for a period of time. But as she was with all things,
Kate Stewart had been unsuccessful.

But perhaps there was one thing she could do.

No one would ever say that Robert Stewart, medical researcher and Nobel Prize–winning bacteriologist, feared any
one human being, but there was something about Kate that
unnerved him. Always had. And now this. Kate had always
possessed an element of the unexpected, and his one fear
was that perhaps she was capable of hurting Hope. That
Kate might not protect Hope the way she was supposed to.

That perhaps Kate Stewart had been pushed over the
edge.

Robert Stewart reached into the glove compartment and
brought out the cylindrical microcassette recorder.

He pressed the play button.

A voice that was vaguely familiar came on.

"Hello, Dr. Stewart. We have your tape. In fact, we have
all your tapes. You egotistical son of a bitch, you document
every damn thing you do, don't you? You take a shit, and
you record it somewhere, don't you? Don't you? I haven't
finished listening to all of them, but when I do, I think you'll

have a lot to explain. Well, see you in hell, doc, see you in hell."

Robert shut the tape player off and tossed it on the floor. He was not a man given easily to anger, and if you were to ask him he would tell you that he never understood why people got angry when there were so many more interesting ways of dealing with problems.

But, he thought, *you can't have her, Grace. The pigeon has flown.*

In his wallet, a photograph of a house on the edge of a town, and he wiped his thumb across the photo. He turned it over. Written in faded ink: "1963, home." Over again, a two-story house, painted white, a black-and-white dog on the front porch, and three boys and a girl squeezed together on the porch swing for a picture.

The dream was coming true, for all of them.

He closed his eyes, trying to visualize what was to come in the next few days, wondering where it would then lead. Robert Stewart was a man who believed in the inevitability of destiny. He had been raised believing in the Golden Rule: "Do unto others as you would have them do unto you."

He was a man who loved his wife and daughter, and felt that marriage lasted into eternity.

He was a man whose family meant everything to him.

Everything in the world.

He was, therefore, a good man who lived by his beliefs.

And he had no fear for the future.

As if it were a good omen, he watched a hawk dive from the limitless expanse of pale sky, straight down into the heart of the canyon, called Taquitz for an ancient Indian demon that lived in a well. The dry, dusty air caught in his throat, and he felt a brief asthma attack come on. He had been prone to bouts of bronchial asthma since early childhood. He had gotten used to them, and so did without the inhalers to which others, weaker than he, had to resort. He held his breath for a few moments, shutting his eyes to concentrate on his breathing. Breathing was completely under conscious control, and if he could reach a state of relaxation, the overwhelming need to cough would subside.

He thought of one word: *perfection.*

It put his mind at ease.

His breathing returned, slow and steady. He had been practicing this state of self-relaxation since he was four or five years old. It kept him from descending into anxiety and stress as well as the wheezing and hacking of the asthmatic.

"Perfection," he said aloud, and the word seemed to comfort him.

Robert picked up the car phone again, hearing the cry of the hawk far below him as it pursued its prey, and pressed the number three on his speed-dialing mechanism.

"Mom," he said, a genuine tear sliding down his cheek, "it's Robert.... I love you, too. Mom, listen. Something's happened. It's about Kate."

6

"GRACE. STEPHEN. TASK FORCE OH-FIVE-OH," HE SAID, TAPping his I.D. tag.

The woman at the front desk said, "Doesn't look much like you." She was one of the middle-aged drudges, not unlike Grace himself, that Special Projects put to work at the front desk before sending them to the glue factory. Difference between the two of them, he knew, was that this woman probably hadn't had to kill for the Company. At least, not yet.

"Assassin," the voice in his head whispered. It was the little creature that had lived with him for many years since the first one. The first killing. The man with the eyes like stone.

After the first one, it got easier, but that voice in his head never quite went away, even on the best of days.

Grace looked from the picture on his tag to the mirror over the woman's desk. In the picture, taken six years before, he'd still had some happiness in those eyes. His sandy hair had been combed neatly to one side and clipped in a regulation haircut—there hadn't been much room for stray strands, anyway—and his smile was pleasant. In the mirror, the man he saw was no longer the one in that photograph, but an old man waiting to happen. "Well," he said, "I do 'good picture.' "

"You're supposed to know the authorization code, you know," she said, smiling.

He grinned, too. She didn't know it, but he had faked his way into higher-security areas than this. "Just here to see a friend in Intake."

"It's to the left, Mr. Grace," she said, waving him on down the hallway. "But do me a favor and get the code next time."

He winked at her, friendly, and nodded in the direction she pointed. It was a club, Special Projects, a country club of the internationally ill, and only the club members were allowed to break the rules. This woman at the desk trusted him because she and he were members, but it was part of Projects' stupidity, trusting the insiders. Hell, enough insiders had gone to the Justice Department, or worse, the papers, with stories that ended up causing embarrassment, at best, for the Company, or, at worst, the disappearance of the squealer within twenty-four hours. *Maybe she figures I'll disappear if I'm lying to her. Maybe she doesn't give a fuck. Jesus, security is lax. A two-year-old could outmaneuver these people. My people.*

His shoes were new and squeaked as he walked across the freshly waxed floor. He passed the turn that he was supposed to make, glanced back at the front desk, but noticed that she was busy going through stacks of papers. He cursed his squeaking shoes, but proceeded down the hallway until he got to the room marked F.

F is for Forensics.

Stephen Grace entered the forensics lab and glanced up at the clock. It was nearly 4:30, and the mother had taken the child hours ago. Holder had stayed his hand, for reasons unknown, and Grace was instructed that he was to be in San Francisco by midnight to await further instructions from the Company. The mother had an ex-boyfriend who was a scribbler for the papers in the Bay area, and Holder was suspicious that the mother would head for him for both protection and money.

Grace looked across the brightly lit room, past the two men in lab coats, hunched over what appeared to be part of a small intestine and a chunk of spinal cord, to the three small offices. None had names on them, so he would have to guess which was Rebecca's. He didn't want to draw attention to himself, or Holder might hear about it. He walked through the room as if he owned it, hoping to pass undetected. *Fucking squeaky Italian shoes.* When he got to the row of offices, each with its door shut, a light beneath each door, he sniffed around for the scent of the Eau de Toi perfume and finally settled on the second door down.

He opened it without knocking, trying to be as silent as possible. No squeaks, either.

Rebecca was leaning over her desk, examining a slide under a microscope when he came up behind her. She leaned back in her chair; he held his breath. She stared straight ahead at the wall, crossed her arms behind her neck, and said, "Grace."

"Hey, how'd you know?"

"First off, who else would be wearing Brut cologne when it's a thousand degrees hot outside. Jesus, you wash in it or something? And second, Holder told me you were in town. You want a date, bub, call before you drop in." Her Brooklyn accent never failed to charm him. She had the beauty, and then that voice.

"Some date," he said. He glanced around the room. Photos of various criminals were on the walls; otherwise, it was bare. Rebecca Lewis disliked clutter in work and in life. He had been easy for her; they had known each other for six years and had worked together on two Special Projects assignments. She was a former policewoman, from forensics, who now worked freelance for the Company, mainly when it interested her.

He watched her work. She was beautiful, with dark red hair and tanned skin that brought out character lines around her eyes and mouth. She looked as if she had lived, not a hard life, but had lived nonetheless and had not turned away from seeing things as they were. That was what had attracted him to her in the first place.

When she had put her slides away, she rubbed her eyes and looked up at him. "You look like shit, Grace."

"Bad week," he said. "I feel like death warmed over."

He saw it in her eyes. *There's that word again: "death." My favorite in the whole fucking world.* Rebecca would've heard about the car accident and the girl and how he had fucked it up. Even his oldest buddy from Projects, Elkhart, had razzed him about it.

"I was worried, you know," she said. "You could've called."

"You thought I'd be outside," he said, using the term for those who'd been expelled from Projects. *Outside* was considered a fate worse than death. Sometimes they threw the Justice Department on you when they put you outside. "I was kind of surprised myself."

"You still could've called. Showing up like this . . . Jesus, Holder would shit if he knew."

"Well, I wasn't so sure I wouldn't be outside. I had to watch my back."

She smiled cynically. "Like I was gonna be the one to blow the whistle on you. What gives with Holder?"

"He says I'm allowed one mistake."

She was about to say something and then hesitated. Then, "Doesn't sound like him, does it?"

"Maybe he has a soft spot for psychos."

She stood up, stretching like a cat. "I've been examining these samples for nine solid hours. I'm just not smart enough. You ever have that happen? You're just not smart enough for some job?"

"Always."

"Fuck you. You gonna take me to dinner or what?"

He said, "Or what."

"Hey," she said, sizing him up, "nice shoes. That where your paychecks go, Mr. Sartorial Splendor, or can't you afford to take a lady out?"

He looked embarrassed. "My sneakers wore out. I blew almost two hundred on these. I feel like a goddamn pimp. Do they look okay to you?"

Rebecca walked past him. "Very Times Square."

*   *   *

She was staying at the Motel 8 down on the Strip, and they ordered Chinese and watched the local news. Rebecca had sprayed the room with Lysol and a fruity potpourri spray because she wanted it to smell like home. She had even started decorating her room: she had the framed photo of her parents on top of the TV set, and some cactus she had just bought along the windowsill.

"Robbery, fire, the pretty baby contest," Rebecca said, clicking television stations for more news broadcasts, "nothing about the hospital. Pretty fucking amazing."

"She had a gun, and she fired shots," Stephen Grace shook his head. "I can understand Holder wanting to keep the disease aspect quiet, but, hell, you'd think a witness might help us track her."

"Holder always has his own agenda." She stretched out on the double bed, and he, alongside her, pushing white cartons full of rice and noodles and sweet-and-sour spare ribs aside. She reached over, unbuttoning his shirt, her fingers stroking the fine hair on his chest, down the edge of what she called his battle scars. "Laos, Libya, Iraq—the history of the past thirty years," she whispered. "You're a map of Holder's bullshit."

"Not all of it was bullshit. Some of it was good."

"Yeah, but he's always got an agenda." He felt her fingers graze his belly. "Not bad for an old man."

"Older than years," he said, reaching out to bring her face closer to his. He kissed her slowly but with little passion. He wasn't interested in making love, not tonight. "I only have another hour," he said.

"An hour's plenty," she replied, kissing the side of his face.

He gave in to her passion and undressed with her, pressing his body as close to hers as he could get, smelling her delicious scent as if it were the essence of life itself, feeling her legs as she wrapped them around his thighs, and then some primal impulse, which other men took for granted but which to him was the very drive of life, kicked in and he was slowly moving into her, making sure that he gave her pleasure, for he drew none from this act.

Always on his mind was the thought of death. Not a fear. But the knowledge that life was precious and short. And that even this feeling of being alive, of being as close as he

33

could possibly get to another human being, was not enough to stop death.

Afterward she said, "You're thinking of Anne."

He couldn't lie to her. "Sorry."

"It's okay. It doesn't surprise me. She was pretty great, I guess."

"No," he said, "she was just herself. It was enough."

"You're such a—what's the word? Enigma, yeah, an enigma. You know that, Grace? I've known you—what?— all this time. You tell me about your wife and how she died, and about your family and about some of the assignments, but you know? I don't know a thing about you. Not really. Others guys I can figure out. But you . . . you're like somewhere down inside there, behind those eyes, you're hiding. Holder says, sometimes—" And then she stopped, suddenly.

Grace leaned back, away from her. He said nothing.

"Jesus," she said, "I talk too fucking much."

"What does he say?"

"I been meaning to tell you." Rebecca propped herself up on her elbows. The room was shadowy, and her breasts were silhouetted against the blue-green light from the TV set. "He says you're not to be trusted."

"He said that about Spinetti."

"Don't go on some fucking paranoid jag, Grace. Spinetti was dead meat the minute he shook hands with Amin. You ain't even in the running. Holder's never trusted you. You're not like that kid in the Bronx with the drug money. But I heard something. Today."

"Tell me, Becca."

"I heard the talk out of Washington is you blew the chance with the girl because you couldn't do it. Holder's thinking of coming out himself to oversee this. That ain't so bad, but down at the lab, I heard something different. I heard that Holder and this researcher, what's his name—"

"Stewart."

"Yeah, Stewart, worked on a chemical warfare experiment with sheep down in New Mexico back in '90. And, Grace, it was this r-seven shit even then. It's a virus, and from what I can see from the blood, it invades cells, and then something different happens. Most viruses, they replicate, they take over. But this one, nothing happens. Nothing, except the fucking tissues start eating each other."

"But the cells remain the same."

"At least from what we can see. There must be something going on that we can't even find. We don't even know where to extract. It's like the virus goes in and assimilates perfectly with the host cell."

"And then all hell breaks loose in the body."

"Only it ain't sheep, Grace," Rebecca said softly.

"Why didn't you tell me this before?"

"I didn't know before. I don't even know now. If anyone knows I told you, I'm out."

"You really believe Holder thinks you won't tell me?"

She looked away, back to the television set. She flicked it on to a channel showing an old cowboy movie, *The Searchers*. She said, "He might think it. He might want you to have that information. Holder's a smart man, Grace. He's smarter than you or me. He's greedy, too, and greedy men always seem to have an angle. I think he's got an angle here that you and me can't even *guess.*"

"I have to catch a plane."

"I can give you a ride to the airport."

"I'll get a cab."

"Now you tell me something, Grace," she said.

"Sure."

"You got the doctor's tapes, don't you?"

Stephen Grace glanced at his watch. He had twenty minutes to make his plane. He didn't answer her, but kissed her gently on the mouth and smelled her hair and the herbal scent of her bath and tasted Chinese food and wine on her lips.

"Rebecca Lewis from Brooklyn," he said, holding her.

"Stephen Grace from Bumfuck, Egypt. You take care of yourself, Grace. I don't know everything about r-seven, but what I see is pretty bad. They're sending pictures tonight of what happened to the poor son of a bitch we got the blood from. You make sure you come back and see me, and I don't mean on a glass slide." There were tears in her eyes, as there always seemed to be whenever they parted. It saddened him, mainly because he felt that she shouldn't be with him at all, that she should be getting out of Projects and on with life. But he couldn't ever get her to do anything she didn't want, and so she would cry. He was a bastard to continue to see her, but she was his only continuity left in the world.

"For what it's worth," he whispered, "I love you."

She pushed him away, making a face. "Break those shoes in, will ya, Grace? The squeaks are gettin' to me," Rebecca said, and went to use the bathroom as he walked out the door and into the fading light of the desert.

Stephen Grace rarely had a drink, but this was the right night for it. He sat in the airport bar, waiting for his flight to San Francisco, and sipped a glass of scotch on the rocks. Someone was playing country music on the jukebox, and a man in a cowboy hat and boots danced with a beehive hairdoer, slow and close. Grace was happy to leave this desert and the painful memory of being in the Mercedes with that girl.

Trying to kill her. Good God.

The bartender, in his twenties with dark slick-backed hair and a carnivorous smile, said, "I hate working at the airport."

"Why's that?"

"You people. You're all goin' someplace, and me, I get stuck right here. I just go back to my place and wait till the next night."

"I'd love to stay in one place sometime," Grace said.

"Not me. I wanna travel the world. See New York, see Hong Kong. Get out, ya know? I play the guitar. I think I could make it in music."

"Really?" Stephen Grace managed a grin. He wanted to tell this feckless youth that he was a hired killer: *I am going to kill a little girl, young man. I am going to break her neck, if I can, because it will be less painful for her. But I don't want her to experience much fear, either, so perhaps a gun would be better. I tried to drive her to a construction site and shoot her a few days ago, but I fucked up. Fucked up royally. You see, kid, even old farts like me have trouble killing kids. It's easier when they grow up, oh, to be about your age, then it's no problem. I see a face like yours, kid, and pulling that trigger is a cinch. It's the little girls that get you in this job. Even if she is a goddamn grenade with the pin pulled halfway out.*

But the bartender moved away, down the bar to get a couple of beers for the cowboy and the beehive, who had stopped dancing long enough to drink.

One more drink. Stephen Grace raised his empty glass to the bartender and waited for that sweet warm feeling inside, from the whiskey, that stopped, for a short while, the pounding hoofbeats of death that sounded in his brain, stamping out what little humanity was left in his soul. The alcohol allowed him such thoughts, and he secretly delighted in them, for he felt, at core, that he was a truly evil man living in a truly evil world. Only his duty kept him from seeking release.

She must die.

Yet his dream, his passion . . .

Seeking death for himself.

"Oh, God, help me," he whispered to no one.

His plane would be taking off in twenty minutes. He had time for another drink, although he wished Rebecca had come with him to the airport, as a lover might, to see him off on a trip to murder a child.

The voice in his head whispered, *"Assassin."*

7

On the Road

November 7
5:00 A.M.

HOPE STEWART HAD LOST ONE OF HER EYES, BUT THIS DIDN'T stop her from believing that she could see out of it, and what she saw in that eye in a brief moment was her father's face.

But she had the sense that she was in what her mother told her was a fever dream, and so she ignored her father and the butterflies that beat their dusty wings against her face.

She thought she saw Denny, but it couldn't have been him, because he wasn't little anymore, he was older, almost as old as she was, and then the pain came back, shooting all through her body, and she was crying a little because it felt like somebody was tugging her skin off, but it was only the ice and the water, and her mother holding her in the bathtub to bring the fever down while Hope kicked and scratched at the side of the tub.

5:42 A.M.

Hope's fever came down, and it looked as if the worst of it was over. She lay in her bathing suit in a bathtub full of ice cubes, shivering, half dreaming. She had been what her mother had termed a hellion when the fever was raging, had screamed and batted at her mother when she'd been thrust into the freezing tub; but it wasn't so bad now, with the room getting to a more comfortable temperature. Fever every day now. She didn't know if the hotel in Las Vegas was part of the fever dream or if she and her mother were really there. The place where her right eye had been throbbed. Not with pain but with a kind of deliciously moist warmth, like a hothouse garden, as if her mind could smell and taste this raw feeling, and enjoy it. She didn't like enjoying it, because it was too much like shame.

Her mother, Kate, reading through the medical encyclopedia, decided it wasn't anything more than a bug, because there was nothing other than the fever and the muscle pain. "It's coming down," her mother said, shaking the thermometer out, "almost to normal. Maybe I was wrong to take you so soon. Maybe another day or two. For recovery."

The girl said, "Mommy?"

"Uh-huh."

"Where did Denny go?"

Her mother looked away for a second, and then back. She had uncreased her face from worry, just as if she'd ironed the smile on. "He's with God."

"I thought I saw him when I conked out."

"I bet you see a lot of things when you conk out. Got everything you need?"

"Can I have Nina?"

Kate nodded and went to retrieve the baby doll. Hope had wrapped a bandanna around the doll's neck. Hope was too old for this kind of doll, and yet she clung to it, something innocent from her preschool days. Nina was plastic, and what little hair she had was coming out. It had been a birthday gift seven years earlier from Ben. And now they were going to Ben.

Her daughter, who was eleven, held the doll against her neck. "We have to leave soon, don't we?"

Kate Stewart nodded. She went to get Hope's sunglasses, which had fallen to the floor in the bedroom when her fever went up. She called out from the other room, "We can cross over into California by ten if we leave by six."

Hope tried not to think of how ugly she felt, how weak and stupid, since the accident. How weird the glass eye felt, too, pushed up into the socket, and the stitches around her eyelid. Sore and throbbing. "Make me an eye patch."

Her mother stepped back into the bathroom light. "Like a pirate?"

Hope nodded. "I'd like it better than having this thing." She pressed her finger against the fake eye. "A patch will make me feel mysterious."

"You *are* mysterious. I may not make a good one."

"I know. But you used to sew me so many things. I liked all of them. A pirate eye patch."

Kate held the sunglasses up. "You still have to wear these in the car. In case someone sees us."

Hope grinned, thinking of herself as a pirate. "What time is it?" The throbbing in her eye lessened. Sometimes the pain went away quickly; she hoped this was one of those times.

"Almost six."

"Is it still dark out?"

"A little."

"No way to go back home?"

"No. You know that. I would rather die than do that."

"Why does it hurt so much? I mean, like when I caught it? I thought it was safe. I only felt it after it was too late."

"I don't know. I want you to avoid it. I shouldn't have let you go by yourself. But no one looked sick. God, how will we know till it's too late?"

"I didn't even know I was doing it."

"Well, it's done now. You can sleep in the car."

"You need to sleep, too, Mom."

"I can't. Maybe when we get to Ben's. When you're better."

"What's really wrong with me?" the girl asked, and her

mother looked at her and wondered the same thing, wondered what had happened in that car accident, before it, what had been done to her little girl by that man called Daddy.

What's wrong with me?

Later, in the Mustang, Kate thought someone was following close behind, but was surprised that whoever it was had not caught up with them. It would've been fairly easy. She didn't understand completely, barely understood what pushed her onward other than her concern for Hope's safety. She'd read about a woman on the East Coast who had gotten her daughter out of the country for similar reasons and had been put in jail for doing it. *They could put me in jail, or worse,* she thought as she drove, as Hope rested in the backseat, *but as long as Hope gets to where she's safe, it'll be all right. Nothing to fear.*

She glanced in the rearview mirror constantly as she drove across the desert to California, to the dream of perfect escape.

But something, she knew, would follow her no matter where she ran.

8

From Robert Stewart's tape

"What did you feel, pigeon?"

"Feel?"

"Inside. Were you cold? Were you warm?"

"Warm. Thanks for the Coke."

"Was it a good feeling?"

"Do we have to talk about it?"

"Yes."

"Oh."

"Was it like fingers? . . . Pigeon? Fingers, inside?"

"It was like butterflies. And a voice."

"Like yours? Or Daddy's?"

"Uh-uh. Like something I've never heard. Like I couldn't understand."

"What did it say?"

"Things. I don't know. I can't remember. I don't remember."

"Did you see inside?"

"I guess."

"What was it?"

"Butterflies and colors."

"But you saw his illness."

"I guess. I don't remember. I saw something wrong. I saw something very wrong. It was eating him. It was like one of those worms under rocks that just eats and eats. When it saw me, when the voice spoke to me, it changed."

"Into what?"

"Something different. Oh, Daddy, I think I'm gonna be sick again."

"What was different? Hope, hang in there. *What was different?*"

"I don't know, I don't know, *I don't know.*"

"You tell me right now. Something was different about it. What was it? You know and I know it didn't turn into a butterfly, so what *did* it turn into, Hope? What was it? Tell me right now. This is very important, because he is in a lot of pain right now, pain you can't even imagine, and I have to find out what you did that made him get that way, why it didn't go right. What was it you saw, Hope? What changed about it? What was different? It began doing something, that thing you saw. What did it do?"

"No! Daddy! *Don't make me!*"

"He needs help, pidge, and I can help him, but you've got to tell me what it was you saw."

The sound of a little girl crying.

"Just . . . tell me. What was different about him?"

The crying continues.

"Was it eating inside him? Is that it?"

"No."

"Don't be afraid."

"Eating itself. Eating itself. Eating itself. Itself."

The child's voice began to sound as if she was exhibiting a multiple personality disorder, for it was different in tone and quality and pitch. She sounded possessed.

9

6:30 P.M.

HOPE'S HEAD WAS OUT THE CAR WINDOW, THE WIND BUFfeting her face. She had to squint to see the farmlands passing by in a colorful blur of purple, green, brown, and yellow. "Can we play the radio?"

"I don't want to hear another country station as long as I live," Kate said.

"Maybe there's some other kind of music, Mom. And I like country."

The smell of onion was smothering, as Hope kept her head out the window of the Mustang going sixty, and she glanced over at her mother, who seemed unaware of the fields and orchards. It had rained, and she could smell everything, even the sweetness of ripened grapes, but the onions were overpowering. Her mother was calling her Lisa for this trip so that no one would put two and two together and know that this was a kidnapping. Hope had known it, and it scared her, that word: *kidnapping.* So many things were confusing, and she hadn't even begun to sort them out. Her father and mother were no longer together, and her mother had explained to her that they were doing something highly illegal, a felony, something her mother could be put away for. The first two days had been hell, but now, closer to San Francisco, to Ben ...

"Pull your head inside," Kate Stewart told her daughter.

Hope glanced around at her. Dark hair streaming across her face with wind, her freckles blossoming, her left eye squinting. She felt up for the patch. It was a basic eye patch, and seemed a little tight sometimes, so she had to tug on it to make it fit right. She pressed lightly down over the top of the patch—always a little pain, and the strange sensation that her right eye was still there instead of the glass one.

"Hope, I will pull over," her mother warned.

Hope sat back down in her seat, snapping the seat belt back into place. "It's flat," she said. "California is flat."

"You slept through the hills. We're just out of Bakersfield," Kate said. "We'll hit some more hills soon enough. The coast is all hills. Hills and cliffs and blue water." A memory, almost painful, Hope could tell, seemed to furrow into her mother's brow. Kate saw her watching and reached over and placed her palm across Hope's forehead. Checking for fever. Combed her fingers up and through her daughter's hair, which always made Hope feel like a little girl when, at eleven, she knew she wasn't. She'd already had her first period, although Missy Hafner was the first one in sixth grade to have hers. Missy would be throwing a party soon for all the girls who had had their first one. Hope wondered if she minded missing the party. She was happy on the one hand that her body hadn't lagged behind, but she was somewhat less than thrilled about the prospect of having this *thing* occur every month for the rest of her life.

Hope watched the pecan groves whiz by on the plain, the shiny newness of the earth after rain, the sparkling jewels embedded in the grasses. California was one of the few western states she had not set foot in before. Her father had spent part of his life here, and his parents were somewhere down south, in San Diego or something, and he didn't like them much. Her mother didn't like her own parents all that much, and between them, Hope had barely heard the word *grandparents*. But they were driving north, a loopy route that Hope had picked out herself because her mother wanted one that didn't make sense. Since Hope was the navigator, she got to find the trails off the freeway, like this two-lane road. "I like it better than Nevada," Hope said, having to shout over the sound of the wind as they sped along, " 'cause of all these smells! Did you smell that stuff like Vicks VapoRub?"

"Eucalyptus." Kate smiled but kept watching the road ahead.

Hope could tell she was tired. Not that they'd been driving that long today, but her mother was tired in a bigger sense—had been tired for the past year, but hadn't gotten any rest. Smudges dug beneath her eyes like hard charcoal. Kate had covered some of it with concealer, but two days without sleep couldn't be hidden.

"Look," Hope pointed to the edge of the road. "Seven-Eleven. Mom, there's a Seven-Eleven. Can we stop? I want a Slurpee." But her mother didn't seem to hear her, and Hope sighed. She wished her mother wouldn't drive so fast. Her mother was nervous and tired, and what was Hope going to do if she fell apart on her again like in Las Vegas? All her mother did was cry and cry, and all Hope could do was sit and watch her fall apart. Hope sometimes wondered if her father wasn't right. *Don't think that. It's not nice.*

Kate glanced in the rearview mirror. "It's back."

Hope didn't turn around to look out the back window. She knew what *it* was.

"Damn it," Kate whispered. "How the hell does it keep finding us?"

"Maybe it's just a truck."

Kate almost laughed. "I wish I was just being paranoid, Hope. Your father's buddies all thought so. But that truck has been with us every day. You've seen it. The gun's still in my purse, isn't it?" She reached to the large blue purse that was propped up between them.

"Not Wednesday."

Kate sighed, and Hope could tell, by the way her mother was taking long, slow breaths, that she was trying to calm down. "Not Wednesday, right. It wasn't around then. One day out of three."

"Sorry. Who do you think it is?"

"No, *I'm* sorry. I'm just a little tense, I guess," Kate said. "I'm not sure who it is. If it was the police, they'd just pull us over. It's got to be someone your father hired. Maybe a detective. Who knows?"

"I can get the gun for you," Hope said, unclasping her mother's purse, reaching into it.

"Don't you dare." Kate slapped her hand, and Hope drew it away from the purse. Her mother sometimes had these mood swings, and she was fairly used to them.

Kate glanced in the mirror again. "Maybe he's just a nut," she half smiled, but her face stiffened into a mask. "He's slowing down. Slowing down."

It scared Hope when her mother talked like this. When they first started out, and her mother thought she saw the yellow truck, Hope had believed her, had even gotten a little scared of someone following them, and had not looked back to see what was there. But then, staying at the hotel in Vegas, looking out over the casinos from nineteen floors up, Hope had known that her mother could not be right about seeing it all the way down on the Strip. It was too far below them—all the cars had looked like ants to Hope. The following morning, while they drove, Kate had seen the truck again. This time Hope had turned around to look. Behind them was a truck, but it was nothing like the one her mother described. "It's not yellow, Mom, it's gray, and it's a woman driving. See?" But her mother kept insisting that it was the same truck she had seen before, the same make, same color, same man at the wheel. "What does he look like?" Hope had asked, and Kate had replied, almost testily, that the man was in his forties, was wearing a straw farmer's hat and round spectacles, and had a long face and burning eyes.

"Don't pretend you don't see it," Kate said, and Hope was wise enough to shut up.

Mommy's just wound too tight. She needs to unwind. It's what her father had said on several occasions.

Hope looked straight ahead, and soon the California flatlands gave way to low hills and her mother stopped mentioning the imaginary pursuer. She was getting hungry.

When they stopped in San Bernardino it had been noon, and she had not been allowed out of the car. They went into a McDonald's drive-through and ate on the freeway. Hope had not been allowed to speak to another living human being since Vegas, when she was sick again. She missed people and wondered if her father wasn't right when he said that Mom was out of sink. There, she could think it without feeling too guilty. She pictured her mother washing dishes, which she *never* did, but having so many dishes that she ran out of sink—too much work, too much stress. Out of sink. That was what her father had called it. He didn't say it to be mean. The people in court, before the accident, when Mom and Dad went in to talk about not getting along too well, they said worse things. Mom's doctors, too. Said things like "manic-depressive," "unstable," "not responsible for her actions," "a time bomb." But her father had been kinder, saying, "She's had a rough time this past year or so. So she's out of synch with things, with her feelings. She needs a lot of love and trust from you, now more than ever." This had scared Hope more than what the lawyers and doctors had said. Scared her, because out of sink seemed dangerous at times, for what would she do if her mother went crazy on her? Who would protect her mother? Not Daddy. Maybe Ben. *But what if I cured somebody and got sick again? and Mom saw the truck, only I wasn't with her? I couldn't help her. What would happen to her?*

Hope remembered the last time her mother had gone off the deep end, and it had lasted a good two months. If Daddy hadn't been there to help, she would've never gotten out of the hospital by herself. Hope had two, maybe three, friends from school and one of them, Frannie Cooper, had told her, "Everyone thinks your mother is psycho. You should be glad they might get divorced. It's better like that." Frannie's parents were divorced, at least twice each. Hope had never thought that her own parents' divorce would be anything but a nightmare. Her mother only seemed worse when her father wasn't around to, as he said, "clean up the mess." Her father never ran out of sink. He had plenty of sink. And then, after the car accident, after she lost her eye— Hope instinctively felt her eye patch to make sure her eye was still gone, because sometimes she thought it was still there—Mom started up with the bizarre accusations about Daddy doing things to her and how it wasn't her fault and that Hope had told her about it—how Daddy had been touching her the wrong way—before the car accident. But Hope knew that it must be in her mother's mind, because she couldn't imagine Daddy ever doing that to her. "The accident," her mother told her. "The accident took away your memory of what Daddy did."

And Hope had to admit that she couldn't recall the week before the car wreck at all, or even being thrown free of the Mercedes when it went into the ditch. Nothing. Blindsight. Lose an eye, lose a mind. Hope was more worried about Mom losing her mind. She'd heard from her mother about how Grandpa and Grandma Weeks were crazy drunks, how Grandpa was a sadist who loved to hurt people's feelings. Daddy had called her grandpa a paranoid-something and said it was a genetic illness, that he couldn't be blamed for his strange behavior. Daddy, being the kind of doctor he was, the kind who didn't really have patients but studied things in a lab, called just about everybody a genetic something-or-other. Hope knew what *genetic* meant and knew that her mother might have the same crazy genes that her grandparents had. What her father called, sometimes, "a case of the nasties."

I might have them, too. Like Mommy. When she gets a case of the nasties. Inside her. Maybe that's what's inside me.

7:10 *P.M.*

"Hey," Hope said.

Kate said nothing; her knuckles were white where she pressed them hard at the wheel.

"Mom, I think we popped one. A tire."

They listened for the sound, and sure enough, they heard the *flap-flap-flap.*

"Shit," Kate said. Her forehead crinkled up like she was about to explode. Or cry. One of the two. "Shit, shit, shit."

Hope ignored this. It bothered her when her mother used bad language; her father never did. It seemed dirty to have words like that around. Her father had once said to her, when she used this very same word, "You have something in your mouth I wouldn't pick up with my hands."

Kate eased the Mustang over to the highway's shoulder. They were still a few hours from Ben, who lived in San Francisco. "God," Kate said, "I hope there's a spare."

"You bet," Hope said reassuringly. She had had to be the support for half the trip, and when they'd stayed in Vegas, after she got over the flu, she had run down a thorough check-list for the car, including checking the oil and water. She knew her mother would never remember to do all of it.

"I've never changed one." Kate laughed at herself. "Here I am, running away, and I don't know the first thing about taking care of simple things like tires."

"I can do it."

"Show me," her mother said. "My father never let any woman get near his car, and your father thought I was too stupid."

"Daddy showed me how to do it when I was ten," Hope said. She was about to open her door, when her mother reached out and pulled Hope beside her.

"Someone's pulling over behind us. Don't get out."

10

THE MAN RAPPED AT THE CAR WINDOW, BUT KATE KEPT IT rolled up. "Got a flat." He nodded. He wore a tan windbreaker zipped all the way up to the collar. His blue jeans were streaked with dirt, like he'd been playing in the mud. His reddish brown hair was thick and greased back, revealing an overhanging forehead. Thick eyebrows shaded his small brown eyes. He grinned, showing large yellow teeth, as if he hadn't brushed for a few days. Then he winked at Kate, stood back from the Mustang, glanced at the rear tire, and leaned back against the driver's side window.

Kate said, "We're fine, thanks." She felt a brief wave of cold air across the back of her neck, as if there were a draft. She tried to remember where the gun was. She would use it again, but only if necessary. She had to think of Hope and what was safe for her. *My purse. It's in my purse.* What if this stranger recognized them? Perhaps something had been on the television news, after all, a photo of Hope or of Kate. She could not bring herself to look at this man for more than a second or two. She was half afraid that he could see through her, read her thoughts.

"You're worried, on accounta I'm a stranger, I know," he said through the window glass. "I know it's scary, especially here, but I can change it if you'll just pop the trunk. Look, my name's Matt. I'm from a little town up the road. I've got a mother and some brothers. I was married once, but now I'm divorced, and I don't smoke, but sometimes I drink Coke. How do you do. Now we know each other. Let me change your tire, okay?" His grin never wavered.

Kate felt a chill spread down her spine. She felt, with her right hand, for her purse. It was nestled down near the clutch. She smiled briefly back at the stranger as she felt the hardness within the purse. The Smith & Wesson. Protection. She said, "I said we're fine."

The man named Matt sighed, seeming exasperated. "Okay. I can go up to Perdito and call the highway patrol to come help you. If you want." He glanced up and down the highway, as if looking for something. She looked up the road, too, as if there was anything but endless highway and cloudy skies.

Alarms seemed to go off in Kate's head. The last thing she wanted was for someone to go to the police. "No, please don't. I know how to change the tire," Kate said. "If I seem rude it's just 'cause I'm in a hurry. But I can change it myself, thanks." She forced a smile that conveyed some friendliness so that he wouldn't get suspicious. *God, let me get out of this situation for Hope's sake. Let her be safe.* She was wishing that she had a pill, any pill, to take to calm her nerves. She wondered if this Matt person could tell that she was about to explode from holding so many things deep inside herself for so long.

"I insist," Matt said, winking at Hope. "Here, you go ahead and pop the trunk, and I'll take care of the rest. You can stay in the car."

"Please," Kate said, not knowing how to get rid of him, but feeling the purse, the hardness in the purse, and wishing it were not a gun but a pill that she could just pop into her mouth and get this whole thing finished. She had gotten rid of the Prozac and most of the Xanax, but she wished she had some now, a big blue pill to swallow and fall asleep with. But "protect Hope" was somehow etched into her brain, and she knew that no pill or gun would solve this problem.

"Mom," Hope announced, looking out through the side mirror, "a cop's coming."

Kate glanced in the rearview mirror. Matt also turned to look back. It was a black-and-white police car, with two cops in it. One of them stayed in the car while the other got out. He was tall and lean and young, with a shock of blond hair falling to the side of his forehead. Kate had never really felt comfortable with the police since Denny's death, when the police had arrested her out at the reservoir—after she'd run from the house and driven eighty miles an hour to get away, only to be arrested and to have to call Robert's own lawyers to get her out. This cop, coming toward the car with his aw-shucks grin, looked like a young Nazi in training. She would not be arrested again. Never.

Kate told Hope to read her book, *Fahrenheit 451,* and not to look up. Matt stood back, sticking his hands in the pockets of his windbreaker, obviously out-aw-shucksing the cop. Kate rolled down her window, and Hope pretended to read.

The cop said, "Any trouble here?"

Matt lost his grin and looked earnest. Like a Boy Scout helping an old lady across the road. "Just helping her change a tire."

Kate grinned. "I can do it myself, really."

Hope whispered under her breath, "No, you can't," and felt a nudge from her mother.

"Well," the cop said, "maybe we both can help you,

ma'am. You want to pop the trunk? We'll have it changed in double time."

Hope felt something run down the back of her scalp, then an intense pressure against the glass eye in her socket. A word formed in her mind, but she wasn't clear about what it meant. A thought, an image. Then the word became clearer. *Unwell.* She whispered, "Keep him away from me, Mom."

Kate half turned toward Hope, and then back to face the policeman. "You're not feeling well, Officer?"

The cop's eyes widened slightly. "Strange you should ask. Just been getting some pains here." He indicated his throat. "Does it show? Am I pale?" He sounded to Hope like a hypochondriac. But Hope was well aware that anyone that she came in contact with, if he was sick, could pass his illness on to her without her wanting it.

Kate held Hope's hand tightly, squeezing hard. "A little. Listen, Officer, I hate to keep you from your duties. This nice gentleman has offered to help."

Matt said, "Yeah, I can take care of this in no time. I've clocked myself at six minutes for a tire."

The cop looked the stranger over, sizing him up. Hope's hand ached from her mother's squeezing.

"What's your name, mister?" the cop asked.

"Matt. Matt Lovett. I live over in Caliente." Matt Lovett retrieved his wallet from his hip pocket and showed the cop his license. He glanced from Kate to Hope, as if he hoped they would corroborate that he had been nothing but friendly.

"Pop that trunk and get to it, Mr. Lovett," the cop said, slapping him on the back. He waved to Hope as if she were a baby.

Hope reached into the glove compartment with her free hand and pressed the button for the trunk. Her mother let go of her other hand.

"Well, go to it, and you folks have a nice day." The cop winked at Hope and then walked back to his squad car.

After the police car drove off down the highway, Kate kept her eyes on the rearview mirror, watching Matt Lovett reach under the mess of clothes and overnight bags to get to the spare. She smiled, falsely, when he looked up at her. Hope was half turned around, watching. When Matt pulled the spare and jack out, Hope whispered, "He's not sick or anything. There's something. I dunno what."

"Everyone has *something,*" Kate whispered. "You may not even be able to feel it with some people. How do we know?"

Hope turned the radio on. It was an old song by the Judds, "Guardian Angels," which was one of her favorite oldies. She wished her life was like the song, that someone, somewhere, was watching over her, guiding her steps. The cop had worried her—if he had gotten closer, if he had come around to her side and she had felt his breath or accidentally touched him ... but she couldn't think like that. Daddy had explained to her what *paranoid* meant, and she didn't intend to be it. She didn't know how she would get around in the future, how she could forever avoid contact with sick human beings. *Maybe it'll just go away. Maybe I won't see any more cures. Maybe I won't catch what anyone has for a couple of days, and then things'll be normal. Maybe pigs will fly.* But the ability had come on suddenly, with the accident, and might go just as quickly. "Some people," her father had told her in the hospital, "believe that trauma to the head like this"—he felt the edge of her eye socket, just where the glass eye went in—"opens up all kinds of psychic possibilities. You know, like ESP. This could be something that was dormant and needed the extra shove. And you got it, pigeon. Of course, your old man doesn't believe in that kind of hooey. I think maybe this is a naturally occurring talent in one out of every, say, hundred million. Maybe you always had it, maybe it developed with the onset of puberty. Losing your eye's probably got nothing to do with it." Hope didn't like it much when her father mentioned puberty or her period, but knew that he was a doctor, so this was not as embarrassing for him as it was for her. But she was sure it was the loss of her eye that had caused the ability. Somehow she knew. In the darkness of her blindsight, she would see things, the insides of people, their blood, and it would have a certain yellow cast to it, and then a word or phrase would form in her mind, and she would know they were sick. She would know that if they got too close to her, she would heal them. She accepted this. She would have been thrilled by it if it weren't for the fact that she herself took the illness on for a while after the healing took place. It was a transfer, like the bus tickets she and Mom used to take downtown. A transfer. I cure you; you make me sick. Fair and square.

"All done," Matt said, clanging the lug wrench and jack together as he tossed them into the trunk. He lowered the hatch and pressed it down, closing it. He came around to Kate's window again, which was halfway up. "You two drive careful. It looked like you went over some glass or something. Headed to the coast?"

"L.A."

"You must be taking the long way." He grinned, friendly. "Nevada plates, all the way up here to get to L.A. Well, you got three choices of pass ahead to get to the coast. You either take Fifty-three or the Paso Robles road, or you can swing out on a two-laner through Perdito and Empire—goes all the way through the Empire Valley. That'll take you north, though. Fifty-three's your best bet. Four lanes, flat. You go sixty, you'll hit the One-oh-one just about two hours up from Santa Maria, and then it's straight sailing down south." He winked at Hope.

"Thank you," Kate said, reaching for her purse.

He lip-farted. "I don't want your money, lady. Jeez, can't even help nobody no more." He ambled back to his car, like he had a limp in one of his legs.

Hope said, "Well, since we have just about enough money to get us to Ben's, what would you have done if he had let you pay him?"

"Something's wrong with that man," Kate said absently, with that faraway look in her eyes that Hope was used to seeing whenever her mother started zoning.

"Yeah," Hope agreed, "he helped us. Nobody's *supposed* to do that." She glanced over at her mother, hoping that she would crack a smile at this comment.

"Hope," her mother said, *"please."* And then, as if from nothing, tears started streaming down from Kate Stewart's eyes. Her entire face seemed to crumple in on itself as if there were no skull to hold it together. Kate covered her face with her hands, but the heaves and sputtering of the tears, and all the pent-up frustrations wouldn't be held back.

Hope reached for a Kleenex and passed it to her mother.

She put her arm around her mother's shoulders, sitting up to do so. "It's okay, Mommy," Hope said.

"No, no, it's not." Kate hugged her daughter tight, still sniffling. "It's like a nightmare. All of it."

"You always wake up from a nightmare," Hope said, feeling like the mother here and not the daughter. "So that means this'll end at some point. We'll get to Ben's, and then we'll figure everything out." Hope knew what her mother intended to do when they got to Ben's home. Kate would tell her story for Ben's paper and then get some kind of police protection or something. And then Hope was worried, because she knew that maybe the police would arrest her mother. That was one of the reasons the cop had scared her. What if they arrested her mother, when all her mother was trying to do was take care of the two of them? Hope barely remembered anything around the time of the car accident, but her mother had told her that, in the hospital, at first, Hope had talked about how Daddy had played with her the wrong way. Hope wasn't sure what this meant, although her mother had then given her a talk on the birds and the bees and how some adults sometimes took advantage of children. Then her mother had told her that even Grandpa Weeks had done it to *her* when *she* was a little girl, and it wasn't right. So that was one of the reasons that her mother had kidnapped her from the hospital. To protect her from her father. Although this confused Hope, she trusted that her mother was doing the right thing. She didn't think that her father was as evil as Kate was saying, but she *was* uncomfortable with her father, and all his taped interviews with her about what her empty eye socket felt like, and all the healing junk. He hadn't seemed exactly like her father anymore—not warm and not affectionate. More like he was studying her like she was some kind of lab rat. Like one of those animals he had at his research facility.

Hope began crying a little, too, as she and her mother held each other. She wondered where all of this would end for them, and what the police and Daddy would do with her mother once they had stopped running. "Oh, Mommy," she said, "don't cry. I love you."

Ben will help. Ben's an important writer. He loves us. I know he does. He'll know what to do to help us. The thought barely comforted her, as her mother's tears didn't seem to end.

11

THERE WERE OMENS FOR JUST ABOUT EVERYTHING, AND THE omen that he had had that morning was the cat he'd run over when he got on the road. It was a black cat, too, and what meant more to him was not just hitting the cat, but the fact that ever since he'd hit the cat, he'd kept hearing the squeal in his brakes, and thinking, There's that cat again. He knew then that it was going to be a good day, a productive day, and looky if he wasn't right. He grinned to himself, just thinking about how long he'd been hunting today, how he thought they'd never show up.

Those two. Mother and daughter.

He'd had to drive the highway for hours, just wondering when the hell they would come across this stretch of road, the point of no return. But he had his faith, and lo and behold if it didn't come through, strong. He knew it was them because of their smell. So strong. Sweet. Pungent. The stink of fear-sweat and pain-cologne, so rich and vital.

Mingled with their natural smell.

He ran his tongue across his front teeth.

Good breeding, he thought when he walked away from the Mustang. *Stink of it. Damn good breeding, like they'd been selected for their looks, for their skin, for their chromey-sones. Not the shitstink of where he lived, but the smell of good perfume and good clothes and good fucking breeding. It was all like Birdy, that smell of it on him no matter how dirty he got. No matter how much blood sprayed across his fingers, he still had it, Birdy did. Just like the woman and the girl.* He looked down at his hands. Grease-spattered, blackened fingernails. He never could get them clean. He tasted rain in the air—it was good for the crops, good for the grapes. He imagined what it would be like to play with her, the girl. Hold her in his arms and monkey with her eye socket.

That was his name, his *real* name.

Not Matt.

Monkey.

He hadn't played with a child for at least six months. He didn't like the Freakchild who lived underground; he wouldn't go near him if he could help it. But the last one, for him, was the boy they got in Monterrey, the one with the prosthetic leg. Imperfection.

Imperfection must be hacked off!

Monkey remembered, with pleasure, the feeling of the little boy's breath on his face when he'd hacked at the boy's imperfection. The smell of the boy, too, like sour milk and rotten bananas. The look on his face when he discovered what Monkey was up to. It always seemed new to him, that look. That look that seemed to say, "Wait, I thought you were my friend. What are you gonna do now?" Monkey liked that best, because with children, everything was like Christmas and birthdays—one surprise after another, all gift-wrapped and eager. And so full of imperfection!

It attracted him, imperfection. Missing pieces, children without certain parts. He could play with them a long time if he wanted. The girl had a missing piece, her eye. "I know you," he whispered into himself as he watched the Mustang drive off down the road. *"I know who you are. I know where you're going. We're gonna play a long time, you and me. We're gonna play with your imperfection."*

Birdy, who also shared space with Monkey inside his body, said, *You can't hurt her until it's all through.* Birdy's voice was always so strong and confident, so fucking clean. Monkey's was like a four-year-old's compared to it. Birdy was smart. *That's what Goodmama said. Goodmama said Birdy's done big things in his life, and Birdy, like Monkey, was coming back home. Birdy never really left. That's what Goodmama said.*

Birdy was silent, and Monkey wondered what he was

thinking. Being possessed by Birdy like this was, at times, confusing, and Monkey was never sure when he was allowed to take over his own body. It hardly seemed fair that Birdy could take possession at any time, and sometimes Monkey fought him, but he never won unless Birdy let him. Monkey had hoped that Harlan would come into him to, but Harlan was silent. Monkey wanted all his brothers to be there, in his body. His body was big enough for three, or more.

Birdy said, *You did good, helping them like that.*

"Thanks." Monkey grinned. "I coulda took her right then. I coulda. It woulda been easy. Piece a cake."

No, it's not the right time. Her mother might've stopped you. And the officer. He was following us for twenty miles. He must've been suspicious. It was good you did nothing.

"You sure they're gonna go the right way?"

Birdy was silent.

The emptiness of the eastern sky behind him seemed to go on and on. He could hear birds in the nearby fields calling one to another in desperation.

"Sorry, sorry." Monkey shuddered, feeling the loneliness come over him whenever Birdy didn't speak. "I didn't mean to doubt."

I love you, brother, Birdy whispered.

Monkey closed his eyes and could practically feel Birdy's hands unbuttoning his shirt, reaching beneath the cloth, touching the cold metal to the skin of his lower belly, and slicing. He shivered, and his nipples went hard. He remembered the small fingernail scissors going into his skin, cutting the fabric of flesh. That was so Birdy could get inside him. *I will never leave you, brother,* Birdy had promised. His voice echoed in his mind, just like he was still in the Pain Room, just like the razors were still scraping at his skin, and the joyous scream of faith coming from his lips as the steam rose up from his hallowed wound.

Monkey shuddered, opening his eyes again.

The highway seemed vast and empty, and the sky was darkening. Somewhere ahead there was a rainstorm, welcomed by a strong wind from the north. If you were to look at this man carefully, you would see that he did, indeed, resemble an ape more than a man, with his hunched shoulders and his long arms, and the patches of red-brown hair growing thick along his neck and down his forearms. He squinted, trying to see if the car with the girl in it had taken the right way, toward the north. The opposite direction from where he'd suggested.

It had.

He saw the gray car about a half mile up the Empire Valley Road, and he grinned. Birdy had been right. He'd said that she was being guided, that the invisible thread would draw her in. It was still up to him to get her, because others were involved, too. Some other man was after her; some other man wanted to kill her.

But monkey wanted to play with her, that was all.

Play.

Monkey opened the door to his mother's car, a Chrysler Fifth Avenue that Birdy had bought two years before as a birthday gift, and got in. The radio was still on, and there was lots of static, but he could hear the classical music, his mother's favorite, Handel's "Water Music." It was like she was right there in the car with him and Birdy, guiding them.

Ah, it was good to be among family.

To be home.

12

STEPHEN GRACE SAID, "I THOUGHT I WAS AN INDEPENDENT contractor here," and held the phone away from his ear so that Holder could yell at him all he wanted. He was so goddamn tired of phones and red tape. He had been in town a couple of days, and all he'd done was run around in circles, waiting for a definite green light, or even some word from Nathan Holder that would cut him loose from this third-rate dick surveillance. And to add insult to injury, he'd been saddled with one of the worst excuses for a car that his boss could find. Most of the Company's cars were outfitted with a telephone; this decrepit Torino from the 1970s wasn't, so he had to use the corner phone booth to call in to Nathan Ass-Holder.

He glanced up at the apartment building, finding the window on the seventh floor, third from the left—Farrell's apartment. After he gave Holder a minute or two to cool off, he brought the receiver back to his ear. "You told me I'd have free rein. You promised me that. Remember? It was only five days ago. Five fucking days."

On the other end of the line, a hoarse voice said, "Five days ago was different. Look, I don't enjoy leaving home to come in and clean up one of your messes."

That was then; this is now. "Hey," Stephen Grace said, laughing, "blow me."

"That's the kind of talk that keeps you in the field, Grace."

"I *like* the field. And I thought we were going to bug Farrell's place."

Holder hesitated on his end of the line, and Grace thought, *He's gonna blow*. But when Nathan Holder spoke again, it was calmly, measuring his words as if they had some intrinsic value. "He's in newspapers, Grace. We bug him, and he gets a Pulitzer for writing it up. And we get crapped on."

"I could take care of him."

The man on the other end of the line sighed.

"Yuck it up, Holder, it's a joke. What's up with the woman?"

Again Holder sighed.

Shit. Grace didn't even have to acknowledge it. They had let the sister go without her answering a goddamn question. Not even a tail to see where she'd head.

Holder said, "It's not like the sister's going to be a security risk. If we need her, she won't be hard to find. What good was she, anyway, Grace? Couldn't have told us anything even if she wanted to."

What good are you, Mr. Boss Man? Playing with fire here with the girl, when all it would take is twisting one of the mad doctor's arms and this whole thing would be over. Two bullets: one for him, one for the girl. Maybe three. "One for you," he said.

"What was that? Grace?"

But Stephen Grace hung the telephone up. He stood inside the phone booth for a few seconds while he lit a cigarette and took a few puffs. A middle-aged woman in a raincoat, with a scarf wrapped around her hair, was waiting to use the phone. She was holding the hand of a boy about eight years old who was tapping on the glass of the booth with his free hand tightened into a small fist. Grace opened the booth door, and stepped out. The woman eagerly went in and dropped a coin in the slot while the boy kept staring at Grace.

"You're a bad man," the boy whispered.

Although Stephen Grace had heard him, he said, "Huh, kid?"

"I said you're a bad man." The boy had wise, haunted eyes, and Grace felt an unnatural wave of something eerie about him. The boy's mother was still speaking on the phone, not noticing her son or Grace.

"Why would a nice kid like you say something like that?"

The boy was adamant. "You're a bad man." And then he pointed at him, but Stephen Grace noticed that the boy was pointing at his mouth. "You're a bad man: you smoke. You're gonna die from those. You're gonna make other people die, too."

Stephen Grace drew the cigarette from his mouth, glanced at it, and then grinned, shivering. "You live long enough, kid, you make a few people die. Trust me on that one."

He flicked an ash and then turned away from the boy. *Fucking San Francisco.* Jesus, he wished he was back in the jungle with the bugs and the endless steam, back in the place where dreams had form, where nightmare had logic. Not in these man-made places where it was all puzzles and games. He crossed the dark rain-slicked street to the Torino. He leaned against it, reaching onto the driver's seat for the photos that Rebecca had mailed from her lab. In the glow of the streetlight, he could make out her note: "Stephen"— and she never called him Stephen unless she was freaking out about something—"Don't go after this girl. She's carrying something more than just a virus. I don't want to lose you to this. I mean it. You are worth something to me. I love you, even if that means shit to you. Don't fuck my life up by dying—Rebecca."

He'd look at the pictures later—they were just autopsy pix. He could wait another hour or two to digest his dinner before going through them.

"Rebecca," he whispered to the night, "don't fuck your life up for me." He tossed his cigarette onto the street, stepping on it. The kid was right: people are gonna die 'cause of me.

He counted up the floors on the side of the building that he faced. It was an old building, dark brick with small balconies, too small to stand on, but each stuffed with plants or flower boxes. When he got to seven, he stopped and watched the seventh floor apartment, hoping that the man who lived up there, the old boyfriend, the confidant, would finally do something, because nobody the fuck else was doing a goddamn thing. No flowers or green ivy on that balcony—just a clear view to the large window behind the low rail. The light was on, and if Grace wasn't mistaken, someone was moving back and forth near the window.

Don't you ever leave your house? Grace thought. *Lead me to her, Farrell. Just help me save the world, and you can write all you want and win the damn Nobel Peace Prize for all I care, and you can make damn sure I get the chair. Just take me to the girl. I want her out. No dancing the Armageddon Boogie with a teenybopper whose breath is gonna spread like fire across all creatures great and small.*

He remembered the mad doctor's tape, the words: "Like any mechanism, it's a matter of triggering the mind, and if it goes, it goes big, and the trigger's already there, just a matter of it being set off. When six and seven connect, it's Fourth of July time."

Stephen Grace was tired of sitting in his car, but what could he do? Until they let him go after Stewart himself, or until the mother turned up, he only had one lead.

Just give me the girl, Farrell, and then all your dreams can come true. After I pull my own trigger.

After I put the bullet in her head.

13

IN THE SEVENTH FLOOR APARTMENT IN SAN FRANCISCO, a man in his early thirties heard the phone ring and then listened to his own voice on the answering machine, followed by an electronic beep.

He was about to pick the phone up, but it was someone he was afraid to speak to.

Especially now.

"Ben?" the man on the phone said. "Ben? Are you there? This is Robert. Robert Stewart. Answer the phone, Ben. Now. Kate and Hope are in danger. You've got to help us. Kate is not herself. She's on medication. She's capable of murder. All right, Ben, I'll call back. I'll try later. Call me."

The answering machine clicked and beeped.

The man in the apartment walked over to the living room window, keeping to the side. He saw the brown car below, and the man standing beside it.

Waiting.

"Where the hell are you, Katy?" he whispered, looking out over the city, as if he could wish her there beside him. "What in God's name is happening to you?"

14

The Boonies

8:00 P.M.

THE SIGN SAID, EMPIRE, POP. 673, BUT EVEN THIS HAD A SLASH through the number, and someone had painted next to it, "pop. 200." Hope giggled when she saw it. The city she'd been born in, Devon, Nevada, had a population of nearly 80,000 and climbing. She didn't think places like this really existed except on TV shows. After they drove by the sign, she expected to see a town, but she saw only an old gas station that didn't seem to be operating, although its fluorescent light still flickered and was stormy with moths and flies escaping the damp night. The rain was spattering on the windshield, and only one wiper seemed to be working at all. So even while they passed some buildings, neither she nor her mother had a good idea of what the town looked like, although it revealed itself with porch lights. Empire,

California, appeared to be all in a line on one side of the road. The few houses she saw weren't like the big modern ones in her neighborhood in Devon. But there was something that reminded her of the kind of place where she imagined grandparents would live. Or what her father would call "the boonies." She had been to a few places like this with her friend Missy, and Missy's mom had called these towns in the Southwest "cow towns."

"It's a cow town," Hope said, liking that word the best.

"California doesn't have cow towns. It's barely a town at all," Kate's speech came out slurred, and Hope knew her mother was running on fumes. They were both exhausted, despite what sleep they'd gotten the night before. Hope felt like the mother sometimes, having to remind Mom when to eat, when to sleep, when to calm down.

"Let's stay here tonight," Hope said. They'd come to what was undoubtedly the only stoplight in town. To the right was darkness, probably an alfalfa field or fruit trees. Hope had quickly discovered that this was mainly what was in California. She had thought it was going to be Disneyland, and had been disappointed that they were heading in the opposite direction from it. To her left stood something that looked suspiciously like a motel, a big green neon cactus in front. "Look." She pointed. "We can get a room. Maybe get to bed before midnight. For once."

Kate shook her head, more to stay awake than in response. "No, I can get some coffee. You climb in back with the pillow. I'll be fine. We need to get to Ben's tonight."

"I bet the rooms are cheap at that place." Hope pointed to the sign above the big cactus: Greenwater Motor Lodge, Reasonable Rates. She couldn't quite make out the rates on the sign, but she knew that she and her mother had about seventy dollars left of the three hundred they'd started out with, and this place looked dirt cheap. She said, pretending to read the sign, "The Backwater Motor Lodge. Reasonable rats."

"Very funny," Kate said, smiling genuinely. The stoplight turned to green again. Kate drove through a dip in the road that sprayed water across the windshield. The traffic light and the splashing water, and even the reflection of a yellow porch light from down the road a ways, created a rainbow across the front of the car. It was almost like someone was hosing them down deliberately. Hope loved it. She took it as a sign.

"We should stay here. Looks like the rain's getting worser."

"Worse. Not worser."

"I know. I was just testing you. I'm hungry," Hope said, and looked out to the left as they passed a burger joint. It wasn't Burger King or Wendy's, but it still looked good to her. She hadn't gotten her full share of junk food on this trip, and she wondered what a road trip was good for if not for regional junk-food sampling.

Kate said, "We'll stop in Paso Caliente. There should be some McDonald's and things there. It's just before we hook up with the 101. It's only an hour. Maybe." Kate was slowing down as the rain picked up and visibility worsened.

"I'm hungry now." Even as she said this, Hope saw something in the road, something moving, but her brain reacted slowly with the information given it, and she managed a "Whoa, Mom," not sure of what she was seeing at all, for it moved fast and was a blur with the sheets of rain coming down around it.

"Oh, shit," her mother gasped, pressing her foot to the brake, causing the Mustang to skid. Hope held on to her shoulder harness, and looked ahead through the windshield. It was just a sudden shadowy rainswept movement in front of the headlights. It must've been a man or a woman running across the road. Nothing unusual, but . . .

Panic gripped Hope for a second, and something came to her—the Mercedes-Benz, the man sitting next to her. It should be Daddy, but she was so sleepy and sick at the same time, and when she opened her eyes—a flash of memory like the lightning that played up in the hills.

In the memory, someone said, "Can't—"

"Can't do it," the someone said, and Hope was so sleepy she could barely get her seat belt buckled.

She couldn't quite see the someone because he was made of iridescent butterfly wings all fluttering around her face. This someone said he'd help her with her seat belt, but in fact he seemed to be pulling the strap away from her so it wouldn't buckle.

"Can't do it," he said, "but I've got to."

"You got to." Hope shrugged, wanting to yawn, but was too tired even to do that. Outside the car, the world was all triangular butterflies batting at the windows. Softly, like feathers. The car had a face where the steering wheel should've been. It was a clown face, like Bozo, only a little weirder. The clown smiled, and when it opened its mouth, dozens of monarch butterflies flew out of it with wings as shiny as new razor blades. They were so beautiful, but it was getting hard to breathe because the orange-and-black butterflies with razor blade wings kept slicing the air in front of her. They tickled her face, and she looked over at the someone driving.

He was a butterfly, large and lovely, all shimmering rainbow, rainbow, rainbow. He said, "Don't be afraid." He looked like her dead brother, Denny, a little bit, but also a butterfly, and also a little like her father.

"I'm not afraid," she told him. "It's pretty. Pretty."

"I'm scared," he said, and she reached out and touched the tip of his wing.

"You don't have to be," she comforted him. "It's all right."

The butterfly said, "Forgive me."

"I do."

And before long she felt the razor blades of his wings come and swipe at her face, digging into her eye socket, and she was flying with the butterflies away from the Mercedes as it rolled over and over and over . . .

. . . *Butterflies, rainbow, over.* Hope held on to her shoulder harness, opening her good eye again.

"Didn't mean to scare you," Kate said, after she'd brought the Mustang to a full stop.

Hope wasn't sure why she was thinking of butterflies. She took in her surroundings, remembering the thing running in front of the car, and the skidding. "What was it?" Her right eye socket had a stinging feeling, just like when she used to have an eye there and it was bloodshot.

"I don't know," her mother said. "A man, a big animal.

Ran right in front of us. I wasn't going all that fast. I don't think I was, anyway."

"It must've been a cow," Hope said, "for a cow town." She didn't think it really was a cow, though. It looked more like a man who thought he was an animal. Hope played animals, too, sometimes, but when she was a lot younger. She wondered why an adult would play animals, but this was the boonies after all. Not a lot to do after the sun went down.

Kate said, "God, that really shook me up. Mind if I smoke?"

"Yes."

"Oh, *well* ..." Kate leaned over and popped the glove compartment open. She brought out the pack of Salem Ultralights, which she'd been saving. She squeezed the pack. Empty. "You threw them out, didn't you?"

"Yep," Hope said, "they stink too much."

"I'm sure I'll thank you one day," Kate said dryly. "But sometimes Mommy needs a little lift, times being what they are."

"Let me smoke one. I need a lift."

"Very funny." Kate sighed, and Hope heard complete defeat in that sound. Her mother took too much medication as it was. Hope knew about people who went cold turkey, and she kind of wished her mother would try it. "Okay," Kate said finally, as if it were a struggle to speak. "Maybe we should stop here for tonight. Get up real early tomorrow, and get to Ben's by ten, maybe. I'm frazzled."

"Good," Hope said. "I don't like this rain."

"That's 'cause you're a desert rat."

"I guess I am," Hope agreed. "A one-eyed desert rat."

The Greenwater Motor Lodge was so named because of the pond behind it, although Hope told her mother, after they'd gotten a room, that she thought it was because of the color of the water from the tap in the bathroom.

Kate managed a smile. "If you run it, it'll clear. It's probably rusty," she said from the bedroom. Her entire body ached, and she was dreaming of suds and warm water. She glanced around the small bedroom. The curtains didn't close completely, but their room overlooked nothing more than a narrow strip of parking lot and an empty field beyond, studded with squat oil pumps. The rain had abated somewhat; now it was only spitting outside. Kate tested the window lock and was not all that surprised that there was no actual lock. Just a good strong shove would've opened it. She looked out at the Mustang, parked in front of their door. She had always wanted a Mustang, and now, on this trip, at thirty-two, she finally had one, albeit a loaner from George and Aileen back in Devon. She actually did not miss the Volvo at all. And still, in spite of switching cars, she knew in her heart of hearts that Robert had someone on her tail. That man in the yellow truck. Following.

Don't think of him. Paranoia will destroy ya. No more Xanax, Thanax, Prozac. No more fear. Hell, no more cigarettes.

Kate had run from many things in her life. First her father, and then the man she was engaged to at twenty-one, and then psychiatrists who didn't think she was quite right in the head, and finally, exhaustingly, Robert. Only now, with this flight, she was finally running *back* to something, although she was uncertain as to what it would mean. Back to Ben, who had loved her in spite of everything. She couldn't be sure she loved him, but he was the only human being, aside from her daughter, whom she trusted.

Between Father and Robert, it's a wonder I trust anyone.

But there was someone else Kate didn't trust, at least not entirely. Herself. She was as afraid for Hope's welfare at Robert's hands as she was at her own. It was all that damned self-doubt, pummeled into her over the years by her father and Robert, with his damned intelligence. Cold intelligence, used not for compassion or love but to categorize, to label, to stamp as useful or useless. And she had fallen into the latter group. Useless. While Hope, for some reason, was in the former. Kate had wanted to kill Robert, too, for more than just what he had done to her, or even to Hope, but for what he had done to her spirit. The weakness she felt around him. The damned insecurity that she couldn't shake in his presence was unbearable. That lingering feeling that, just as had been said in court after Denny died, she was unfit to be a mother.

* * *

The day she took Hope from the hospital, she had felt sure that every cop in the state would be down on her. She had driven carefully—the traffic that afternoon had been heavy—and in order to do this, Kate had stopped taking any medication. She had been shaking a little, and Hope, rather sweetly, had reached over and placed her small warm hand over her mother's. It was calming. Kate had wept, and Hope had combed her fingers through her mother's blond hair. When she was ready, Kate had said aloud what she had memorized, about Hope's Grandpa Weeks and about how sometimes people we love touch us in the wrong ways, but she'd forgotten the rest.

"I can't remember anything like that. Not with Daddy, or anyone," Hope had said, blushing.

"You told me, the day before the car accident, and I ignored you. I was busy. I was wrong to do that, honey. My mother pretended to ignore me, too. It's called a chain of abuse, sort of. I was doing what my mother did. But not anymore."

"I told you, I don't remember—"

"Hope, I'm not sure why, but I think your father drove over the detour on purpose."

"I don't even think it was Daddy in the car."

"He says it was. He had the bruises and the concussion. Your memory may have gotten a little shaken up. That happens in accidents. Your father thinks I'm crazy. But crazy or not, we are going to Aunt Aileen's for the night. And tomorrow we'll drive to Ben's. It'll take us a couple of days, maybe. But we'll be safe."

"What about later? Aren't we gonna call Dad?"

"Baby, no. Please trust me. You know I love you."

And then, they had both been crying, and Kate had started the Volvo up and driven them away from the city to a sparse suburban development where they spent the night and Aileen gave her their Mustang so Robert and the police might have trouble tracking them. Kate had called Ben that night. He had been wonderful, even offering to fly them to San Francisco. But Kate had refused mainly on a point of common sense: if Robert had called the police, the first thing they would check would be the airports. To say nothing of her basic fear of flying. As much as she trusted

Ben, she couldn't shake the feeling that it was wiser that he stay out of this side of it. He would do enough for them once they arrived in San Francisco.

Tomorrow. Nice to have maybe one night of peace and quiet. In the cow town boonies of Empire.

15

IN THE EVENING, IN THE AUTUMN, EMPIRE WAS ALL COOL shadows, and people stayed indoors nine nights out of ten. Most of its residents were proud of their quiet life, their life in miniature, in which the rhythms of the earth were heeded, where night meant sleep and day meant work. They watched the same TV as anyone else in the country, but it bore no relation to their lives. The young in town had restless hearts, and sometimes they abandoned the place of their childhood. But more often than not, they returned to this town, this way of life, this acreage of God's earth. They lived what others would call the life of boredom, but it was, perhaps, the actual experience of living in a small town at the end of the twentieth century.

In Empire County, the town of Empire was itself the smallest. Paso Caliente, out the Sand Canyon Road, was the largest with a population over 4,000. Perdito was of a middling size, and it was at the edge of Perdito where the Empire State Facility sat like a warning to people driving through the valley. But Empire, once a thriving farming community, now just gathered dust and some grapes. Most of its residents commuted to Salinas, or even to Silicon Valley to put food on the table. Almost half the population had put their houses up for sale by 1987. They had moved on, leaving several empty homes that had yet to be bought.

And there were others in Empire who had no wish to leave.

There were those who could imagine no other life.

16

8:15 P.M.

GRETCHEN FEELY WORKED THE FRONT DESK OF THE Greenwater Motor Lodge, but they were having all kinds of trouble with the phone lines because of the storm. And with only one guest in the entire place. She'd been hoping that her boyfriend, Gus, would call. He worked the day shift at Empire State, the correctional institute. He was a recreational therapist, which to her meant that he kept crazy people playing basketball and weaving baskets. Gretchen hadn't heard from Gus in almost six hours, which, if one knew Gus as she did, was highly suspect, since he usually checked in with her every hour on the hour. She was almost sure he was two-timing her with Lois Hicks, because Lois always went for what everyone else had, and she'd run through most of the married and willing men in town. Gretchen had seen Lois eyeing Gus with that detached hunger that other girls in Empire had come to fear. Barracuda eyes.

Gretchen sat at the desk, bored, wondering about Gus and whether she could trust him to keep his thing in his pants. She tried the phones again, but the lines were still down. *Dang wind.* Something outside, through the glass doors, caught her attention. Something moved. Maybe a guest, or just one of the Miller boys playing pranks again.

Well, I will just pretend they don't exist. She had had to wash the windows of each and every room after Halloween when the Millers threw five dozen eggs at the front of the motel. Teenage boys were such unimaginative creatures. *Eggs. As if I care.*

But Gretchen looked again. There was definitely someone standing out in the parking lot. Just standing. No crime in that. It came in handy that she was almost engaged to the sheriff's son. Nobody in town, except maybe the Miller boys, ever bothered her. Once, when those creeps who ran the vineyard tried to get her involved, Gus had threatened to knock their lights out. She had nothing to fear. She reached beneath the desk and lifted up the silver flask. She unscrewed the cap. Gus had been off work for three hours. Why wasn't he here yet?

The taste of the scotch was warm and almost bitter. It always put her head in a good place. Especially on lonely nights. Stormy nights. Windy nights. A drink never hurt anyone.

Bravely she got out of her chair and came around to the front of her desk. She heard her own footsteps, loud as nails being driven through wood, but she walked right to the door, opened it, and said, "Hey!"

The man standing at the edge of the front parking lot shot her a glance.

She asked, "Mister, you want something?"

But the man turned away and loped toward the side road, beneath the dripping oaks.

"Well," Gretchen said, thinking maybe he'd hear her, "I better not have to use my daddy's rifle, that's all I can say."

Then she looked out into the spitting rain, listened for the familiar sound of her boyfriend's Chevy, and felt the gentle chill of night. She hoped Gus wasn't hanging out with that psycho houseguest of his father's, Fletcher, the one who always made Gus think the most Looney Tuney things. Why in the name of all that was sacred, she wondered, had Sheriff Stone ever taken that insane man into his house at all—and to what purpose, given the fact that Fletcher only seemed to influence Gus for the worse?

8:17 P.M.

Fletcher McBride was insane by anyone's standards. His favorite pastime was barking back at dogs from behind the chain-link fence in the yard. And there was the story of his having axed his wife back in the mid-1970s. *Judged* insane, in fact, by a jury of his peers, sent to Empire State, got out, and now lived with Sheriff Kermit Stone and his son, Gus, in a house on Olive Street, just off the main drag in town. Fletcher actually occupied the one-room-with-kitchenette guesthouse behind the Stone place, but most nights found him inside the main house, watching horror movies on video with Gus.

They were watching a movie called *Bury Me Not* when Fletch turned to Gus, who was drinking his third Heineken and feeling no pain, and said, "You afraid of that?"

"What's that?" Gus mumbled.

"Like on the movie. Premature burial. I read this story once like this—maybe they did this movie on this story I know—but it was a true story. It's about this guy who gets buried. When he was alive, see, he was afraid of being buried alive. So, in his will or something there's this thing about putting a phone—one of those cellular jobs—in the casket. Well, only problem with this is, ya see, a month after this guy's buried, the phone company comes up with two calls on his bill. The fucker called somebody. Only, turns out, life is shit, and death's forever, 'cause he must've panicked and dialed wrong numbers from the grave. Ain't it a pisser?"

"Lovely story, Fletch," Gus shook his head. Fletcher McBride had been like an uncle to him ever since he was about twelve and his mom had passed away. That was thirteen years back. But Fletcher had his dark side, as Gus and his dad had known from the murder trial. Headline: "Mad Doctor Operates on Wife with Ax." It sometimes got to Gus and gave him the willies when Fletch went on about these kinds of things. Gus kind of liked it, too.

"Well, I got a point, son. This movie gave me a notion. And that notion is, you know, if I die soon, anytime soon, I want to make sure they cut out my heart or some such thing to make sure I don't wake up in a coffin. Or on my way down the slide into a crematorium."

"You're weird," Gus sighed. "Is this some kind of premonition?"

"You bet. Promise me you'll do it."

"Hokay, Fletch. Scout's honor."

"And when you die . . ." Fletcher's eyes grew dreamy and started rolling up into the lids. He looked like a big old marine sergeant, with his crew cut and jug face, about to faint.

Damn. Gus sipped the last of his beer. He set the bottle to rest with the others beside the sofa. *Here it comes.* It had been six months since the last one. He didn't get spooked by Fletcher's possessions, just dog-tired of them. Fletcher believed that spirits took him over all the time.

"Hey," Fletcher gasped as if he were drowning, "something's gonna happen."

"Yeah, Fletch, the world will spin."

"No. I can smell it. Someone just came to town and brought along the end of the world. You know how good my nose is."

"Give me a break."

"I'm telling you. It's like the tide of the universe is upon us. As in the last days. We better start repenting real soon if we want to make it to heaven. Or Valhalla. Or Nirvana. Reincarnation won't count for shit—won't be nothing left to incarnate *in*to. Jesus, and in this valley, too. What will they think up next?"

Gus had to work hard to find his grin. "Maybe you and me's been watching too many monster movies, you think?"

But Fletcher's faith was unwavering. He looked almost stern, although there was always something a little comical about Fletch even at his most serious. "I wish it were a joke, son. But I can feel the tide pulling. Some dark being just came upon us here. As a shadow upon the light of day, to snuff it out." Fletcher's eyes seemed clearer, almost radiant now in the white light of the halogen lamp that Gus had bought up at the J. C. Penney in Caliente. Fletch shook his head, as if to expel all the notions rattling around in it. "All's I can say, son, is you better go get yourself laid in the next day or two. What you got between your legs might just drop off before too long."

"Maybe I'll just do that," Gus concurred, thinking of

Gretchen all alone over at the motel. And all those empty rooms. "What are you gonna do?"

Fletcher McBride's eyes twinkled. He scratched his big belly through his T-shirt and thought a minute. "Me, I'm gonna just go out and enjoy the evening for what it is, son. I'm gonna smell the sky and walk barefoot on the grass. I'm gonna think on women I've been with and women I never got the chance with. I will remember my glory days. It's the best I can do, given the endless night that's about to be upon us. Your dad at his office?"

Gus shrugged, rising up, tucking in his shirttail, making sure the buttons on his 501's were all secure. "He should be. Carlos quit on Monday—moved up north, got sick of it here. And you know how Dad is. Won't stop working."

"Well, then," Fletcher McBride said, "think I'll take me a walk over to Main Street and see if our sheriff's got wind of the eve of destruction."

"Won't he be pleased." Gus laughed, slapping Fletcher on the back as they both headed out the front door.

8:25 P.M.

Gus's father, Sheriff Kermit Stone, looked like a man who had seen a ghost. But, of course, it hadn't been a ghost he'd seen, exactly, but one he'd heard. Just before the phones went down, he'd received a call and listened as a voice said to him, "I don't want trouble. You know what I mean."

And Kermit, who was forty-seven and holding, and who felt that he had lived two lives—the first one, where he'd made all the mistakes, and then the second one, when he found new and different mistakes to make—now wished he'd never been born.

8:25 P.M.

On the western edge of town a woman waited patiently for the arrival of her children.

17

THE TELEPHONE RANG IN THE MOTEL ROOM, AND KATE STEW-art almost jumped.

Don't answer it.

Hope opened the bathroom door. She stared at her mother, with worry furrowing her brow. Then she shrugged.

The telephone was a rotary, and rang like the bell on a bicycle.

After seven rings the phone was silent.

"Got to be a wrong number," Kate said. She rubbed Vaseline Intensive Care lotion into her hands. Her skin had been drying, from air and stress, the entire trip. She looked at her hands, rubbing in the lotion, not wanting to show her daughter how afraid she was of something as simple as a ringing telephone.

Hope went back into the bathroom and shut the door. Kate heard the fan click on inside it.

She stood up, thinking about the phone, and then heard the flush of the toilet. Water ran in the sink.

Who could possibly know we're here?

Aloud, Kate said, "That's silly. Nobody could possibly know."

Kate went and sat down in the stiff pine chair beside the telephone stand. She picked the receiver up and dialed the motel manager's office. A young woman answered. Kate asked about the call that had just come through.

"That was me, Mrs. Gardner," the woman said, using the alias Kate had given when she'd signed in at the front desk, "just to tell you that the phones are back up. They were only down for an hour. The wind takes 'em out about four times a year, but it's usually just a branch, maybe, or something on the wires in Perdito. You can use the phone if you want, but we keep your deposit if you don't pay up in the morning."

Kate hung the phone up. She wanted to laugh, but the panic had seized her as it always did. She didn't want to reach in her purse for the Xanax, but it seemed so easy and convenient. She resisted, for Hope's sake. *What's the use of having an anesthetized mother? What good would I be if Robert or the police found us?*

She heard the sound of running water in the bathroom sink. She thought she heard Hope say something through the door. For a moment she felt the panic descend again. *What if someone's in there waiting for her? What if someone has her? The police—Robert's using the police or a private detective to hunt for Hope. What if she's—*

But Hope repeated herself, shouting this time. "They use real glass!"

"Baby?"

"They use real glass," Hope swung the bathroom door open like she was going to take it off its hinges. She came out, carrying a small fat glass filled with tap water and held it up to the light. Particles of rust and air bubbles still swirled in it. "I thought all the motels used plastic."

"Only motels built after World War Two. I don't think this place has been occupied since the Gold Rush," Kate said, leaning over and brushing dust off the green-and-gold bedspread. "But, hell, ten bucks a night plus a five dollar phone deposit. Pre-recession prices. Pre-depression prices."

Hope said, "The windows don't lock. You notice that? I tried them. The only way to open them is from outside. At least the bathroom windows."

"Yeah." Kate nodded. "The front ones, too. I'm sure this kind of town doesn't have much crime."

Hope volunteered, "We can use some electrical tape from the car and tape it all up. Or something. Man, am I hungry."

"You had a sandwich. Didn't you? And Fritos?"

"All the chili cheese Fritos. The entire bag. Almost four hours ago, though. I'm starving."

"Well, let me take a bath, and then we'll go down the block to that burger place. Sound good?"

Hope nodded. "You gonna call Ben?"

Kate glanced at the phone. Then, as if shaking off resistance, she picked it up and dialed a series of numbers. On the other end, it rang and rang. Kate made faces at Hope, who made them back, and she expected Ben's machine to pick up any second.

"Hi, this is Ben Farrell. Please start confessing at the beep."

She waited through a long pause for the beep, and when it came it was long and ear-aching. When it was done, she said, "Ben, it's Kate. Are you there? Oh, come on, pick up, pick up."

She heard laughter on the line, and Ben said, "Gotcha."

"That was you? Oh, *Ben,* I wish you'd grow up."

"Please start bitching at the beep." Ben chuckled. "So, you're still alive, are you?"

"Stop it. I don't think that's funny at all. You don't know Robert. He's capable of a lot. Especially if he thinks I'm running to you with something that's going to be on the front page of a major newspaper. He's probably worried about future grant money."

"Aren't you two coming tonight?"

"We've stopped . . . somewhere. We're both exhausted. I think we can be at your place by ten tomorrow morning. I'll call when we get to the city."

"What, are you in San Jose or something?"

Kate held her breath. She knew it bothered him to be kept in the dark about their route and schedule. *A journalist in the dark is not a happy camper.*

Ben muttered under his breath. Sighed. "All right, Katy, I'll play by your rules. You sure nobody's following you?"

Kate couldn't bring herself to tell him about the man in the yellow truck. She hadn't seen him since they'd turned off to Empire, anyway. Ben would think she was crazy if she told him. So she lied. "Uh-huh."

"Well, I think someone's shadowing me. Me and my shadow. I don't know if it's police or Robert, but this guy is some kind of detective. Showed up when Robert started calling, though."

Kate held her breath for several seconds, trying to swallow her panic. She had known Robert would figure all of it out—going to Ben's, to the press. "Who knows, with Robert. Who knows? It could be a detective or someone from one of those army think tanks trying to stop a scandal involving one of their top researchers."

"Or," Ben volunteered cheerily, "it could just be a fly on the windshield of life."

"Ben. Making jokes. I wish you'd be more serious. And I am so tired. I can't wait till this is over. There's something I have to tell you."

"Shoot."

"Not on the phone. Tomorrow. When this is over."

He laughed. "You think it's going to be over anytime soon? You must be dreaming, K-K-K-Katy."

"Don't you K-K-K-Katy me. Oh, God, Ben, you don't think your phone could be tapped, do you?"

He took a moment to answer, as if this was something he hadn't considered. "Jesus. I don't know. Maybe. Listen, I better go, but give me a call when you can. And tell Hope that she's too old to be afraid of the dark, willya?"

"Bye."

"Katy, I—"

But she hung up the phone before he could finish. The thought of a wire tap seemed more and more plausible to Kate. Once Robert had spoken with Ben, felt him out, tried to cut through the bullshit, then the next logical step would be to bug the phone. See if Kate would call and tell Ben when she was arriving. Which she had just done. *Shit.*

"What'd he say?" Hope asked. "Why didn't you let me talk to him?"

Kate was morose; when she spoke, her voice was flat. "I think someone may have been listening in on Ben's phone. He said hi to you, and he wanted me to tell you that thing, what he always says. About the dark. Listen, I'm beat. I'm going to take that bath."

"Can I get a Coke?" Hope asked, grinning sweetly. Her hair fell across her eye patch in long dark bangs that needed cutting.

She looks so much like her father, Kate thought. "This late? You'll be up all night."

"How 'bout a Seven-Up?"

"Okay. Only don't talk to anyone, okay? And if someone doesn't look so great, walk the other way. You don't need to start getting sick on me."

"Don't worry," Hope said.

Kate brightened for a moment. "I know what it was that Ben said. He said, 'Don't be afraid of the dark.' You know, like that old joke you two had. He always says that, doesn't he? You like Ben?"

Hope nodded. "Yeah. He's neat."

"How did that thing go? When you were six? He came out for a visit—"

Hope's face grew serious without ever losing the smile. "Just after Denny died. He came for about a week. Daddy didn't want him around. You were kind of sick, and I was scared at night. I kept thinking I heard Denny crying. Even though I knew he was dead, and you and Daddy told me about how he went to heaven. All that stuff. And Ben, when I was upset, said, 'Don't be afraid of the dark,' and I said, 'It ain't the dark, pal; it's what's *in* the dark.' And then he told me about how everyone has this light inside their bodies, like a firefly, and they can switch it on, only most people are too stupid. And he taught me how. I mean, I'm too old for all that stuff, but I don't know ... it makes me happy, sometimes, to think about it."

"That's right," Kate nodded, remembering. "Now, how do you turn your light on?"

"You close your eyes and you put yourself into tomorrow, when the sun's up, and pretty soon it *is* tomorrow. Well, I mean, it worked when I was six. It doesn't work as well at eleven, does it?"

"Guess not," Kate sighed, "and when you get to be in your thirties, it doesn't work at all. Believe me on this point." God, Hope was such a mixture of incredible maturity and so much childishness. It was sometimes easy to forget she was just a child, but then, a second later, she might seem younger than her years.

Kate noticed that Hope still had that habit of reaching up and touching her eye patch, as if she thought her real eye was still there. As if it hadn't been torn out by glass when Robert's Mercedes-Benz went off the road and into that construction site.

Touching around the socket's perimeter.

Nodding her head at an angle, turning to the right.

It's as if she thinks she can still see with it.

18

Grace Under Pressure

From Robert Stewart's tape

"What's it shaped like?"

"Daddy, I told you."

"No, I mean when it's not a butterfly."

"Like a long tail. And a head."

"You mean like a worm."

"No. Almost. But it's all bones."

"Look at this picture. . . . Like this?"

"Kinda."

"That's a spinal cord. You know what that is."

"Yeah, Daddy. It's a face."

"Where do you think you see this?"

"Inside. Them and me. At the same time."

"No. I mean, where does your sight come from?"

"The light inside me. In my eye."

"The one that's gone?"

"It's somewhere, Daddy. Everything's somewhere. And wherever it is, I can see."

Stephen Grace flicked the tape recorder off. He picked up the manila envelope from the table. He had drunk too much coffee. This whole business gave him the creeps. He should've just done the job when he had the chance. Instead, he'd fucked up. Now Nathan Holder was out here, camping out in one of the Project's offices, waiting to fry his ass. Some fucking world. A girl was somewhere between Nevada and San Francisco, bringing with her a plague from—where?—the skies?

He slid one of the photographs out of the envelope. He had seen it before, close up. It showed what had happened to the woman from the hospital. He had to stare at it long and hard to get used to it, because he didn't want to overlook anything, no matter how nauseating.

Just the remnant of a woman, an eye here, perhaps the collarbone in place. It was like looking at something that had been half eaten. A piece of meat.

And still moving. Moving so fast that it blurred the picture, where her spine still batted against the cot in which she was restrained. *She?* More like *it*. Still alive, heart beating, but tissue burned away. By what? By this girl's touch? By her look? By her breath? By a virus that could be caught from just the touch of a child?

More photos of the woman, taken from different angles. She'd had the bad luck to see the girl, to get near enough to her to feel her breath.

And then, another photo beneath these.

A little boy. Picture of health. Pink cheeks, brown hair, freckles, smile right out of Norman Rockwell. His chubby fingers held a Snickers bar in one hand, a glass of milk in the other. He had also been touched by the girl, but he was better for it. Healthy. Cured of, of all things, AIDS.

Creator and destroyer, Patch—that's what you are. I should've done it right before. I'm kind of glad you cured this kid, though. But I won't fuck up next time. Next time I'll have no mercy.

Grace glanced at his watch: 8:30. Time to make a few more damn calls, to go sit in the stinky car again and try to find out what the hell kind of game was being played. *Christ, I'm tired of all this phone shit, all this waiting.* Time to get the show on the road, before anyone else ended up like that woman in the photo, the Thing with No Skin and the Whip Spinal Cord Tail. He couldn't get the image out of his mind:

Her spine beating against the cot as if what remained of her nervous system were trying to rejuvenate necrotic tissue.

19

Devon, Nevada

STEPHEN GRACE CALLED AT 8:33 CALIFORNIA TIME, AND
Dr. Robert Stewart took the call. He was sitting in the study
of his house flicking channels with the remote control of the
thirteen-inch Sony Trinitron. He had been waiting for this
call ever since he'd left the message on Ben Farrell's answering
machine. He switched the phone to speaker and leaned
back in his chair, still changing channels on the muted
television.

"You've made contact," Grace said. "Got the hookup a
half hour ago. You and Farrell. He's talked to her."

Robert didn't respond. He kept his finger still when he'd
gotten to the Discovery Channel, and watched as a caterpillar
spun its cocoon; through time-lapse photography it wriggled
through its pupa phase and then to its adult, emerging
as a dusty moth in a few seconds.

"You're wrong to keep secrets from us, doc," the voice
said. "I found out about this woman, Poppy, things about
her background. She likes to talk about her past. Especially
when it involves you."

"I don't know her, Mr. Grace. I believe she was a correspondent
of my wife's. She might even have been interested
in blackmail, concerning our dead son. This woman also
fueled my wife's paranoia. She is perhaps someone from my
early childhood whom I don't remember, or who has illegally
been put in touch with my family by some unethical
agency. And my wife, susceptible as she is to every crank
and charlatan ... Well, why waste my breath? I suppose

your agency enjoys wading through filth, given its past activities." Robert looked up at his clock. The show he wanted to watch should've already started. This nature bit was running too long.

"Doc?" The voice from the speakerphone asked. "You there, doc?"

Robert said wearily, "Yes. Please don't call me doc. I find it rather annoying."

Grace ignored this. "Poppy says she's your sister."

The credits came up on the TV screen, over the moth as it flew out into the pale blue sky. The show was ending.

"Well, she can't very well be my sister, can she? The only one I know of is in San Diego and is named Vonna Stewart."

"Is she the only family you have, doc? My boys seem to have come up with a few others around the state."

"Like I said, you're wading through filth."

"You can describe your life like that if you want, doc."

The next show was coming on, and at this he turned up the sound. The voice-over said, "And in the world of bacteriology, the experiments of men such as William Grasse and Robert Stewart combine the best of our space research with . . ."

"Turn the TV down, doc. I can't hear myself think," the other man said. "Jeez, I'm familiar with your work, I don't need to hear some self-congratulatory broadcast."

Robert muted the sound. "Look, this Poppy from San Francisco, you must know from speaking with her, how absolutely loopy she is. I have no doubt you've already been through the mail. The notes she sent. That sort of childish—"

"She told us about your second mother, doc."

The image of the screen showed his acceptance of the Pasteur Medal for Achievement in the Field of Microbiology. Then a brief shot of him with Dr. Grasse in the isolation suits, walking through the Prewitt Laboratory in Denver. Making the thumbs-up sign as he held up a dropper with liquid r-7 in its tip. He wondered if the filmmaker had decided whether to portray him as a leader in the field of bacterial research or as a pawn of the government war machine. Only he knew that he was neither. Only he knew what the significance of r-7 would be. And he would keep it that way so that no government could ever use the virus for its own political purposes.

"Doc? You still there? Hello?"

Robert Stewart glanced with annoyance at the telephone. "I think you should stick with your assignment, Mr. Grace. I've told you, my wife is very ill. She cannot be held responsible for her actions."

"You've told me lots of things in the past month. None of them true. Why don't we start with the truth? Didn't your mother teach you the value of truth, doc?"

Robert stared out of his study window.

The voice said, "Why don't we start with where your wife is going?"

"Well, you have my tapes. And I thought you'd found out about Farrell."

"Yeah, but he's a weak link. A know-nothing. There's a hidden agenda. A secret. We know that, don't we, Doc?"

"Thugs."

"Doc?"

"You're a bunch of thugs. In India, the thugees were an order of assassins who waylaid travelers and strangled them along the roadside. They believed they appeased their goddess of destruction, Kali, who was also the principle of creation. What god or goddess do you worship, Mr. Grace?"

"None of your damn business. So, you're a man of science with a mystical bent. Do you worship a god, doc?"

Robert twisted a paper clip in his hand, unbending the wire. "I worship the world of the possible. I think it is possible that you might help my wife and daughter, if you and your thugs had any trace of simian resourcefulness."

"Oh, doc, don't you worry. Help is on its way. But no more bones."

"Bones?"

"Yeah. You heard me. Bones tossed to dogs. Trails to nowhere. I think you know what I'm saying. Poppy has been real helpful on clarifying a few points. It didn't take any persuasion. But you must know how she loves to talk. A mouth that goes on forever, doc. You might be happy to know we found her all strung out and sleeping on the streets. A shame what life's done to her. You'd almost think she got tortured somewhere along the way, you know? We cleaned her up a little, but she went back to living on the streets. But you're a man of compassion; you understand that type of thing, don't you?"

"Tell me something," Robert said.

"What's up, doc?"

"Was it you?"

"Was it me what?"

"Was it you who tried to kill my daughter?"

The man on the other end of the line broke into hoarse laughter. Robert recognized it as a response to long-term stress. He had dealt with this response before—with Kate.

"Was it you who tried to kill her?" Robert repeated, and felt the anger, the rage, at what this man and all his monsters meant to do.

The voice on the speakerphone said, "Doc, I got to tell you. I don't know from *try.*"

20

From Dr. Robert Stewart's tapes

"R-seven is a unicellular life-form, but it mutates and seems to build upon already existing cells without destroying them, so it cannot properly be termed a parasite. It is a kind of powerful transformer. It seems to exaggerate, in the specimen, what is already there. Thus the aggressive rhesus monkey becoming more so, and the rats with accelerated rate of illness. Four-oh-four-eight-five seems to have increased capabilities, but was perhaps injected with r-seven too soon. Onset of mammalian adolescence seems a requirement for a nondestructive effect. I am hoping that six-two-two-eight-two proves my point. It is quite a phenomenon, a miracle from the stars, as it were. Life building upon life, a melding of two separate life-forms to create a whole greater than the sum of its parts. With this synthetic approximation, who knows? A leap into the future of evolution. Evolution observed, in process . . ."

Special Projects had an office on the fifth floor of the Pacific Rim Bank building, just down from the Hilton, six blocks from Farrell's place, but Stephen Grace was beginning to think that Holder and the boys were keeping him out of the line of fire on this one anyway. What the hell did it matter if Farrell got a line on something? Grace wanted the girl, not the mother's old flame. He would've waited for the elevator, but he was restless; he jogged up the stairs, entered the office by the back way. On the office door, it said, "Orestes Consultants, Technical Group." A different name for every month. Grace wondered what they did it all for, why all that creativity went into name changes and cover-ups and hidden bank accounts, when nobody ever seemed to get found out or prosecuted. Maybe a few did, through the Company's history, but they were the ones who were no longer needed and who perhaps would be dangerous if they were *not* tossed to the Justice Department. He didn't for a minute doubt that one day he would be the sacrificial lamb; with each assignment he always kept something for himself, some kind of protection as a guarantee that he would not end up behind bars. For this assignment, he had gotten hold of Stewart's research tapes. He knew that, whatever stunt Holder might pull, he had him by the balls. *If I can only put together what the hell Stewart's really gabbing about.*

Once through the doors of Orestes, he got the third-degree search. Company Security tended to be cop discards or agent wanna-bes, all of whom smelled of nervous sweat and had some kind of attitude problem. This time Security came in the form of an overweight slob in an ill-fitting blue uniform. Grace made a mental note: another operative who had never finished basic training but had gotten a kick up the payroll from Washington. In Projects, you got either the field or the desk. One meant streets smarts and one meant book smarts. But when they hired you for fucking Security, it meant you had no smarts.

"Hello, Homer," Grace said, passing his I.D. to the man.

The guard said nothing, but waved him through the double doors.

Grace smiled for the three cameras. Totally unnecessary, since nobody gave a shit if Special Projects was up here or not; it was just the suits' way of pretending to have power over the rest of the mere mortals. Or else it was their way of making sure that their own operatives didn't come up one day and slit their throats.

He went past a pretty secretary. She was new and looked to be about twenty-six. They never hired unattractive ones, and this one smiled at him until she noticed his fatigue jacket and jeans, and then she must've thought he was too downscale for her attentions. "It ain't *GQ*." He winked at her as he passed. He wondered what kind of government-issue sexual harassment this woman was in for from a lech like Holder. Nathan Holder, former big businessman, former ambassador to Germany, former psychiatrist, current asshole-in-residence, at least for the duration of this assignment. Organized the Laos chemical spill in '66 and tried to double-deal the Libyans in their own terrorist game. An all-American kind of guy. Holder, known among the other operatives as Ass-Holder. Holder, the same army psych who once upon a time diagnosed Grace as paranoid, possibly schizophrenic, with no chemical base, possible psychotic, definitely dangerous. Who woulda thunk the Ass-Holder would make director of Special Projects at the Company just because of a chemical warfare success in Nam, and start recruiting the misfits of the Big Bang? And a nice guy named Stevie would end up having to suck up to him just to get the kind of job he was good at, after the Wars of the World were done? *You and me, Holder, we got a goddamn history.*

Finally Holder's personal secretary, Jean, met Grace in the outer office. She looked exhausted—must've caught the red-eye from Washington that morning—and her face was getting old before its time. Her husband had been in the field and then got the boot, but Jean was a Company pro and was better at keeping secrets than her spouse. *I remem-*

ber when you looked real. Too much stress working for a former war hero and psychiatrist.

"How's the Son of God today?" Grace asked as he shook her hand.

"Shh." She attempted a smile, but none came. Her desk was immaculately organized, and he noticed that in her in box was a memo with the heading, "r-7 test file." She must've seen him looking; she picked up the memo and the file beneath it and slipped it beneath some others. He made a move for it, as casually as he could, but she was equally as casual in pushing him away from her desk. "Do you feel as bad as you look, Grace?"

He grinned, giving up. "Always with the compliments."

"He said he could take a call."

"I'm fucking sick of the goddamn phone. Methinks the old fart is dicking with me."

Holder's voice came over the intercom: "Try to remember there's a lady present. That gutter mouth of yours won't make rank, Grace."

Jean pointed to the camera above the door; she whispered, "Smile."

Stephen Grace looked at the camera and said flatly, "Big Brother is back."

"Get in here," rasped the voice on the intercom.

"You ever read Tolkien, Jean?"

She shook her head.

"That's what Holder's like, something out of *The Hobbit.* I think its name was Gollum. Yeah, slimy and sucking up to anyone in authority. Holder even looks like him, a little, if I remember right. You should read it, it's really terrific." Stephen Grace winked at her and then leaned forward, closer to the intercom, saying, "You, too, sir, should read Tolkien. It's all about creatures who want power."

"We've found the girl," Holder said, dispensing with greetings as Grace closed the door behind him, entering the inner sanctum.

"Okay, so where do I go?" Grace hung back; the inner office was unfurnished except for the desk and the computer and phone. Not the opulence to which Holder was accustomed along the Potomac. *Must be a comedown for the man with horses and acres and servants and a wife and at least three mistresses that anyone knows of. Slumming it, are we?*

"You can come sit here." Nathan Holder indicated a chair beside the desk.

"No, thank you, sir. You remember, sir, that my favorite movies are *The Godfather* trilogy?"

"Please, Grace," Holder said with disgust.

"Well, one thing I learned from them is that you don't sit too close to someone because he might slice your fuckin' neck open. Especially if he's an old friend."

"We're not all out to get you, Grace."

"And just because you're paranoid doesn't mean people *aren't* talking about you. That's Woody Allen, Holder. I like my movies. Like my books. You really should read Tolkien, sir. So, where's the girl?"

"I said we found her. I didn't say we had her. This has to be a careful assignment, Grace. You know that."

"Yeah, right. So she's someplace, but we don't know where."

"We think she's heading here, after all."

"You're so smart, Holder."

His superior ignored this comment. "A highway patrol officer gave us the tip."

"We got a report from a cop?" Grace shook his head. "I got twelve men on the fucking road from Nevada, and we get a highway cop who knows more? Jesus. Jesus. You know, Holder, you should've let me handle this in my own way. The department's got nothing but fuckups."

He stood, his back to the wall, near the door.

"Grace," said the man behind the desk, "when you want to talk like that, go find a sewer. And for someone who didn't finish his work on the girl a week ago, I should think you'd see the irony of your own comment."

Yeah, and I'd like to ream you a new asshole, Mr. Washington D.C. Stephen Grace smiled, baring what fangs he had. Holder was such an officious prick, Grace wondered how the hell he'd gotten to the position of power he was in. *Ass-kissing goes a long way on the East Coast. If only I had the shit that girl has, maybe I could get him to lose some skin.*

Holder sifted through papers on his desk; he let his glasses slide down the bridge of his nose. "What's with Farrell?"

"You know."

"What do you think?"

"What I think is going on, sir, is exactly what was in my report. I know you think it's bullshit, but Stewart has some other agenda. Not just the misuse of r-seven. But I told you Friday, and it doesn't make a dent. I don't see why we don't just pick the motherfucker up and make him sweat. He's the one holding all the cards here."

Holder said nothing.

Yeah, asshole, what is it? The doc's got you and military intelligence by the balls somehow. So you want me to nuke the girl but not the father. But Stephen Grace was also silent.

After a minute Holder said, "Farrell's been on the phone to the mother."

"Yeah, yeah, so what? The guy's got zilch. Why don't you look at Stewart? He's the master planner. He's the fucking mad scientist here. Farrell's an old boyfriend of the mother's. He's just a cipher."

"I want you to stay with him."

"Jesus."

"Grace," Holder said, admonishing, "I hope you're going to stay within bounds this time. No side pursuits. Not like last time."

"No, sir. I'll be good." He laughed, turning to open the door. "Hey, you hire a psycho, Holder, and you never know *what* the hell's gonna happen. How're your business holdings in the Middle East doing?"

Nathan Holder must have gotten used to the gibes; he didn't acknowledge this last one. "No one here thinks of you as a psycho, Grace."

"Oh, yeah, they do." Stephen Grace didn't even turn around to look at Holder. He knew he'd see that smug pseudo-psychiatric sympathy shit in his eyes. He sighed, muttering under his breath, "And I *am* one, too. Pushing fifty, and still crazy after all these years. That's Paul Simon, sir; I like to acknowledge my sources. Don't you?"

He walked out of the office, wondering how the hell he was going to catch the girl if he was sitting on Farrell's tail all night.

21

AFTER HE'D HUNG UP THE PHONE WITH KATE, BEN FARRELL
sat and stared at the wall. Waiting. He hadn't told Kate
about the second call from Robert, the one that had come
at 7:45, too close to her own call.

He had taped the call on his answering machine, and now
he played it back: "Ben? This is Dr. Stewart again. Bobby.
Listen, something I didn't tell you when last we spoke. And
you were so rude. I'm glad I got the machine this time. It
won't hang up on me...."

But it did, Bobby boy. Ben chuckled to himself. *It's only
programmed for four minutes, you arrogant prick.*

"I've spoken with Kate's psychiatrist, Dr. Jardin. She was
on a prescription for psychotropics. Lithium, too. I found
the bottles beneath the bathroom sink where she left them.
She might possibly be in her manic phase. I understand your
concern for her and for my daughter. But I think if you do
hear from her you could call me, not the police. I don't
want her to end up in some state hospital where it'll take
every lawyer in the country to extricate her. I want to do
what's best for her and what's best for my daughter. I don't
want—"

But then the tape had cut off.

Robert had called back, perhaps twice. The third time, he
continued his message: "I see you found an electronic way
to hang up on me, Ben. As I said, I don't want anything
bad to happen to Kate or to Hope. They have both been
through plenty to last a lifetime. If you hear from them,

please call me, day or night. If you do hear from them and you don't call, then I'll hold you personally responsible for whatever happens to them. Kate is not herself, and Hope is in danger because of it. You must believe me. Thank you."

The worst part about this message was that Ben was afraid he was beginning to believe Robert. He had called him the Mad Doctor back when he was an undergraduate, but only because Robert had stolen Kate from him. In the end the marriage had worked out, and Ben had realized that it was meant to be. He and Kate would never have worked out as a couple, for various reasons. That had never stopped him from caring about her, and it hadn't kept him from feeling that unreasoning jealousy of Robert, who was worldly and brilliant and rich.

More than anything, Ben hated the idea that Robert might actually be right. Over the past three years Kate had begun talking about things she was seeing that no one else seemed to notice, and she spoke about voices and an incipient paranoia that grew with each passing day.

Not Katy. Not Katy Weeks who used to make him corn bread and fried catfish for dinner because she said it was something she knew well, "white trash cooking." Not Katy Weeks, who had held on to her virginity for two valiant years while Ben pressured her, until she finally decided it was high time, but only if it was going to be ridiculously romantic, so they had run away to Cambria for the weekend. Ben had spent every penny he had on a cabin, and they were so exhausted from bicycling that they barely had the energy to kiss. Until Sunday. Their last day. And then it had been something unexpected, a physical, spiritual thing, unlike being with the two other girls he had known in high school. It had been breathtaking, exhilarating, and he'd had the energy to jog six miles up and down the road by the ocean afterward just to come down from the high. It hadn't even been lust, to which he was accustomed, but an incredible sharing.

This woman Robert was describing was not Katy.

Not my Katy.

Ben erased the tape and wondered when Hope would beep him.

He had given her the code: "Tell Hope she's too old to be afraid of the dark."

It was his signal to her that they needed to talk in private.

It usually took her ten or fifteen minutes to get somewhere where she could beep him.

If he hadn't lost the beeper again.

Ben Farrell quickly glanced over his book-and-magazine-heavy apartment and wondered how he could have lost the infernal machine in less than ten minutes. He could wait until Hope beeped him, but that might be a while, and he would have preferred to grab it and get out, maybe down to Chinatown, to make the call. He wadded up old newspapers in an attempt to find it, and then came up with the brilliant idea of beeping himself. He picked up his phone, dialed the number, tapped in his own home number, hung up.

Waited.

Within thirty seconds, the high-pitched sound, calling all dogs, doctors, drug dealers, and reporters whose editors liked having them available at all hours. He tossed several paperbacks off the worn couch and dug down behind the cushions. There it was, nestled with seven potato chips and his keys. He munched on a chip and pocketed the keys and beeper. It had been chilly in the afternoon, so he grabbed his tweed jacket from the back of the kitchen chair, threw it over his shoulder, and hustled outside.

"Come on, Hope, come on," he mumbled his mantra. He was in a mantra kind of mood, having just done an exposé of some New Agers who were ripping people off over in his old stomping grounds, Berkeley, and he'd even gotten a pat on the back from the big guy himself. The next story, the one that Kate herself would tell him, and for which she would be paid the small fortune of three thousand dollars—to Ben, a great big fortune, actually—might even get him some national attention, and it would get Kate what she wanted: protection for Hope. So he was in a good mood, and even seeing his Shadow didn't faze him.

"Hello, Shadow." He waved to the man sitting in the brown mid-size car. The man was not ugly, as Ben had at first thought, just unpleasant. Someone who didn't enjoy getting up in the morning. Or going to bed at night. Or the in-between stuff. His Shadow actually nodded courteously.

Ben's car was parked up the street, but he figured Shadow might follow him, and he didn't want that. He jogged down to Pierce, took a left, and didn't look back to see if Shadow was trying to figure this out. He walked into Daryl Woodward's store, ostensibly to buy cigarettes, but once he had his Marlboro Light 100s, he walked out back to the stockroom to say hey to Daryl and his son, and he hung out there awhile, even though it was cold and some very fleshy meat was hanging from the ceiling, too much for a vegetarian to keep quiet about. So he had an argument with Daryl's son, Paul, who was nineteen, about how cattle were raised and the chemicals pumped into them; Paul, to his credit, asked Ben not to smoke around the meat. "Never mind the chemicals," Paul said rather snippily. "Think of the nicotine."

"Okay, you win." Ben crushed the cigarette out.

"Sneaking away from an irate victim of your yellow journalism?" Paul asked.

"Not quite. Some detective's following me. Shadow, I call him."

"You want to lose him?"

"He's waiting right outside, I'd venture to guess."

"We got another way out." Paul led Ben through the house of horrors filled with hanging sides of beef, and Ben was feeling a little green from it. There was a small stairway—a half-dozen concrete steps down to a low cellar. "You go through there, and there's another stairway leading up the other side. You can get over the back fence if you're feeling acrobatic, and cut through the yard beyond. That is, *if* the owners don't shoot you for trespassing."

"Great, thanks." Ben ducked and went down the stairs into the gray-lit room, the low ceiling keeping him hunched over. He maneuvered his way around boxes of soda and candy and came out into the alley.

The car was just one store down. Shadow had guessed his every move.

Ben didn't know what to do, other than smile at the man sitting behind the wheel. "You son of a bitch," he muttered.

The man was smoking a cigarette. *The great and mighty Shadow smokes.* Ben was feeling ballsy, so he walked right up to the car. Shadow's window was down.

"Got a light?" he asked.

Shadow didn't say a word. Just reached up to the dashboard, picked up a lighter, and flicked its flame up for Ben's cigarette.

Ben saw the face for only a second, but it wasn't what he'd expected. If Ben had been at his parents' for Christmas, this would have been his cousin Griff, young and old at the same time at forty. Deep-set green eyes, almost like a snake's, but not so cold. Not so cold at all. A high forehead and the kind of blond hair that had darkened with age, but still fell in a thin field down over the right side of his brow. A hairline scar running from his right nostril down along his smile line to the curve of his chin. And tight lips, glued together. When Ben had the cigarette glowing, he moved back, and Shadow rolled his window up. Ben was about to say something, rap on the window, anything ... *Damn! You're a reporter, Farrell, and this guy intimidates you like he's a ghost or something. Jesus, you can get in the line of fire of a bunch of pro-lifers, and you can question the morals of a Mafia family to the godfather's face, but you can't even open your mouth to the Shadow.*

The Shadow drove on down the alley, out to Bush Street, and Ben knew this was a fuck-you, if he ever saw one.

You're telling me that you can find me anywhere, anytime, Shadow. You're here whenever I turn my back. You're the actualization of all my inherent paranoia. I'll look around, and you won't be there. I'll run away, and you'll be where I run to.

And then the high-pitched beep from the device in his pocket. *Must be Hope. Perfect timing.*

22

New Friends

FIFTEEN MINUTES BEFORE CALLING BEN IN SAN FRANCISCO, Hope walked out into the damp night; it was drip-dropping rain now, mainly from the live oaks perched just beyond the pavement. She looked for the soda machine but never found it. Then she walked down the cracked sidewalk, lit by the porch lights of half a dozen houses next to the motel, down to the hamburger place. It was called AttaBurger. There was a pay phone inside, and the pictures of the hamburgers and french fries looked good. She counted her change and went in.

"I'd like the King AttaBurger and a large fries, and a small Coke," she told the pimply-faced boy behind the shiny counter.

"Three-oh-six," he said.

Hope took a minute to count her change out. She was fifteen cents short, but was hoping he wouldn't notice.

He, too, counted out the quarters, nickels, and pennies. "Got another dime and nickel?"

She sighed. "No. I guess I won't have the fries."

Behind her a girl said, "Ah, jeez, you ain't gonna starve her just 'cause she's short a couple of pennies, Jake?" The girl's hand moved into Hope's line of vision, tossing a twenty dollar bill on the counter. "Break that, Jake," she said.

"My name's not Jake," the boy huffed.

"Everybody in this pissant burg's a Jake."

The girl was standing on her right, and Hope couldn't see her. When she turned around and looked at her with her good eye, she saw that the girl was only slightly taller than

she was, but definitely older, probably sixteen. But something about her made Hope think maybe she was only
twelve or thirteen, but had grown up really fast—kind of
like the way Hope felt on the inside. "Thanks," she said.
Hope didn't think the girl had any illness, although she felt
a tugging in the space where her eye had been. She saw
something there in the darkness—what her father had called
her dark of eye, just like she used to have a white of eye—
some shape, but it might've been a blip, like snow on the
TV screen. That happened sometimes, and it didn't mean
anyone was sick.

"Hi, where'd you get that patch?" the girl asked, and it
didn't even seem rude. "It's so cool, just like a pirate, so
mysterious, so glamorous. All you need's a hat or something.
You can't be from around her, 'cause nobody's glamorous
or nothing in this pissant burg, just mean and cold like they
got enemas up their butts that didn't take, you know?" She
had a baby-girl kind of way of speaking, and Hope thought
it was the way her doll, Nina, would sound if she could talk.

"I'm not supposed to talk to strangers," Hope said, feeling
like she must sound like a four-year-old.

"Well, I'm Iris Lefcourt from Minnesota, and I'm thirteen,
and I am not a virgin since I was twelve, and my mother
was Catholic and my father is Lutheran, and I have never
liked oysters or tomatoes. My favorite color is *not,* and my
least favorite part of life is going to the bathroom, and let
me tell you, if I could pay someone else to do it, I would.
There, now I ain't no stranger." Iris Lefcourt and Hope both
noticed Jake staring at them at the same time, and Iris
barked, "Change, please!"

After she and Iris had settled onto the taped-up red stools
by the front window, Hope excused herself to go call Ben.
She punched in his phone code and beeper number, and the
pay phone number and then hung the phone up. She glanced
over at Iris who, she noticed, was sneaking her french fries
as if being caught at it were an enormous crime with a
dreadful punishment. Hope smiled and mouthed, "Have as
many as you want."

She looked at her Swatch watch: almost 9:15. *Mom's
gonna be out of the tub and worried. Hurry up, Ben.*

A few seconds later the phone rang.

"You okay?" Ben asked.

"Yeah. Just tired. Ben, I been thinking about what you told me last time. I think Mom needs help. I want it to end now. She keeps thinking people are following us when they're not."

Silence on the line. Then Ben said, "Okay, Hope." He sounded sad. "So are you going to tell me?"

"Okay. We're in a town called Empire. It's real small. I think the sign said a hundred miles or maybe just a little more to San Francisco. We're east, and a little south, from you."

"You're at a motel?"

"The Backwa—the Greenwater Motor Lodge. Room number six. I have to go back, Ben. She's going to panic if I don't get back now."

"I'll be there soon, sweet pea. An hour if I drive fast."

"Ben," she whispered into the phone, "drive *very* fast. I'm scared. For Mommy." She hung up before he could say anything. She felt her eye patch. It hurt a little. Tingled. Something was weird, but maybe she was just getting one of her humongous headaches. Sometimes her glass eye rubbed against the inside of her skin all wrong.

Through the glass door of AttaBurger she saw a man and wondered why he seemed familiar.

And then she knew.

It was the man named Matt who had changed their tire that afternoon.

23

KATE STEWART WAS TRYING NOT TO LOSE CONTROL. HOPE was probably fine. Kate had stayed in the bath too long; the skin on her hands had wrinkled like a preview of old age. *If I make it that long . . .*

Actually she had been relaxing for the first time since Hope's accident. A hot bath, lots of bubbles, the music on Hope's transistor radio turned up. The two choices of stations in Empire were country and classical with a Muzak mix, and she'd chosen the latter. She had no idea what the selection was, but when she'd closed her eyes and sunk down into the small tub, the strings and the woodwinds took her somewhere else. It was the closest she'd ever come to an out-of-body experience. Amazing. One minute tied up into so many knots, feeling so many pains in her chest and her head she thought she'd end up with a coronary and an aneurysm all in one. And then, floating peace. And no double-header Xanax, either. No experimental psychotropics from Dr. Jardin's evil garden. She'd been on the drugs so long that she'd forgotten how smooth reality could be without them.

She opened her eyes, briefly, sleepily, to regard the bathroom: tile, yellowed and stained, a brown mildewed plastic curtain, a black-seated toilet—very clean, actually, as was the tub, still smelling of Comet and Clorox. Hope's doll, Nina, sat up on the windowsill—Hope must have set it up there when she used the bathroom. The doll was as grimy as the window itself. Nina had been through a lot of wars.

Hope clung to certain early-childhood things as if for dear life—the baby doll, the dog-eared and dog-chewed copy of *Goodnight, Moon,* the stuffed owl her father had given her when she was two. Kate had always loved Hope even more for this habit of hanging on to childhood; Robert wanted Hope to grow up quickly, pressuring her to skip grades, to learn beyond a young child's capacity. These childhood treasures were a sign, Kate figured, of Hope's rebellious nature. Kate hoped to encourage this in her daughter. She herself had buckled beneath the authority of her own parents and of Robert for too many years; she wanted a better life for Hope.

Kate closed her eyes again, trying to just forget the pain of the past two years. Forget the accident of two weeks ago. Just wanted a cool darkness, like a bed of warmth and suds, and soon she was falling asleep.

And in her dream, lasting only a few minutes, the day of the accident was replayed, as it always seemed to be, for the terror had not left her.

Drunk on pills. Shit.

Glance around the bedside table. Nothing but pills. Lithium for the madwoman. Hate doctors. Hate Robert. Hate my father.

Phone ringing somewhere in house. House too big. Too big, but not big enough for Robert. Needs his privacy. Needs his home office. Locks his home lab. Needs privacy. Well, what for, Bobby? You got porno movies in there? You bring in dead animals to dissect? You keeping secrets from me again?

I want a divorce, Robert. You know that, Robber-Bobber. Never sleep together, never talk together, never see each other. But Hope, you see Hope a lot, don't you? You even take her in that office. You and Hope out for a ride today. I could kill you if you are doing anything to hurt her. I would get a good lawyer, but you have 'em all to yourself, all those damn lawyers. Well, I'll find a female lawyer and a female judge, and they'll know what I'm babbling about. They'll know what it means when a father wants to bathe his little girl and when a father takes her into his locked office. I may be crazy, but I ain't stupid.

I am walking up the stairs to the third floor, down the hall, sliding in bare feet on the slick wood floor, feeling drunk on pills, and wondering what it is that Robert Bluebeard keeps in his home office, his lab away from lab. Maybe all his other wives' blood in cauldrons, maybe dead animals or maybe Penthouse *magazines with pages sticking together. I come to the office door, part of the house add-on, B.K.—Before Kate—and it's like he left in a rush again. Leaves the door unlocked, maybe part open, done that at least twenty times before, but his mousy, doped-up wife is too chicken to look in, like the girl in* Rebecca, *just too intimidated by the big cheese, but this time wifey's got balls of steel, and she pushes the door open and sees what she expects. Boring. Painted white and smelling like rubbing alcohol just like his lab in the desert. Just like Robert. Diplomas on wall—she smashes one of them, but only cuts her fingers. She is into symbolic expressions of hostility. Dr. Jardin told her that. He also told her, last time she bothered going, that when she attacked Robert with his own surgical shears she was angry at his job and she was taking it out on him. She was borderline just about everything. She will do it again if she has to, she thinks. She hates the fact that Robert's so overeducated when she had to drop out as an undergrad at Berkeley because she had to marry him now-now-now. . . . She walks into a steel closet, and it feels cold, and wifey didn't know that hubby had a walk-in fridge in his enormous office, and she does something stupid: she lets the door shut and then realizes she can't get out because the latch is on the outside. Oh, well, screw it, he can just find me here. I own half this house, too. I think, she thinks, wifey thinks, and hopes when she walks out the door finally she will find out this is true from her female lawyer and female judge. Then she notices the shelves, first the wrapped sandwiches and the milk—Robert prepares his own lunches when he's up all night working—and then the other things, each with a label and in Baggies or petri dishes, and she feels sick even with the pills, because it's all dead animal tissue and parts, the kind of stuff she figures goes into hamburgers on the fast-food strip, but still repulsive. Then she finds one that is newly labeled, and she doesn't recognize it at first, but when she does, she screams like it's the end of the world, and then laughs until she feels the cold of the fridge and the effect*

*of that last Prozac she took coupled with her hyperventilating.
As usual, she fails at reality. She blacks out.*

*And wakes up in bed, a dream, a dream, because she
doesn't the hell remember what it was she saw that took her
breath away in the walk-in fridge.*

Kate opened her eyes. She was in the tub in the bathroom
in the Greenwater Motor Lodge in Empire, California.

"Hope?" she called out.

The strings and the woodwinds played on the radio, with
only a little static.

"Hope? Baby?" Kate asked again, rising from the tub and
reaching for a bath towel.

24

"SEE THAT MAN OUT THERE?" HOPE ASKED IRIS.

"Yeah. I seen him before." Iris smacked her lips as she
ate, french fry grease making her lips all glossy. "He's like
the village idiot here, lives up in the commune. I been here
three days, Christ Almighty, and already I know the local
yokels."

"Something's wrong with him."

"Yeah, he's a half-wit. You gonna finish your burger?"

Hope shook her head, and pushed the sloppily assembled
double-decker hamburger across the table. "I mean, something's really wrong. I almost can see it."

"You can't see much with only one eye in working order."
Iris laughed, and then grinned apologetically for the bad
joke. "My mouth gets ahead of my brain sometimes."

"Some kind of fence."

"Hope? You spacing?"

Hope again, almost hypnotically, "Some kind of fence. Like I can almost see through it, but not much. Like he's not sick, but he's different. Like there's something missing."

"You read a lot into first impressions, kid," Iris said.

Hope realized where she was, and was silent. *I should go back to the motel. Mom's gonna be furious. And weirded-out. But what if he's a bad man? What if he's like the man from the nightmares? The one who held me down so I couldn't move, the one who opened a door and threw me out from it?*

What came to her next was something she had only marginally experienced before.

The vision. In her lost eye. Inner eye. As if it could still see. So vivid, so real.

He was not a man, but some kind of hairy animal, and he held her down on a cold floor and peeled her patch back, and with his grimy finger he began sawing against her eye socket.

She knows who you are.

Monkey Lovett shivered uncontrollably as he stood just beyond the light from the AttaBurger parking lot. It had been like she was inside him, tickling his armpits, teasing him. *Oh, Mama, make it stop. Make her stop. She's just a monster. Birdy can't be right. She can't be the one!*

But she is, Birdy said, *and you can go in there right now and get her. You have to act fast, Monkey.*

But it hurts so much, Birdy, I just ca-ca-can't. Now it was like a river of ice, pain running beneath the frozen surface, beneath his skin.

He broke his gaze from the girl's and went running off down the road, knowing that he would have to get her somehow, somehow, maybe with Birdy's instruments, but not when she was looking at him, not like *that.*

"Hey, you okay?" Iris waved a french fry in front of Hope's face.

Hope blinked, and then her vision adjusted. Iris was pretty

in a way that Hope liked: no makeup, no pretense. She just was. "Is he still there?" She cast her gaze around.

"I can't see him. Wow, Hope, why'd you freak out?"

Hope said, "I think he wants to hurt me. I think maybe he wants to kill me."

"Baby?" Kate, half covered with a large white towel, opened the bathroom door. She dripped water across the cheap brown carpeting as she walked quickly to the outside door. She opened it, stuck her head out. "Hope!" she called.

She went to the bed and picked up her watch: 9:38. "Shit," she muttered, dropping the towel, getting back into her jeans, pulling a sweatshirt out of the mess of bags and tugging it over her head. She stepped into her sneakers and grabbed the motel key on the way out. Slammed the door, but it didn't stay shut, and she had to slam it twice—but what the hell did it matter when anyone could break in through the windows so easily?

She checked the car and then went around to find the soda machine. The girl at the front desk told her there was no machine. "But AttaBurger ought to be open down the block." She pointed to the left.

Kate peered out the office door. The air still smelled of rain and the fertile odor of California live oak, like a strange aphrodisiac. She stepped out onto the shiny asphalt drive and smelled sweet fruit, beyond ripening, coming from across the road, from the field, carried by an easy wind. For a moment her panic eluded her. This town of Empire was lush, or the rain had made it so. The houses down the road were poorly lit, but she could see two-story buildings from the early 1900s with wraparound porches. And silence. She had never been for more than a few minutes in a place like this, so small you could walk from end to end in a few minutes; a complete tour would take you around three blocks. Nothing could happen to Hope in a place like this. A lone dog barked from somewhere up the road, and then she heard someone yell at the dog to be quiet. Like her hypnosis tapes, this place seemed to have a calming influence. As she walked out along the road, stepping up onto the thin and crumbly sidewalk, Kate glanced about, thinking she would see Hope through the shadows. She heard unidentifiable country music from a stereo as she passed a large house with a feeble yellow porch light; on the other side of it she saw the movie-screen white light of the AttaBurger, and there, sitting at the window, Hope.

Kate smiled, more relieved than angry, until she noticed the girl sitting next to Hope, an older girl, a girl who had her arm out, and something in her right hand—a pencil? a stick? a knife?—pointed downward at Hope's own arm.

Kate Stewart walked faster and faster, but no matter how fast she went, Hope and the girl and the burger joint all seemed to recede and get farther and farther away from her.

Don't hyperventilate, do not, do not, Kate commanded herself. She stopped for just a second, cupping both hands over her mouth. She felt her warm and slightly sour breath against her hands and face.

Now she could see clearly what the girl sitting next to Hope had in her hands.

A syringe.

"I got to poke myself like this," Iris was saying, "every now and then when I eat something like this." She indicated the spread of food wrappers and paper cups with a nod of her head. Iris's hand quivered a little, holding the needle just above the crook of her left arm. "The trick is, I'm left-handed, but my right arm's sore, so I got to poke the needle in my left, even though I'm a little shaky."

"Doesn't it hurt?" Hope asked.

Iris withdrew the syringe, setting it back in its small red case. "It's like anything. Gets to be part of the general pain of life."

"Yeah." Hope grinned.

"Like you'd know, buckaroo." Iris nudged her.

"I do."

Iris pointed out the window. "It's a night for weirdos," she said. "What do you think *she's* on?"

Hope looked at the glass door, swinging shut, the same as Iris, and saw her mother walking toward her with that look on her face. But it was the last thing Hope remembered for the next few minutes, because Iris touched her shoulder, and Hope suddenly felt the nerves jumping behind her right eye, like her eye was being re-created out of nothing, liquid from her brain pouring into some remnant of optic nerve, creating the white, the pupil, there behind her eye patch. The pain was brief, more an afterimage of pain, like something clutching and letting go of her there, and clutching again. She heard a word, and as always, she didn't understand the word, it was phonetic, but repeated several times.

And then, the vision, the clawing darkness, the light breaking through like flashes of lightning, rhythmic and steady, closer and closer.

"Baby," she heard her mother's voice as though at the end of a Dixie cup telephone, and then clearer.

She awoke to an intense feeling of heat beneath her skin. Her mother hugged her tight.

The light from the long fluorescent tubes above her seemed burning.

Her mother called out, "Get me some ice! I need some ice!"

A voice, her guardian angel, repeating one word again and again: "Perfect." Glowing yellow and orange lights like lightning bugs against a dark night. "Perfect," the Voice whispered. Comforting. A thousand butterflies fluttering along her face, crawling into her mouth. Beautiful orange and yellow butterfly wings slapping her gently. Taste of butterfly dust on her tongue. "Perfect," the Voice said.

The Voice died away, the vision faded. Hope looked at her mother, not recognizing her at first. And then she couldn't remember what the Voice had said to her. Her face was warm; she reached up and touched her nose and lips to make sure they were still in place. She'd had a feeling of her body changing, of something growing inside, like maybe she was getting taller.

"Baby?" Her mother said.

Hope was sitting up in her mother's lap on the red stool at the AttaBurger in Empire, California, on a back road to San Francisco. She remembered: it had begun when Iris gripped her. Iris was now sitting across from them, sullen.

"I almost went," Hope whispered, embarrassed.

"You need to go now?"

Hope raised her eyebrows. "Yeah."

"Okay."

There was a rest room behind the concrete block wall, and Kate unlocked the door with the key that the boy selling hamburgers had given her. The room stank.

Hope said, "It might be dirty."

Kate went and wiped the toilet seat off. She had kept calm inside the restaurant, but now, here, she let her anger out. "Jesus, Hope, I was about to jump out a window, and you're sitting there with some stranger, who has God knows what disease."

"Dia-something," Hope said.

Kate held her breath for an instant. Then the knowledge seeped through her, and her eyes grew wide. "Dia*betes*, oh, Christ, Hope, she has *diabetes?*"

Hope began crying uncontrollably. "Why does this keep happening to me? Why can't you make it stop? Make it *stop!*"

Kate clutched her stomach, leaning over the sink, suddenly nauseated. Like cramps, only worse. She looked at her face in the mirror and barely recognized it. Bit down on the corner of her lower lip so hard that a pearl of blood appeared. *God, the pain was intense.*

Hope, speaking in weepy hiccups, said, "Mom? Mommy, are you okay? Mommy?"

Kate leaned forward and turned the faucet on. She thrust her hands under the lukewarm water. She wiped the palm of her right hand across her face, sprinkled water along the back of her neck. *Better.*

"Mommy? Are you sick, too?"

"No, baby, I'm fine," she said, but she lied. Maybe it was the pills she needed. Maybe it was rest. Maybe this stress was going to drive her over the edge, the way her mother had gone. Dr. Jardin had said, many moons ago, "Different people are affected by different stimuli. To some, a rainy day is a joy. To others, it is frightening. From what you've told me about your relationship with your mother, her alcoholism, her bouts of anger, and your father's sadism, I would say that family, and even the idea of family, is your rainy day. When you think of mothering, you think of rage. When you think of sexual activity, you think of pain. When you think of your daughter, you think of illness. You have programmed yourself to believe that a mother is a woman who lies in the shadows of her living room, nursing constant headaches, feeling imaginary pains."

Kate had argued against him then. "Not everything's a hangover from the past. Just because my parents were that way doesn't make me like that."

"Mommy?" Hope asked.

Kate, looking at herself in the cracked, spotted bathroom mirror, could not believe she thought of herself as a decent mother. "Baby?" She turned, not just to see Hope, but to *not* see herself any longer.

Hope was unrolling toilet paper, wiping at her eyes. "When I get upset, you always get sick. Don't you?"

"It's not you. Are you better?"

"Still have to go."

"Okay. I'll wait outside."

It had gotten much colder in just a few minutes, and Kate stood outside the restaurant wishing she'd worn a sweater. The night was dark and slick; she could hear distant thunder.

Someone was walking toward her. Kate recognized her: the girl who had been sitting next to Hope came walking up to her. "She okay?"

Kate worked at smiling. "I think so."

"You her mom?"

"Uh-huh."

"She's nice. I don't meet a lot of nice people. But Hope's nice. I hope you get to San Francisco okay."

"Thanks." *Shit, Hope, you're not supposed to tell people where we're going.*

"I need to get to Salinas. You think you could give me a ride?"

Kate sighed. "I'm sorry, but . . ."

"Naw, you don't got to say nothing. I get you. I'm just some stranger and you don't pick up hitchers."

Kate was silent.

Then Kate said, "You had diabetes, right?"

"I got it."

"Not anymore," Kate said, and felt anger toward this girl she didn't even know. She wanted to scream at her: How could you be so irresponsible as to allow my baby to cure you? But it wasn't this girl's fault. It was the way things were now. Some miraculous damn gift. Some nightmare that had flowered inside Hope.

Robert had termed it a psi gift, a result of the trauma to her head. The car accident. Her right eye studded with glass. And this ability. Talent. Curse.

Kate had seen this kind of ability before. In Kentucky, where she'd grown up. Her grandmother, Granny Weeks, living just down the road, laying on hands on the Sabbath, curing whooping cough and sprains and healing wounds. Kate had loved Granny Weeks, and had gone to her for protection from her own parents. And then Granny Weeks had died when Kate was seven, leaving her alone to face her father, and what he did to her.

Granny Weeks had died at fifty because of an accumulation of ills. She had taken on so many sick people that she had brought upon herself a cancer from which she did not recover.

Kate had truly believed that Granny Weeks was a healer, and when, after the car wreck, Hope had exhibited signs of healing, Kate feared for Hope's life. But Hope seemed to have a gift that was different from Granny's; she took the illness on for a couple of days, and then it went away. So far, Hope had unwittingly cured a case of leukemia, a migraine headache, and perhaps the flu. Each time, she had all the symptoms of each ailment, and it was painful for Kate to watch her, the same way she'd watched Granny Weeks grow sicker and sicker.

And now.

Diabetes.

So simple. So treatable. Nothing horrifying.

But it was not her disease. She didn't deserve to be a receptacle for everyone else's physical problems. Not after what she'd been through.

"Ma'am?" Iris said, looking at her with a curious expression.

Kate sighed. Counted to ten silently. "Look, please just leave me alone. It's a bad time, okay?"

Iris started to turn away, shrugging, and then looked back.

"Was it that man? The one who was following her? Is that what made Hope get sick?"

"What man?"

The girl clucked her tongue, as if the answer were obvious. "The village idiot. Hope said he scared her. She said he helped with your car. He lives here. I seen him lots. His name's Monkey. Is he the one who's got you spooked, too?"

25

Followers

Letter sent the morning Kate Stewart took her daughter from the hospital in Nevada

Deer Kayt,
Y dunt yu anser me? No more spearmints, you here?
No mor spearmints.
Sinseerly,
Poppy.
p.s. me take cayr of it. dunt wurry.

The woman named Poppy was weary from the past several days.

It had taken her a little over two days to travel on foot what would have taken two hours in a slow car. But she had been determined to make it there, especially after the policeman had told her that Kate had kidnapped her daughter. She wasn't too bright on the surface, but Poppy was smart where it counted, underneath, down where the machinery churned itself to movement and turned jumbled words into thoughts. She thought, at first, that they were following her. Then she figured this was good. The more the

·merrier. They had asked her a hundred questions, and she had given them a hundred and fifty answers, hoping to convince them, but they weren't prepared to hear her. Not really, not the way she could be understood. But she knew from years of trying that they didn't really want to know what was going on in the world; they only wanted to know what they already knew.

The weather had been good—cold, but the right kind of cold for her—and she had spent the first night sleeping on the side of the highway, covered with fallen branches and aromatic leaves, beneath an enormous eucalyptus tree. It was better to be among trees and grass, after all, than in Salinas, which she hated. That place had been good only for migrant work, and even then, she'd barely made enough to survive. The other workers thought she was nasty, and she couldn't blame them: her deformity was truly something to behold.

She didn't even mind when they called her Freek.

Freek was what she felt like inside, what her mother had called her, and all the rest of her family.

She liked her birth name, Poppy, better, but what the hell.

She had acquired Freek later in life, when she was nine or ten. She couldn't remember. She was thirty-seven now, if she had counted right. When the cop had asked her name, her *full* name, she'd told him what she thought was the truth: Poppy Freek. It hadn't come out the right way, though, so he didn't figure it out. Cops and people like that never listened to her, not the way she could be listened to.

She liked Freek things, like the storm that she herself had called up as she descended into the Empire Valley from the northwest. She'd been tired, her feet had practically burned through her shoes, and she had wanted a little water. Only a little, though, not this much.

Between the lightning and the thunder, she'd gotten scared, and because she had only one thing left to do in life, she decided she had better not catch pneumonia before she did it. So when she got to town, she headed for her hideaway and, during the storm, almost got hit by a car that skidded around her. Mr. Death almost had her in his grasp. But Mr. Death wasn't going to get Poppy Freek. Not yet. *Not before I done what I was meant to get done.*

She could see the hideaway ahead of her, hidden from the road and town by a circle of cypress trees. A sign was tacked haphazardly on one of the trees: Hillside Memorial Park. There was a path into it, but it was overgrown now with berry bushes. She had tended it when she was a girl, but now there was no one to take care of the dead. The cemetery was an acre around its edges, and muddy. Its markers were flat stone or wood, and a few of the graves were marked only by a shrub and a stake to indicate that someone had been buried there. Poppy stepped over the low wrought-iron gate, lifting her dress, which was soaked, and after stamping her oversized Nike running shoes, from the Goodwill Store, to get the mud off, she walked along the flat stone markers as if she were on a hopscotch path.

When she reached the largest stone marker, with the name Albert Wooten on it, she bent forward, digging her fingers beneath it. She remembered dropping it on her foot once, and how much it had hurt, and she didn't want a repeat, so she clung tight. Her belly jumped as if tugging it was too much of a strain, and there was a sucking noise from the mud, but the stone came up.

"Oof," Poppy said.

The hole beneath the marker had gotten washed in from this rain, and others, but she used her fingers to scoop some of the clay out. Then she squatted down in the depression and pushed with her butt, shimmying deeper into the hole. The feeling of mud, and maybe worms, made her shiver, but she was sure this was the only place that would be safe for her.

As she scooted down farther, the hole widened, and she felt the edge of a skull, and then another. They were still there, waiting for her after all this time.

They had not abandoned her.

Their bones were warm to her touch.

26

10:41 P.M.

BEN FARRELL WAS SURE THAT HIS SHADOW WAS FOLLOWING him, even though he couldn't see any car behind him on the interstate. His orange Volkswagen bug stuck out like a sore thumb, though, and he just hoped that he wasn't screwing things up by driving to Empire to try to get Hope and Kate before this detective of Robert's did. Maybe if Ben got there first, he could at least keep the cops at bay. It was the girl's mother who had taken her, after all, and that was not necessarily a crime, except in the hands of Robert's twisted lawyers. Robert Stewart had gotten Kate declared incompetent once before, after Kate's son had died.

Wipe that out of your memory; you know it wasn't Kate's fault.

But he couldn't. Back then he had gotten on the next plane out of San Francisco International, and was in Nevada only six hours after the tragedy had occurred. Nine years before, and two and a half years after Robert had swept Kate off her feet, and away from Ben—she had given birth to a son, whom she had named Daniel Benjamin Stewart. Two weeks after the delivery, she and the baby had been back home only a day before something—Robert's lawyers had termed referred to it as excessive postpartum depression—had led to an unfortunate accident. The baby was found dead, dropped or, as the lawyers saw it, thrown by the mother. The lawyers had paraded out all kinds of psychotropic drugs that had been prescribed for Kate by her psychiatrist. Robert, who had initially blown the whistle on her, came to her defense and became the hero of the day. But he had gotten it inserted into Kate's legal records: Kate Stewart was an incompetent mother, she was manic-depressive, she was not to be trusted.

So if Robert wanted to, right now, knowing that Kate wanted a divorce, he could call the cops and the FBI down on his own wife for taking his daughter away from him. Ben could hear Robert's excuses replayed in his mind: "her own good," "doesn't know what she's doing," "dangerous," "not responsible," "unhinged," "no sense of reality."

God, what if Robert was right?

What if Kate really was crazy? It might be because of the drugs, but she could be capable of anything. When Ben had asked her, years later, about her son's death, she had said that she was so zonked from medication she might actually have done it. She didn't know. It was like someone committing slow suicide.

Yet he *knew* Kate, had known her since they were both eighteen. She could be a little impulsive and devil-may-care, but nothing like what Robert believed her to be capable of.

Maybe, though, it would be better if she turned herself over to the authorities and straightened this whole mess out.

The road he took was dark, but it was the shortest distance, according to the map, into the town of Empire. He knew that he needed to get there, to Hope, and to Kate, before anyone else did.

11:04 P.M.

Behind him, with headlights off, Stephen Grace drove under the speed limit—just under—keeping Farrell's car in his sights, like a patient hunter stalking its quarry.

"Ah, shit," he said, watching Farrell turn off onto Sand Canyon Road, going southeast. "The back way. Damn. Now why the hell are you making it so hard on me? You could take Twenty-six or even Caliente, but you want to make it hard on all of us, don'tcha?" He had traded cars with Kerrey, a man whose taste in cars ran to the expensive—thus, the Corvette—and the dilapidated—*and so, we have here an engine making strange noises, like a dying swan, and a clutch that sounds like it's grinding bones.* At any moment, he figured the Vette could die on him in the middle of Bumfuck, Egypt. Car phone probably didn't work. *My luck.*

He could tell by the route Ben Farrell took that he was heading for Empire. Grace knew this route, because well before this day, he had driven the opposite way into the town, just to see what was so great about it. He knew about going into a place and trying to see what someone else saw in that place. Didn't always work, but this time he had his journalist-hero driving there to save the damsel in distress, no doubt, and he had some information, leaked from the doc himself, that indicated Empire.

He could've called his subordinates; Silva and Elkhart could have been there before him. He trusted both of them. Silva had been with him since Laos, and Elkhart, through the Libyan operation in 1978. Neither man was attached to Special Projects by his umbilical cord the way most of the others were. Both men despised Holder, at least approaching the way Grace did. He could depend on them when worse came to worse.

But he wanted to wait. The others could be there at a moment's notice.

What was she thinking, the girl? Was she asleep as any girl her age should be, or didn't it let her sleep? Did she toss and turn in very real pain, the bones and the tissue and the blood at odds with one another? Did she know what was fermenting beneath her skin?

Had she been aware of the death in Las Vegas? It was obviously connected to her: a middle-aged man had had the flu and then suddenly had felt better. This according to his wife. Silva had seen the man after the implosion. He described briefly, the damage to the vertebrae, the apparently burned skin—dead skin, the consulting medical expert had corrected—all the signs that the woman from Devon had exhibited. What struck Silva was not the death, not the fact of the death, anyway, but that the man's spinal cord continued to writhe, even after the disfigurement.

Even after brain death.

The wife had said, to Silva, when he showed her the picture, that she remembered the girl. Very well. The girl had come through the casino on her own. She asked the husband, who was coughing, where the front desk was, because she was lost. The wife wondered if the girl had some life-threatening disease. She asked because she wanted to know whom to sue, who was responsible. The wife was still in custody. *What the hell are we gonna do if all these people end up in some limbo custody? Christ, we might as well sell tickets if we don't have the girl soon.*

How do you tell a woman that her husband ain't really dead? Not in the sense of dead as a dog. He'll keep wagging his tail for a few days to go, and maybe even then he ain't gonna kick. Maybe have to bury him while he's still moving. Or burn him. Not pretty to look at, but hell, it's better than looking at him wriggling around for the next forty years, huh?

A fucking wounded animal.

To be put out of its misery.

He lit another cigarette and turned up the radio to listen to the religious station. A preacher was on, and Grace shook his head, laughing, because the preacher was talking about a blight on the land in the form of corrupted youth, perverted sex, and the worship of the golden calves of the sinful world. "The false gods of science and medicine, of astrophysics and anthropology," the preacher shouted, "all are servants of mammon, all are humanists, deaf and blind to the spiritual path! Our children practice sexual deviations, indulge in carnal appetites, because of this lack of guidance. We need to bring God back into our lives, moment to moment, day by day. We need to open up our souls to the voices of salvation! We need to heal those who are sick."

"Don't heal anyone else, Patch, not till we meet," he whispered, and the mental image formed of himself, imploding, the molecular structure of his being shattered like the Fourth of July, and yet the electrical impulses running up and down his spine, the twitching of nerve endings, into eternity.

"Eternity . . ." said the preacher on the radio.

It's a long fucking time, he thought, and almost went off the winding two-lane road. Stephen Grace began playing Robert Stewart's tape again, and although he had heard this passage before, there was a code within it that he could not decipher.

From Dr. Robert Stewart's tape

". . . need to work fast. Special Projects wants to send an operative . . . have six-two-three-eight-two prepped and ready, set the timer and program, and now have to ensure that the bomb goes off before they get six. . . . I do it for the future and what it can bring, even if I go because of it. The new generation will be the revitalization of life on this planet, and we who have come before will be dust. I can't do this sanely, but I do it with the knowledge that a better world will come of my actions today, and I only ask forgiveness for what has been in the face of what shall be. I know that within me they will direct my actions, and within us all we will bring ourselves out into the light from the shadows."

27

11:05 P.M.

KATE HELD HOPE'S HAND, SQUEEZING IT TIGHT, PROBABLY too tight, but she was angry and frustrated and nervous. If Hope *had* cured this stranger of diabetes, who knew how long it would be before she exhibited some full-blown symptoms—a convulsion, perhaps, or damage to her internal organs. Jesus, maybe even total blindness. Sometimes the indications of the disease that Hope took on didn't show up for an entire day. There was the leukemia, after she cured the man in Nevada. Hope didn't start feeling the pain until the middle of the second day following the healing. It had lasted only a few hours, but Kate had begun to estimate that it took Hope a full forty-eight hours to work the bugs out of her system. Kate had never known anyone with diabetes, but she knew from her reading of Robert's medical texts that the convulsions and spasms from insulin shock could be painful and terrifying; and a lack of insulin at the right time could lead even to death. Just like Granny Weeks, healing people, healing them with her enormous black Bible, and then their ailments finding passage into Granny's bones, until finally Granny died of something she had saved someone from. It wasn't fair that the best died and the bad ones lived.

It was getting colder than she would've thought, almost wintery, with a wind blowing down from the north. She heard wind chimes tinkling as they passed by a Monterrey-style clapboard house that seemed out of place so far inland. Hope kept glancing back to the burger joint, but Kate kept herself face forward. She didn't want to turn into the kind of scolding mother her own mother had been, and her head desperately ached for a good dose, however unpleasant, of lithium, but she knew it was better to be lucid, if angry. "You know you're not supposed to talk to strangers, and you're especially not supposed to heal them."

Hope said something inaudible.

"What?" Kate asked tensely.

"I said, I didn't mean to. I can't help it sometimes. It's like it jumps out at me. Remember how you showed me how the iron filings go to the magnet? That's what it feels like, only I'm the magnet." Hope's voice was tearful, and Kate let go of her hand for a second. They both sighed at the same time.

Kate put her hands in her pockets; Hope mirrored this.

Kate said, "Look, we have to be careful. I told you how your father works sometimes."

"I feel a little dizzy," Hope said. Kate immediately felt her forehead. Hope's skin felt clammy.

"I don't know much about diabetes, but I do know you're going to see a doctor about it tomorrow morning. In San Francisco. Which we are going to tonight."

"I thought you said tomorrow."

"Tonight. That man named Monkey—I think your father may have hired him. He's obviously following us."

"But ..."

"I can't chance anything happening until we get to Ben's. Then, once we get you somewhere safe, your father and I can figure this thing out."

In the periphery of her vision, she saw the car coming down the road, slowly at first, then picking up speed, until it seemed to be coming at them at sixty-five miles an hour; Kate pulled Hope up onto the pavement, but the vehicle stopped on a dime about three yards in front of them.

"Oh, my God," Kate gasped.

Hope turned and stared at the road. "What?"

"It's him. The man driving the truck. It's the same truck, Hope. Can't you see it's the same truck?" Kate grabbed Hope's hand and pulled her farther into the shadows of one of the front porches, just off the road.

The truck was a dull yellow and looked as if, in spite of its age, it was well cared for. It was a '58 flatbed Ford, and if she had never recognized it before, as she had seen it follow them on their trip from Nevada, she now came face-to-face with it, with what it was, and something in her mind seemed to click like a camera shutter, as if tamping down some information, sending it on, not examining it.

But she knew, and for a moment she also knew this was not possible, for it had been so many years ago that Kate Stewart had seen this truck, in the hills of Kentucky, in a small town called Berlin, fifty miles from Louisville, and as if that camera shutter were coming down to take a picture, she was sent into a memory from her past. . . .

When Kate was little, her father said, "Now, don't move. Stay real still."

She said, twisting her head away, "Don't."

"That's right, don't move," he said.

He was taking a picture, and she moved so the photo would come out all blurry. She heard the animals in the background; the hens, the goats, the pigs. She was crying because of Granny Weeks dying, and he wanted a picture of her on that day.

Behind her father: the yellow truck he had owned since as far back as she could remember.

Mommy?

Mommy, you okay?

"Mommy, you okay?"

Kate stared straight ahead, at the place where the yellow truck had been only a second before.

She blinked. The afterimage of the truck remained, as if it were lit up behind her eyelids. She opened her eyes again, and still no truck where she thought she'd seen it on the road. She remembered what Dr. Jardin had said about the psychotropic drugs, how they might produce side effects lasting well beyond the end of their prescriptions. *This is it. A flashback. A compartment of my mind that those drugs reopened. I am not really crazy, just under the influence.* It was almost a relief, and she could deal with it now intellectually, understand that it was not her father's truck but the photographic memory image of the truck recalled. But in spite of that, a part of her that was still little Katy Weeks was shivering, terrified that her father was going to run her down, the way he'd tried to the day that Granny died.

"Mommy?" Hope asked again, backing away from her.

As if she's scared. Of me.

"Oh, baby, Mom just lost another marble for a sec. Let's go back to the Backwater and get packed before she loses any more." Kate and Hope walked swiftly along the street, not glancing at the houses, although music still played in one of them and a dog continued to bark in the fenced-in yard of another. Kate tried to shake the afterimage of the yellow truck; it disturbed her more than her knowledge that Robert had molested Hope the same way Kate's father had molested her.

Robert: Father.

It was like a voice in her mind. It repeated again, *Robert: Father.* Kate felt suddenly warm, as if her blood were heating up. Her head began pounding again, and she wanted to stop and rest a minute, but she knew if she didn't get Hope back to the motel and out of this town something bad would happen.

Robert: Father.

It was Robert's voice in her head, repeating the two words, almost a whisper. What the hell did it mean?

Crazy. That's what it means.

A truck, a normal truck, not yellow, but big and long, carrying fruit, drove by. She was relieved to see it. The driver of the truck waved, and she smiled. This was a friendly place, after all. Some weirdo of Robert's was watching them, perhaps, but it was nothing more than that. Her head felt as if it had been put in a vise and squeezed, but now relief came, and she didn't even feel like taking prescription drugs. Her sinuses cleared, and she smelled the damp air, the wet grass across the road. Some kind of vineyard there, running along the opposite side of town. The clouds had moved to the east; the sky was clear and brilliant with stars. Kate almost laughed, thinking of what a neurotic she was, programmed that way since childhood, no matter how she tried to escape it.

But Hope will escape it. Hope will have a better life. We'll get to Ben's tonight, get Hope to a good doctor to treat this diabetes for the time being. She will be fine.

The driveway into the Greenwater Motor Lodge was shiny and wet. Hope pointed out that the neon cactus had gone out.

"I don't think there're any cactuses in this part of California," Hope said, with some authority. "Lots of grapes, though. I saw a poster in the AttaBurger that said they had a grape festival. Wouldn't it be awful to live in a place where you had a grape festival?"

"Might be fun," Kate said. They walked through the breezeway to the back of the motel. The girl who had been at the front desk peeked out from the linen closet. She was wearing an ill-fitting maid's uniform. Kate guessed, from her expression, and the quick way she hid something among the towels, that this girl was sneaking a drink.

"You finding everything okay?" she asked. Her breath was laced strongly with scotch. She was in her early twenties, and had the hangdog look of someone who knew she would never get out of this town. She reminded Kate of the alternate universe version of herself in her twenties, if she hadn't taken Granny Weeks's inheritance and gone to Aunt Cheryl's in Berkeley, California, a few thousand miles from Kentucky. And started college, and gotten away from her past.

"Yes." Kate smiled. "Everything's fine." She didn't want to tell her that she was getting ready to move on. *Nowhere is safe,* the fleeting thought occurred to her. Nowhere and no one—and she couldn't tell the girl who worked at the motel that she and her daughter had to leave before they'd stayed one night in this godforsaken town.

The girl's grin was lopsided. "We don't get a lot of folks comin' through. Least not this time a year."

The girl obviously was drunk, and a thought raced through Kate's mind: *What if she's an alcoholic, and what if Hope cures her alcoholism and takes it on? Jesus, anyone and everyone could give Hope their infirmities.* There was no letup to the paranoia. But then she remembered that she herself had certain psychological problems that Hope had no effect on. And there had been a five-year-old boy in the hospital whom Hope had cried about because she couldn't cure him. *It doesn't always happen. But how am I ever going to know when it will?*

Hope said to the girl, "We're leaving tonight."

Kate gave her hand a squeeze. *You're not supposed to tell anyone. You're not playing this game right, Hope.*

The girl shrugged; she didn't care. "You just got here," she said. "Can't blame you for goin', though." She went back in among the linens, shutting the door behind her.

Kate walked on ahead of Hope, to the room. A light was coming from beyond the small pond in back of the motel. Kate saw shadows of what she figured were oil pumps in the light. These were ubiquitous in California, turning up on the strangest hillsides. The light was no doubt some porch light off a side road some distance back. She saw the silhouettes of rows of houses and shops off the side streets, and heard a car skidding somewhere on a distant road. A sliver of moon was off to the south in the sky, and Kate wondered what sort of man was out there, looking for her daughter, looking for her.

And she wondered what that man would do once he had them both. Would it be prison or a mental hospital for her? Would it be something too awful to imagine for Hope?

But the countryside, even with the oil pumps, was beautiful and seemed like a haven of tranquillity around her. Empire was a town she would've liked, a place where she could've raised her daughter peacefully. A place where she wouldn't have to go crazy just to do the right thing.

From Dr. Robert Stewart's tape

"Oh, Jesus, what am I playing at? But every man who has ever delved into the science of the living organism has made sacrifices. In the blood and tissue of the human body is the soul. Beneath the skin of this world lies another, and this is for the sake of human, or super-human, potential, not for me, not for six or four or for every stupid moron who walks the face of this planet, but for the children, and for the planet in its totality, for the riddance of vermin and despair, but Jesus, Jesus, what am I playing at? R-7 is not stable, and the human being is not stable. Life, not being stable, in flux, liquid, moving, always moving. R-7, too, moving forward, in sync with the animal, just pushing the inevitable forward, the death of a star, and the creation of a new race. Six will be the one to go right, and maybe four will go later. It is the only solution to the problem of humanity. We can no longer abide within; we must expand and let loose our selves . . . transform."

28

HOPE FOLLOWED HER MOTHER INTO THE MOTEL ROOM AND started packing her clothes back into the big brown suitcase. She was resigned to going on, but she knew that Ben would probably show up sometime before morning, and she hated to leave. But she would never tell her mother about calling Ben. It was a tough position, and it was made worse by a strange dry feeling in her mouth that she'd had since leaving

AttaBurger. She attributed it to the illness that she'd cured Iris of, perhaps, but this feeling wasn't as important as her worries. About her mother, about Ben. About Dad. Why didn't Dad come get them? She didn't understand. She didn't comprehend any of this running away, but she had a feeling that her guardian angel was looking out for her and for her mother.

She would have to leave a note or something for Ben.

Kate was doing more pacing than packing. Hope watched her for a moment and then said, "We could stay and leave real early. I'm sleepy and I don't feel so hot."

Her mother was not smiling, but had a look on her face that was almost a smile. *Wound too tight.*

"I wish we could." Her mother said the words slowly. Tension tugged at the corners of her mouth. "It's important that you see a doctor. Diabetes can lead to all kinds of complications. It may not go away."

"They always do," Hope said.

"We don't know that for sure. It's only been a few days."

Hope was about to open her big fat mouth again—as she thought of it—to inform her mother that her father had run about ten different tests after she'd cured the man in the hospital of leukemia. She decided against telling her mom. *Just keep it shut and things'll work out.* Hope continued packing, and as she went through her stuff, she made a mental checklist of things: jacket, sweater, scrapbook, *Goodnight, Moon* book, charm bracelet, underwear, socks times three, sneakers. . . .

"Where's Nina?" She asked, looking around the room and seeing everything but the doll.

Kate was on her way to the bathroom; she knew how stressed she was, and figured a quick bird bath at the sink might help. There were prescription pills, too—just some Xanax—in her makeup kit on the bathroom sink. *I might just swallow one. Only one.* Or she might smoke one of the cigarettes she'd managed to hide from Hope. "You look around for your doll," she told Hope as she shut the bathroom door behind her, "and I'll be out in a sec."

Hope didn't particularly like looking under beds, but it occurred to her that perhaps she'd dropped Nina while she was sitting on the double bed, and maybe the doll had rolled a little. This had happened in her bedroom at home enough times to seem plausible.

She knelt down beside the bed, squinted to see beneath it, found she could not.

Ben would tell me not to be afraid of the dark.

She stuck her hand beneath the box spring, felt the underside, wondered if there were spiders and things that she would prefer not to think about.

Then she felt it. For a millisecond she was sure it was the plastic face of the baby doll.

Only it was warm.

And it grabbed her hand.

29

THE CIGARETTE HAD BEEN HEAVEN, ALTHOUGH KATE HADN'T liked sneaking it. It felt too much like being a teenager again; and then the lung cancer and stroke fear had surfaced, so she'd put the cigarette out after a few puffs.

Kate turned the water off, not quite remembering having left it running, and she looked at her face in the mirror. Her hair actually looked clean, which surprised her because she always imagined herself as being vaguely filthy, greasy from the road. In the mirror she saw the doll sitting up on the windowsill next to the radio.

Hope must've left it there when she first used the bathroom.

She leaned over and flicked the fan off and, in doing so, heard classical music on the radio. From her hellish days of piano lessons, she recognized "Für Elise."

Something was wrong.

The screen was off the window.

The doll, Nina, sitting on the sill.

Something was wrong with the doll.

Hope. Kate's first thought.

Nothing matters except Hope.

Something was wrong with the doll, but she didn't know what. She went over to the window and pulled the doll from the sill.

Then she realized what it was, and she felt the first short breaths sucking at the back of her throat, the early stage of hyperventilation, and she knew she couldn't give in to it, but *oh, God, oh, God, Hope, Hope* . . .

The right eye.

The doll's right eye.

Like Hope's.

No longer in its socket.

From Dr. Robert Stewart's tape

"We must go forth from ourselves and expand into others. . . ."

Kate Stewart was almost afraid to open the bathroom door.

A second passed, or perhaps it was an hour, or perhaps no time elapsed from the moment she saw the doll with its missing eye and the moment she flung the door open and ran out into the room, through the open outer door, into the parking lot.

And saw the yellow truck with the farmer in it, the farmer with the red coal eyes and the spike-toothed grin.

The farmer who was her father from twenty years before.

Daddy.

And then there was no man, no truck, but the sound of screeching brakes and the smell of burning tires as someone in a car sped away from the Greenwater Motor Lodge.

Kate grabbed her car keys and ran out of the motel room. Her only thought was to chase down the monster who had stolen her child from her.

30

From beneath the double bed in the motel room: breathing, and the smell of a wild animal.

PART TWO

Empire

November 8, Darkness to Dawn

Behold, I show you a mystery; We shall not sleep,
But we shall all be changed, in a moment,
in the twinkling of an eye.

—Corinthians 15:51

31

Monkey Business

12:03 A.M.

BREATH AS SWEET AS THE FIRST MILK FROM THE NIPPLE OF A dog, he thought, holding the delicate odor in his nostrils for a good minute, his face near hers.

Beneath the bed, in the Greenwater Motor Lodge room, Monkey Lovett held his hand over Hope's mouth until he was sure she was out. She'd tried to bite him, but he had kept the pressure on her neck until she had stopped struggling. He didn't want to kill her; sometimes when he pressed too hard around a kid's neck, the small bones there snapped, and that could mean problems. Maybe even death. But he was careful with this one, this girl. Only enough pressure so that her throat would close up, and then, if held, it would stay closed until she passed out.

The air smelled like dust balls and mildew under the bed, and a spider crawled across his forehead, down the bridge of his nose, pausing there, at a nostril. It then must have realized that it was on a living being, for it scampered down his lips, and he barely got his tongue out in time to catch it.

But he got it, closed his mouth, bit down, and felt the gentle squash between his back molars. Bugs were perfect. They had all the right parts. They were one with nature. Whole organisms were good.

He waited there a few seconds after the girl's mother drove off. The girl was so warm and so still. He had caught her. Birdy had been right: fate had brought the girl to them.

How he longed to play with her. The smell of her hair was like wheat-sweat after rain. And her skin, so smooth. He heard the pounding in her neck, her pulse, still going, still washing blood through her, carrying nutrients, carrying oxygen, the red blood that was, he knew, the purest form of water, the origin of life. And she was imperfect. The word grew in his head.

Imperfect. *Imperfect little children should do what they're told. Imperfection is bad, and all imperfection should be hacked off.* Monkey saw the words in his head just like it was a blackboard and he had written them on it a thousand times. *I will not be imperfect.*

For a moment he saw the Exact-o knife, its razor edge dull and corroded. It moved through his mind like something sprouting. *Memory sprouting behind my eyes.*

All imperfection should be hacked off.

Remembering:

Harlan, his hands, the way they twisted around whenever he tried to repair anything.

One turn to the left, two to the right.

The Pain Room.

The steel washtub with the rusty lip.

Harly's hands, how small they were.

Imperfection, the GoodMama said, should be hacked off.

Blood, when it sprang from the rips and tears, how it was like a shower, how you could take a shower in the spray from another human body.

The girl without the eye. She was imperfect.

And he wanted to play with her.

He brushed his lips against her shoulder and, without thinking, bit down gently on her shoulder blades.

Birdy, inside him, said, *Stop it, stop it right this instant.*

"I want to play," Monkey whined softly.

Later. Birdy did something inside his head, fiddled with his skull and brains until he felt the sharp cold prick that ran from the base of his skull down his spinal column. It made Monkey wriggle slightly.

The prick of conscience, Birdy said, *because you don't have one.*

"Yes, I do," Monkey felt an ice coldness along his teeth. "I have you."

He pushed the girl out from under the bed and then rolled out himself. He'd parked the Chrysler Fifth Avenue on Brown Material Road, just over the other side of the pond.

He lifted the girl up—she seemed light—and jogged across the parking lot, through the break in the fencing. He felt a surge of something through him, like a small victory accompanied by a sense of unbounded joy at the prospects that life offered. And life continuously renewing its offer with each child placed in his path, but this was like being a child himself again, with all the strength and bravery and innocent heroics that he had felt then.

Children, all of them, together, happy memories in the Pain Room, Birdy, Harly, Monkey, and Poppy.

The special prayer they learned to say when Harly's small hands twisted.

Childhood! Like a faroff land of dreams, echoing back to him, in the back of his head, the back of his throat, the back of his lips.

The taste of childhood in his mouth kept him awake the rest of the night.

12:03 A.M.

Fletcher McBride, who had already been down to the sheriff's and talked about the end of the world right here in Empire, was peeing into Greenwater Pond, thinking how nice it was for a man to piss out in the open like he was meant to. The pungent, rancid smell of chickens was nearby, no doubt from Jim Feely's place three doors south of the motel. Fletch thought he might go steal some eggs on this last clear night of the great wide world, for he had never stolen before and he wanted to know that experience before the fires rained down. Fletch didn't consider himself an intellectual; he had studied hard as a youth and had become a doctor by a kind of default. He enjoyed being near dead bodies, although he never cared to examine his motives, and being a doctor was a good way to be around them. Perhaps he had flirted with mortuary work once or twice, but it seemed a job for perfectionists, whereas doctoring had seemed more suited to his interests. Thus he had run into some trouble with the rather high mortality rate in his practice, and eventually had been falsely accused of having caused his wife's death. The story had gotten so far out of hand that it had become a hand ax he had killed her with, rather than the simple fact that she had died under anesthesia on his dining room table while they were playing out one of their more beloved games with each other. But Glory had died with a smile on her face, and "in her sleep," which was how Fletch himself would someday like to go. Glory had been an attractive woman in life; she attained a rare beauty in death. Fletch wasn't into the kinky stuff, although he knew a few surgeons who were, but the hand ax came after she died, as he'd explained when he tried unsuccessfully to argue his case in court. He had realized he would have to get rid of Glory's body, and the small ax was the only tool available to cut Glory into manageable pieces.

Occasionally Fletcher McBride had flashes of self-recognition, and knew that this was perhaps not the smartest move he could've made.

But he had always believed that instinct should be obeyed over intelligence, and his first instinct, at the time, had been to go for the hand ax.

He thought of her, of Glory, on this last night of the world, and when he had finished peeing and putting it back in his trousers and zipping up, he saw Monkey Lovett come hopping along the other side of the Greenwater Pond, and he said a friendly "Hey," although he didn't think Monkey heard him. He saw that Monkey was carrying something, maybe a child, maybe a big old dog, and then he felt like he was in the operating room again and he was cutting with a scalpel, but not on some patient. "Heal thyself." The words came into his head, and it was like he was performing surgery down around his heart, the flaps of skin pulled back, the greedy fingers fiddling with the fat around his pumping valves. Something in Monkey's gait, his shambling, rambling hitch-and-slide walk, made thoughts come into Fletcher's head that hadn't occurred to him before. It was like Monkey was playing a damn piano with his feet, like he was cutting the tissue around his heart.

The end of the world, he thought, and began shivering. Monkey had it with him, like a disease. Whatever he was carrying, whatever package was in his arms.

It was *them.* They had promised they would bring it upon the face of the earth. Years ago. And it was here.

"What to do, what to do," he said aloud to the stink of

chickens in the air. He wiped his brow of sweat. If he hadn't just gone, he knew he would've just pissed his pants. Fletch had tried to tell Kermit Stone, the sheriff, but talking to Kermit sometimes was like talking to a rock. And Kermit thought Fletch was crazy, Fletch knew, and so no matter what he said, it was of no consequence.

But it was here. The fulfillment. Those fuckers had been right on the money.

Just like Judgment Day.

"What to do, what to do," he said, and then a smile crept across his face. He thought of Gus over at the motel, probably getting laid with his girl, and of his old buddies back at Empire State, and the poker games they played late into the night. But most of all, he thought of the experience of life and knew that the last of anything was always the best. And it must always be embraced. That was the one thing the people who had died under his knife had taught him: to embrace destiny.

Between now and the end of time. He looked up at the infinite blackness with its white sputtering stars. *God, you've given me life, you've put life in my hands, and you've shown me death. And I have played you. But from now until the light of the world dies, I will be an animal.*

And Fletcher McBride, embracing his animal nature, searched the skies for a sliver of moon, and howled long and high. The sharp, pungent stink of chickens called to him.

12:10 A.M.

"Aw, shit." Gus Stone sat up among the piles of laundry, and, beneath him, Gretchen Feely sighed.

"What you stop for?" She sounded annoyed. Her eyebrows were crossed over each other like two woolly-bear caterpillars mating.

"It's Fletch. He's out on his werewolf thing again."

"Well, if he gets into my daddy's chickens one more time, I don't know if Daddy's gonna be so nice as to scare him off with rock salt like before. Can't you control that man?"

Gus smoothed his hair back, scratched his chin, thoughtfully. "No. I hate him sometimes. He was talkin' about the end the world again. You know what happens when he does that."

"My daddy thinks he should be in jail still. My daddy thinks he's insane. My daddy thinks he shouldn'ta never gotten let go in the first place."

"I wish your daddy would shut up sometimes. God. I hope Fletch don't come home with chicken feathers on his teeth again." Gus shook his head and dropped his hand back down to Gretchen's breasts and turned each nipple like it was a knob.

"That don't turn me on," she said, slapping at his hand. "Stop it, willya?"

Gus stopped twiddling with her and put his arms around her. He whispered, "I don't think the world's ever gonna end, do you?"

Gretchen shot straight up, with the towels and sheets from the linen storage room dropping off where they'd clung to her body. She was naked and scrawny, and he found himself staring at her knees, then up to her snatch, and then her face. She was angry now. "Gus Stone, that's blasphemy, of course the world's gonna end, and the wicked shall perish and the righteous shall rise again from the dead. Have you already turned away from the Lord?"

Yes, he thought, but knew it was not what she wanted to hear, especially after she'd saved him seven Sundays back, which was the only reason she'd allowed him in her pants in the first place.

12:13 A.M.

Iris Lefcourt stood on the edge of the two-lane highway that bordered the vineyards on one side and the town of Empire on the other. She was feeling a little shaky and more than a little cold. She thought she might go down and sleep at the bus stop, but she'd been kind of hoping that lady and the one-eyed girl named Hope could give her a ride or a place to stay. But folks just weren't friendly anymore, not like in Minnesota, where nobody would even leave a rat out on a cold night. She had her insulin with her, and a small pillow and blanket, so she would do okay and maybe get a ride with one of the trucks that came through at four in the morning. She'd done that before, and truckers were actually really nice and generally didn't try anything. She hadn't liked sleeping in the boarded-up house in town, though. Too many mice and too much peace and quiet for her taste. And then there'd been the way all those townies seemed to look at her, like she was white trash from L.A. or something. Like she was the outsider of the universe invading their pissant town. Enough. She'd get up to San Francisco soon, and then make it big somehow. In a place like San Francisco, they knew things that places like this only dreamed of. Her older sister, Louisa, was there, too, and she'd take Iris in and help her get started. Louisa had gotten started when she was only fourteen or so, so she knew the ropes. It would be cool, and maybe she'd make something of herself.

These were her thoughts as she stood there, waiting for whatever fate would bring her way.

As long as I don't sleep through the night and miss the trucks, maybe I'll get a decent ride.

Already there'd been some traffic, even this late, so who knew? Maybe she'd get a ride in a nice warm car all the way to Salinas.

And then, as if in answer to her prayer, a long dark car headed toward her from down the road, and she stuck out her thumb.

Monkey Lovett slowed the Chrysler down when he saw the young girl standing on the side of the road with her thumb thrust out into the headlights' beam. She came running to the passenger side of the car, and he set his foot down hard on the brake so she would know to get in.

Iris slid into the car almost before he had the door unlocked, and he smelled immediately that she was still a child, barely into her monthly curse.

She glanced at him and said, "Oh, it's you. Maybe I better get out."

Monkey smiled and said nothing, pressing his right foot down hard on the accelerator.

His right arm was out, hand in a fist, and he knew to hit her across the bridge of her nose, because he'd done this before with kids half her age, and he was shocked that it took three good poundings to really knock her out, and he hadn't expected that look of bewilderment to cross her face, and he wondered if she was thinking, *Are we gonna play later?* or if she was thinking, *I can't breathe.*

Finally she slumped down in the seat, but not before he practically went off the road onto the shoulder, almost into the gully just this side of the vineyard. He brought the car to a complete stop and put it in neutral, his foot still on the brake. He held the girl at the point where her spine intersected with the back of her skull. He felt the life pulsing there, and found that he was aroused just touching her. He thought he tasted her memories as he squeezed a little harder. There was blood on his ragged fingernails as they punctured her skin.

And then he found what he wanted, right there, at the base of her skull—three moles, in a triangular pattern.

Imperfection.

He sliced his fingernail up under one of them, but it wouldn't come off right away, and he didn't want the girl to wake up. A voice in his head told him that he had to get back home soon or he would be in trouble, but all he could smell was this other girl in the Chrysler with him. Her imperfection filled his nostrils like the wrenching stink of a brewery. He let go of the back of her neck, and she slumped, again, down in the seat.

Monkey glanced out into the night. The vineyards almost glowed from the recent rain. Rows of vines, tangled, twisted, gripping the earth and each other. The vineyard was like family. It was just like family, how it gripped and writhed and kept you in its arms until you couldn't breathe.

Harlan's small hands, their fingers wiggling.

He tried to pretend his erection would go away, because he knew that was an imperfection.

All imperfection must be hacked off.

It never got very erect anymore, only a little, and only when he felt blood in his hands.

GoodMama held the small scissors up in the shining light. In her other hand, the coarse black thread. "We'll stitch it up nice and good, Monkey baby, we'll make sure the bleeding stops. Birdy reads up on all these things, Monkey. And just think, your imperfection got cut right out. You're gonna be just fine now."

"Hurts," he whimpered back to her.

And then she smiled. The GoodMama smiled. She had the warmest, sweetest smile in the whole world. Her eyes squinted a little, and the crow's-feet came out around them. Her lips peeled back so he could see the pink gums above her white, white teeth. "Hurting's good sometimes," she said with the coolest, sweetest breath in the world.

Monkey saw his reflection in the darkened car window. Anyone else might have seen a man of about thirty-five, worry lines creasing his forehead, eyes red and teared-up, lips parched, teeth yellow and scummy.

But Monkey saw the most perfect little nine-year-old boy in the whole wide world.

Old Mason jar on the shelf. The imperfections, both of them, floating in the smelly water.

As he put the car back in drive, taking his foot off the brake, Monkey began to imagine just how he would hack at this hitchhiker's imperfection until it was clean off. He could chew it off with his teeth, but then the imperfection would just grow back.

Better to hack.

Hack it off, once and for all.

GoodMama held the two small lumps in her hand and showed them to him. In the Pain Room, over the steel washtub. Finger painting in blood, the withered fingers. Birdy said, "They're called testicles, but everyone calls 'em balls."

"Your imperfection," GoodMama said, still stitching there between his legs even after he woke up. One stroke up with the black thread, one stroke down, and the needle; he didn't even feel the needle, it was like a little prick of conscience digging into his bag of skin, in and out and all about, up and down and all around.

"Balls," Birdy whispered, holding the jar up to the light with his bloody hands.

32

12:15 A.M.

THERE ARE SOME PLACES THAT SEEM FAMILIAR, AS IF VISITED before in a dream, or a nightmare. Kate Stewart felt this about Empire now, only after her daughter was taken, as if she knew the slick wet streets, as if she knew where the five-and-dime was, where the Safeway stood, and when Peppertree Street came up, with its row of six Victorian wedding-cake houses, For Sale signs up in the front yards, bordered by olive and pepper trees along the well-lit sidewalk.

She felt her entire body shake as she drove, and although the speedometer read fifty-five, it felt like she was going ten miles per hour through molasses. The road was shiny and wriggled like an eel beneath the tires; her head ached, and she thought she saw tiny points of light along the edge of the trees and from the windows of houses. Her fingers on the wheel kept tensing, tensing, as if they could not grip it tight enough, as if her fingers and the steering wheel were melding. The car that had taken Hope away always seemed to be around the next bend in the road. She heard its squealing tires as it turned corners; it led her through the town of Empire, past the Fox movie theater with its brilliant marquee still blazing white, through the only stoplight in town, flashing yellow, drawing her farther into what seemed not a town at all but a labyrinth. But her mind lagged behind her motor functions, and she kept her foot pressed to the floor, even when the Mustang skidded as she turned a corner and sprayed water up across her windshield, blinding her for a few seconds. But all she wanted was that car, whatever car it was, all she wanted was Hope. Whoever had her could leave. If it was Robert or one of his henchmen, she would fight him to the death for her daughter.

Within ten minutes she realized that no amount of crazy driving was going to catch up with whatever car was ahead of her, and so she tried to slow down, but found that she could not. Her right foot would not come up from the accelerator, and her hands would not let go of the wheel. Something tugged the wheel to the left and then to the right. *Why can't I stop?* she wondered. *Why am I doing this? Why is this happening to me?* Another voice, a bit scarier, whispered in her ear: *It's because you're crazy, lady.* She panicked, and realized that she was taking the sharp turns through town at sixty miles an hour, and she had no control. There was no other car to chase, nothing in front of her on the road. The Mustang was moving so fast that it slowed the entire world down around her, and she noticed the signs on the storefronts along Main Street, the light coming from a bar called King Tut's, the light from the windows of houses on the distant hillside, and she thought that she must be heading for death. *Can't let go, can't let go, can't let go.* The tears that came to her eyes momentarily blinded her, and she closed them for an instant, and when she opened them, her muscles seemed to be driving without her knowledge, without even the need for her eyesight. She almost laughed when a word came to her mind, about the town, about this countryside.

Quaint.

She passed through a small shopping area, with Grapevine Avenue running through it, all old western-style buildings that had been gutted and renovated; a street with nothing but three-story town buildings, and then the library, which looked like a miniature Spanish mission; a railroad crossing, the old train station with its columns and empty cars; and then the houses, some Victorian, some bungalow, some cheap stucco, but most just basic post–World War II California three-bedrooms with wind chimes hanging from the porches. All of it was a blur, and then she saw it all clearly, as if she were driving in slow motion up and down the street grids.

Fucking quaint, and I'm going to smash my brains out in all this fucking quaintness.

"What the hell—" She tried untensing her muscles, but the effort was useless. She realized the voice in her head was not hers, but belonged to Robert, and that useless bastard had even taken away her own inner voice, replaced it with his own, replaced it with his wise, smarmy upper-class nasal doctor voice, like he was lecturing to students during a difficult surgical procedure.

Get out of my head, Robert.

Get away from my daughter.

Up ahead, in the direct path of her car, was a statue, in the middle of the road, and she didn't wonder if it was a statue of a soldier or of the town's founder, but she wondered at the fact that she was going to drive right into it, and she would probably die without knowing why she couldn't take her foot off the accelerator.

12:25 A.M.

Sheriff Kermit Stone was in King Tut's, downing the better half of a boilermaker, even though it was the cheapest whiskey he'd ever tasted. His hair was white, although he was only in his forties, and if you were to sit across the bar from him, you might even mistake him for sixty, on account of the hair and the fact that his skin had a pale, translucent quality with pulsing blue veins on either side of his forehead. And his eyes were old, too, but without wisdom. And still he was younger than many in the town, and he still felt sixteen in his head whenever he saw a pretty woman or a fast car, and so it was with some interest that he saw both whiz by the open door of King Tut's.

Lennie, the bartender, whistled and said, "She looks like she's going smack into the middle of the Known Soldier."

"She does." Kermit nodded, shaking his head. "Shit."

"You're sheriff."

"Don't remind me."

They were both silent for a moment, and being the only two in the bar that night after midnight, Kermit felt like they were in a bomb shelter waiting to get nuked. The bar usually cleared whenever the sheriff went in for a late-night drink. He never knew why; he rarely arrested anyone for anything.

"Well." Lennie shooks his head; Kermit noticed there was a fine sheet of sweat above his eyebrows.

"I guess she missed it."

"I guess she did."

"Kinda dangerous. A woman driving like that. What do ya call it—reckless driving?"

"Reckless with a *w.*"

"I think maybe you been sheriff too long."

"Oh, yeah," Kermit agreed. He stretched and got up off the barstool. He reached in his breast pocket and pulled out a stick of gum. "Want some Wrigley's?"

"Only if you got two."

"Oh, well." Kermit unwrapped the gum and slid it into his mouth. "I guess I should go pull her over."

"Think she's one of them?" Lennie asked.

Kermit looked in the mirror behind the bar, more at himself than at Lennie. *Ancient of days,* he thought looking at his out-of-shape body and the veins on his nose.

"I hope not, Lennie. God, I hope not."

This hour of the night was Kermit Stone's least favorite, because it was after midnight that he remembered things from his youth he'd've preferred to forget. As he stepped out of King Tut's, he had a feeling from the past, like a chill wind, and he wrapped his arms together in front of his chest and wished he had a heavier jacket on. He stood in the dim blue light of the bar doorway and looked down the street toward the statue of the Known Soldier, the local joke. It was a life-size carved stone image of what many figured to be a Civil War soldier, or perhaps Spanish-American War— no one knew for sure which. And then around World War II, somebody declared that it was the image of one of the Confederate deserters who had founded the town of Empire and had displaced the Spanish settlers back in the late 1800s. So it had gone from being the town's Unknown Soldier to being its Known Soldier, also its shame. *Whole town's a damn joke,* Kermit thought.

The Mustang that had been speeding was gone, although he heard its squealing wheels down one of the tree-lined streets, and he wondered if she was one of them.

Them.

Because he knew *they* were still here, that they had unfinished business.

Family. The everlasting family. With a capital C.

And if she was with them, he hoped to Christ she would crash and burn.

Eternally.

Then Sheriff Kermit Stone turned about, having decided that it was time for another boilermaker.

Kate managed to pull the Mustang over to the shoulder, but she could not stop shivering. All she thought was *Hope.* She knew she would have to calm down or she would never be able to help her daughter. But if Robert had her, if one of Robert's spies had her, what the hell was Kate going to do?

If I go to the cops they'll put me away.

And he'll have Hope.

To do with as he pleases.

Her brain felt like it was going to burst out of her skull.

"I'm scared," she said, not realizing that she was talking out loud. "Scared, scared, scared."

For a second she calmed, as if saying that one word was a soothing mantra. Then Kate saw the yellow truck in her rearview mirror.

The yellow truck of nightmares.

You're my little girl, Katy Weeks, you and me together, forever.

It had pulled up behind her, and now the farmer with the burning red coal eyes was getting out from behind the wheel, and he looked very angry.

"You don't exist," she said, averting her glance from the mirror. She stared straight ahead. "You are not my father, and even if you are, you're dead, and dead people can't hurt anyone."

She felt an inner calm all of a sudden, as if she had just lost the nervous edge that had sustained her for the past week. It was like a second wind, and she shut her eyes and felt for her pulse to make sure she was still alive.

When she opened her eyes again, she stared straight ahead. The sturdy houses and shops were still; their windows reflected the streetlamps; insects fluttered and flickered around the white glow of the lights.

Without even looking back, she started the car up again and calmly drove back to the Greenwater Motor Lodge, because she had nowhere else to go.

12:30 A.M.

Elsewhere in town, knowing that their sheriff was probably getting good and soused, and that perhaps a wife-killer was out prowling among chicken coops, the good people of Empire were, for the most part, asleep. Kermit's son, Gus, was actually lying among wads of laundry in the linen closet of the Greenwater Motel and wishing he was someplace else. Gretchen Feely snored beside him, and he wondered if she really enjoyed the sex with him or if it was just her way of ensnaring him. Across town from the Greenwater, a woman named Loretta Swink watched the road out front for the crazy person who had been driving so wildly a few minutes earlier. And then she saw another car, a Chrysler Fifth Avenue, drive by her place and on down the Asistencia Road, alongside the grapevines. This reminded her of something she had to do, so she left the front window of her farmhouse and went back into the kitchen, and opened the Dutch door to the root cellar. Her little grandson was beside her, following her steps. Why a little kid like that should be up so late, well, only Loretta knew for sure. A woman named Joanne was taking off her blouse in another house, down on Grapevine Avenue, just as the man who'd won her in a pool game was passing out in bed. A boy named Abraham, although his friends called him simply Bram, was sneaking down to the TV room in the house he shared with his mother; she was snoring away, and he would get to stay up and watch monster movies until at least three. Karl Swanson awoke briefly, thinking his long-dead wife was standing over him asking him for directions, but it was only a dream, not a nightmare, for he missed her, and he fell back to sleep, happily and peacefully, hoping to glimpse her again in his sleep. A man named Hub Radcliffe had managed to cover himself with enough newspapers to stay fairly warm, and was asleep on a bench in the oval of park that sat downtown almost like an old-fashioned town common. It was an ordinary night in Empire, as far as most of its residents were concerned.

And beneath the ground at the Hillside Memorial Park, a woman who called herself Poppy Freek slept with the bones of children in her arms.

12:30 A.M.

Fletcher McBride tasted raw chicken and thought it was good.

12:30 A.M.

Hope Stewart awoke for a few seconds, but the smell of oil and gas and the darkness swallowed her down again into sleep without pain. She had a sense that she was traveling in a car, probably in the trunk, but it could've been a dream, and it felt a lot like the day when she had seen the butterflies and had flown out of the car. The day her father had the accident. In her dreams she saw the creature that she'd told her father about when he quizzed her back at the hospital, the creature with the twisting vertebrae, the one that began eating itself, and she realized that it was only a caterpillar, and when it changed again it would be like one of the pretty butterflies.

Its face was like someone she had never seen before, and it said to her, "No pain. I'll make sure. No pain."

"I know," she said, and then was engulfed in the darkness of warm sleep.

33

12:36 A.M.

BEN FARRELL HAD ARRIVED IN TOWN JUST A FEW MINUTES before and had even seen the Mustang driving swiftly and recklessly by, but he had assumed it was full of kids out on a wild ride. He stayed to the main drag, thinking about Kate and the mess she was in. Anger still boiled somewhere inside him, anger that was directed not only at Robert but at Kate as well, anger that had grown from a scar he'd received years ago. "Why the hell did you ever leave me?" he asked his reflection in the rearview mirror. Ben was a man who had never quite gotten his life right, never actually got on track, and he was well aware of the reason. It was that he hadn't grabbed his chance when he'd had it in his hands, when he and Kate were together, when they were both happy. When Kate told him about Robert, how Robert loved her and wanted to marry her, all Ben had been able to say was "Well, if it's what you want ..." That, rather than what was really on his mind. What he burned to say: I love you and you love me, and I don't want you to ever leave me. But he hadn't said that. Perhaps, he thought, he had been too young. They had both been too young. But somewhere in his being he knew that that was not true. He had just not been brave enough. He had just not been man enough, or human enough. And it had led to this suppressed rage; that was exactly what had done him in. He had been with other women over the years, but none like Kate, none who lingered in his memory as she did. He was one of those men who needed a particular woman to make him grow up a little, take some responsibility, choose his direction and head in it. He had spent most of his adult life doing exactly what he damned well pleased, and this was where he'd ended up: in a town he'd never heard of, coming for his life, his love, his reason for getting up in the morning. Two reasons. Kate and Hope. He was determined never to let them go once they were with him again.

He stopped in a doughnut shop that was going to close in another fifteen minutes and grabbed a Styrofoam cup of coffee. He asked the woman who was wiping the counter where the motel was, and she pointed on down the road.

Ben looked through the glass, in the direction of her finger, and saw Shadow's car idling on the other side of the road. He knew it was Shadow's, even though it wasn't the same one he'd been driving in San Francisco.

"Shit," he muttered.

"Mister?" The woman said.

Ben apologized. "I just can't run fast enough from my shadow."

The woman shrugged, poured him another cup of coffee. "The more you try the more it finds you, and that's the truth. You been drinking tonight, mister?"

When Ben arrived at the Greenwater Motel, he drove around to the back and found the room number that Hope had given him. The door was open, and the light was on. He parked, got out of his car, and went to the doorway. He knocked on the doorframe. "Kate? Hope?"

Soft music came from within the room, and Ben stepped inside. It smelled of mildew and Lysol. The colors were yellow and red, and for a moment he felt as if he'd entered the wrong room, as if someone else was here, because there was another smell in the air, another color beyond sight, as if an animal had been set afire here. He noticed grease stains on the wall, as if someone had rubbed his head against it. For a moment he remembered another room, another place, another time, and a rooster walking in between the small pale white bodies, naked and stitched with blood and shiny glass, and the network of plastic tubes connected to the children's wrists and legs, siphoning blood out even while they breathed their last.

Ben blinked, his eyesight becoming unfocused and then clear again. He saw the motel room. That was where he was, not in that other place. He caught his breath and held it. Counted to twelve, just as he had back in those days when he'd seen the dead children. Exhaled. His hands were tight fists; his fingernails dug furrows into his palms.

A suitcase lay open on the bed. "Kate?"

Water was running in the bathroom. He heard the tinny sound of classical music, also from the bathroom. He went through the room, almost tripping on a pair of shoes—Kate's. The bathroom smelled like rust, and he was shocked by his face in the mirror: haggard. Old.

In the bathroom he turned the faucet off. Kate's makeup kit was there, and he saw cigarette ash in the soap dish. Same old Kate. Things everywhere. No organization. The paint had begun peeling along the wall by the medicine cabinet mirror. Hope's doll lay on the floor. He bent over and picked it up. It was falling apart. Ben remembered walking into Toys "Я" Us and picking it out from among the many others, wrapping it carefully, taking it to Hope when she was three. He remembered, too, how drained and withered Kate had seemed on that visit, how she had been forgetting to eat, wash, brush her hair. But he had attributed it to her son's recent death, and knew she was strong enough to pull out of it.

And then he heard the sound of a woman weeping from the bedroom, and turned toward it, as if recognizing the sound of his own heart beating.

34

KATE BARELY FELT THE ARMS THAT CIRCLED AROUND HER back. She had thrown herself on the motel bed and was sobbing. Ben Farrell seemed to speak to her from a dream. She knew now what Robert had done to her, probably using Dr. Jardin to keep her supplied with every psychotropic drug known to man and then some.

"You're a hallucination," she said, turning to Ben. She could barely focus on his face because of the tears streaming down, washing against her vision. "You're some hypnotic suggestion he gave me, or you're part of my brain going haywire. You're not really here." As she spoke, she felt stronger, somehow.

"Kate," he said, "it's me. Ben. What's going on? Where's Hope?"

She was silent for a minute. She glanced around the room to make sure she was not hallucinating further, then back to Ben. She wiped her eyes. Ben touched the side of her face. His hand was smooth and warm. He looked into her eyes; she noticed that his own eyes were brimming with tears.

"Where's Hope? he asked again.

If you're Ben what the hell are you doing here? she wondered. *And if you're a hallucination, how can I feel you?* She tried to sort through the layers of confusion that were keeping her from thinking straight.

"Katy?" Ben leaned forward and kissed her, just to the side of her lips. "Baby? Where's Hope?"

She drew back from his kiss, scrambled along the bed as if she were terrified of his touch. Her lips curled into a snarl, and Kate said, "How did you know where to find me?"

Ben backed away from her. "Katy—"

"You've been speaking with Robert, haven't you?"

"Kate. Slow down. Hope called me. She told me where she was. Now you tell me: where is she?" Ben felt warm, as if someone had turned the temperature up high in the motel room. He broke a sweat, thinking that he was too late, that Kate had done something—probably accidentally or while on some medication—or maybe ... Oh, God, maybe Hope was safe somewhere. He hated himself for jumping to these conclusions, but Kate seemed to be in such a state, and his fears about Hope's safety, particularly after Robert's phone calls, were enormous.

Kate looked at him shrewdly, as if she would read his thoughts. "Why don't you ask Robert? He knows where she is. One of his trained lab ràts must've taken Hope. Oh, God." She began sobbing again, and he could not help but go toward her. "Ben, they took my baby. I don't know what to do. Robert's messed me up too much. He's twisted my mind."

"It'll be okay," he said.

She turned to face him again. He could feel the warm tears on his neck.

And then she pulled back just as if a snake had bitten her.

"Get that out of here, get that out of here," she cried.

She was staring at the doll, and only then did he notice something strange about it.

The missing eye.

"Look what those sick people did to it. *Look at it.*"

He picked the doll up, turned it around. Someone had scratched various designs into the plastic, none of which meant much to him. But there was one design, a small diamond within a circle within a large diamond.

And Ben Farrell wondered how the hell Kate and Hope had wandered into this hellhole.

"It's not Robert," he said, feeling the blood draining from his face.

"Who else ..."

He shook his head and set the doll back on the bed. He worked at keeping the tears back from his eyes, because he didn't want Kate to sink further into despair. And perhaps he was wrong; perhaps it was only a nonsensical design scribbled by someone to scare them.

Or to scare me. He had heard they'd gone south, or far north to Canada, or to the jungles of Brazil. He had been able to put them out of his mind for almost a decade, put out of his mind the scene he had come upon years before in the old Victorian down by the waterfront in San Francisco; the memory came back like a strong smell, the memory of the bodies, the children's bodies along the stairs, hanging from the banisters, the blood on the walls, the flies buzzing as they feasted on the two-days dead. The betrayal he'd felt when he'd covered the trial for three days for his undergraduate newspaper, how he'd been suckered into believing that they were taking care of children, providing them with shelter and food and alternative education.

And in perfectly drawn lines of blood, the same symbol on the yellow living room wall of the Victorian. Their mark.

Kate said, "Who?"

Ben Farrell closed his eyes, saying a prayer. "Not Robert. Something else. We have to call the police. Before ..." But he could not finish that thought.

He thought he heard something just beyond the doorway. He remembered his Shadow, and wondered if he was waiting outside.

Or if it was something far worse.

35

ON THE OTHER SIDE OF TOWN, HOPE STEWART SLOWLY CAME to. A gag over her mouth. Tasted like gasoline. A rag dipped in gasoline. Tied around the back of her head. Tight. The rag that had been pulled across her eyes was tight, too. She had to pee really badly—her consciousness of her bladder made it seem enormously out of proportion to the rest of her body.

She knew she was propped up somehow, but her senses were overwhelmed.

The air around her stank, like dirty things, like bathrooms and gutters and places where animals lived.

Cold, the smell of dirt, humid, the sound of dripping water, moist, like after peeling back a scab, that kind of feeling. Hope tried to see in the place where her eye had been. It hurt to force it like this, to scrunch her forehead all up and really press down hard on the socket because sometimes the glass eye rubbed against her skin all wrong.

Gotta pee.

Her hands were tied up to sticks so that her hands stuck straight out. One of her hands was pressed against what felt like a solid dirt wall. Her feet were tied together, also. She was attached to some kind of pole, thrust in the dirt; her knees were bent, and her feet were in the dirt. But the dirt smell was so strong that it seemed like she was almost surrounded by dirt.

She saw nothing in her head.

She felt warmth coming for her, like a bird swooping

down for a beetle in the grass, or a child reaching beneath a rock for what lay wriggling in the cold and damp. Whoever it was, he didn't touch her, but passed his hands over her face and shoulders without touching; she felt the air between his hand and her skin.

Without wanting to, she began crying, and she remembered being taunted by some boys when she was only five and how they called her a *crybaby, crybaby, crybaby, cry*. The memory only made her tears come faster, as if they were pearls on a string sliding off, one after another, faster as they went.

A damp hand grazed her cheek, catching the tears.

Then, she realized it was not a hand at all.

He's licking my face.

But she tried to think of it as a hand, a warm, moist, rough hand, *not a tongue, not a tongue,* because she was going to throw up if it was a tongue, and if she pressed down on her missing eye hard enough she could *make it into a hand in her mind, not a tongue.*

The man said, "You're the one. You're like the deformed one, ain'tcha? Only your deformity's on the inside. I can smell it. Real strong, like rat shit."

He had a different voice than the man called Monkey. It was not gentle, but it was comforting.

Someone else, farther away, sounding like a little boy or perhaps a woman imitating a boy, "Welcome to the house of pain."

And then, even closer to her, near her right ear, the breath of some animal, and Monkey's voice: "I want to play with her. I want to hack off her imperfection." She felt his rough finger dip beneath the rag that covered her vision, and then a pressure as he pushed her glass eye, and it was like a millipede slowly crawling along the eyelid, trying to insinuate itself between her skin and the glass eye. "You promised we could play with her. You promised."

The man standing in front of her said, "It's not playtime yet. Remember what I can do. Under your skin. If you don't behave. We have to milk her first."

Monkey whispered, just for her, "You're not perfect, are you? You're like all children; you're not perfect. We'll play later on. After they leave. After you take care of Harly. He's been asleep too long. Then we'll play a long time."

He loosened the gag. It had cut into the corners of her lips. She tasted blood. Blood and gasoline.

"Tell me," he said, "what you like to play."

And then she began shivering uncontrollably, not out of fear, but with a feeling like something under her skin, plucking at her nerves, sliding along her spine like it was playing her, and sweat began prickling the back of her neck.

I'm feeling his sickness, she thought in the jumble of thoughts that were short-circuiting her brain. *Madness, crazy, mind, my mind, all wants, three, three in one, three in one, three in one. Do ... Do ... Do ...*

"What are you doing to me, you bitch? What are you doing to me, you bad bad girl! You naughty child!" Monkey screeched, and she felt pressure against her skull as he pulled the blindfold off.

"Get her out of me!" Monkey could feel the girl's grubby fingers digging through the gray matter of his brain, squeezing it into long ropes that pulled him every which way, and then he saw. *He was seven again.* BadMama was standing there with her fingernail scissors saying, "Can't go to church until they get clipped, Matt, you know that." Her hair so yellow and wavy, her dress long and brown, and the scissors just clicking back and forth. She reached for his fingers, but he drew back.

"Please," he whimpered, but she grabbed his left hand and brought it against her stomach. Then she took the scissors and pressed them up to his fingers.

BadMama pressed down on his fingernails, slicing them just below the skin line, drawing blood, and the shock ran through him in wave after wave because he knew he could not scream and move or it would be worse, because to go to church he had to have his fingernails clipped and clipped good.

"Ah," she said, her breath fluttering, "now, let's take care of the other hand."

Hope felt as if she had just thrust her fingers into an electric socket. Her right eye socket throbbed and she felt that she could see *a woman with a small pair of scissors, and fingers without their nails, all pink and puffy. And then other things, too, other children, other houses, two boys playing in a bathroom.* This was superimposed on what she saw with her left eye, which was *the yellow-lit room, and the man named Monkey near her face.* His eyes were bloodshot and wild, and there was a yellow light around his head like a halo. And his face no longer seemed human, but was contorted in pain. "Birdy was wrong! You ain't God. You're just a bad bad little girl who needs to have her imperfection hacked off just like the others!" The words began gargling and choking in his throat, and Monkey stepped back from her.

Her shivering stopped as quickly as it had begun. The vision in her right eye faded to black.

"And I won't let you play with my friends." He grabbed a torch that was thrust into a wine cask, and then squatted down so that the torch light fell upon a child's face.

It was a little girl, just like Hope.

And then Hope recognized her.

It wasn't a little girl at all. It was a teenager's head, her tongue flopped across her chin, her eye sockets completely empty, and two thin streams of blood dried along her forehead.

It was Iris, from AttaBurger.

When Monkey lifted the girl's head up by the back of her scalp, showing that there was no body connected with it, he said, "See, I hacked off her imperfection, and now we play whenever I want, but you can't play with us because I don't like the kind of girl you are!"

Then another voice came out of his mouth, and it was as if a ventriloquist were using him as dummy, for the voice was deeper, more resonant: "Put it down, Monkey. You're scaring the poor girl."

Then, in his own voice, Monkey said, "Well, now she knows what it feels like! Don't you? *Don't you!*"

But Hope had been holding her breath since she'd first seen Iris's head, with its slack mouth and its gouged-out eyes, and she was sure she would pass out.

She peed in her underwear and felt shame and fear and

revulsion all at once, until she felt like she was going to crawl out of her skin and leave it behind, like the way her mother told her that spirits leave the body after death. *Just let me die and not be here. Please, God, please, God, just let me out of this body.*

She heard Monkey screeching as he ran into the darkness.

36

MONKEY RAN DOWN THE PASSAGEWAY, FEELING HIS WAY along the cold walls until he found his bunk. He slid into it. "You saw what she did to me," he whispered.

Birdy, inside him, said, *You brought that on yourself. You have to be more careful with her. You know what she can do.*

"And she did it, too. She's a very bad girl."

But you liked it.

"No, I did not. And you can't make me think I did."

I know you, baby brother. I know what you like. You like the scissors.

"I do not."

Remember how I cut you? You like that.

"It's different. Not like when Mama used to."

You mean your bad mama. Not your good mama.

"Don't fuck with my mind, Birdy!" Monkey covered his ears. He listened to his pulse.

Birdy was gone.

Then another voice rose up inside him and spoke aloud through his lips: *"You're both driving me nuts. Monkey, I want you to hurry up and do what you're supposed to. I'm fucking rotting away, and you're dicking with her."*

Monkey calmed. He could feel the fur of his brother's scalp rubbing against the inside of his stomach. "Okay. Okay. But I don't wanna touch her again. You hear?"

"Whatever you want, little brother. You don't know what it's like here. What they make me do. How they make me ... Where are they?"

"What?"

"You know."

"In the jars. Still."

"You took care of them? Good. Can't let Birdy know. He don't want me back. He wants me here. But you know. You know how."

Monkey nodded. "The Pain Room."

"Right on, brother. The shower. Her. The girl. What's inside. But I need it soon. You know where I am."

"I know," Monkey said, feeling tears in his eyes. "I miss you. I like it when you're in me."

"I'll always be here if you want me. My little Monkeyman.".

"Sing for me. Like before."

"Do you know the Monkeyman, the Monkeyman, the Monkeyman?" the voice sang. It echoed down the long corridor, past the children of the harvest as they lay in the bunks along the walls, and Monkey knew what he would have to do when the song ended.

Monkey had come to Empire when he was almost seven, after the BadMama. He had never known the BadMama too well, even though she was all he had known since his birth. She was very ugly, and someone told him when he was five that she was really his older sister, and only his mama because she had let herself go astray. He had never known his father. They had found Monkey locked in the closet, and when he asked them about Ginger, his little sister, they said nothing, but he read about Ginger in the paper—at least he saw the pictures, and someone read the story to him. And as a result, he learned about his family and what had become of them. The photo in the paper had been of their bungalow in Indio, with the date palms rising up behind it. The green Chevrolet was in the driveway, and the blinds were pulled down except where the dog had torn the one down in the garage window. There had also been a map of the area, showing the spot where Ginger had been found. Then there was a picture of Ginger when she was three. She was not pretty, and looked too much like the BadMama even then, but he had felt some affection for her because she took most of his whuppings for him. The BadMama mainly liked to hurt Ginger, which was perfectly fine by Monkey's standards because Ginger never cried out no matter what the Badmama did to her. In the paper, the people called her "autistic," although he had always known that Ginger was just plain quiet. The paper talked about Ginger's burns and how she'd been left in the Borrego Desert, in the hills, and was only half alive. He never saw Ginger after that, but he missed her. The paper didn't mention his name, but it did mention that there was another child who was being taken care of by the county. He knew that it was the biggest county in California.

He was happy to leave the BadMama's house, and he went to a couple of different homes, until finally he'd ended up in San Francisco with the GoodMama, or just plain Mama, and she'd taught him spiritual values and how to take care of family. And it was a real family, just like on TV, with a father, a mama, two brothers, and a sister. And no one ever locked him in the closet unless he was really bad, and no one tried to scare him. His new mother showed him that by using his memory, by going back into it, like prayer, in a quiet place, he could enjoy things that had previously scared him. Even the fingernail scissors, if they were used right, could be his friend. "Sometimes," the Good-Mama used to say, "what hurts us makes us better. Sometimes you can turn pain into something that feels nice, if your mind is in the right place. You have to put your mind in a perfect place and listen to the inner voices that tell you what to do. If your mind is aligned with perfection, then you can never go wrong. And imperfection should be hacked off." She used to say this while she rocked him on her knees, and then she would give him the fingernail scissors and ask him to do what he was afraid of. "Only when we are most afraid do we become strong and brave. Face your fear, my little Monkeyman, and turn your pain into something good. Align yourself with perfect thought, perfect light."

And then it didn't feel so bad. At first it hurt a little. At first when he tugged at his own fingernails there was pain just like before. But then, with time, he enjoyed the sweet feeling of cutting down to the cuticle, of that strange sour taste that would rush into the sides of his mouth like the stuff the dentist used on his teeth to clean them, and then there were his fingers, how they looked different than they had before—he grew to enjoy it, take pleasure out of it. He would sometimes take hours alone in his room, peeling back layers of skin just below the cuticle; or he would eat the outer layer of his lips. His brothers would help him, Birdy especially; he would take the scissors and make small cuts around Monkey's nipples and on the bottoms of his feet.

When he was eleven, Monkey tried it on a little boy who lived in the apartment above, but the boy screamed and ran away. When the boy came back, Monkey told him that it hurt him because he wasn't perfect. "All imperfection has to be hacked off," he said. The boy was a little scared, but Monkey convinced him it was for the better. The boy was four and was a little slow, but Monkey was sure he could find his imperfection if he looked, and if he listened to the counsel of his inner voices. Back in those days, the inner voices had sounded like the GoodMama or like Monkey himself. He had examined the boy all over his body; gotten him to pull his shorts down, and then his daddy pants, as Monkey called underwear, and checked under his armpits and between his toes. After about ten minutes he had located the boy's imperfection in a place he hadn't thought of: his left ear. The ear was filled with wax, and it smelled. The inner voices agreed that this was indeed the boy's imperfection.

The boy had yellow hair, all curly and too long for a boy. His other ear looked like a fat dried apricot. But the left one looked like a curly fig. It was repulsive, and Monkey had to swallow some vomit when he got too close to it. *Imperfection must be hacked off.*

"You ain't gonna cut my ear off," the boy said.

"Uh-uh. I wouldn't do that," Monkey reassured him. They were in the bathroom, sitting side by side on the tub edge. He got the boy to pull his pants back up and button his shirt. The boy's mother knocked on the bathroom door; it was locked, and she wanted them to unlock it. She was drunk, and Monkey wasn't really scared of her, because she was stupid.

She said, "What are you boys doing in there?"

"Nothing," Monkey said.

Her own son said nothing. Monkey knew something about him then, because he saw the boy blush. The boy had liked the way Monkey examined him; he had liked pulling his shorts and daddy pants down.

"Say something," Monkey whispered to the boy.

"I'm coming, Mommy," the boy said.

"Open this door now," his mother said. She rapped her knuckled on the doorframe.

"Okay." The boy made a move to get up and do as he was told, but Monkey held him in place.

"If you put your mind right, this won't hurt," Monkey whispered to the boy as he aimed the point of the fingernail scissors at all that nasty wax in the wrinkled fig ear.

And he jabbed. Again and again and again.

Monkey rocked back and forth, knees to chest, faster and faster, as if rocking would take away the pain that the girl had caused him back in the cellar. *She's so imperfect she doesn't even know it, but I'll hack it off, hack it off, hack it off, and then I'll make her eat it! I don't care what Harly and Birdy say. I'll hack if I want to hack!*

37

HOPE STEWART KEPT HER GOOD EYE OPEN. THE HEAD THAT lay in front of her no longer terrified her. She smelled her own urine and felt the discomfort around her thighs where it seemed to burn. But the panic and shame she had felt before were gone. In their place, she felt something that she didn't know she could feel at all. It wasn't fear so much, although that was there. Ben would tell her, "Don't be afraid of the dark."

And thinking of him helped a little. Only a little.

But there was something else, like the voice that was there when she healed someone.

But not a voice, exactly.

Maybe it was just a thought, a word.

An idea.

Power.

She had felt a kind of electricity flowing through her, a jabbing pain in the empty eye socket, but from that, the feeling of power, like a taste and a smell and a touch that shivered from her eye socket through the nerve endings in her body, a kind of friction that she had experienced, drawn from the man named Monkey, as if he had some sort of low-intensity energy inside him and she had plugged herself into it and sapped what he had. She had seen images in her head, not of the butterflies but of two little boys playing together, on the edge of a bathtub. One of them was Monkey. It was as if she had crawled into his skin for a minute, seen from *his* eyes. It had felt so good to do it, like eating ice cream or watching a fun scary movie, that feeling—*power!*

Like she could crawl through his brain, and press down on memories—*power!*

Like it was not him but *her* who directed him to take a pair of fingernail scissors—*power!*—and stab them deep into the other boy's ear. She couldn't control the motion, and yet she felt in control. It was dangerously sweet, that feeling.

Power!

What she had enjoyed the most from it, before she was tugged back into her own consciousness, was the sense that he had felt her inside him, that she had scraped a path into his mind, bored a hole like a worm. And he had felt it, and had fought it, but because she was somehow using his own energy, claiming it as her own, he could not fight too well. And she didn't have to fight at all—it was natural, like opening an eye, but not one with a lid and an iris and cornea and pupil. This was an inward eye, a sense beyond just vision.

This was more than just sight.

This was *power*.

This was something she could *use*.

Exhausted, exhilarated, she fell asleep quickly, as if her body knew when to shut down, to rest. She slipped painlessly into a sweet dream of a time when she was four, when Denny was a baby and still alive. Back before her mother and father had gotten worse, back before Denny died and went to heaven. She rocked him in her arms, smelling that sweet baby smell of his, so clean, so wonderful. "I am going to love you for always," she told her brother, kissing his little blond head, "for always and a day."

Her brother smiled, and her dream went on and on as she slept.

38

A BOY AND HIS GRANDMOTHER WERE TALKING IN THE DARK:

"We don't need her. We're fine like this."

"But it's the time of reckoning. You know that. That's why we're here. It's our mission."

"I like things the way they are."

"I know you do. I love you so much. You know how much your grandma loves you?"

"More than the world and life and everything. I know."

"That's right. And you're special, too. You are part of this, too. Make me proud, child."

"I just don't see why we need her. I don't. You know what I can do."

"Soon. Come here. Sit on my lap. Let me hold you, child, let me see my most beautiful of children."

39

The Shadow Knows

DR. ROBERT STEWART DREAMED OF THE CRAWLING DARK, its many hands reaching for him, its centipede body wriggling, pulling him to its pulsing body. This was not a nightmare; he felt warm and comfortable. When the crawling dark opened its jaws, it began making birdlike chirping noises, and Robert fought the sound, but finally opened his eyes, looked at the clock, and reached over to pick the phone up.

No one was on the line. Annoyed, he slammed the phone into its cradle. He'd fallen asleep only within the past hour. He stared up at the ceiling, switched on a light, flicked on the television, flipped through twenty cable channels before turning it off again.

He got up from the bed, his knees aching a bit from the jogging that evening, and prepared to go to the bathroom. His underwear rode up, so he pulled it down in back, and that was when he noticed that the hall light was on. He was sure he'd switched it off. He stopped, stood still, sniffed the air as if he could detect a predator. He took a few steps backwards, toward his dresser. He pulled the top drawer out halfway, felt through the socks until he found the cold steel of his pistol. Even Kate hadn't known that he kept one there.

As he withdrew it, a voice behind him said, "Didn't mean to scare you, Dr. Stewart."

He looked around, and recognized a man in military uniform. "Corporal," he said. "You could've tried the doorbell."

"Yes, sir. I did. There was no answer, and given the circumstances . . ."

"I understand."

"There's a man from Special Projects who wants to see you."

"Grace?"

"I don't know his name." Then the corporal said, half-joking, "You know Special Projects, sir. They change their names faster than a woman changes her mind."

Robert didn't appreciate the joke. "I know several women who would shoot you for that comment, Corporal. My wife included."

The corporal rolled his eyes, and then said, "We have a car waiting."

"Has he found my daughter? My wife?"

"I'm afraid I'm not at liberty to say."

"Of course not. Hear no evil, see no evil, speak no evil."

"I understand you're not fond of us, sir."

"I'm not fond of this government taking over my research. I'm not fond of suspicion. Or dirty tricks. Isn't that what you call Special Projects? The Dirty Tricks Department? The Search-and-Destroy Boys? The Nuke and-Puke Department?"

The corporal said nothing, and Robert Stewart felt like aiming the gun at this man's balls, but knew that it was too late: his balls had already been yanked by Nathan Holder from Special Projects. You couldn't even get mad at these guys: they were following orders, never questioning. It was a military commandment, do or die.

Robert set the gun back among the socks, and went to get a fresh shirt from the walk-in closet. "How long will it take?"

The other man said, "You should be there by oh-five-hundred. We have an escort for you, a young man who is waiting now at the airport. Perhaps he will be able to fill you in in greater detail than I. But we need to get to the airport within the next hour."

Five A.M., Robert Stewart thought. *The dawn of a new era.*

40

3:45 *A.M.*

"SHIT," STEPHEN GRACE SAID. HE STUBBED HIS CIGARETTE out against the wall of the motel with his two hundred dollar Italian shoes, all squeaked out at last. *Nights like this go on forever.* It was so silent on the slick streets, he wondered if the town was dead. He knew places where night was so raucous, so explosive, that the calm came only with the first light of the sun. He liked those places better than this place, this Empire. It was in these towns, off the back roads, that a country was most dangerous. The cities and the jungles, those were for enlightenment, for exchange of ideas, and for peace. But a place like this, with its living silence. He knew what was here, in one of these houses: something he could not put his finger on, like smelling something and recognizing it from memory without identifying it.

And before dawn, before this town awoke, he would have to make sure things didn't get out of hand. No leaks to the press, no gossip, no misunderstandings.

His job here, as always, was to throw himself on the live grenade.

In this case, the girl.

But to perform it like surgery, so that no one was aware of the operation.

In that motel room, which he watched, Katherine Weeks Stewart and Benjamin Farrell. She: wife of the acclaimed doctor and medical researcher. He: small-time San Francisco newspaperman. The town: Empire, known in the 1940s for its grapes, known now for nothing.

So why here, Stewart? Why here? Why is this place the end of the line?

Is this the place where the dark tide will rise? And what the hell is the "dark tide"?

Stephen Grace had spent the past forty-eight hours reviewing all of the doctor's tapes, noting the maddening gaps in logic in them, the code words, the numbers all run together. One section of the tape that was only now making sense to him. *If only I could torture you, doc, then there'd be none of this game playing.* But that wasn't how he worked; it wasn't his assignment. The girl was his objective. And once she was out of the way, then he could deal with Stewart. But only then.

From the tape, he had scribbled these notes: "Mentions dark tide. What the hell is that? And change and numbers and rise of dark and grand experiment=girl?=mother=??=why #6 & 4? Signif.? 6 & 4 what? Experiments?"

He hated puzzles—never was good at them, never had the patience to solve them. He could do a job, but he couldn't always figure it out. And every time he thought he was on to something, the suits from Washington kept tying his hands.

Holder, coming out from Washington to San Francisco, had been no help, and Grace knew that the mad doctor was being protected by Special Projects, probably because this r-7 shit was such a hot commodity. *The dark tide, doc. What time does it rise? Just after midnight in some godforsaken town on the edge of a vast plain of nothingness?*

What the hell have you done with her?

Then, some movement at the doorway of the motel room. Grace smiled, nodding.

Ben Farrell stood, half in shadow.

41

"Figured you'd be here," Ben said. He looked to his right and then to the left. "My shadow."

"Now that's a nickname I like. The real one's Grace. Stephen Grace." Stephen Grace lost his smile; his face became an impenetrable blank, something he had perfected over the years.

Ben seemed to be listening for something. Grace had sized him up correctly: Ben Farrell looked for things. There were men who never did, who took what came their way, who ignored what was around them. Those men were possibly better survivors than Farrell. But Farrell looked for things—signs, portents. He was quick, and he was curious. *Seek and you will find.* "Are you alone?"

Grace held his hands out, palms upward. "No one else here."

"Yet," Ben said. "You with Stewart? The army? The FBI?"

"All of the above," Grace said, wishing he hadn't run out of cigarettes, "none of the above. I don't suppose you've got a smoke on you? I mean, we all smoke, I notice, all of us self-destructive types."

Ben didn't respond to this request. Now Stephen Grace felt as if he were being sized up; Ben squinted into the half-light of the motel. Then he said, "You're from that group of kamikazes, aren't you? Special Projects. I interviewed one of your guys back during the Gulf War. Didn't buy the guy's story, though. He told me he'd been sent to get Hussein.

But I think he was there for other reasons. Maybe to get one of our own guys. You know the weird thing, Shadow? He was a junkie. I found him living in the streets. He worked for some big-time government, and he was a junkie. Is that what they do to you after they've used you—get you hooked on something and then throw you out on your ass? You're all kind of crazy, aren't you?"

Stephen Grace grinned, then dropped the grin just as quickly. A blank screen for a face to hide everything. "You got to be crazy to love this job."

"You kill people, don't you?"

"Enough questions, Farrell. Where's the girl?"

"I thought maybe you had her."

Grace shut his eyes, pained. He said nothing.

"I've got another question," Ben said.

"You write for the rags, it's your job to ask questions. Go ahead; meter's running."

"Does this have anything to do with Cthonos?"

"Tha . . . ?"

Ben hissed under his breath, as if fed up with everything. He became impatient. "Christ, a girl's missing. Anything could be happening to her. I'm talking about the cult. Cthonos. The death cult. Or was the doll just a setup to blame someone else?"

Grace's eyes lit up for a second, a flash of distant lightning on the horizon. But he wasn't going to reveal anything. He glanced across the motel's back parking lot, as if sensing someone else. But there was no one. He said, as if to himself, "So that's it. Something more than just bad science."

Ben Farrell watched the man as if he were watching a snake turn in its coils. Adrenaline pumped just beneath the surface of his skin; he was ready for a fight, if there was to be one.

Stephen Grace had impenetrable eyes.

What's he thinking?

Grace said, "Listen, I want you to take a ride with me."

"Like hell," Ben said. *And disappear like some of the others who crossed the path of Special Projects? And leave Kate here alone? No thanks, Shadow.*

Stephen Grace kept on grinning, and Ben Farrell thought he might be talking to a card-carrying psycho. Upon first seeing him, Ben had figured Grace to be a man in his late fifties, but now it was apparent that he was maybe in his late forties or so, and young-looking, at that, but aged in the eyes and around the lips, as if maybe he'd had to scream one too many times, as if maybe he'd been put through hell before he was twenty-one and had come back with the kind of eyes that had a knowledge of whatever abyss there was in this world.

"Farrell," Shadow said, "I'll only repeat my invitation once."

He reached deep into his army fatigue jacket and withdrew what at first looked like a garage door remote control. It had two small antennae coming out of it, a thin copper wire strung between them. Shadow wiggled it in his hand; it emitted a series of clicks. "Space-age gun," he told Ben. "Can't even figure it out myself, but trust me: it works."

"I would've pegged you for a sawed-off shotgun, from your looks," Ben said. "That's a government-issue Uni. Well, not *our* government, unless I'm mistaken. Highly illegal in this country, isn't that right? I know what it does. I've seen pictures. You have to be careful, though, Shadow. I understand you can burn yourself pretty badly if you aren't careful."

Grace gesticulated with his hands as if he couldn't please everyone. "You know a little bit about a lot."

"I've done enough exposés of your agency. The CIA disavows all knowledge of you people, but you and I know how close your agency gets to theirs, don't we? Or don't you read exposés?"

"I don't read. At least, nothing written after 'In Xanadu did Kublai Khan a stately pleasure dome decree.'"

"Liar. You've at least read all my work. You spoke with Laurie Gilman in research. I know. She told me a man from some police investigation came in to grill her. She said you flirted with her. She told me you were only interested in *my* stories."

"Okay, jig's up. I read it all. Even about Ca-thonos. Back from your student days. Or should I say, your more idealistic days."

"The *c* is silent. In Cthonos. The *c* is silent."

"About that ride," Stephen Grace waved the Uni about, gesturing toward his Corvette, but also as if he didn't really know what the hell he was doing with it. "I have another one. Standard issue Smith and Wesson, but, Farrell, between you and me and the wall, it doesn't make as good a first impression."

42

4:00 A.M.

"Ben?" Kate said from the doorway. She had been lying on the bed, feeling like every bit of her was dead, even feeling that Ben had been a phantom, a dream, part of some demonic hallucination plaguing her.

And when she looked out through the open doorway, she saw him.

The man with the eyes of burning coal.

Behind him, the yellow truck.

He said, "My little darlin', come to Papa." He spread his arms wide, and she saw within their span a body riddled with disease, like tattoos along his naked chest and down his sagging stomach; the pockmarks of a visible cancer spreading from his armpits; rips and tears along his skin as if his bones were trying to push through the flesh.

Her eyes were dry; she would be brave. She was not going to let this make her go crazy. "You're not my father. You're something Robert put in my head."

"I missed you, darlin', I missed our times together. Come sit on my lap, come sit here. I won't bite," he said, his red eyes

glowing brighter, his smile broadening into a feral grin, his teeth like yellow corn kernels pressed into his bleeding gums.

Kate Stewart shut her eyes tightly. *I own my mind. You don't own it, Robert. No matter what you did to me, you don't own it.*

She opened her eyes again, and the farmer stood there laughing at her, patting his knees now, whispering, *"Come to Papa, little darlin'. Come on up here and let me see how fine my girl's grown up to be."*

She felt the heat of fear and terror rising up through her body, just as if she were about to burn up; she heard her own breathing as if it were distant thunder.

"Little darlin, you can see your old papa with your own two eyes, not like my granddaughter with only one to look at you, but two, two eyes, the better to see me with," he said, his voice becoming disturbingly real, and she wondered if perhaps she wasn't insane after all.

Kate thought of Hope, and there was something about what the father image was saying, about Hope's eye, about seeing Hope in her mind, seeing her whole, with both eyes intact.

Like a strong, stinging electrical current, shooting volt after volt through her body, Kate shuddered and let out a cry from her innermost being, a cry that had been there, buried so deep inside her for so long that it felt like another Kate was there, buried beneath her skin, a Kate she had forgotten about, a Kate who had been pushed aside while this other Kate had taken over her life.

The world before her exploded in a white-hot flash, and for a moment she thought someone had shot her in the head and now she was dying, for all she felt was numbness, and the pain of a memory of another Kate who was only now pushing herself up from inside, like a moth from a cocoon.

And she remembered.

Two weeks before, talking to Robert about a divorce, the argument, going to her medicine chest and taking the pills, the entire bottle. She just wanted to die. She just wanted . . .

4:02 A.M.

"Jesus, Kate," Ben turned, moving toward her; he sensed Shadow behind him, but was not scared of Shadow, not when Kate was shivering and staring, sweat pouring from her skin as if she had run a marathon.

And then she collapsed on the concrete before he could catch her.

She drank as much water as she could, afraid she would choke on the yellow-and-red capsules, not even sure of what they were, just wanting to die. His voice was rising from the downstairs foyer, "There's nothing you can do, Kate! I will make sure that she knows about what happened with our son, and I already have enough evidence to prove you unfit, so just face the fact that you've lost her!"

She blocked out his voice by humming, and the pills crawled down her throat slowly, painfully, catching against the base of her neck; she had to drink more water; they went down easily after that. Was that door locked? She frantically moved to it; it was.

Then it hit her.

This was just what Robert wanted her to do.

He had gone for the chink in her armor, as he always did.

He had used the memory of her dead son to press a button of weakness.

He had played her the way he played the piano—badly, but hitting all the notes he intended.

Robert had stopped yelling at her.

She heard the silence of the large house, the deafening quiet of loneliness.

Her stomach churned; it was full of the yellowjacket pills. She was pregnant with drugs. She would give birth to a giant yellow-and-red pill. She began to laugh, and had to cover her mouth because the laugh echoed through the cathedral she was standing in, a cathedral with a bathtub and a sink and the mirrored medicine cabinet looking back at her and laughing, too, looking like a burned-out woman in her thirties.

"Get over your self-pity," the woman in the mirror said.

But then she was shaking, and gravity got turned up high, because it was pulling her to the cold black tile floor. She heard a key going in the bathroom door. The knob turned. She could see the brilliant silver of the round knob twisting.

The door opened.

There was no light from the hallway, only a form, and then the form became a man, and then the man became Robert.

She knew she was drooling, but she couldn't help it.

"You're not going to die in my house," he said, scolding her.

She felt like a little girl, and she could not stop drooling.

And then she was in bed, and the other doctors came, and they told her they had pumped her stomach. She couldn't remember why she had even taken the pills, and she asked Robert where Hope was, and he said, "You don't want her to see you like this, do you?"

But later she got out of bed and went through the house, up to his study, into his private laboratory, into the walk-in refrigerator.

And she saw the thing in the covered petri dish.

The gelatinous oval, like a cracked egg, its white and yolk held perfectly in the round dish.

Except it was filled with yellow-brown pus.

A small piece of white tape attached to the side explained what it was in code: 6-e

But she knew what it was without having to crack the code.

It was an eye.

She wanted it to be the eye of a sheep or a monkey or a dog.

But she recognized something familiar in its iris, in its pupil, in the specks of colors there.

4:10 A.M.

"Katy?"

It was Ben's voice she heard, and she opened her eyes. Even the darkness of early morning was too bright for her, and she had to shut them again.

Someone else said, "I wonder if she's got it."

Ben said, "Katy?"

Without opening her eyes again, she said, "Hope's eye. He took it out. Before the accident. Hope didn't lose her eye in the accident. My God, my God, he *operated* on her."

When she finally opened her eyes, Ben kissed her on the cheek, and she tasted his tears as they reached her mouth. "I love you, Katy Weeks. Don't you die on me, not now, not now, not when we're finally together," he whispered, and his breath against her was like inspiration.

43

DR. ROBERT STEWART GLANCED AT THE YOUNG MAN SITTING next to him on the plane: a private in the army for this mission. *Christ*. Both men had been silent on the way to the airstrip, and they had barely exchanged two words since climbing into the jet. There was no one else aboard except the pilot.

Robert broke the silence. "Who is it you work for, Private?"

The man smiled. "You can call me Jim. I don't enjoy the formal titles with civilians."

"Jim. Are you one of Holder's men in disguise?"

Jim regarded him with a smile, as if he thought that Robert Stewart was some joker. "We'll be landing in a few minutes. There's a car waiting at the airstrip. It's another thirty, forty minutes to Empire. I enjoy a good drive when the sun's coming up. You ever do that? Sun's rising off the horizon, and nobody else is on the road? My dad used to take us for long drives. Someday when my wife and I have kids, I'll do the same—drive all over the country." He reached into the inner pocket of his jacket and withdrew his wallet, opened it up, displayed photos of his wife. She looked like she was still in high school. "Her name's Hilary. She's three months along with our first one. I want to name him David."

Robert looked at the pictures. A family man. He liked men who were proud of their families, especially their children. After Jim put the photos away, Robert said, "I'd like you to give me an answer. Do you work for Nathan Holder?"

"I work for the United States Army, sir." Jim's face became a blank; he turned away from Stewart for a second, then faced him, composed. He was tense. A trickle of sweat rolled down along his hairline. As if to clarify something that might not be clear, he said, softly but with pride, "I serve my country."

Robert almost grinned. *Fucking Special Projects and their patriots.* "We all serve our country. Perhaps you serve other interests, too? With a baby on the way, I doubt the army pays you enough."

Jim didn't reply."

"Do you know why I am going to this town in California?"

Jim nodded. "Task Force oh-five-oh."

"So . . ."

"So, you're with the Company. Or you're a contractor. It doesn't much interest me."

"Old hat to you," Robert waved his hand as if lazily swatting flies. "One task force is pretty much like the next."

Jim was getting to the point of opening up or breaking down, one of the two. He must always have in the back of his mind a suspicion that groups like Special Projects sometimes made the wrong decision or did the illegal thing. So Jimmy would develop a conflict between the "my country, right or wrong" attitude and his own conscience. Robert liked men of conscience, because they could see the point of things more easily than men who relied on pure common sense. He preferred conscience to patriotism, and if he could get Jim to crack in exactly the right place, then he would have all the information he needed on Holder to guarantee a successful operation. Conscience in human beings kept them from acting in sensible ways; they were easier to lead in the right direction if there was a moral spark. Robert had seen it back in Devon, in the government lab: Special Projects was run by mavericks, but the people under them were sheep. Sheep were impractical, but they followed whoever seemed to know where he was going.

I experiment on sheep, Jim.

Jim said, "I do my job. I'm an escort. I make sure the right people get to the right places."

"Do you know why you're going to drive me to Empire?"

"Orders," Jim said, almost looking surprised at the notion that there could possibly be another reason.

"How long have you been with Projects?"

Jim said nothing. The sweat still shone across his forehead.

You don't know as much as you'd like about this operation, do you, Jimmy? But you're lying. You do work for Holder, Robert thought. He could tell by the way the man's eyes had moved just a little when he'd mentioned Projects again. *Shit, I'm dead center in the game. Holder could put a gun to my head before this is up.*

Holder or that psycho operative.

The one who wants to kill my daughter.

Christ.

Robert Stewart wondered if the man named Grace had taken his research tapes to Holder. He thought not. He suspected that Holder employed so many damn live wires in his organization that nobody in Special Projects knew for sure what the hell was going on with any of the others.

If any of them did know, would they even want this particular very special project?

This man, Jim, for instance. Did he know what he was putting himself into, just by being the escort? It wasn't going to be like any other assignment Jimmy had ever had before. Jimmy would be part of it. He would be reborn in one lifetime.

Radiance.

Robert Stewart glanced away from the private named Jim and looked out at the night as it passed; back to the east somewhere the sun was rising, but ahead, only darkness, darkness and, perhaps, if all went well, destiny.

He thought of his daughter, and prayed that she was unharmed.

44

Townies

SHERIFF KERMIT STONE GOT HOME, A BIT DRUNKER THAN planned, and found himself locked out of his own house. Not wanting to wake Gus, he walked around to the kitchen window, which was always easy to push open, and tried to maneuver his way in. But it was a struggle, and then the dog started barking.

Damn beast. Kermit winced; his hand had caught on a nail. Because of drunkenness, he didn't feel pain, exactly—it was more like something cold and then hot and very hard pressing into the palm of his hand. The dog, a chocolate Lab, stopped barking from inside the house, having already sniffed out the fact that it was someone familiar breaking in. Kermit could hear the panting dog on the other side of the window.

He felt the cold and hot nail in the palm of his hand, and then pulled up hard away from it. The nail turned in his hand, and shredded a thin layer of flesh just before it came out. Kermit dropped back to his haunches, on the ground, nursing his wound. *Another couple of inches, and maybe I would've reopened an old memory,* he thought, feeling the raised braille of another scar that lay down toward the center of his hand.

Gus called out upstairs—*damn it, wouldn't you know he'd be home before me and now I'm gonna get a lecture before I pass out*—Kermit squatted in silence, hoping Gus would go back to sleep.

And then, from somewhere across town, he heard a howling, as if a wolf were staring up at the slivered moon at the precise moment that he was.

But it ain't no damn wolf, that's for sure.

Fletcher McBride on one of his wolfman trips again. Holy Mother of God, what was he gonna do with Fletch if Loretta Swink or Sam Feely actually got one good shot in while Fletch was raiding their chicken coops? And if he'd been getting down in those old catacombs and interfering with the sewage pipes one more time, Kermit would have to cart Fletch back to State on account of he was getting too damn expensive to care for.

Fletcher McBride was covered with feathers, and blood was smeared across his face and down the front of his shirt. He had a big old grin slapped across his face, and his howl resonated in the ramshackle coop just like it was an opera house. Around him lay the remains of three chickens, while others huddled in a corner, now settled down, oblivious to the fate of their sisters.

"The sky's falling," Fletch said.

Chicken blood always made him a little dizzy, especially when dawn was on its way and the wolf part of him was wearing down.

He turned to a noise, and a scent. Not chicken.

Human.

There, just outside the torn length of chicken wire, stood Loretta Swink. She hefted the rifle in her hands, aiming for his head.

"Last time you gonna get in my chickens, Fletch," she said. Loretta Swink had a voice like a squeaky door, but Fletcher figured it was on account of the time of morning.

"Don't shoot," he rasped, but realized, too late, that his wolf nature had garbled the words. That, and some chicken feathers that hadn't shaken loose from between his teeth.

"I'll do what I please," Loretta Swink said. In the shadowy light from the back porch of her farmhouse, she looked like his grandmother for a second, and then like his dead wife, Glory, and then, with each blink of his eyes, she looked like some kind of blue-haired country angel with both barrels of a shotgun pointing straight at him. She raised the gun up for a moment and fired it into the air, then brought it down again so he was staring right into the barrels like he was next.

Kermit Stone heard the gunshot, and said, "Aw, man, and it was a peaceful night, too, goddammit."

45

"YOU OKAY, MRS. STEWART?" SHADOW ASKED. HE STOOD back, away from where Ben held Kate, but he still had the Uni in his right hand. Ben thought, for a second, he'd heard a gun go off somewhere, and he kept his eyes on the Uni. *One of those things can fry you faster than a microwave,* Ben thought, and whispered to Kate, "Don't say anything."

"Oh, Ben, Ben," she murmured, "he used her for some kind of test. He operated . . ."

Ben kissed her forehead, but she pulled away from him. A sound of trucks, out on the distant highway outside the loop of town, came at him. He wondered what the hell kind of normal cargo they carried: fruit, chickens, canned goods. *Not some Uni.* The trucks seemed to get louder and closer, and Ben thought they'd come right by them in a moment or two, but they did not. He looked at Kate: her face seemed small and fragile despite her stony glance. He reached out for her hand, and she allowed him to take it into his. She was warm, and he felt that sense of love, so small, like a flame that had been turned down on a gas stove, so blue at its heart, but burning there nonetheless. She pressed that warmth into his hand, and then let go.

"Sorry to interrupt this," Stephen Grace said, his voice possessing another kind of warmth that surprised Ben, "but, Farrell, we have to take that drive."

"All I want to do is get Hope. Someone has her now," Ben said through clenched teeth.

Grace gestured with the Uni, almost casually. Ben knew that

it was a very specific instrument, and if Grace even *tapped* lightly on it the wrong way, it would fire. "You think maybe this cult has her?" Grace said. "Or Dr. Stewart? Or maybe someone crazy?"

"Oh, God," Kate moaned, "my baby."

Ben said, "I don't know what I think. If you want to fry me with that thing, you can go ahead, Shadow."

Grace looked at the Uni in his hand. "You know I'm not going to do that."

"I don't know fucking anything," Ben said.

Kate pulled herself up, out of Ben's arms, and said directly to Stephen Grace, "You better call the police and get my daughter back. She has cured a girl of diabetes, and that means that for the next forty-eight hours she has diabetes herself and whoever has her doesn't know that, and if the disease isn't treated in that time, she might very well go into shock and die. Do you understand me?" Tears evaporated from her eyes. She looked stronger, more sure of herself than Ben had ever seen her.

"Katy," Ben said. "You don't want him to find her."

Kate looked from Ben back to Grace. A look of puzzlement crossed her face, and she seemed about to say something, but no words came from her mouth.

Ben said, "Shadow wants to kill her. Don't you, Shadow? Isn't that your job?"

Stephen Grace said nothing, but reaching into his vest pocket, he brought out a pack of Marlboro 100s. He slowly opened the the pack and withdrew a cigarette. He slipped it between his lips. He grinned and spoke from the side of his mouth, "Either of you got a light?"

4:42 A.M.

Ben finally agreed to a walk rather than a ride, and Stephen Grace figured he could use the exercise. Ben took Kate back into the motel room.

"I want you to rest for a while. Not long; maybe fifteen minutes." He shut the door behind them and checked the bathroom out to ascertain if there was any immediate danger of someone breaking in, or to see if there was a further clue as to who had taken Hope.

"I can't rest, not when Hope . . . That man—who is he? Why would he want to hurt my daughter? Ben?"

"Where are your pills?" Ben was trying to stay calm, but losing it by the minute. "Your tranks?"

"I don't need those anymore."

"No, but I do. Where are they? Don't you have some Xanax or something?"

Kate stared hard at him. "There's some in my makeup kit in the bathroom."

"Thanks." He returned to the bathroom. Her makeup kit was propped up on the sink. He picked it up, opened it, sorting through what to him was one of the mysteries of woman: the various pencils and sticks and small jars of cream, until he found a Baggie with a few small oblong pills. He took two out, checked to make sure they had "Xanax" stamped on them, and swallowed them dry. He turned the water on in the sink, cupping his hand beneath the thin stream, and drank from his cupped hand. He avoided looking at his face in the mirror, and, wiping his wet hands on the sides of his khakis, he stepped back into the bedroom. Kate was sitting up straight, almost stiff, on the edge of the double bed. She looked as if she was about to start screaming, her face was so tense, her eyes clutched in tightened lids, her hands curled into fists at her sides.

Ben went and stood over her. "I can't even begin to tell you what I think this is all about, Katy."

She looked straight ahead, not meeting his gaze. "You said you loved me."

"I do. Always have."

"Then tell me."

"I don't know enough. After I take a walk with this guy, I'll be able to tell you more." He wondered if he would come back alive from taking this walk, although he had the sense there was something on the level about his Shadow. Something actually decent, somewhere down in all that brainwashed shit. "I'll find out what kind of information he's got. You just try to stay calm. I'll be back soon, and we can figure this thing out."

Kate shook her head. "No way. No way are you going to leave me out of this. You know, Ben, that's one of your worst qualities, acting like you know what's best for me. Well, I'm tired of hearing men tell me they know what's best for me. I am so tired of it." Then the tension in her face, in her body, *went*, just like a dam exploding, and she began crying and shivering.

Ben sat down beside her, holding her tight. He did not hear the motel room door open.

Stephen Grace, at the door to the room, said, "She okay?"

"I can't leave her," Ben said.

"Look, Farrell, these people aren't after her. They got what they wanted. If they'd wanted the mother, they would've nabbed her with the girl. Believe me, I know what the girl's worth."

Ben asked, "What's she worth?"

46

KERMIT STONE WENT OVER TO THE SWINKS' PLACE AS SOON as he could get Gus out of bed and into the car. "I can't drive," Kermit told his son, "and anyway, I thought you were gonna keep an eye on Fletch tonight."

Gus mumbled, "He's his own man."

"He's a damn lunatic, and I am tired of chasing him around town, even if I do owe him one," Kermit snapped. He kept his window down in the old black-and-white Ford Torino—he needed the air to help him sober up. He hadn't heard another gunshot after the first one, but he hadn't heard Fletch hightail it home with chicken feathers in his mouth, either.

When they arrived at the Swinks' farm, he ran around back. Gus waited in the car.

Kermit was beginning to sober up a bit, and just as he entered the backyard and ran around behind the spring-house to the coops, he heard another shot somewhere in the distance. He wondered if he was so drunk he couldn't tell how close or far away any gunshot could come from.

"Sweet Jesus," he said.

Loretta Swink kept the gun pointed at Fletch, who sat there, not shivering, but grinning, red and white tufts of feathers still drifting from his mouth. They heard distant gunfire. Loretta briefly glanced in the direction from which it came; then she fixed her eyes back on Fletcher McBride.

"I don't mind if you shoot me," Fletcher said.

Loretta shook her head and spat, "I wish they'da kept you locked up in State for the rest a your life."

From behind her, a shadow appeared among the coops. A young boy, looking all of nine, extended his hand to Loretta.

She went and took it. "Lex, you were playing here, too?"

The boy nodded. His eyes were sunken into their sockets; there was some kind of scar across the left side of his face that looked as if the skin had been burned there, from the corner of his eye down along the cheek, almost to the lips. "Chickens got sent."

"Yes, they did," she said. Then she glanced back at Fletcher McBride. "I catch you in here one more time, it's gonna be your head that goes."

She heard another noise: the sound of a man running.

Then the voice of the sheriff, approaching, shouting.

When he got there, he surveyed the scene, saw that Fletch had not been shot. He looked at Loretta and then at the boy. He said, "Who's he?"

Loretta said, "Ye gods and fishes, don't you know my grandson? Lex. You seen him before, don't tell me you ain't."

"Visiting?"

"Has been since July. He got in an accident in Mill Valley, and he needed to see his grandma. Didn't you, Lexy?"

The boy looked from his grandmother to the sheriff and then back to his grandmother. He reached up with his hand and stroked the place where his flesh had melted near his nose. He was silent.

"And while we're on the subject of interrogation, Kermit," Loretta said testily, hanging on to the shotgun, "what in heaven's name is this lunatic doing in my chicken coops?"

Fletcher piped up, "Biting the heads off 'em. It's my wolf nature coming out. We all have an animal inside us."

"Now, just keep it shut, Fletch," Kermit said, and then turned to Loretta. "I'll get him home, and then tomorrow we'll see how much damage he's done, and we'll figure out how much he owes you."

She turned to glare at Fletcher. "You don't owe me nothing. Just get off my land and let me get a night's sleep."

The boy named Lex went over to her, took her free hand, and they both turned and walked back toward the farmhouse.

Kermit said, "It's too early in the morning for this, Fletch, so just go get in the car, and me and Gus will put you to bed. Tomorrow we can figure out the rest. Is *everybody* shooting their guns off tonight?"

Fletcher McBride rose to his feet briskly, brushing himself free of straw and dirt and feathers. "You know what this means."

Kermit said nothing.

"You know something's going on. I can feel it. I can smell it."

"All I smell is chickenshit."

"You just won't look at it," Fletch continued, "because you're afraid of it. You're immobilized by fear. But I admit my animal nature, Kermit. I am not afraid of the end of the world. I am not afraid of what she can do."

"Who? Loretta Swink?"

Fletcher McBride smiled, and his teeth were stained berry-red with chicken blood.

47

Walk to the Graveyard

4:50 A.M.

STEPHEN GRACE AND BEN FARRELL WALKED DOWN THE RAIN-slicked streets. The AttaBurger was dark, as were the houses they passed. They came upon a poorly lit path—only two ancient streetlamps gave off enfeebled yellow light—that led into what seemed to be an open field. Beyond it, the squat oil pumps sat like miniature Eiffel Towers in dark pastures. The town itself was just a clustered shadow to the immediate south; to the north, the old mission vineyard; to the east, the houses that shielded downtown Empire from the Empire Highway. Grace pointed out the graveyard he'd noticed, just beyond a stand of eucalyptus and willow. "The names on tombstones in small towns fascinate me," he said. "Always only seven or eight names, at the most."

"It's too dark to read them," Ben said, keeping a step behind him. "And that's not why we're here, is it?"

The sign on the low gate read Hillside Memorial Park.

A small graveyard for a small town. Stephen Grace lit another cigarette, offered one to Ben, who declined. Grace said, "You asked before what the girl was worth. Don't you know?"

"Because she has this healing thing?"

"Jesus, you've been brainwashed like everybody. Sure, she heals somebody now and then. But not all of them get better."

"I don't understand."

"I'd show you pictures, Farrell, but they'd make you fuckin' puke. I think you need to stay lucid right now. You already look like one half-dead motherfuck."

187

"Your mother never wash your mouth out with soap, Shadow?"

Grace whispered, "My mother never washed out *any-fuckin'-thing* with soap, Farrell. She always had maids. Now, you want to hear about this Hope Stewart or what?" Dropped his cigarette, stubbed it out with his shoe. There was a silence, and then he thought he heard something. He glanced about, among the trees, across the road to the uninterrupted acres of vines. Not even a truck out on the highway. He returned his gaze to Ben Farrell. *A pair of miserable sons of bitches.* He was tired of the cat-and-mouse aspect to his job. He would've liked for just an instant to be able to tell this man everything he knew. Things he knew that no one else knew except the mad doctor. "She's a carrier, Farrell. Have you ever heard of Typhoid Mary? Little Patch has got the motherfuck of plagues. So far as I know, she's only passed it to half a dozen people. A few only got the good part of it, the so-called healing. But two others ... well, they're not dead, but their hearts have stopped beating and their tissues ... How did one of the medical team put it? He said, 'Their tissues are ...' something. Shit, I forget the term, but their tissues just began a fuckin' feeding frenzy on themselves. Not much of what you'd call a human body afterward, either. But they're still alive and kicking, Farrell, and not a damn thing can kill them. They don't even need food; but they're still alive. Some kind of living hell. Living death is what I call it. And you were right, you know, back there. About my job."

Ben sighed. "To kill an eleven-year-old. Some job."

"You wouldn't think of her as just a child if you knew what she's capable of. You'd see her for what she is: she's walking napalm. She's C-4 without a detonator. Maybe worse. You scared of cancer? Of AIDS? Worried about your prostate blowing up to the size of a basketball? Well, worry no more. What she's got's worse than all those, and the beauty is, you don't die of this disease; you just go on living and suffering. What a concept. Not many people have been exposed to her. Yet. Those of us who have, who knows what the hell's going to happen to us in the next few weeks. Maybe we'll get healthy, or maybe we'll be like the medical photos. All of us. Vegetables with a wriggling brain stem. Head and spinal column and maybe the remnant of an arm."

Ben shook his head. "I don't believe you."

"I don't give a fuck what you believe," Grace said, snapping as if he had lost patience with the human race and the blinders that protected it from nothing. "Tell me about this cult."

"You already saw the files at the newspaper."

"I want it from you. The stuff that didn't make it into print. Your college paper. The story you did. You were twenty, and you had this friend who knew these people down at that nightclub, the Anubis."

"I don't think you've got the time for this one."

Grace pointed off to the east. "Hey, the sun ain't even up yet, Farrell. I'll tell you right now, nobody's going to kill that girl. At least not whoever has her right now. She's too valuable. I seem to be the only one who wants her dead."

Farrell was exhausted. He had that pre-catatonic look that came from mental confusion as much as from lack of sleep. He had grown old in one night; Stephen Grace wouldn't't've been surprised to find newly sprouted gray hairs on both of their scalps when the sun finally hit the sky. Grace disliked journalists, particularly men like Farrell who clung to some belief that the press had enormous power over the way the world went. The only thing he admired about Farrell was his tenacity. He was like one of those little yappy dogs, unable to let go of an ankle once its teeth were in it.

Farrell pressed his hands together, as if praying, and then slid them across his mouth, and down his chin. "God, I'd like to just fall into bed right now."

Grace lit another cigarette and inhaled deeply. It tasted good. *Screw lung cancer.* When a man had to face things like what this girl was carrying, lung cancer, emphysema, and heart diseases seemed like the gold rings of life's carousel.

Ben Farrell looked a bit like a man who had just lost his soul. He said, "I had this thing going where I thought I'd be this hotshot journalist if I could just crack the right story. I'd been trying to get on the staff of the *Trib* since my freshman year at Berkeley. I got the story on the Aries killer—remember that guy?"

"He's still around, too, right?"

"Well, if you can call Empire State Institute being 'around.' The cops couldn't crack that story, but I knew all these old hippies in the Haight, and they helped me out with some information. Then, when this one group was doing all this charitable work—making sure poor kids in the city got hot lunches, helping the homeless, that kind of stuff—they came under attack by the establishment."

"How very sixties of you, Farrell."

Ben continued, "Well, I figured it was political corruption because they wanted to close the group's halfway house down. The group didn't have a name at that point, but they were claiming tax-exempt status because they were a religion. And the Anubis was in full flower then—post-seventies punks and graying flower children dancing to synthesizer music or playing Chinese checkers in one of the game rooms. You could only get into Anubis if you knew someone—the cops were always trying to close it down. I was as preppy as they came back then, and knew I'd never get in there. But I knew this guy Siggie who had a pet rooster and preached the gospel of love down on Market Street. He used to tell me the best jokes. Just the best. Like he knew every joke backwards and forwards. Siggie. He had a problem because he liked to play with fire—literally. He was always getting himself into minor trouble for suspected arson, but he was trying to straighten himself out. That's why he joined this one group. He said that this group was going to take over the Anubis for one night, so he gets me in there. They were different—half their members were there, whole families, with lots of kids playing and dancing. It was great—until the cops came in and arrested everyone. Including me. But remember, I was this college journalist–type, and being arrested suited me just fine. So I spent the night in jail, got their stories, printed them, and won a hell of a lot of awards. The *Trib* offers me a full-time job upon graduation, and I feel like I'm on top of the world. Great, huh?"

"Then the group got a name."

"Oh. Yeah. Seems they already had a name, but you had to be pretty tight with them, almost to the point of initiation, to find out. I thought it was Gnosis or something like that."

"But the name was Cthonos."

"Yeah, I looked up Cthonos. It's the word for the place

beneath the earth where the spirits dwell. That's them. So I start a series of articles. Lots of good stuff. My friend Siggie's going through their initiation process, so I learn things. Bit by bit. They base their religion on snippets of other religions: a little Old Testament, a little New, some Buddhism, some Mithraism, some Druidism, some even older than those. Fascinating stuff. And then . . ."

"They get that tax fraud stuff thrown at them."

"Right. And one of their members is set up by some other cult in the Haight. And there's that trial. And Siggie calls and tells me there's something going on down at the waterfront house. It was one of their four houses. He's kind of scared, so I tell him I'll be right there. I leave the trial of this member named Irby, and drive to this Victorian and walk in, right into . . . Jesus." Ben closed his eyes, as if trying to drive the memory of that sight out of him. But he opened his eyes again and stared straight into Grace's eyes. "Shadow, it was a *slaughterhouse*. Children's bodies were everywhere, and the cult's law was written on the wall, a law I thought meant something completely different, every time I saw it. I thought it meant something nice and light and sweet and warm. But it was a law with teeth. It was a law that bites. Their law was 'Do unto others as you would have them do unto you.' "

"Nice interpretation of the Golden Rule."

"Jesus. I tried to find Siggie, but he was gone. I heard he went to South America or something. Probably setting fires down there. It was a fucking death cult, and some of the children had been dead for two days. The family of Cthonos had been teaching them how to murder. And I had made them out to be the grass roots social services department."

"Eh," Stephen Grace said, shrugging, "you're human, you ain't perfect, and you were twenty. We all fuck up now and again." He reached into the pocket of his raincoat, bringing the Uni out again.

Ben said, "What? You're going to shoot me?"

Stephen Grace didn't smile. "You've told me all I need. I'm sorry, Farrell, but I've got to get the girl. I know you'd understand if you had seen those pictures showing what she's capable of."

"I don't believe you'd kill me. Not like this." Ben tried to keep his voice steady. "I don't believe it."

"Ah," Grace said, almost with regret, *"belief.* After what you know Cthonos did to those children, do you still believe in the inherent goodness of man?"

"And you're going to be the savior of the world, Shadow?"

A smile flickered across Stephen Grace's face and then disappeared. "Saviors get crucified, Farrell. I'm an assassin."

"Gee," Ben said soberly, "I thought I was in America. Home of the free and the brave. I guess I walked into some repressive fascist police state. Oh, well."

Stephen Grace held the Uni up at chest level, aimed at Ben Farrell. "There are two Americas, Farrell. There's the one you believe exists, and then there's the one that *really* exists. The Company runs the real one, and it's about terrorists and little girls who need to get hit and small microchip laser machines like this Uni. Did you know that this weapon was invented as a tool of medical technology? It was. It was gonna be used for detailed cauterizing and delicate surgery. But that ain't what it ended up being used for. I used one for the first time in Saudi, couple a years back. It was a rougher model than this one. Takes some getting used to, the kind of surgery you can do on human beings with this little gadget. Makes me feel like James Bond sometimes. It goes on low beam or high beam, and it just does a job. Not exactly the surgery it was meant to do, not by the researchers who developed it. Ain't that just the way. You've been living in that other America too fucking long, Farrell. Sure, you've been writing about the bits and pieces of the real one, but you never had the scoop on it, did you? Or maybe you thought that by writing about it you were safe from it. But it's here now. You walked out of the dream and into the reality, and it looks like this, Farrell. It *feels* like this." The Uni emitted a succession of clicks, sounding something like a child's video game.

Ben Farrell, in what Stephen Grace was sure would be his last moments, looked quizzically at him, as if maybe his face wasn't on right, or maybe ...

Grace thought he heard something behind him, some movement, and he was about to look over his shoulder when he felt a cold numbness in his left hand, and then heard a blast.

Shit, and I'm left-handed, too.

When the bullet caught him in the left hand, Stephen Grace lost control of the Uni; it fell, shooting a beam of razor-sharp light into the trunk of the eucalyptus tree that Farrell was standing against; burning like miniature lightning into the bark of the tree; Grace spun around to identify where the shot had come from; he sensed blood rushing from his hand, but he'd been shot often enough to know that he could stop the blood fairly easily, especially in the hand—dead center in the palm—and that the pain would come later. Right now he felt only a frozen numbness.

Behind him, Kate Stewart.

48

"I couldn't sleep," Kate said, with a degree of calm that belied her shivering hands. She held the gun straight out in front of her, working hard to keep it steady. It was no longer aimed at Stephen Grace's hand. It was at heart level. Perhaps she had meant to hit there and had missed.

"Kate," Ben said, making a move toward her.

But she pointed the gun at him, too. "I don't know who to believe right now, but I do know that my daughter is here, somewhere, and if what either of you said is true, then I need to get help for her. Understand?"

"Katy." Ben sounded hurt, almost like a little boy.

"Ben," she said, "you didn't tell me everything you knew,

either. I can't risk Hope's life because I trusted the wrong person."

Stephen Grace was wrapping his left hand in his handkerchief. He knew that, with the right amount of pressure, he could cut the blood flow off. His voice was soothing. "Mrs. Stewart," he began.

"Don't call me that!" she shouted as if reacting to the worst insult. Then, more calmly, "I'm just Kate."

"Kate," Grace conceded, "this may be difficult for you to understand right now, but—"

She grimaced. "I am so tired of men telling me what I can and can't understand. I don't give a fuck what you think about my daughter, asshole. I don't care if she's the Beast of the Apocalypse. I'm going to find her and take her someplace safe."

Grace tightened the makeshift bandage that circled his palm. He bit his lower lip.

"Katy . . ." Ben tried again, but his nerve failed him.

"Ben," she said, nodding toward the Uni on the ground. "Get that, and any other gun he's got on him. And you," she said to Stephen Grace, "you try anything like karate or something, I'll empty what's left in this gun into you."

Grace handed his gun over to Ben Farrell. He never took his eyes off the woman. "You're going to have to kill me," he said, "if you really want to protect your daughter. Because as long as I have life, I will not give up until that girl is dead and buried."

He saw rage in the woman's face, as if these words had the opposite effect on her that he had wanted. He had thought she would break down or weaken her resolve, but her face seemed to light up with intensity and newly released hostility. She hadn't been as frail as he had assumed, and perhaps the psychotropics the mad doctor had been feeding her had finally kicked in. Bad timing. He was about to mutter, "Aw, shit," but these final words were taken from him before his lips could move.

She said, "No one—"

But that was all he heard, because the noise was deafening, like the sound of an enormous bomb exploding, only inside him, and he looked at Kate Stewart with reverence and awe as he felt at least three bullets ram into him, around his heart and in his left lung; he tasted blood in the back of his throat; his knees buckled; he fell to the ground like a sack; his eyes retained the image of this woman's face, the fury in her eyes burning through him, boring holes into him, burning out his life.

Noises.

He heard the ocean. Not the ocean. But a sea of noise, from the leaves rustling in the eucalyptus tree to the sound of beetles chewing beneath the bark and beneath his head. Also, people, but he had no consciousness of who was speaking. Someone was near him, for he felt the heat of breath, and then a chill spread from his chest out to his arms and legs, up to his neck. He felt something like a large rock being lifted from his stomach. The noises lessened.

He felt like he was in a small dark place, for he saw nothing, but had *consciousness* of surroundings, as if this were a room and his nerves were hooked up to the walls and floor and ceiling, so he knew its diameter, its shape, its feel. But no sight.

The name Stephen Grace meant nothing to him, although he thought he heard someone say it.

"He's dead," someone said. "My shadow, Stephen Grace. Fake government I.D. Hope's sixth grade picture, too. Jesus, Kate, what the hell are we going to do?"

But he was beginning to lose the feeling of the place he was in, and he felt as if he had forgotten how to breathe. There was no room to panic, just a sense that breath was unnecessary.

Dying.

Consciousness enough to know that.

Then the darkness became a series of intersecting dribbles of color, as if a child had spilled watercolor paints down the walls of a room, and then the color became geometric patterns—hexagons, spirals, pyramids of blue and yellow and purple—and then the geometry expanded outward, as if a triangular door were opening . . . and it reminded him of butterflies, the way the colored triangles moved against each other, intersecting at one point and then separating to connect at another. He remembered a girl's voice he'd heard on some tapes saying that there were butterflies, and he knew, as his energy dissipated, that what she had seen was the strange and wonderful color of death.

49

Family Ties

5:28 A.M.

"I KNOW THE AREA," ROBERT STEWART TOLD HIS DRIVER.

Jim, behind the wheel, nodded. He was sleepy and a little hungry, but this was his first big assignment outside of regular duty, and he didn't want to screw it up. He was tired of seeing every other jerk in his regiment get ahead; he wanted it to be him. Hilary did, too. She was going to have the baby, and damn if he didn't need the extra cash just to cover the hospital bills. "Just point me wherever, sir."

"There's a dirt road up about two miles," Dr. Stewart said. "You go left onto it from the highway. Nothing but vineyards. Miles of them. And you follow the dirt road all the way until it hits the main road through town. You cross the main road, and there's a house."

"Sounds like you know Empire pretty well."

"I grew up there. Quite a town."

"Old home week?"

"Jim?"

"Well, sir, if Task Force Oh-five-oh is to be effected here, and if this is where you lived before, I assume that you're combining business with pleasure."

"Jim, do you have any idea what we are going into?"

"I'd really appreciate hearing from you on that subject, sir."

Robert Stewart glanced out the side window of the Cadillac. Jim watched his face in the rearview mirror for a fraction of a second. Stewart seemed calm and not the least bit exhausted. The hills were low and gently rounded, and seemed to go on forever to the north. The town to their right was Perdito, and soon they were past the chain-link and barbed-wire fence that circled the perimeter of the Empire State facility, and headed toward Empire.

Stewart said, "It's about ten minutes to town, but you'll notice how the hills divide the area, how even though we are really just a few miles from Empire, we can't see it. There are no houses between the towns, just farmland and empty hills, too coarse and rocky to plant much on, although the grapes do well here. My family lived off the land for most of their existence, although my father, like me, was trained to be a doctor. But he chose a different kind of healing. He was a healer of souls."

"A minister?"

"Of a sort. He was a man of great spirituality, and he established his church up and down the coastline, coming inland only when he found the persecution to be extreme in the larger cities. Small religious movements have always flourished inland in California. I have always thought it was because of the weather being, for the most part, so temperate. Each day is very much like the one before. It is not too much different from the notion of eternity, which is changeless. Most of life is predicated upon the assumption that everything must and will change. Do you know, even now, that the tissues in your body are sloughing off, dying, to make way for new tissues? Life feeds off the dying. Buddhists call it a wheel of suffering. Christians might call it sin or error."

"Your father must've been quite a man," Jim said, but without much interest; yet he felt it was important to impress this man so that there might be a recommendation at the end of Task Force 050.

"But my father believed that this was unnecessary, that the wheel of suffering could be stopped, that there was no need for a concept of sin. The study of medicine is similar. As a medical researcher, I believe there is no need for suffering, for death, for lifelessness. I believe that these are simply errors in perception that can be . . . corrected, if you will. Turn here, Jim," he pointed to a break in the highway—barely a road at all.

"It'll be muddy," Jim said. "We'll get stuck."

"Less than a quarter mile of it's dirt; the rest is gravel,"

Robert said, and then closed his eyes. "Are you hungry, Jim?"

"I could use some breakfast. I'm sure there's a McDonald's opening up in this town within an hour or two."

"No, you don't want fast food, Jimmy. My mother's an excellent cook. Real down-home cooking. You'll like her; she'll take to you, too. Now, see, up ahead, there's Empire," and Jim looked beyond the trees and the tangling, unkempt vines, the stink of overripe grapes and rotting fruit on the wet morning air, and he felt Stewart's hand on his right shoulder, and heard a gasp from the doctor, like the sound of a man who's finally been let out of prison.

"Been a long time since you've been back, sir?"

"Oh," Stewart said, "a very, very long time. And yet, what is it with some places? You feel that you've never left them, that they've always been with you. How old are you, Jimmy?"

Jim beamed with pride, "Just twenty-one, sir."

"So young. Where do you hail from, boy?"

"Virginia, sir."

"A southern gentleman. Do you realize that the year you were born was the last time I was here, physically, in this town?"

"Don't believe in visiting family much, then?"

"Only when it's the right time, Jim, only when it's the right time. And this is it. This is the right time. My research has kept me very busy."

"I guess." Jim felt he could breathe easier here, let down his guard a little. He wasn't sure what Task Force 050 was about, other than that it had to do with some kind of animal experiments, and he was aware that the people who were against that sort of thing were dangerous—thus, the secrecy of the experiment in 050.

"Jim," Robert Stewart sighed, "Jim, oh, Jim. Empire hasn't changed. I used to play here, among the rows of vines. I had a dog, a Doberman, and we'd run all over—and my brothers, and my sister. All out here."

Jim slowed the car. To his left was a white mission house; up above it was a town that was right out of a movie about small-town America, complete with rooster weather vanes and white church steeples. Trees were woven into the fabric of the streets, and behind it all, the low oil pumps that gave any rural area of California an industrialized look, as if the surface of Empire might appear quaint and serene, but underground there was constant pumping and drilling, and destruction. "It looks like a nice place," Jim said, not really liking the look of it at all. What the hell was Projects up to here?

He continued up the road until he came to the Empire Road; Stewart told him to take a right, and then an immediate left into the potholed driveway of a small farmhouse with a barn behind it. It smelled like chickenshit and horseshit.

"This is it," Stewart said.

Jim glanced in the mirror again, and saw something that made the hair on the back of his neck stand on end.

And yet Dr. Stewart hadn't changed. Not really. He had the same look of composure and calm; his hair was neatly combed to one side, and he didn't even appear to have any stubble.

Jim's wife, Hilary, enjoyed reading vampire novels, and so Jim had, when he was bored, read a few of them. And that was just what Stewart looked like to him just then, in the draining shadows of morning, a vampire, his face white, his eyes piercing and hypnotic, and something wild there, beneath the skin. For a second Jim saw something else, too, something less lunatic, less imaginative.

He saw a torturer.

"Something the matter, Jimmy?"

"You were going to tell me about Task Force Oh-five-oh, sir?"

Dr. Stewart shrugged, screwing his face up as if this were an absurd subject to go into so early in the morning. "Jimmy. Private Jim. Later. Couldn't you use some coffee? Some fresh eggs, scrambled to perfection, fresh hot home-made bread, and pork chops?"

A large, although not particularly overweight woman with a gray beehive hairdo and thick spectacles propped up on her nose was coming toward the Cadillac, and although she smiled, Jim Park was scared shitless, because in her left hand was a chicken, its neck freshly wrung, its skinny legs still twitching.

50

MONKEY LOVETT SLEPT FITFULLY, STILL DREAMING OF THE imperfect girl who was supposed to be the one who would make them all gods. He awoke, as he had several times in the night, feeling that someone was staring down at him. Next to him, his brother Harlan. He whispered, "You scared, Harly?"

Inside his skin, Harlan replied, *Nothing to be scared of, Monkeyman.*

Monkey nuzzled closer to his brother's chest. The dead smell rising from the cavity on Harlan's left side had worsened. Monkey didn't like bad smells so much, but he was more scared of the imperfect girl than he was of Harlan. "You promise you won't ever leave me?"

Birdy replied, *We made the oath, Monkey, remember? We cut into you and bound all three of us together in blood. Remember?*

Monkey closed his eyes, feeling comforted. He didn't like the imperfect girl much, just as he hadn't like the imperfect boy. The boy scared him, too, and he had spent most of his life avoiding him whenever possible. But the boy left Monkey alone; the girl was different. Monkey had looked into her, past her skin and her blood, into the marrow of her being, and had seen her missing eye, within her. The darkest eye he had ever seen.

Inside her.

He shivered and clutched Harlan's arm, pulling it around his neck. *Good to be back with family.*

Harlan had been dead for years, and still Monkey felt the warmth of life in the skin, and the blood that settled along the side of his lower back. Harly was shriveled, a little, sort of like a dried-apple-headed doll, but he looked the same. Still some wisps of red-blond hair around his dried-apricot ears. Still the look in his eyes, even though the eyes were marble now.

"Gonna play soon," Monkey told Harly.

Harly didn't reply. He was usually quiet.

Birdy said, *You can play with the girl once it's started. Once it's started, she's yours.*

But Monkey was silent. He wasn't sure if he wanted to play with this girl at all.

That inner eye scared him.

The darkest eye.

And then he slept well, with his dead brother's arm around him and the smell of death like a memory of comfort and security. Sleeping with the dead was part of what the cult had taught him.

"No separation," the GoodMama had said. *"What is dead and what is alive, all the same. What inhabits the body in life still inhabits it in death. But the body becomes a prison. We must seek to liberate the dead from their prison. We must seek to make the body continue even when the heart has stopped its beating. This is the purpose of Cthonos. This is the joy of Cthonos. We are the chosen who will destroy the barriers between the living and the dead."*

But he smelled something in the dark passage where he slept—not death but the other.

The deformed one.

The boy.

Monkey pressed closer in to his dead brother's body, hoping the deformed one would pass him by. The deformed one had powers from Cthonos. Monkey had seen what he could do with animals, how he could make them *change*. It was awful. He had some kind of disease, that boy did, that abomination.

51

5:32 A.M.

IT WAS DARK IN THE TUNNEL, ALTHOUGH FLARES WITH BRILLIANT red-yellow flames lit the path at the turning points. The boy hoped the old woman hadn't heard him sneak down here; she wanted him to wait until everyone was home. If he had followed the roads and the fields, it would've taken him half an hour or more, but the underground route, where the Spanish had carved out tunnels for their dead, was more direct, and if he ran, he could be there in ten minutes. He saw the other children, the sacrifices, their bones nestled together in the previously unoccupied recesses of the catacombs, and he remembered the rituals he'd been taught: how to hold a child when it was being sent as a messenger; how, when the child gasped, his job was to stroke her hair and to whisper about what she was about to see when crossing over into the other realm, the place of Cthonos, the dwelling that was already in the subconscious. Although he didn't really understand the word *subconscious,* he knew it was like dreaming.

The boy had lived much of his life in the catacombs and was rarely awake during the day. When he went out in the sun, he wore dark glasses and tried to keep his face covered. His skin was sensitive to natural light, and, as he had a fair complexion and had suffered burns, he knew that he must be careful of the sun. He felt most at home beneath the ground and had found the place where the catacombs, running beneath Empire, crossed through the sewer system, where the divergent paths of the 'combs went, sometimes ending at a wall of dirt, sometimes ending out beneath a moonlit sky, on the edge of a stream.

It was his world, and he had ruled it since as far back as he could remember. Except for Monkey, who had shown him many of the paths beneath the earth and the ancient graves that held the dust-bound remains of the early Spanish, no one knew the 'combs better than he did. Monkey had shown him only out of fear; the boy knew why Monkey feared him. The boy was glad of Money's fear—it gave him a kind of control.

A kind of *rule*.

And he was only nine.

He passed the last flare before the old stone stairs. The smell here was cleaner; someone had spread eucalyptus leaves down in the narrow corridor.

He jumped the low, worn stairs two at a time and then pushed his way up through the heavy trapdoor. It took a tremendous effort. The last time he'd tried this on his own, the door had almost fallen on him, and the old lady had started crying because she was afraid it would crush his skull. *But I am not afraid of death, old woman!* he wanted to tell her. How could he be? Death was just a ride out of this flesh, into a higher form.

And beyond the thought that death might mean leaving this flesh that he was so attached to, he knew he would not die.

Ever.

For he was a kind of god. Baptized Lex Talionis, from an ancient law, the old woman had told him: "An eye for an eye."

"You are the vengeance of Cthonos," she'd told him, ever since he was a baby. "You are the spiritual heir of Justice."

Lex crawled across the packed earth and felt his way to the edge of the room. There was no light, but his eyes worked well in the dark. Dry sticks and leaves, all around.

I am the incarnate.

I have no fear.

He stood and, passing the larger barrels, entered the wine cellar. The lower half of the cellar was still part of the earth. Here there was no smell of the moldering dead. Just the stink of dirt, of spilled wine, of adobe brick.

He sometimes drank wine from the casks, although if the old woman caught him, she whipped him something fierce. Someday, when he was more fully god incarnate, he would get her back for all that whipping. But he liked the taste of wine, and more than once he had played games with scissors and needles on Monkey when both of them had sampled the casks. But he had not come for wine.

Not this morning.

He had come to see her.

To see what she looked like.

He had heard that she was a god incarnate, too.

That he would grow up one day and marry her.

Lex didn't like the idea of marriage too much, and he didn't care for girls, either. But he was not one to argue. He had a hard time expressing himself, even to the old woman, although she was able to divine his thoughts if they sat close enough to each other. Sometimes, particularly in the daylight, he felt ugly, the way his face went, the way his tongue seemed too large for his small mouth, the way his lips hung down on one side. But at night he was a beautiful child again, and it didn't bother him to be this bold, to seek out the girl, to maybe even touch her face if she wasn't too ugly.

He had heard she was beautiful.

In the dark he would not be able to see her well. He sniffed her out; she was tied up and slumped over in exhausted sleep. He could smell, from a distance of eight feet, her hair and the sweat-fear stink of her skin. He recognized it as the same odor the other children produced through fear, just before the scythe came down across their necks.

He didn't enjoy that smell, not as much as he thought the others did. The old woman seemed to enjoy it the most, and then Monkey, because he liked everything about the ritual.

But Lex tried to block that odor out whenever it was near. He often held his breath when he was around the other children. The smell made him think things he wasn't supposed to; it made the hair on his neck, just beneath his scalp, stand up.

It made him remember his ugliness.

But he approached the shadow of the girl, just to see her face. He just wanted to see if she looked nice, because if she did, then he might not mind marrying her. But only when he was a lot older.

He had a pen flashlight—his father had brought it to him after one of his trips. It was the kind doctors used to look down people's throats or in their eyes.

The boy brought it out of the pocket of his jeans and flicked it on. He held it up to the girl's face.

And then felt something.

Dark. Dark down dark 'combs. Held down. Fire, heat, exploding gasoline—mindfire.

And dropped the light on the ground.

He was silent, holding his breath.

But she didn't wake up; he heard her gentle breathing.

But it had been like looking into himself, into the heart of his ugliness. He could hear the rush and crash of his own blood as it pumped through him. The sound was deafening; the world went completely silent, and it spun, or else he became aware of its spinning, faster, and yet he stood there while it moved; everything was moving fast, heating up like a bomb that was about to explode, or like fireworks bursting across his vision.

I am so ugly, I am so ugly, nobody is gonna love somebody so ugly. He hid his face in his hands, feeling the crevices along his cheek, the way his hairline started so high on one side, the way the blisters still grew along the ridge of his earlobe.

Tears came to his eyes, and instead of a god, he felt like an ugly little boy, and he hated everyone on the face of the earth, including this girl, and his father, and the old woman, and Monkey.

Lex ran across the cellar, up the wooden steps into the main room of the great house, down the corridors, until he pushed open the dark wooden door, and rushed out into the vineyard.

He fell to his knees, weeping, wishing someone were there to hold him, but not the old woman, not her, not any of the others, but someone he had only dreamed of, someone who would hold him and not care that he was ugly, not even care that he was a god incarnate, but just that he was nine and himself.

He pounded his fists into the ground as he wept, wanting

to bring out what the old woman called the blood of the earth. It never seemed to come, but he kept pounding, pounding.

One day I'm gonna get back at all of them for what they did to me, he vowed. *One day I'm gonna make them feel what I got inside me!*

And then, as the tears subsided, he saw the first rays of the sun, in the east, beyond Empire.

A bird—it looked like a dove to him—flew across that early light. *I'll make her wish she'd never been born!* he screamed inside his head.

Even if she is my sister!

52

Townies, Continued

6:30 A.M.

THE SUNLIGHT WAS SLOW TO OVERTAKE THE SHADOWS IN Empire.

There was an unusual noise of trucks out on the outer reaches of the main roads; normally the trucks went through town, but this morning none did. Empire, California, had only two churches, both on Main Street, inside the loop of town, across the circular park from each other. One was very old and had been, many years before, San Miguel, a Catholic church, but then, when most of the Catholics started going to Saint Bernardine's over in Perdito, it fell into the hands of the Episcopalians, although the Seventh-Day Adventists shared space on Saturdays; the other, a more modern building, was Christian Science and was the smaller of the two churches. But both clung to dying congregations, and even the Right Reverend Hub Radcliffe, who preached while standing on a milk crate right in the middle of the park, Fridays through Sundays, had to admit that Christ had pretty much passed Empire by, at least as far as settling down went. All the more reason for Hub, who had slept in the park since losing his horse trailer in a rigged poker game, to keep preaching, because all around him were the minions of darkness. Including the New Agers and the former hippies, whom he considered quite pagan and corrupt, as well as those in town who had just petered out on religion, at least in any formal sense. As he awoke, he looked across the street at the statue of the Known Soldier, and then down to King Tut's bar, where a sinner lay, passed out and snoring like thunder, on its steps. He watched as a little boy rode by on his bicycle. At first Hub thought it was some paperboy, and he was about to ask if he could buy a newspaper from him. Then the boy braked his bicycle alongside the curb of the park and let it fall, its wheels still spinning, as he ran off to the center of the park, where the pigeons gathered and cooed with the annoying crows and the occasional dove. The boy set something down in the middle of the birds and then stepped back. Hub scratched his head. Had the boy set down birdseed or bread crumbs?

And then the birds began attacking whatever the boy had brought them.

Hub figured the birds must've been starving; the boy must've fed them something good.

And then the boy, as if sensing the preacher lying upon the bench, turned to stare at him.

One side of the boy's face was discolored, almost like a port wine stain, but it seemed to obliterate his features.

Hub Radcliffe did not believe the devil resided in gambling (unless he was losing that night), nor did he believe that the devil resided in the loins of men or women (unless the woman he wanted was not interested in him). What he *did* believe was that the human capacity for evil was enormous, and that each human being had a key with which to lock the door to that very capacity.

Or they turned the key in the opposite direction, and that capacity for evil was loosed upon creation.

He knew this from his time spent at the Empire State facility, after having been put there for drowning a baby, accidentally, while baptizing it. His lawyer had been good, and so Hub had spent ten years at Empire State before being released. In that time, through Bible study and grace beyond knowing, he had learned about the evil in man and how it could be controlled.

When he saw the boy, he knew.

The boy had turned the key and opened the doorway within him, and behind that door: *the abyss.*

The boy grinned, as if reading Hub's thoughts, and then ran off to his bike, lifting it up, and riding away on it, down the streets of town. He flew past the rows of shops and the houses, and zigzagged in between parked cars and around the garbage truck as it came through the alley to load up from a Dumpster. He would do what boys did when they rode bicycles so early in the morning: own the town.

Hub shuddered with the thought, with the chill that was both outside and within. He watched the pigeons finish whatever meal the boy had offered. Hub Radcliffe started praying, frantically and furiously, as if saying the words fast and aloud would ward off whatever that boy had let out from himself.

Other people lived in Empire, too, although its population had been dwindling since the early seventies. But there was a woman who got up every morning at six-thirty to jog up and down the Empire Road and three miles up the Sand Canyon Road before making a loop on a dirt road and jogging back to her house. Her name was Ellen Fremont, and she had come to Empire in 1973, from Los Angeles, having married a man who was destined to do nothing with his life, while she was a recreational counselor at Empire State, having gotten her degree and her first taste of the criminally insane, by the legal definition, down at Patton State Hospital in San Bernardino. She had a lot of stress in her life, both from her husband and from her job, so she found jogging to be one of the best cures available. She stayed in good shape, and at forty-seven was often mistaken for someone much younger. The air was clean in Empire, and she enjoyed it, in particular, on this morning, after the rain, when she could smell the grass. She noted that the mission *asistencia* needed a new paint job, and she wished those weirdos who owned it would keep it up. She had tried to organize some kind of grass-roots historical society to preserve some of the more interesting homes in town, but no one seemed to be interested. It bothered her when things weren't taken care of.

Like her husband—not that he could even take care of himself, let alone anything else. She had had some affairs when she was younger and living in southern California, but she knew somewhere deep inside her that she hated sneaking around and cheating, and she also knew that she couldn't leave Ricky because she loved him—unfortunately, she realized—the way some mothers love their sons, so completely and unconditionally that she would always have a place in her heart for him, no matter how small. But jogging set her in some kind of balance for the day, so that when eight-thirty rolled around and she had to clock in at work, she could take whatever hassles the patients doled out.

As she ran up the low rise of the Sand Canyon Road, she caught sight of what she thought at first was an overturned truck. She slowed down, and as she approached it, she realized it was not the result of an accident. The truck had been intentionally parked lengthwise across the road, so as to block it.

It was an army truck, the kind she'd seen so many times going up and down the 101 when the military was going out on maneuvers or to wherever military men went.

Several soldiers were standing around, too, and when they saw her they waved, friendly.

She began walking, catching her breath.

One young man walked out toward her. He wasn't wearing the olive drab shirt and pants and black boots that the other soldiers wore.

He wore something that looked to Ellen, at first, like a space suit from a science-fiction film. She had always been active in discouraging the use of pesticides in the farm areas of California, and she wondered if some sort of poison had been sprayed on the local crops. This thought frightened her a little, but confirmed something she had sensed for several years about the possibility of disaster related to chemicals used in the soil.

The suit looked less and less like a space suit the closer the man got to her. She could tell that some kind of oxygen-tent hood covered his face, but it seemed to be not much more than an expensive Baggie, and the suit was white, and look, like it was made from parachute material. He held his hand out to shake hers. He smiled, and she smiled as she greeted him.

"What's the matter here?" she asked.

The man said, "Unfortunately there's been an accident about six miles up the road."

"Oh," she said, not very surprised. She had always expected something like this to happen someday, with a nuclear power plant twenty miles to the west, and with toxic waste being carted up and down the freeways as if the trucks were taking the large canisters to the farmers' market. "Are we downwind or something?"

The man looked at her a moment, almost as if he didn't understand her.

One of the soldiers back by the truck was telling a joke to another. The other laughed and then was silent.

The man in the space suit said, "You're perfectly safe. It's just that the road is rather dangerous until the spill is cleaned up. Nothing more."

"Oh," she said. She didn't know what else to say. She wanted to ask him more detailed questions, but he seemed to want to return to the truck, and to whatever was beyond the truck, and do his job. She said, "Was this on the news?"

But he ignored this question and turned away.

She scratched the side of her forehead—the sweat made her itchy. Then Ellen also turned away, jogging back toward town, wondering why she hadn't heard about this particular spill on the radio, or if, perhaps, it had only happened within the past hour.

6:38 A.M.

While Ellen was still jogging toward the Sand Canyon Road, and while the morning clouds still hung low like a canopy beneath the white brightness of the early sun, Karl Swanson was checking the racks in his market, making sure the fruit was still fresh from the night before. Empire didn't have a Safeway or an Albertson's or any other brand-name supermarket; even Swanson's Market was going under these days. Most folks seemed to want to go to the supermarkets or farmers' markets over in Perdito and Caliente, or even as far as Paso Robles if they wanted the more exotic fruits or gourmet items like pâté or caviar. Karl and his wife had run his market since the early fifties, and he had thought his two sons would take over the business once they got out of high school; but neither boy had been interested, and both left town to go to distant colleges and to live in faraway places— far away from Empire, anyway. So Karl, now sixty-seven, still ran the store and figured he would until the day he died. Jenny had already passed on, and each day was more difficult to face without her. So, alone, he ran his business. He spent some days completely alone—no customers. That was just fine by him. His house was paid for, he had some money set aside—although not quite enough—and he just liked the routine of setting up the market. Local farmers brought in produce once a week, and he managed to unload it one way or another, either by selling it in the store or by taking it home himself twice a week for his own larder. He considered himself a fairly selfish man, particularly since Jenny had died, and enjoyed his privacy and his being able to run things his way.

He normally didn't open up his store until seven-thirty, but he heard someone rapping on the door. When he lifted the shade up, he saw a little boy pressing the right side of his face against the window.

Karl didn't recognize the boy, but then, he didn't even think of little boys living here in town. He couldn't put his finger on why, but children were things he didn't notice. Barely had noticed his own sons while they were growing up.

Empire was a fairly safe town.

He knew that.

He had lived in this town since 1952, and the only bad stories he had ever heard were about incidents that had occurred around 1971. There were some more rumors in the early eighties, but he had never witnessed anything related to those stories. He hadn't believed that the hippies in town were all that dangerous. It was all the reactionaries in Empire who spread those rumors. Karl Swanson considered himself a conservative liberal, and never thought too much bad about his fellow man. Why, he had even spoken with that crazy man, Fletcher McBride, who had murdered his own wife, and Karl had felt the warmth of the human heart even in that man.

So as Karl opened the door to his market, he had no idea what he was letting into his life, what kind of gift this boy would give him this day, this morning, this life.

Karl said, "What happened to you?"

The boy looked a little sad and pretended not to understand what Karl Swanson was saying.

The boy coughed and then sneezed, and Karl was about to turn to get the cold medicine that was on the counter—either Contac or Alka-Seltzer or Sinutab—but something made him pause.

And then Karl Swanson felt something warm against his skin.

7:00 A.M.

Heck Foster was still on the john, and, as he suffered from narcolepsy, his old lady, Judy, had to look in on him every few minutes to make sure he hadn't fallen asleep there. But: behold! There he squatted, his tank top stretched over his knees in false modesty, a copy of the *Weekly World News* between his stubby fingers. He had the hairiest legs she had ever come across, which had been the initial attraction for her; that and what was between his legs, but she had been younger then, she figured, and still bought into the whole male-fantasy *Playboy* sex kitten thing. That was back when they met, in 1968, in Frisco, at the Playboy Club, where she was nineteen and a Bunny, and he was a horny overweight businessman with a charge card that was as hard as a rock and ready for action. She'd run into him again on the streets—he was a kind of hip square who liked to partake of acid and love-ins—so she'd invited him to a party at this cool old church on Polk Street, and that was when she'd seen the hairier parts of his body. She was calling herself Butterfly French back then, but she wised up and got her consciousness raised well before Watergate, when she learned that the male establishment in America was for shit, and then after a brief but ecstatic extra-old man affair with a commie from Ann Arbor, in which she learned that the Reds were particularly expert at premature ejaculation, she decided she was just plain Judy Marshall again. At about that point, around 1972, she had decided to marry her horny businessman, who had changed his name from Herman Franklin Forrester III, to just plain old Heck Foster, and they had moved back to the earth. First they had gone to this ashram in New Mexico, but she had grown tired of the other guys pawing her and of the weird turban they required her to wear; then, Heck heard about this gig in Berkeley where they could work this farm and keep some acres to themselves, so they worked it, and Judy was picking strawberries in the back quarter one March day when she had a revelation from something beyond, something divine. She knew, from the tingling in her heart, that she and Heck and their three babies must go south, must find the place that was meant for them alone.

Heck, who had given up IBM in favor of huaraches and shirts sewn by Guatemalan refugees, by now was in thrall to Judy and her visions, so they up and packed, and took not only their three babies—Clay, Rocky, and Sandy—but also a few hundred dollars from the farmers' market where they worked on Saturdays. They drove up and down the coast of California, but could not find the right place. And then the Buick dropped an axle in a small town called Empire, and they had been there ever since.

But Judy was getting another stirring in her heart these days—it was about what she called the Family. They had come before her to these parts, mainly to escape the persecution of the spiritual children of the 1960s. She had detected them in Empire when she and Heck first rented the house they still lived in; they had that look, something she could identify. She had spoken to a few of them, although none had been very forthcoming. But she understood that.

But in the past few days she had seen them around more, going into the main drag of town, talking with each other on the street.

She had approached one of them and said, "Hey, sister, hard rain's falling."

The woman had looked at her kind of funny.

"It's the last decade of the millennium," Judy said, hoping to find a common ideological ground with this woman, but the woman had said, "Excuse me? I'm afraid I don't know you."

But Judy had known *her,* and that was all that mattered. The Family was pretty strange, but then a lot of people kept their distance in this place.

Heck called from the toilet, "Breakfast ready yet?"

She ignored him. She wasn't his slave, and he knew it. The age difference between them was beginning to show. He was nearly sixty, and she was only forty-two. She barely had turned gray, and it looked good on her. On Heck it looked just old. She pushed her crimped hair behind her shoulders; she would need to get it cut soon.

Sandy was still asleep. Judy looked in on her; the kid's room was a mess, but she was seventeen and a looker. Clay was already taking his shower. She missed Rocky, but knew that he would someday get out of jail once the great white gods of corporate America decided that sexual activity between adults and children was perfectly acceptable the way it had been in ancient Greece.

Judy went to get some chicory coffee, wondering when the hell that old man would get off the john so she could use it. She hadn't put in a call to her parole officer lately— that damned armed robbery in 1974 still haunted her—and they had become such good friends, she hated to lose touch. So she poured some coffee, picked the phone up, and dialed.

She heard a series of clicks and buzzes, down some distant wire, through the microstrands of sound tubes, or whatever they were, that the phone company used.

She hung the phone up and tried again.

Still no sound other than the buzzes.

Clay was getting out of the shower. He came into the kitchen already half dressed—he was so scared of nudity— and she was annoyed that he hadn't toweled off. A pool of water formed at his feet. "Hey, Judy," her son said.

"Clay," she said, cradling the phone in her hand, "did you hear a lot of lightning last night or anything?"

He grinned sheepishly. "I was kind of out of it. I was watching *The Little Mermaid* with Angie, and hit the sack by ten."

So square, she thought. "It's just the phone's out. We forget to pay the bill again?"

She heard a thump against the roof of the bungalow. "Shit, man, maybe a tree came down on the line."

Clay said nothing; he turned and went to his room.

Heck finally came out of the john, and Judy said, "Babe, I think something's on the roof. Can you go out and check on it?"

Heck scratched his fat belly and grunted his assent. He went out through the kitchen door, and she waited, sipping her coffee.

She had to be at work—selling homemade baskets in Perdito—soon or the damn Indians would get the best spots in the town square, and she'd be peddling beaded gimps at the Caliente Airport by noon alongside the Hare Krishnas.

Impatiently, she went out to the back porch.

Heck stood there, holding something in his hands that at first looked like a bird, then maybe a lizard, and then she thought: Behold! *It's Quetzalcoatl, the feathered serpent. The myth of the Aztecs has come to pass, as shall all things.*

But Heck had another idea. He shouted excitedly, "It's fucking acid rain! Finally got the damn crows! Holy shit!"

His voice echoed and ricocheted throughout the neighborhood.

Judy sighed. "Damn, babe," she said, "if they're all gushy like that, we ain't gonna be able to eat 'em no more."

But then she screamed when the skin of the bird slid right off its bones, and the crow itself, its innards curling like fingers around its wriggling spine, began shrieking, in turn.

7:10 A.M.

Bram Boatwright sat up in bed. His mother had stopped calling for him to get up for school, which was pretty darn eerie considering this was her job in life. He had had some weird dreams, but that was par for the course, ever since his mom had begun her campaign of terror, making him stay up late to finish his homework, even though he didn't really care much about high school, and ever since she had made him stop seeing "that girl from the other side of Perdito."

It was tough being fourteen, particularly when he just wanted out. Out of everything: school, home, *life*. It sucked the big wangola. Ever since Dad had run out on them like that, with that shameless hussy from Seattle, it had all seemed to go downhill. At least for him. Mom seemed to be having a great time busting his chops with discipline, discipline, discipline. He wished, sometimes, that she had gone ahead and sent him to that military school on the Coast that she used to threaten him with. But Now He Was All She Had Left In The World.

Somewhere, down deep where sometimes even *he* couldn't find it, he knew he loved her. It was just that she was too much sometimes. He was smart enough to realize that she was just making up for the fact that his dad was such a flake, but that knowledge didn't seem to help him when she went on one of her rampages about his messy room or about his grades or about his lack of religion. That last item *really* bit the big one. She read him passages from Revelations just about every night, and she'd tried to drag him to that bizarre church in Paso Caliente, the one where everyone started shaking and speaking in tongues, but he had successfully avoided it so far. She kept doves in a home-made cote out back, and each time she wanted to cleanse him of sin, she let a dove go so as to symbolize the release of the spirit from the bondage of error, but it just made Bram want to sin again so she would get rid of all her stupid doves. The way she went on sometimes! All about how she was seeing the Beast everywhere in Empire, and the Whore of Babylon riding in from the mountains—he hoped she wasn't off her rocker. Times like these, he understood why his father had hit the road.

One day, maybe when he was sixteen or so, he would leave too. Just take off for parts unknown. Maybe find his dad. Maybe go down to L.A. and get in the movies or something. Preferably monster movies, maybe as one of the monsters with a lot of special effects makeup on. He knew a lot about monster movies—he read two magazines that had a ton of information about them. One was called *Fangoria,* and was the best because it had color pictures, and the other was called *The Scream Factory*. He dreamed of one day either being in that kind of movie or maybe making one. He never told his mother about this dream because he knew she'd think it was as sinful as jacking off—which he didn't tell her about, either.

As he sat there, the covers still up around his stomach, he began to wonder if maybe something had happened to his mother, something bad. It was a weird childhood fantasy of his, not that he *wished* for something bad to happen to her, but he always had a feeling that, knowing *her,* something terrible would inevitably befall her one day.

"Mom?" he called out.

The house was silent.

Then the door to his bedroom slid open just slightly.

He held his breath.

His cat, Sophie, wandered in and began meowing as soon as she leaped up to his chest. He stroked the cat's smooth black fur. She had dropped something on the small oval rug, and he didn't want to look down and see the dead mouse beside the bed. Sophie was too good a mouser, and he hated to have to take the little rodents out and bury them in the backyard every other day.

Bram felt silly, being scared as if there was some kind of monster in the house, when it was just a dead mouse. *You're not nine, you know,* he told himself. *You're fourteen. You don't believe in monsters. Only in the movies or in stories.* He pushed the cat off him and slid out of bed.

The floorboards were cold.

Winter was coming. Even here. He had been born in Eugene, Oregon, and they had moved down here when he was seven. He still remembered the chilly winters up there, and hadn't, back then, expected to ever think this part of California could be as cold. But, just like anything, he had grown used to it, and eventually even when it dropped to fifty degrees it could feel like it was freezing.

Bram had gotten out of bed on the opposite side from where Sophie had deposited whatever small creature she'd caught. He stood, stretched, yawned, shuffled across the floor, out the bedroom door, into the hallway.

He glanced about the kitchen: no coffee on, no smell of eggs.

But water was running in the sink.

His mother was a stickler for waste not, want not, and it seemed more than a little strange that she had left the kitchen faucet running.

"Mom?" he asked the empty hallway that led to her bedroom.

A picture formed in his mind, and he had no idea why. It was a picture of his mother, in her bedroom, with the gold-plated letter opener in her hands, blood on its tip, blood on her wrists, and blood smeared on her lips as if she had decided that she wanted to taste her life as it ran from her veins.

But when he arrived at her room, he saw she was not there.

Then he returned to the kitchen and shut the water off.

He looked out the window above the sink, into the backyard, which was overgrown with weeds and piles of junk.

His mother stood there, turning slowly around and around as if she were trying to make herself dizzy. She had no unusual expression on her face, although he wondered if perhaps she had lost one of her contacts in the grass and wasn't sure where to start looking.

Bram never quite understood his mom most of the time, so he went out back and said, "I'll make my own breakfast today, okay?"

His mother stopped turning about and looked at him.

He felt a chill run through him.

For a second he was sure she didn't recognize him at all.

"Mom?" he said, almost shivering.

"My birds," she said, and tears came to her eyes. "My little sweet birds."

Bram looked down at the grass, and there, among the weeds and the broken-down wheelbarrow and the spring from the old twin bed, were his mother's doves, the ones she claimed reminded her of the Holy Spirit, all flopping on the ground like fish out of water, barely able to breathe.

"Some godforsaken sinner has *poisoned* my birds," she said, bending down to gather the suffering creatures in her arms. "Who would do such an awful thing? It wasn't you, Abraham? It wasn't you?"

One of them turned its soft-downed head against her breast as she cradled it. It pecked at the thin yellow material of her nightgown once, and then, pecking twice, drew blood from her breast.

And when it pecked her again, she dropped all of them

back to the ground and looked at her son and cried out, "Sinner!"

Behind him, from the house, he heard Sophie his cat yowling like she was in heat—only she couldn't be because she'd been spayed a year ago—and he wondered what it was she could've brought into the house, maybe not a mouse, maybe a dove, one of these doves, with some poison coursing through it, and Bram found himself running from his mother, back into the house, hoping his cat hadn't gotten poisoned, too.

7:22 A.M.

"Just a quickie?" Larry asked, but Joanne shook her head. The way she did it was so sexy that he got harder just watching her golden yellow hair spray down over her back.

"I thought the doctor told you no more nookie."

"He didn't mean *forever,* darlin'." Larry grinned. He had a tooth missing up front, and it bothered him sometimes, but it never seemed to bother Joanne, so who the hell was he to worry about it? He closed his mouth self-consciously.

"Well, I feel fat. You know I don't feel like it when I'm fat."

"Hey, sweetheart, you know what they say: the bigger the cushion, the better the pushin'."

She glared at him. "And what about your wife?"

He shrugged. "You know what they say: eatin' ain't cheatin'."

"Crude," she said, "but my type of man."

"I won you in that pool game fair and square, and you're supposed to deliver."

"I don't *do* deliver."

"You weren't like that last night."

"How the hell would you know, Larry Brady? You were so drunk down at King Tut's you could barely call me by name."

"I got me a photographic memory, darlin'. Nothin' slips by me. Nothin'."

"Where's Marti, anyway?"

"At her mother's in San Jose. Old lady's sick, and she goes up a week every month."

"And you play all week long."

" 'Member when I first saw you? I mean, that kinda chemistry when you first come to town? How long ago? You and them hippies. I always did like hippie girls."

Joanne began to look sullen; her brows curved downward in the middle. "None of us was hippies. Not really."

"Whatever. Wild things. Free spirits."

A tear came suddenly, shockingly, to the corner of her left eye. She wiped at it. "Not free, either."

Larry Brady had barely an ounce of human warmth in him, but what little he had, he extended. He leaned into her, wrapped his arms around her, and kissed her gently on the neck, just below her ear.

She whispered, "It's why I spend every night I can with you."

"It's not that often, darlin'."

"I don't mean just you," she continued, sighing. "Other men, too. I hate being alone. They're still here."

"The other men?"

"No. *Them*. The Family. They're always here."

"They can't hurt you or anything."

"You ever want to leave this place, Larry? Leave your home, your wife, all of it?"

"Leave Empire? I never thought about it. I was born here. I'll die here. It's part of what I'm all about."

"I wish I could leave."

"Why don't you, then?"

She began sobbing. "I can't. You don't know. I *can't.*"

Larry Brady had been horny and hung over, but he began thinking about how long he'd known Joanne, known about her problems, her deep dark secrets, how he had first seen her in 1981, when she was only fourteen and living with the weirdos from San Francisco, and how sad and pretty she'd been then, but with that same haunted, unrelenting look in her pale blue eyes.

Then she straightened up, and he saw in those same eyes a wisdom beyond her twenty-six years. "Something's happening here," she said, "and I can't tell you what it is."

"Why not?"

"They put this *thing* in you. It's like a self-destruct button or something. And if you say anything . . ."

"Darlin', I don't get it."

"If you say anything or do anything ... It's like mind control. They did it with drugs at first, and then ... I can't say it."

"Just try," he said. "It's only me here. Nobody's gonna get you in trouble or nothin'."

She shook her head, looking away. "You don't understand. Even if I *think* it, it starts to hurt. Inside. In my head. You ever hear of a brain aneurysm?"

Larry lied. "Sure."

"It's supposed to be something like that."

"I'm sure it'll be okay," he whispered, kind of sad that they both lived lives that neither one could ever get away from. Maybe that was what had attracted him to her in the first place, that kind of recognition of familiarity, of being *stuck*. He was stuck in his marriage, and she was stuck in her past with the hippies.

Joanne rested her face against his neck, and he felt her warm tears again.

Larry Brady had an epiphany, just there, with this woman in his arms, and in spite of his fucked-up thirty-six years, he felt like the heavens had opened up for him, and he made a decision.

And there would be no turning back.

Ever.

We've been slaves, he thought. *We've let ourselves be enslaved. Me, because I'm a weenie, and Joanne because she's hurt somewhere inside and can't see around it. Hell, Marti's gonna be better off without me, anyway. I'll be doing both of us a huge favor.*

"Baby," he whispered, "let's you and me get outta this hole and go make a new life someplace else."

"I don't think I can. I just—"

"I'll protect you from everything else, I'll make sure our life is good together," he said, and felt more like a man than he'd ever felt in his life. "We'll get packed, and I'll gas up the Hyundai, and we'll go to Mexico or someplace, and I'll be a fisherman, and you can make tortillas or something."

"I don't think I can," she repeated, but he knew, now that he had made this decision, she would come with him.

7:25 A.M.

Bram Boatwright stared at the thing that his cat had brought in from the outside. At first he didn't recognize it as a human finger, because it was still wriggling.

7:28 A.M.

Anne Potter worked as a nurse over at the infirmary in Empire State, but every morning, before she took off for work, she drove her two little girls to the day-care center in Perdito. It was a roundabout way of getting to work, but it was the only day-care center she trusted. As she was walking out her door, making sure that Charlotte and Michelle both had their lunch bags, she sniffed the air.

Weird, she considered, wondering if some new form of pollution was coming from the West. *Smells like necrotic tissue.* It was a smell that always made her sick to her stomach, and when she had been around dying tissue in her school days, she had gone to the infirmary herself with severe headaches.

But she got her girls into the station wagon and knew that she'd better get up the road or she would be late for work.

7:35 A.M.

At the Hillside Memorial Park, beneath the ground, Poppy Freek awoke slowly, groggily. In her arms, the skulls of her children, and she kissed each one lightly on the tops of their white bone heads.

Her first thought: *No more spearmints.*

In a few minutes she would crawl up out of the grave that had for so many years been her hideaway, and she would face someone she had been running away from for many years.

Tucked into her belt, beneath her sweater, was the knife she had used to clean so many fish when she lived as a much younger girl down by the waterfront in San Francisco.

She heard something among the graves.

They had been invaded by the living.

8:00 A.M.

Kermit Stone's phone had been uncharacteristically silent as a tomb, so it wasn't until Ellen Fremont jogged right up to his door and began banging on it as if he owed her something that he finally had to face the day. He glanced out the bathroom window and saw her standing there, as lovely as the first day he had ever set eyes on her, and as difficult as any woman he'd ever known. Once he had hoped she would divorce her husband so Kermit could feel free to pursue her; but then, as he grew to know her, he realized that she was a stubborn, hard individual, and he had enough on his hands to take care of. She always kept in shape, that Ellen, but she was often too stern for his taste.

He knew this wasn't a social visit.

He was just finishing shaving, and Gus was upstairs in the shower; Fletcher was still sound asleep in his bed in the guest room. Kermit wasn't sure what was about to hit Empire, California, but as he set down his razor and pulled his bathrobe around him, he knew that the end of the world, which Fletcher had spoken of, was somehow being set into motion.

Right here, right now.

Somehow, they'd managed to start their dark tide. Kermit didn't know how, didn't know why.

The thoughts coursing through his brain brought on a slight headache that grew more severe, more painful, the more he thought about it.

He went down the hall to face Ellen Fremont, his head feeling like a train was running through it at full speed and derailing just when the pain in his head seemed to be at its peak.

Kermit opened the door. "Good morning, Ellen."

"Kermit," she said, catching her breath, "there's some kind of spill out on the highway. They've cordoned the town off. I ran up Sand Canyon and out the Empire Road to the east, and we're blocked off on all sides. What the heck is going on?"

"You have breakfast yet, El?" Kermit said, opening the door wider, and then the pain became so intense in his skull that the world seemed to black out around him until he knew he was falling but never felt himself hit the floor.

These were just loose skeins in the tapestry of the town. Others went about their business, going to their small shops or to their gas stations and shoe stores to open up for the day, unaware of the birds that had fallen, unaware of the military vehicles that had blocked the roads to the outside world. And if they were aware, perhaps they shrugged and thought, *None of my business, no concern of mine. Don't care so long as it's a good day here. If it ain't on the news it can't be happening, anyway, not really, and nothing's on the news about some toxic waste or poison gas or end-of-the-world bullshit. Get me my coffee and a Danish, if it ain't too much trouble.*

Gretchen Feely slept late, dreaming about the children she was going to have with Gus Stone one day. Gus slept late, five doors down from her, dreaming of playing with eight different breasts on four different girls right out of *Penthouse.* A man named Hugh Best was already wondering if he should call his wife in the hospital in Perdito to see if the test had come up negative, but he was worried that it would be positive. A seventeen-year-old named Nancy Welker just found out, from her home pregnancy test, that the rabbit had died and her first thought was of throwing herself out a window, only there weren't any buildings in town tall enough to allow her to do the job right.

Things were still ordinary for most of the townies. It was just a day. It was just an hour. It was a little cold, a little boring, a little of the same old same old.

In early November the weather in Empire could run hot or cold, although with the recent rains, it leaned toward the cool. Storms that came this far inland tended to originate in the Gulf of Alaska, and by the time they got to Empire, they died a quick death and never went much farther east. But the chill didn't die until April or May, so with the rains came an early but mild winter. By the standards of much of the rest of the country, this was no winter at all, but in Empire, once the temperature dropped, it might as well have been the Yukon, and sweaters were pulled on, hats worn, and sometimes even gloves.

It wasn't until someone needed to use a phone or get to

the next town over or buy fruit or milk at the local market that anything other than the change in the weather presented a problem.

Birds were omens in ancient cultures. Carriers of good news and bad news.

In this case it was, for Empire, California, bad news.

These residents, waking up, finding the birds dying, finding some of their pets dying, too, would soon feel what might come to them by touch or by a breath, and might think that some kind of headache was coming on. From the youngest to the oldest, how many of them would fall within minutes? How many within hours? How many would have a natural immunity to what a little boy named Lex had passed on to them?

A virus from the stars, that was what r-7 had been labeled by Dr. Robert Stewart years earlier when it had been brought back from a space probe.

It was a virus that seemed to work right only in children.

From Robert Stewart's tapes

"If six responds, then the recombination of the two, of the charge of the two, six and four together, the signals that each possesses, the electrical rewiring of their minds, with r-seven, will culminate in the evolutionary moving forward from this age of destruction into a new age, a turn of the tide, where life and death are dualistic notions in the head of a romantic, if indeed romantics will still exist beside the greater good. But I need a test group. These aren't sheep to be slaughtered afterward. I need the right place. I need a test tube too large for ordinary lab work. But how to convince the complex is the problem. Maybe convincing isn't enough. Maybe ... maybe I should just go ahead and do it. Convince them later. 'Do unto others as you would have them do unto you.' Some will build up an immunity if they're around either six or four when the recombination occurs. I need her in a completely new environment, someplace where she hasn't had contact, where no one is yet immune."

PART THREE

Welcome to the House of Pain

November 8, The Day of Reckoning

"Her father," continued Baglioni, "was not restrained by natural affection from offering up his child in this horrible manner as the victim of his insane zeal for science.... What then will be your fate? Beyond a doubt you are selected as the material for some new experiment. Perhaps the result is to be death; perhaps a fate more awful still. Rappaccini, with what he calls the interest of science before his eyes, will hesitate at nothing."

—"Rappaccini's Daughter,"
Nathaniel Hawthorne

53

Awakenings

8:00 A.M.
The Fairmont Hotel, San Francisco

NATHAN HOLDER HAD LOST NO SLEEP, AND AS HE WOKE, HE glanced at the girl lying next to him. Seventeen, at the most, although she had lied and said she was over twenty. He had hoped she would leave in the night, but since she was still with him, and so invitingly naked, he began playing with her breasts, and then, as she woke, he directed her head down to the place between his legs that would really make for a day-brightener. "That's it," he said, enjoying the fact that she would do this for him just because she thought she had fallen in love with him overnight, as much as enjoying it for the physical sensation. It had been easy getting the girl, as it always was when he was on Company business. There was always a list of "availables" in each of the major coastal cities, and interestingly, this girl, Melanie, was the daughter of one of the older availables. Nathan wondered if he could persuade the mother to participate on some night in the future.

When he was satisfied, he pushed her face away from his crotch. He was always extremely sensitive to any kind of touching afterward, and Melanie seemed to want to hold him. She was pretty, but very selfish, he decided, and as he lay there next to her for a few minutes, he realized that she was using him to get a job, and he didn't appreciate that one bit.

"Out," he said, as sweetly as he could. "I've got business to do."

"We could order room service," she said, so needy, so pushy.

"I've got important things to do this morning, honey. I'm sorry. Tell Chuck that I said you should get double per diem pay."

"I'm not a whore," she said, getting up slowly, as if hoping he would pull her down against him again. "And I'm not some kind of Company perk, either."

"Of course not. I didn't mean to suggest that. I meant for the secretarial work we'll have you do up at the office today. As a test. How does that sound?" He scratched his stomach, and then realized his testicles were itching, and he panicked momentarily—what if she had crabs? He hated hunting down the cure in some pharmacy and then spending the day with the stinking elixir all over his lower body. He was fairly sure she didn't have any venereal diseases, because Chuck tended to check them out for that before assigning them.

He watched her dress; she was looking less attractive by the second, from the first moment she dropped her pale behind into her black lace panties, to the zipping up of her skirt while her breasts still hung down like they'd been nursed dry. Finally, as she buttoned her blouse up, she said, "Well, it was fun, anyway."

"Good," he said, his mind moving on to other things. "Good for you."

After she was out the door, he picked up the phone and dialed a number.

A woman answered. "Lewis," she said.

"Rebecca? It's Nathan. Anything on the blood?"

"I've been up all night, Mr. Holder, working on it. This lab is pretty limiting, you ask me. L.A. could handle it better."

"I don't want L.A. handling it. What've you come up with?"

"Well, Stewart's right on target. It's a whole new blood type. Takes over what's already there. The r-seven virus seems to be the catalyst. The girl started life as O positive, and she's now ... this. I still don't know what the fuck it means."

"Rebecca, you know how I dislike rough language."

"I want to send a sample of this to Majesky."

"Impossible."

A pause on the line. "There're other things, too, sir. The tissue we extracted ... we don't need to keep it alive. It won't die. We've even tried killing it, and it shows all the signs of necrosis, but it comes back."

Nathan Holder sighed. "I wish we had Stewart's balls in a vise on this one. But there's no messing with genius."

"Sir?"

He had said more than he should've, and that wasn't like him. Rebecca Lewis was the rising star in forensics for Projects, just as her father had been, but she was too close to Grace. Who knew if Grace was somehow still in communication with her? "Stewart is some kind of a genius," Holder said, thinking as best he could on his feet, "or madman, whatever he's done."

"You've seen the sheep trials," she said.

He couldn't deny this. "Right. In 1990 in Los Gordos."

"Stewart didn't get it right, not then."

"Rebecca?"

"He only got it right with his daughter. She's a manufacturer of this blood type. She's a new species, Mr. Holder. The r-seven didn't take with the sheep, but it worked on a human being. When she spreads it, it doesn't always take, maybe because it needs to be spread through a certain kind of contact. Or maybe the girl needs an emotional stimulus. Maybe when she knows she's doing it, there's enough of one there. The boy in the hospital, he came to her sick. She knew he was sick. So she healed him. But the guy in the casino, hell, she just passed him by; she was just mindlessly sending this stuff out. Now, in those sheep trials in New Mexico Stewart tried to do what any good scientist does: inject some animals with this virus, and then see if something can't be made of their blood—you know, create the strongest version of the r-seven virus and then inject that into other sheep. Well, this is what I think he's done with his daughter. She's the test tube for r-seven compatability. It worked on her, and she turned out fairly healthy; the changing process did only minor damage, maybe. And so she's gonna manufacture perfectly processed blood of this type. I think that's been Stewart's plan all along."

"I see," Nathan Holder said.

And thought: *Good.*

"I'll keep working on this and see if I come up with anything more, sir."

"Great work, Rebecca. Terrific."

"And sir? Have you spoken with Grace?"

"We're not in communication right now. That's as it should be."

"If you do get an opportunity to speak with him, tell him I owe him a beer."

He heard the click as she hung up the phone.

Then he dialed another number. The man who answered said, "Task Force Oh-five-oh in effect."

54

At dawn

POPPY HAD BEEN AWAKE SINCE 5:00 A.M., WHEN SHE'D HEARD the series of gunshots. The sound had been enough to wake the dead, and she moved from the mud and leaves that she'd tamped down around the children's bones, and dug her way back up to the outside world. She knew she stank, but stinking on the outside was better than stinking on the inside, as she was so well aware. Her brothers and her mother all stank on the inside, as if they'd had their innards opened and dumped out while somebody sewed human excrement up inside them. She felt along her waistband, for the knife— *protection.* It was still there. Good. she couldn't be sure that this wasn't some kind of trick her family had used to try to flush her out. She was fairly sure they knew she was on her way, and they were capable of anything.

Anything.

She gripped the old tombstone that covered her hideaway, and pressed hard against it, using the mud as lubricant to get the stone moving. It was heavy, and she wasn't the most muscular person in the world, although her legs could carry her anywhere. When she was fairly sure she wasn't being watched, she made her move. It was still pretty dark out, and she couldn't see much, except for a man and a woman standing by the eucalyptus trees near the streetlamp by the road.

Then they dragged something out of the bug-fluttering light, and between the trees. Poppy didn't pretend it was anything other than a human body.

More murderers.

She lay still for a while; had to flick a milky white maggot off her fingers. It had left a trail of sticky silk behind, and, being hungry and practical, she licked at both the trail and the maggot, knowing from her reading on survival, during endless nights hiding out in public libraries—that nourishing protein and carbohydrates could be found in the most un-likely places.

After the two murderers left, she heard some trucks out on the highway just north of town. She sent her feelers out, but got nothing back but vibrations and the sound of birds. Perhaps she picked up a radio signal or two, but nothing she could understand.

Finally, when she was sure that the coast was clear and the daylight was just coming up, she crawled out of the hole, and managed to stand up, slightly stooped from the aches of sleeping in such an uncomfortable position. She loped out to the trees, and there, beneath several thin eucalyptus branches, lay the man.

He was beautiful, not like her at all. He was the way people were supposed to be, and she would've begun crying, except she was afraid she might be heard. She was self-conscious of the vestiges of her vocal cords, the windy, raspy sound they produced, and although her feelers couldn't de-tect anybody, who knew? Perhaps someone was waiting nearby just for such a sound. Who knew what they would do to her if they had her now? Who knew where they would sell her? How they would cut into her? She wept the tears of decades of the small shiny knives they had used on her, the hours of lying on an operating table, strapped down because they offered no anesthesia, of screaming so much that finally they had operated on her neck to keep her quiet as if by not screaming there was also no pain; how she had to train herself to stare up at his face, *his* face, and hypnotize herself into believing that she was somewhere else, someplace where it didn't hurt, where he wasn't doing those things to her, he wasn't making her into Poppy Freek.

She wiped her muddy fingers across her eyes. As the sun rose, she began picking up signals—a car was coming up the Mission Road, and the birds were calling one to one another as if a predator were loose among them. She lifted the man's arms and dragged him back to her hideway, back to the place where she'd buried all the young children that she had taken for hers, and had blessed as they'd died. She'd given them a place where their bones, at least, might rest.

55

At dawn

" 'TRUST'! DON'T EVER SAY THAT TO ME AGAIN," KATE snarled, and Ben felt as if he were watching some wild animal sniff the air for danger. She held the gun loosely; it wasn't a threat anymore, but he wasn't sure he trusted her. Not now. Not after what she'd done to Shadow. They had walked back to the Greenwater Motor Lodge, and he had almost relaxed.

Almost.

And then he had suggested that she should trust him, and

suddenly the expression on her face had changed from fear and exhaustion to unbridled rage.

A few minutes later she had calmed.

Now she undressed down to her slip, still holding the Smith & Wesson. He had already put the Uni aside, on the dresser by the bed. "I don't need help from men. Never again. Men like Robert, men like that man I killed. They all want to hurt my little girl in some way, and I will not stand for it." She was working hard not to break down and sob. He wondered how she could still be standing there, how anyone could, after the ordeal she'd been put through—through most of her life.

"I'm not Robert," he said quietly.

He closed his eyes. God, he was tired. And hungry. But mostly, tired. Dead tired.

When he opened his eyes again, Kate stood there, and even then, even with her snapping at him, even having watched her gun the man down, even with her exhaustion and fear and anger, he knew he loved her. He had wasted so much of his life standing back: standing back while she had gone off, so mysteriously, with Robert so many years ago, standing back even now, when all he wanted to do was hold her, feel her close to him.

Perhaps it was what he had just said, but something in her eyes had calmed. She reached up and pushed the stray hair from her forehead. It was beaded with sweat. "I know you're not Robert. I know you wouldn't hurt Hope. I just don't know what to believe, Ben."

She went around to the side of the bed and picked the phone up. She began dialing, hung the phone up, tried again, but again pressed the receiver back down into the cradle. "Phone's dead. The lines went down last night during the rain. Damn boondocker. God, I'm tired." Now the tears came, but he sensed not to move toward her. It was not what she wanted. "I am so goddamned tired, and I don't know who to turn to. I've spent my whole life needing help I couldn't even get, and now that Hope needs it, I can't seem to help her. I can't seem to do—" Her voice became shrill, and then she stopped in mid-sentence. Again she calmed, catching her breath. "I don't know how Robert did it, but I know he put pictures in my head . . . thoughts. All those pills he gave me. It's like he spent half our life together rewiring my head, as if he was just waiting for ..." She clutched the sides of her head with her hands as if the confusion were too much to bear. "Who in God's name are these people who took her? What do they want with her? What does Robert want with her?"

Ben said, "It's hard to believe he'd put his own daughter through this."

And then, with a voice drained of blood and warmth, she whispered, "Hope is not his daughter."

"Does that surprise you?" she asked a few seconds later.
"No."
"Do you understand?"
"Part of it. Why didn't you tell me before?"
"I couldn't. You were going to write your great American novel, travel to foreign wars, fight the good fight through journalism, remember? You went on police raids, and you almost got killed at that protest down on Market, remember? What was I going to be, to you? What would a baby have done to you, Ben? I knew you. I knew what you'd tell me then. You'd want me to get an abortion. We talked about family, remember? You told me that you didn't really want children. Not for a while. They'd get in the way. What should I have done? You tell me."

"You could've at least told me."

"I guess I could've. But I was going through a lot. It seems silly now. I knew it was wrong then, but I did it anyway."

"And you ran off with Robert."

"He was there. He was different then. He wanted this baby. He ... was different. He wanted a family more than anything."

Ben was silent, almost brooding, as if he'd been thrown back to that time. Not the best of times, when Kate had left him. Not the best of times. Something was wrong with her story. He hadn't wanted a family, not right then, but he had talked to her about children and babies, and how much he enjoyed them. He would never have suggested that she have an abortion. Not back then, at least. Not when he was sentimental, and the world seemed a brighter place to a young journalist who had yet to learn of death squads and cults and Special Projects. "You're lying, Kate," he said, finally. He moved closer to her, as if to put his arms around her, to embrace her, but instead he grabbed her shoulders and held her almost roughly. "Tell me the truth, damn it, Katy. Tell me why you left me!"

She began crying and tugged herself free of his grasp. She covered her face with her hands, as if she had done the most horrible thing in the world, the most terrible act a human being could do. Her hair hung down across her hands; she was rubbing the palms of her hands furiously up and down and across her nose and eyes and lips, as if she wanted to obliterate her features.

Ben softened. "Katy? What is it?"

She collapsed against him in wave after wave of sobs. "I'm a monster," she said through the tears.

"No," Ben whispered.

"I never wanted to have Hope," Kate Stewart said, working hard to keep the tears back, "not ... not because I don't love her. I love her more than life, but it was ... It's hard to explain. . . . I was going to get rid of the baby. I was three months pregnant. You didn't know yet; I had just found out. Remember? You went on that trip to Washington to cover the ... What was it?"

"I don't know," he said. "Some protest march."

"You were gone for six weeks. I didn't want the baby. I knew what my father had done to me starting when I was four. I didn't want a child to grow up and maybe have that happen. I didn't even have my own shit together—how was I going to protect a little baby? My mother couldn't protect me. My grandmother couldn't. She tried, but she couldn't. Family only sees what it wants to see. How would I care for this child?"

"You could've trusted."

"I did." She took a deep breath, and the tears stopped momentarily. "I trusted that an abortion would solve the problem. I also trusted that I would never be able to look you in the face again. I was wrong. About a lot of things. I went to this abortion clinic—my friend Julie had it done there. So I go, and I give them all this information, and then I freak. And I go for a walk. It hits me then, Ben, that I'm carrying your child. That it's not just mine. And all the stupid sentimentality of that notion. Like I'm living in the nineteenth century. And then I start to really hate myself, and I'm thinking of jumping off a bridge or finding a gas oven to put my head in. I don't know where to go. So I go back to your place. I had the key, and I just let myself in. I sat there, crying. Half my life I've spent crying. I listen to your Springsteen records. I hated Springsteen even then, but I felt closer to you. I was silly. I started to feel giddy, almost. I had a drink, maybe two. Your friend came by."

"Friend?"

"Oh, that crazy one. The aging hippie. The guy who was always walking around talking about nirvana, and he had that—remember? That pet rooster."

"Jesus, Kate. Siggie. Siggie Wasilewsky."

"Yeah. He said there was a party. I was down and happily drunk and suicidal. I was looking for you. Anyway, I went. It was different. He said you'd been there before, a lot. It was like a side of you I hadn't seen. Different. And I met a man there. He was different, too. Different from the others, not weird at all, but in a suit, standing tall like he mattered, and he looked *into* me, Ben. He *saw* what the matter was. It was like he knew."

"Kate. Jesus. The Anubis."

"Huh?"

"You went to the Anubis. It was a club run by Cthonos. Robert," Ben said. "Robert. Cthonos. Hope. Jesus."

But Kate wasn't really listening. She was like someone walking in her sleep, acting out a drama that was in her head alone. "He gave me some pills, right then, to relax, to sleep. And then he took care of me, Ben. I was a screwed-up, immature woman with a baby in my body, and he took over. I should be shot. I should be shot for what I did. What I allowed."

Finally the tears were released again, from her eyes, from her soul.

When he knew that she was too tired to go on, he kissed the top of her head and leaned down into the bed with her so that he could hold her while she slept.

They weren't supposed to sleep, he knew. They were supposed to find the police, or do something—anything. He didn't intend to let her sleep for more than a few minutes.

They had left a dead man, a Special Projects agent, no less, out by the road, and Hope was being held by someone else. Someone worse. Some . . . The only word that came to mind was "fiend."

Hope was being held by some fiend.

Sleep, for Ben, should not have been on the agenda.

Hunger, perhaps. That doughnut shop he'd hit on the way into town, perhaps that was opening up.

He imagined an entire breakfast—room service, wheeled in on a shiny cart, with fruit and cereal and coffee.

He felt the wet rain of the last of Kate's tears along his neck, just beneath his chin.

No sleep.

Not today.

Sleep is death. Can't die. Not me. Gotta get up out of bed, gotta take a shower, gotta make my list of things to do, gotta get this show on the road.

The wet rain of tears on his neck. So warm and cool at the same time. He thought, *We wreck our lives. We tell half-truths just so we don't interfere with each other, just so we don't crash and burn. Just to avoid an accident, we swerve away from each other. And that's when the wreck comes, when we seek to avoid it. I've spent half my life wondering why she left me. And now it doesn't matter. Here we are, caught up in the same wreck, running toward each other even when we think we're running in opposite directions.*

These thoughts prepared the way for sleep, and he fought them. He fought the drifting-down feeling where thoughts were interconnecting patterns of a quilt, where tears were rain, where warmth was a memory photograph.

He felt Kate's hand open and close slightly across his chest in a weakened struggle against the inevitability of sleep.

But when she was quiet, her face pushed gently against the side of his neck, when he heard the slow, deep breathing of long-desired sleep, when her fingers lost their grip on his shirtsleeve and relaxed, he turned his face into the pillow, and Ben, too, slept and was allowed to dream about a small cabin by the sea when they had both been children, and safe.

56

At dawn

"MAMA, THAT'S THE BEST, JUST THE BEST," ROBERT Stewart said, wiping bits of grease from his lips. "How was it, Private Jim? You used to a country breakfast? Pork chops, mouth-watering good, and fresh orange juice, right off a tree. Did you know we have an orange tree out back? The oranges never get too big—it's the wrong climate to grow them in, but Mama made Daddy bring up this seedling from down in Anaheim, back before I was even born, and they planted it here, right here in back, out by the chicken coops." He leaned back in his chair and pointed through the kitchen window that overlooked the field in back with the coops and the barn and a few scattered fruit trees. "And Mama's got such a green thumb that anything grows where she decides, whether it's the right climate or not. 'Member that plum tree? Monkey set it on fire when he was nine, but before that, oh, the plums we'd have in August. Not like Nevada. We never really got fruit or vegetables in Nevada. It's kind of a wasteland there."

Jim grinned lazily, too sleepy to say much, but his stomach was pleasantly full. "Best," he echoed. He sipped his coffee, hoping the caffeine would kick in.

"My mama's the best cook in the world." Robert reached across the table and gave his mother a brief rub on the side of her arm. "Good to be home."

"Ma'am?" Jim asked.

"Call me Loretta, honey. I hate 'ma'am.' It's either Loretta or Mrs. Swink or Mama, but no 'ma'am.'" She didn't smile, and Jim got an uncomfortable feeling just sitting across from her.

"I'm kind of tired, Loretta, and I was wondering ..."

"Sure, Jimmy. You can take Monkey's room and have yourself a little lie-down." Loretta Swink had removed her thick glasses, wiping at them with a Kleenex. Her eyes seemed smaller, almost nonexistent. The irises were almost completely round and black and gave the effect of being dark marbles thrust between two tight little eyelids. Jim had heard something once, from a friend who had worked Psych for Projects. *"You can always tell when you're in the presence of a psychotic," the friend had said. "The dangerous kind, anyway. They're like another species, with special powers. You feel cold at first. Really cold. No warmth at all, doesn't matter if the sun is beating down on the top of your head. And then you start to feel dizzy, light-headed, and maybe you giggle without knowing why. When that happens, get the hell away from this person. This person will kill you. This person will do unimaginable things to you, if he gets the chance. He is the worst kind of human being, in so much pain, in so much conflict over every minute particle of the universe, that even while he rips your lungs out with his bare hands, he thinks you are in control, you are making him eat your liver."*

Jim was suddenly not so tired.

Because, just before Loretta Swink propped her glasses back up on her stubby nose, she glanced at him with those dark eyes, and he felt the chill of winter.

Jim giggled.

"What's funny?" Robert Stewart said.

"I guess I'm just dog-tired."

"Well, ten minutes or so of a nap won't hurt you."

"Who's Monkey?" Jim asked Loretta.

"He's my other boy. Got three. Monkey, Birdy, and Harly."

Robert shook his head, grinning, as if hearing the most wonderful memory. He looked at Jim and said, "All nicknames. I'm Birdy."

There was a noise from back near the sink and pantry, and Jim noticed that there was a Dutch door, as if leading down to a root cellar. The door creaked open, and a boy poked his head up, and then came up the steps into the kitchen, tracking mud.

"Hello," he said sullenly, looking at Dr. Stewart.

"Lex," Robert responded.

Only then did Jim notice that the boy was deformed on one side of his body. The left side was fine, and the boy had reddish brown hair and a few freckles. But the right side of his body looked like as if it had been burned in some terrible fire. The damaged tissue was separated from the clear flesh by a scar line running from his forehead down along his nose. The right edge of his lip was torn and ragged, and pink scar tissue ran along his neck. His right arm was smaller than the left, and he limped when he walked; Jim guessed that he had a curvature of the spine.

"Introduce yourself to our guest," Loretta said stonily.

"Hello, my name is Lex. How do you do?" the boy said, pronouncing each word slowly, as if trying to mimic a foreigner learning the phrases for the first time. Then he said, "Are you here for her, too?"

Jim grinned. "I'm a friend of Dr. Stewart's."

"Oh."

"You're up early," Loretta said without looking at him.

"I want to take my bike out," Lex said.

Loretta turned and nodded her head. "You see her?"

"She's asleep. I don't see what's so great about her."

Loretta and Robert exchanged glances, and Jim was feeling sleepier by the second.

Lex continued, "I can do a lot more than she can, anyway. I can make things the way I want. You know what I can do, mister?"

Jim shook his head. "What's that?"

The boy named Lex grinned, and Jim saw that half his teeth were missing on the right side of his jaw, which accounted for the slight lisp. "I can make things change. I have a cat like no cat you've ever seen. And I have a dog, too. I have birds, lots of birds. They don't even fly."

"Shut up, Lex," Loretta whispered, but kept her eyes on Jim.

"I can breathe on a rat and make it melt. You ever see a rat melt? It looks like butter in a skillet, mister, just down, down, down, and bubbling all around," the boy said.

Jim looked over at Robert, but the doctor had closed his eyes with an apparent headache. Jim looked at Loretta, but her eyes were so intensely focused on him that he had to look away, back to the boy.

"Do you want to see something, mister?" Lex asked, coming around to him. "You want to see something real different, mister?"

Jim wanted to push himself away from this table and get out the door and back into the Cadillac, but those weren't his orders. His orders were to escort Dr. Stewart wherever he needed to go. And Jim always followed orders. Always.

"Look at this," Lex said, coming closer to Jim, and cupping something in the palm of his hand, something he had been hiding there since he walked in.

Private Jim peered into the boy's deformed hand. The boy's three remaining fingers uncurled from around his prize, and Jim saw something that seemed to be stitched into the palm of the boy's hand, carved into it.

A human eye.

Pale blue.

The dark in its center dilating as light from the kitchen window spread across it.

As if it were watching him.

Jim saw his own reflection in the eye become distorted, and he felt something like a river of ice run from his heart out toward his skin, his extremities, and he found that he could not look away from this eye that had been sewn into the boy's hand, and he screamed as loud as he could, so loud that Loretta and the doctor should've known how much pain he was in, as if his flesh were being scraped right off the bone, but he also knew, even in that steel slice of raw pain, that they were watching him—the boy, the woman, the doctor, and the eye within the hand.

Jim watched them watch him, and then he glanced at his hand, and watched as the fingers distended and curled backwards on themselves and his elbow twisted around in its socket. The pain, while excruciating, was not the worst thing.

The worst thing was the smile on the little boy's face.

57

Resurrection

TRIANGLES OF COLORED PAPER LIKE ORIGAMI CRANES *flapping their geometric wings as they glide downward into a hexagonal lake of calm, causing interruptions of yellow-red butterflies. A door opens. The lake expands to reveal a world of laughing fire.*

Not fire, but light.

Normal light.

Day*light.*

"Shit," he said, coughing up whatever had been in his throat. "I'm alive."

A voice, in his head but not of it, said, *You are.*

These were the things that came to him, these were the memories: his name was Stephen Grace, and he had to kill a girl named Hope Stewart.

Someone, maybe his mother from heaven or hell, was feeding him something that tasted like Campbell's chicken noodle soup, cold. There was very little light, although what there was shed enough illumination on his surroundings to let him know that he had been buried.

A few moments later, more memories: Stephen Grace had grown up in Richmond, Virginia, and had watched a playmate die playing on some railroad tracks while they dared each other to run in front of the trains. His mother was sick most of his life, and his father was never there. He went to Vietnam at the age of eighteen, and didn't return to the United States from Asia for ten more years; by that time he was working for the Special Projects division of the Company. He remembered his wife, Anne, her golden brown hair, and her eyes, like an endless fire. Undying fire. Looking into them and seeing eternity, seeing beyond the human flesh and blood into something that would never be lost. *Love.* And then her face was rent in two, and he was staring at a man's face, a face like a steel wall.

He remembered Nathan Holder.

He remembered working for Nathan Holder, director of Special Projects since 1980.

He remembered what Nathan Holder had said when Stephen Grace's wife, Anne, had died in the jet that exploded over Paris in 1983.

Holder had said, "Ironic, Grace. That was probably our C-4 from Task Force 032. Once our allies, now our enemies. It's the nature of the business."

That was really the beginning of Grace's hatred for Nathan Holder, and it was his reason for living.

But something in his memory told him that this was no longer the reason.

That perhaps there was no reason at all.

You can't die, not now, a woman's voice said through the wind that was blowing in his mind. *You've been touched.*

Who the fuck are you? My fairy godmother?

Look at me, the woman said, and suddenly his eyes were filled with a brilliant light, more shocking than a thousand suns.

Stephen Grace opened his eyes completely. It hurt, as if he had sand in his eyes, and he wanted to rub them but could not move his arms or hands.

A match had been struck, and that was the only light in this dark place. He inhaled and smelled dirt and a moldy odor. When his eyes adjusted to the match's light, he saw a woman whose face was half covered by swaths of torn clothes, patchwork. But he recognized her.

"You're the sister," he said. "Stewart's sister."

The bottom of her face, along the scarred jawline, curved upward in what he assumed was a smile, and the eyes, where the skin hadn't melted over them, shone fiercely in the feeble yellow flame. *Poppy,* she said.

Her lips hadn't moved, as he had known they would not,

because when Projects had found her living in the streets, they had discovered that her tongue had been cut from her mouth, and the teeth had been torn out from her gums years before. She had only been able to write in broken English, and very little of what she had written was useful.

"How are you speaking to me?" he asked.

It is my gift. It is the one success of Birdy's experiments. It is bestowed upon me from the gods of the dark, and for this I am grateful. To them I have lost only my tongue, but to the same gods, my brothers have ransomed their souls and their minds.

Then Grace thought: *I'm hallucinating.*

The final memory that came to him, after all the others of his lifetime, was a picture of Kate Stewart pointing a gun at him and firing into him, his lungs collapsing, his heart stopping, and then, forgetting how to breathe out.

"I'm fucking dead," he muttered, "and I'm hallucinating."

The woman's voice was silent in his head.

And then pain shot through him in the places where the bullets had driven in—his chest, his left hand, beneath his neck.

He had been hoping that after death there would be no pain at all. But he felt nothing but pain, and he did something that he could not remember having done since he was a boy, not even when Anne had died or when he had held his mother in his arms on her hospital bed and she, too, had died: he cried, and heard himself weeping as if from a distance, and he thought, *What a sad, sad sound.*

This is the story of the first death and resurrection of Stephen Grace, as it came to him then, lying in a dark hole between life and death. He felt as if she were sucking the story out of him as she breathed, and as he thought it, she repeated it back to him in his head: *It was the girl. She kept you alive.*

Poppy reached out with her scarred right hand and patted the edge of his cheek. Her hand felt warm, and then the sensation of warmth grew like a smoldering fire until he no longer felt cold. Inside his mind she told him her story, and the pain seemed to lessen as she spoke.

"Who I am," she said, *"is Poppy Freek, daughter of the judge of Cthonos."*

"My first memory of life was at three, in the dark closet beneath the stairs where my mother and father kept me. I had several brothers and sisters, but I never saw them. But they locked something in with me then, when I was three, and it was a dog. It growled at me whenever I moved, and I felt its spit as it moved its filthy face along my naked body. I screamed and screamed, but no one would come and get the dog off me. This happened every day, each time the dog climbed on top of me or mauled me or pissed across me or nipped at my shoulders. I grew terrified of dogs, and my parents seemed to enjoy my cries and shrieks. My terror never ceased until one day the dog died. My next memory was at five, when the police came and took me from the closet. Someone photographed me for the local papers. That was in Riverside, down near Los Angeles. I never saw that house again, or my natural parents. I was put in with a family in San Jose, the Carsons. They were nice people who had a large house with a pool. I learned how to speak and read from them. Although I was behind in school, I was smart, and caught up with my age group within a year. I dreamed then that all my nightmares were behind me. I wore pretty clothes in San Jose, and the Carsons, who were previously childless, were loving and caring. That's where my life went wrong, you see. If I had never known what a decent home was like, perhaps I would've adapted better. Perhaps this"—she motioned with her hand to her mouth— "would never have been necessary."

She brought his fingers up to her lips, but Grace pulled them back.

He said, *"How can you speak so well ... in my mind, like this?"*

"I just throw the images at you," she said, "and your mind puts the symbols—the words—to the pictures. You're seeing my childhood, my life. It's you that makes it make sense. I'm only as good as your mind is, at least as far as putting the two together."

I know about your tongue, he said.

"No, you know it's gone. You don't know how they took it. You don't know why."

The Carsons. They were part of Cthonos?

"No. I told you they were decent people. They treated me decently; they taught me how to be decent . . ." But her words were running away from her, or else the images were running too fast in Grace's mind, and suddenly he saw:

A young girl, ten or eleven, getting off a yellow school bus, her books strapped together under her arm. She wears a dress and saddle shoes, and as she walks down the street, she notices the house that she lives in has a large white Volkswagen bus parked in front of it. It has a lot of bright green and yellow flower stickers on it, and she goes to look at it and then at her house. The front door has been left open, which the Carsons never do, so she walks hurriedly up the flat slate steps along the green lawn. Just as she gets to the open door, she smells something acrid—it stinks in there—and it reminds her of being three, in a dark closet in a basement. She calls from the hallway to her mother, although she has only just recently stopped calling her "Mrs. Carson," when she sees the dark liquid on the white living room carpet. The drapes have all been drawn in the house, and she then feels her heart lurch, and she is about to turn and run when she hears her mother calling from the television room, so she continues on through the kitchen and the narrow hallway. And when she arrives in the room where her mother is calling, she sees Mr. Carson, and he is sitting upright in a chair, with a wire tied around his neck and along his waist, with an extension cord wrapped around his legs. His eyes are bulging, but not with fright, for she sees that he is no longer alive. This is something she doesn't quite understand at first, because she feels like she just stepped into a dream. Mr. Carson's checked shirt is an enormous stain of muddy red, and she sees what looks like the handle of the large meat cleaver from the kitchen butcher block that Mr. Carson uses to cut the steaks and the ribs. The girl can't seem to open her mouth to scream, more out of wonder than fear because it hasn't reached her brain yet, just what this means, and she's partially gone somewhere, too, into a closet in her mind, where a dog is beginning to rise up and press itself against her.

She hears someone call to her, and she turns around.

It is Mrs. Carson, her mother, perhaps. Perhaps not.

The woman who sounds like Mrs. Carson is lying on the floor near the television. A man with long hair is leaning over Mrs. Carson. The girl thinks Mrs. Carson is naked, although she is not sure, because there is so much blood. The man with the long hair looks up at her. He is barely a man. He has the strangest face—like a boy, only older, like a little boy whose body has outgrown him. A little boy who looks like a monkey in a zoo. He grins briefly.

From between his teeth, as he grins, something is dangling.

It is a piece of human flesh.

He eats this greedily, slurping as he swallows.

All that's left of her mother's face is her eyes. Even her lips have been skinned off. The girl can't look back at her. Can't! Can't look back down at Mrs. Carson's body because it doesn't look like her anymore!

Just as the girl is about to scream, a boy, not much older than the girl, rises off the couch and comes over to her. He grabs her and hugs her and kisses her on the cheek. A man walks into the room, a man with a long white beard, and for a second the girl thinks she's dead, and this is God in a dark suit.

And as the man takes her hand in his, she hears Mrs. Carson's voice, a whimper, pleading, "Oh, God, please kill me, please kill me. Get it over with. Just kill me. Oh, God."

And then Poppy's voice, in his head, slowing down, erasing these images. . . .

She said, "They had known me from the newspaper, you see. They had been looking for me for years. They searched for their children carefully. They wanted the ones most suited to their purposes. They knew, from my early years in a closet with a dog, that I was right to join their family. It was Birdy himself who had found the clipping in the Riverside papers. About me. About the baby girl who couldn't speak, who had spent the first five years of her life locked in darkness. They believed, you see, that it created a kind of mind, a will. A resilience to torture, perhaps, as well. But more importantly, such a situation created children who might be willing sacrifices to a dark god. Let me tell you about Justice Swink. He was the man with the beard, and he looked like a god at times, a vengeful, condemning god. He created a religion from his own nightmares and hallucinations, and he found willing converts among child molesters and sadists, among people who were willing to move in darkness, who enjoyed the taste of blood and the sight of human sacrifice. Others, too, people who thought he was some kind of prophet of the last days, who saw his mysticism and power as signs of divinity. And he was a powerful man, make no mistake. He was a Rasputin, a Crowley, part showman, part mystic, part manipulator. He could find human weakness and exploit it to his advantage. I have watched while he brought a stillborn baby back to life, just with his breath, and, in doing so, converted a woman and her husband to his religion. But I have also seen him take the same woman's child, at six years old, and tie the child in a sack with the child's own pet cats, and sink them into a swimming pool. I can still remember the sound of the little boy's screams and the shrieks of those cats as they tore him to pieces in their panic while they drowned. I witnessed the killing of seventy-nine children before I was fourteen years old. Mostly in ritual. Justice and his inner circle of followers believed that the sins of man could be appeased by sacrificing innocents to this god, Cthonos. Each child would then be a servant to the god in the land of the dead."

"And he was never caught?"

"How do you catch the beloved of the devil, Mr. Grace? For although you may not believe in Cthonos, I will tell you that I do. I have seen this god. He has been conjured. Just because a power is evil, you see, doesn't mean that it doesn't exist. I became part of their family. They had special children—me, Harly, Monkey, and Birdy. Harly was found chained in a shed in Bakersfield. He was wearing a diaper at the age of eight and could only say the word 'bitch.' Monkey had been legally adopted through the foster care system. Birdy was Justice's own son. As family, I was part of the inner circle. But Justice saw how I was favored. Birdy was allowed to experiment on me, Mr. Grace, because I saw something that none of them saw, and Justice Swink and his natural-born son, his only son, did not want me to be the beloved of the god. They were jealous. They didn't want me to tell what I saw. I showed them the face of their god, you see. I showed them the face of Cthonos."

Stephen Grace whispered, "That's crazy, there's no—"

"No god? You are willing to say that, after being brought back from death?"

"That's different. That was the girl, Hope Stewart. She's infected with a virus. I must be, too."

"I have seen the dark god, Mr. Grace. Monkey called it the paingod. Those who see the god's face never forget it. It is an image beyond madness, beyond human reckoning, beyond what our feeble languages will allow. And his abode is not just the land of the dead, as Justice Swink believed. It is in the realm of pain. For the mission house became the House of Pain, and the room beneath it, the Pain Room. It is at the extremity of torture that one sees the paingod, Cthonos. It is when pain meets with a kind of pleasure, the pleasure just before release from life. I saw it when they tortured Mrs. Carson, you see. She laughed just before they killed her. She giggled hysterically when the scythe was brought down across her neck. There is really no such thing as being beyond pain, Mr. Grace. There is only the transformation that may occur, in which the fire that burns, freezes, the knife that cuts, heals. I know. Life and death are not just biological functions. There's more. I have seen it. And I showed it to them, to Justice and to Birdy, but they cut my tongue out for it. They held me down, both of them, and Harly wiped my forehead. Birdy whispered in my ear to just think of the pain as a gift, as something to cherish, and then I felt the cold metal of the scissors, and Birdy whispered, 'No one really needs a tongue. No one really needs one. Don't scream. Don't scream. It's almost over.' It was later, when I woke up, that I found myself on the table. He had drugged me, mainly with heroin, and then I had to watch while I was partially conscious, as he began cutting into my stomach just like he was already a doctor, peeling the skin back while I watched. While I watched. And then the acid. Pouring it across the open wounds. The steam, rising out of my body. Across my hands, too, destroying the muscles in my fingers, so. And the razors. All of it. The needle pressed into the soft flesh where my tongue had been. I was an early experiment of theirs, for I wasn't allowed to die. They say that pain cannot be remembered, but I will tell you: every nerve in my body remembers. My nerves are the record, if you will, of my memory. Pain is always with me. Like that dog, Mr. Grace, and the dark closet, the animal as it slobbered across the back of my neck. Others watched. Others, in Cthonos. They are still here. They still watch. Their god has not left them."

"What others?"

She didn't answer at first.

And then he knew: it came to him not in a word but in a sweeping view of a small town that lay along the gently sloping hills with vineyards and oil pumps.

Empire.

"It can't be," he whispered. "Not the entire town."

"Everyone," replied the inner voice, "hostages to Cthonos."

"I don't believe you."

She said, "believe what you like. There are the innocent few have settled here in the past five or six years, I'm sure, who have never heard the name of Cthonos. But anyone else, be he seventy or twenty, has gone through the initiation. It is a complex and arcane ritual, but it uses some of the more up-to-date techniques of sensory deprivation and suggestion, combined with a less subtle torture of living burial for each of the initiates."

"Brainwashing. Special Projects knows all the tricks, too."

"You remember Jonestown, Mr. Grace? Hundreds of people died because of their obedience to a leader? And Waco? Well, this is slightly different, although the technique is the same. Most of the residents of Empire are former members of Cthonos. Inactives. Their memories aren't too good, especially when it comes to their association with the religion. But should they divulge anything relating to Cthonos, a most peculiar thing seems to happen. It is nothing that can be medically proven. One must have faith for proof. The person experiences sharp pains in his head, just behind his eyes. I've heard it described as a feeling that some sort of worm is inside the head, like an apple, eating away at the rotting brain. Death comes within minutes, in the form of a brain aneurysm. I have seen this demonstrated. I believe it."

"What about you? Why isn't your head exploding right about now?"

"Mr. Grace, I have told you. I was adopted into the Swink family. As strange as it sounds, Justice and Loretta loved us. Torturing us was their way of expressing that love. Families can be like that, can they not? If they had wanted me dead, I would've died a while ago. They love us all—Monkey, me, Birdy, and Harly. Especially Harly. What they did to him ... I don't think Loretta Swink really thought it would kill him. I think she really thought he would survive it and learn from his error."

"How did he die?"

But the images appeared again, flipping and speeding through his head like a movie was being run behind his eyes: A boy of thirteen, with a wisp of blond mustache on his upper lip like a milk smear, with his hands kneading something—what?

The whiteness of flesh.

The body of a girl with beautiful yellow hair. Dead. He pushes long slender needles slowly into her lower lip. "Don't tell, but, see, I done stuff to her and I don't want her telling when she gets to where she's headed," he says to her, but she stares at him, almost casually, but without blinking. Each needle goes through, and the black thread follows, sewing once up, once down, through the tender, torn lips of a girl of twelve. When he is done with that, and her lips are stitched together with thread, he proceeds to sew her eyelids shut.

He turns to his sister, who is standing over him. "I did it just like Mama, din't I?"

"Uh-huh," she says, but she can't look back down at the girl. Instead she looks up around the bathroom and counts the tiles.

She can hear him as he sews another part of the girl together, down beneath her stomach in the bad place that their mama is always warning them about.

When he is done, he says, "Okay, you can look. Watch this."

The boy is almost pretty. He has strawberry-blond hair that is too long over his ears and down his neck, and his lips are red as a rose, his eyes a sparkling blue. What mars his face is a kind of indelible sorrow etched just beneath his eyes in dark circles, and a tightness around his thick lips. He has a shiny curved instrument in his hand.

"No," his sister says, "you'll get in trouble for that. It's sacred."

He smiles back at her, scythe in hand. It seems bigger than normal, maybe because it's in his hands. "Don't worry. They'll never know it's gone. Look what I can do with it."

He sweeps the scythe across the left breast, barely a nub, of the dead girl with her eyes and mouth sewn up and pierced with sewing needles.

"No blood," he says. "Ain't that something?"

"Paingod drank her blood already," his sister says.

Someone is standing at the door to the bathroom, in shadow from the hallway. It is their mother. "Playing with things we are not supposed to be playing with?" she asks, although both children know that she doesn't want an answer.

And then, their mother is calling in their two other brothers, Birdy and Monkey. Harly is crying already, saying he won't do it again, that he'll do his penance like normal, and even though his sister tries to take the blame, Harly pushes her away and swears it's all his doing.

"My needles!" Mama is crying, "my thread! Your father's scythe! I let you children play, and look how you take advantage of me!"

Harly is sobbing uncontrollably, and gets the bright idea to say, "It weren't me, Mama. It's my hands, they get ahead of my head, you know, my hands." The children know how Harly had his left hand crushed with a stone after he put his hands down into his underwear one night, but that was long ago.

"It's your hands, my poor baby," Mama says. "Of course it is. My baby boy wouldn't ever want to do anything like this. It was your hands. Good heavens, if your right hand offends you . . ."

And in one swift move she grabs the scythe from his hand and drags him over to the sink. He is crying, and she is saying "Take your punishment," and he is saying what he's supposed to, through the tears and shudders: "Gladly I come in the name of our god."

And his two brothers and one sister watch as their mother holds both of Harly's wrists together with one large, determined hand and, with the other, hacks at them with the scythe. And the blood, as it sprays from his hands, is like a waterfall to his sister, and his falling hands, as they leap to the floor, disconnected, seem like a surgeon's gloves, red-spattered and glorious.

"No more," Stephen Grace said, blocking the flow of images, "I can't— I can't take this—what I'm seeing . . ."

"I understand," Poppy said within him. "It is beyond what most men can face. Even men like you, whose job it is to kill other humans."

Even dead men must rest.

Stephen Grace tried to keep his eyes open as Poppy finished her story, but for once in his life he could not force himself into a state of wakefulness. He closed his eyes, thinking he would rest only for a few seconds, but found, behind his closed lids, the image of his wife, Anne, shimmering against a blue sky.

Happily he pursued that dream.

58

Hope

"I'M HUNGRY," HOPE SAID. SOMEONE HAD REPLACED THE blindfold across her good eye. But she could smell him, that man. That Monkey. He was standing somewhere to her left. He was working hard at holding his breath, but if she listened carefully, she could hear him.

"I said I'm hungry. I know all about kidnapping. You probably want a ransom from my father. But if I starve to death, nobody gets paid." She had watched enough TV shows to know exactly how kidnappers plied their trade. First they kidnapped you, and then they went after ransom, and then the police came just when they were about to kill you. And you lived. She was afraid this was different, though, because of seeing Iris's head. *Try to block it. Don't cry. Not allowed to cry.* Hope Stewart had awakened a few minutes earlier feeling strangely revitalized, although she wasn't sure why. She vaguely recalled a dream in which her dead brother Denny was calling to her from heaven, or from somewhere in the clouds with lots of light. Just that dream-memory was enough to make her feel stronger when she awoke. She was no longer tied to a pole, but had been laid down on a bed. The bed itself smelled of cedar chips, so she assumed that whatever quilt that had been laid across her legs had been stored in a chest for a long time. Her favorite books, growing up, had been *Harriet the Spy* and the Nancy Drew mysteries, so she was trying to piece together her environment the way a detective might.

"I won't bite you," she said to the man named Monkey, who seemed to have moved a little closer. "I'm just hungry. Do you have anything to eat?"

He whispered, "No."

"How about water?"

He said nothing.

She felt the warmth of his hands as he reached up and untied the blindfold.

She had been moved from the wine cellar into what looked to her, at first, like a long dark corridor made of stone. There was some light coming from red flares, and these gave a pink cast to the walls. She heard water dripping slowly somewhere, like there was a sink nearby. The noise echoed. The smell of dust and something like incense—the kind her father used to burn in his office when he wanted to "get rid of that lab smell." She wanted to remember precisely where she was so that if she ever got out, she could lead the cops back to catch the kidnappers. She could well imagine being featured on *America's Most Wanted* or being interviewed on *A Current Affair*—two of her favorite shows. Of course, as far as she could tell, there was only one kidnapper. While she was scared and worried about her mother, she felt something else, too—a kind of excitement, like she was at the center of some great adventure. She almost felt guilty about feeling like this, but until the car accident, nothing much interesting had ever happened to her.

The man in front of her was the same man who had helped them on the road. His red hair seemed darker, dampened and matted down. His nostrils were flared like two raisins puffed up with air. He was scowling, so that his forehead came down over his small eyes like a cliff.

There was blood drying on the edge of his lips. She noticed—*teeth marks?*—on his lower lip. He'd been biting himself.

"Your name's Monkey," she said, working hard to steady her voice. "You said it was Matt when you changed our tire."

The man said nothing.

"Is my mother okay?" Hope tried to ask this in as clear and unwavering a voice as possible, but the thought that her mother might be dead had occurred to her several times in the night. She knew that her own imagination could be her own worst enemy at times. She held her breath, waiting for his answer.

"I dunno," Monkey said.

"Did you hurt her?"

As if he were trained to be obedient, he said quickly, "No, I did not. I did what I was supposed to, that's all."

"You killed my friend."

"Nobody dies," Monkey said. "Don't you know that? They just go home. The more you suffer, the better it is later on, when you're with the paingod." He barely moved his lips when he spoke.

"I don't understand."

"I mean what I mean. Shut up. Please."

"I'm really hungry. That's my stomach growling. Hear?"

She was silent, and tried to look pained. Although she wasn't supposed to, she had sneaked downstairs one night at home and watched *The Silence of the Lambs,* so she knew that you were supposed to make your captor see you as a human being instead of as an object. In the movie, they did it by repeating the woman's name and by showing pictures of her. Hope wondered how she would do this. The idea that this man might skin her, like the man wanted to in the movie, kind of scared her, although she knew that what happened in movies never really happened in real life.

"My stomach's really growling. Honest."

"I don't hear nothing," Monkey said.

"Shh," Hope whispered. "Listen . . ."

She swallowed and prayed that he could hear the gurgling in her belly.

"They gonna feed you when they gonna feed you," he said finally, disgusted. About to turn away, he swiveled half-way around, but then turned back again to face her. "You seen the paingod, too?"

She didn't know how to answer. She said, "Please. I'm hungry. And thirsty."

And then she said, "I'll let you play with me. If you feed me."

Monkey brought her some grapes and bread and cheese, in a small paper sack. He fed her the grapes first, one after another, almost stuffing her mouth. Then the bread and cheese, washed down with warm milk in a glass bottle.

"Can I touch your eye hole?" he asked, sounding like the boy she remembered from first grade who wanted her to show him her thing after he showed her his, which she had refused to do.

But now she said, "Okay. But you have to be careful."

The closer he got to her, the worse the smell from his skin. Like baby spit-up.

His finger was almost touching her eye socket.

Hope remembered the surge of power through her when he had touched her there before.

She brought up all the anger, all the rage, she had inside her. She was going to let it loose when he touched her there.

Like an electric socket.

But before his skin touched hers, he began whimpering, lowering his hand from her face. Tears filled the lower half of his eyes, and his face was crisscrossed with wrinkles. "You're so beautiful," he whispered. "You're more beauti-ful than anyone. No matter what Goodmama says."

He covered his face with his hands.

"Touch it," Hope said.

Monkey was shivering, wiping at his tears, sniffling. "Harly was beautiful, too. His hands couldn't help it. She said we never die, but sometimes, sometimes, it's like he's not in me at all. Sometimes I'm just empty, and I think it's all pretend. Freakchild ain't like you. He's ugly and mean, and tries to hurt me. But you've got an imperfection, too, only I can tell you're like Harly. I tried to protect Harly, too, only Goodmama said he didn't die, but I never see him. And I keep asking the paingod to see him, but he never lets me."

"Don't cry," Hope said, losing the energy as she watched him. All she felt was pity.

Monkey ran his hairy arm across his face, wiping away the wetness of tears. When he looked back at her, his eyes were bloodshot. "If I let you go, will you never come back here and leave us alone?"

Hope nodded.

"I can't." Monkey shook his head. "Birdy—he's inside me—he won't let me. Everybody's all inside me," he moaned, clutching his stomach as if struck with a sharp pain, "and I can't let them out. Why won't they get out of me?"

A voice, back in the darkness, coming from where the sink with the drippy faucet was. A white shaft of light cutting across the shadowy tunnel, as if a door had just been opened.

It was the voice of a little boy.

"Why don't you touch her, Monkey? *Afraid?*"

Monkey stood still, as if paralyzed.

"I heard every single word," Lex said.

Monkey began gibbering excuses, but the boy cut him off. "Just shut up, you," he commanded. He grabbed Monkey by the wrist. Monkey reacted as if he were being handcuffed with barbed wire. Then the boy turned to Hope. "What makes you so special?"

"I don't know."

"You're not so great," he said. "You don't look so great. You don't looked like a god."

"I'm not a god."

"Well, *I* am. Watch this."

He began twisting Monkey's arm around his back. Monkey remained silent. "You know why he's not screaming, huh? Not even fighting me? Because he knows what I can do."

"Leave him alone," Hope said.

"Fuck you," Lex spat out. "You're the ugliest thing I've ever seen. You look like you got puked insteada born. You gonna cry, little girl? Go ahead, cry, baby, cry, baby. You think you're so great? You think *you're* so special?"

There was a moment of silence, as Hope listened to his shouts echo through the underground chamber.

And then he said, almost softly, "Well, look at what I can do."

And then he leaned over Monkey's arm, pressing his face against the skin just above the wrist. When his mouth came back up, it was covered with blood.

Monkey's eyes bugged out, and he began to open his mouth in a comic-book-drawing slow-motion scream.

Hope watched as Monkey's skin began ripping from his wrist up to his shoulder, exposing the dark red meat, spitting blood.

Monkey threw his head back, a howl of pure pain beginning and then dying, as the skin of his face peeled off like rice paper.

Lex finally let go of him. Monkey sprayed blood at Hope, who struggled to get away from it.

Monkey stood for a few seconds more, his heart clearly visible as more skin fell from his chest. The shredded skin lay at his feet. He rocked on the balls of his feet, as if finding his balance. This was a brief moment, for Monkey then fell in a heap, his body convulsing.

"I bet you can't do that," Lex said.

And then he turned. He looked back at Hope. "You hear that?"

She kept her eye closed. She was beyond feeling.

"You pussy," Lex said. "Can't stand the sight of a little blood. You ain't so special. We're only gonna use you like a rat. You ain't a god like me. If you can do so much, why don't you? 'Cause you just plain *can't,* that's how come."

He turned again, as if hearing a sound. "It's them."

Hope tried to put herself somewhere else in her mind.

She knew now that she was going to die. That all this—Monkey's death, seeing that girl Iris's head, and the bones—they were all preparing her for her own death.

But, like a buzzing electric wire, she felt somewhere in her that power, that energy that had not been switched off yet. What did it mean? All she knew she could do was heal some people. What did that feeling mean? It was almost like having had a sore throat and then getting better, only still feeling the soreness a little, down in her throat.

Only this feeling was in the eye socket.

"They're calling me now," Lex said, "but when we come back, we're gonna take care of you. I'm gonna do it myself. Then maybe you'll get your chance to show me your magic. If you have any. But you're weak. They're all wrong. I'll show them." He ran off, back in the direction of the light from some doorway.

Within half an hour, Hope opened her eye. The light was still on from the doorway. She tried to keep from looking down at the skinned body at her feet, but she found that she could not. It was fascinating, and no longer looked human at all. The skin, tattered, lay in a circle around the bones and organs, some yellow-white fat having slid to the side of the stomach. It was weird, but she didn't even feel sick. She felt sorry for Monkey, despite the way he had scared her and all the things he'd done. He had killed Iris, and other children, too. Monkey was a very bad man. But to die like that seemed horrible, because she had felt that Monkey was suffering from some incredible disease, the kind of disease that she could not cure no matter how much she wanted to.

She started to cry again, but then told herself, *No more tears. You're acting like a two-year-old. Never again. You need to make sure Mom is okay, and then get her and get on up to San Francisco, and go to the police and the newspapers and make sure that Dad knows you're alive. This is a crazy place, and the people here are insane. But you've got the power inside you, and you will make it through this. No more self-pity, no more crying. Grow up right now or just lie down and die.*

Hope felt the wire around her wrists, tying them together. *How am I going to get out of this?*

She began moving her wrists back and forth against the wire. Her skin burned there, and she knew she must be bleeding, but all she felt was determination. She tried to think back on better times, when her mother wasn't so frazzled, when they had spent afternoons swimming in the pool in the backyard. Her mother had taught her how to swim and then how to dive. This was like swimming, for, at first, it was like drowning, and then, gradually, as she got used to breathing differently, she could handle the lack of air, and she could move. *I can do this, too,* she thought as the slicing pain made her clench her teeth. *I'll do what I need to do to survive here, just like underwater. It won't hurt. It'll just be different.*

She sawed.

And sawed.

And sawed.

59

The Dark of the Eye

ON A LAPTOP COMPUTER, THE WORDS CAME UP:

Task Force 050
Time: 0900
  r-7 virus/rate of epidemic × population density
Endtime: 1200
Command: * s & d 1
  search & destroy/ all living organisms with
      apparent abnormality/1200
Abnormal = Death
Normal = Release/debriefing/control group

Nathan Holder leaned back and filed the information in his computer. He turned to his assistant and said, "You have the epidemic cover for the media? And the report ready for the CDC?"

She said, "Yes, and yes."

"It's going to be a tough one, with that madman running the show."

"You mean Dr. Stewart, sir?"

"I mean Grace. It's important that he's taken care of as soon as Projects moves in."

"Sir, the helicopter is waiting."

"By noon," Nathan Holder said. He thought of what would come if Stewart's strain of r-7 held. He thought of the prizes, surely, but also of what this could mean for the future of mankind. And of how this would take care of two birds with one stone, of how Stewart had presented the town as the perfect location to "accidentally" leak the r-7 virus, which would both test its effectiveness and put the blame on a group of cultists if the experiment went badly. But also, Stephen Grace would be taken out.

He embedded a further command on his computer link with the men who had set up the roadblocks around Empire:

Access: 050/classified
Eliminate Special Projects Agent Stephen Grace/
contaminant

And then, beneath this: *Search for and protect.* Then two pictures came onto the computer screen. One was of Hope when she was ten. She looked happy.

The other was of the boy, Lex. The experiment that, according to a report from Dr. Stewart from some years previous, had failed.

But Lex was alive.

The computer-generated image was from a photo that Stewart had given to Nathan after Kate had taken off with her daughter.

Nathan Holder remembered that day well: the fear he had felt at first when he was told about the kidnapping, and then the relief when Stewart got in touch with him.

* * *

"Nathan," Robert had said solemnly, "plans have changed because of your operative."

"Yes. Grace."

"Was it your orders that got him to try to murder my daughter?"

"Yes."

"I'm glad he failed. As you should be, too. If she died, what would die with her? The future of mankind. Most viruses are throwbacks to the past, a stunted evolution. But r-7 is transformational. What it can do to the genes is remarkable. If she died, where would you find another child who would take so well? Remember those others? Nineteen boys and girls. None of them took."

"I can't take him off her trail."

"You'd better. If he kills her . . ."

"He won't kill her. I'll keep him sidetracked. He'll never even get near her. Now, my friend, you must tell me what part you have had in this. With your wife."

"My wife doesn't know this yet, but she and my daughter are heading for a certain town. I am not going to divulge its name until I can be sure that you keep your word. I won't chance this experiment to the caprices of Special Projects and its various agendas."

"Understood."

"This town will be the test tube. I will release the virus. My previous experiment—"

"The boy."

"The boy, correct. He has a certain ability, not as highly developed as Hope's, but powerful nonetheless. When I give you the name of the town and its location, I want a roadblock set up so that I can put in three hours of uninterrupted work."

"Only three?"

"That's all that's necessary. And then your men can take those who have been infected into custody. As we know from our previous attempts, we have a one-in-twenty chance of success. The less hardy specimens will have to be destroyed. A few will even die natural deaths."

"Of course."

"And the two children are mine to study. Do you understand?"

"You will have complete access to the Projects labs and equipment."

"Good. When we meet again"—Robert Stewart almost smiled—"it will be a different world, my friend. I promise you that."

Were you to drive into town for the first time, you would remark first on the silence. Not just the silence of cars, of radios. But the silence of birds and the stillness of the earth as it was held, firm and solid, between the sloping hills. You would drive down the Sand Canyon Road, feeling the quiet of a small town, not knowing that its inhabitants had been struck down.

Empire was very much the same as it had been just hours before. The streets still crossed each other, neatly, with carefully folded corners. The lawns were still damp from the previous night's rain; some were well manicured and lovingly landscaped, although most were overgrown with weeds. The wedding cake houses on Main Street stood empty, unsold, with the real estate office signs thrust into their front lawns. In the center of town, the shops remained closed, and no one cooked pancakes at the Flap N Jacks. The town square with its lush park, was still a deep green, with wildflowers still blooming, soon to die with the chill that would grow and spread through the month of November. A trash can in the park had been overturned, and its contents lay beside it—a dog had, perhaps, gone digging in it for treasure. A Toyota Celica was parked on the right side of Half-Moon Street where it curved; another, an Audi, had left skid marks behind it and had crashed gently into a eucalyptus tree that guarded one edge of the park.

Yet it was a particularly lovely morning, for the early light of autumn cut in spears through the slate gray sky, and there were even patches of the clearest blue to the northwest. The trees, as was characteristic of much of California, clung to their still brilliant leaves; and the sweet scent of wild onions and eucalyptus wafted on the breeze. To the south of town, the fields of tall yellow grasses had been tamped down by the night's rain, and shone silver and gold when the sun's light crossed over the fields. The rows of grapevines that conquered the land on the north side of town were heavy with overripened fruit that had not been harvested earlier in the fall as it was supposed to have been. The skies were overcast, although the hidden sun would shortly peer out from between the clouds.

Within its first hour of release the virus had wiped out most of those who lived in Empire.

Those who still lived had not yet encountered it.

Or they were immune.

This was the way a virus worked, and this particular virus, which had been capable of infecting humans as well as birds, dogs, cats, and rodents, worked faster than most when given the opportunity.

In his house off the Sand Canyon Road, Kermit Stone had lain on the floor for nearly an hour and a half before he opened his eyes again. He remembered an enormous headache, and when his vision focused, he saw something that was difficult to identify lying a few feet from him. He had seen several victims of car wrecks in his career with the police, many worse than this.

It was Ellen Fremont, the jogger, who had come to tell him about the roadblocks outside town.

Her skin and blood and organs seemed to have been melted down by some kind of acid, leaving her skeletal remains twisted about themselves, like the boughs of a thin, gnarled tree. He knew it was Ellen because traces of her face still remained, as if pasted against her recently deformed skull.

And yet this was less of a shock or surprise to Kermit than he wished.

He called up to his son, Gus, who had been in bed when he'd come down to answer the door.

But there was no answer.

I will not go up there, he thought. *I don't want to find out anything. I don't want to know anything.* He tried the phone, but the line was down.

They had promised this.

The end of the world.

The death of the old ways.

The birth of—what? The Beast? The one who would bring about the new millennium?

On his way out of his house, he passed something else, lying dead and cut open, too, and knew this was probably the dog. He didn't glance down the block—he had no desire to find out if there were others, too. For he knew there *were* others, and whatever curse had been unleashed upon this town, perhaps, for the most part, the town of Empire deserved what it got.

Not one person in this town was innocent.

His head was pounding as if a truck were driving through it, a big Kenmore, hauling butt through his mind, skidding, speeding, rumbling. "Comes with the territory," he said to no one.

Then he did something he hadn't had the urge to do in at least a dozen years. A private compulsion, perhaps. Kermit found some matches out by the barbecue, beneath the side porch roof. He lit a match and pressed his thumb and forefinger together against it, putting the flame out. A slight burning sensation, but only for a moment. The memory of pain.

Nothing'll burn when the grass is this damp, he thought, walking back toward the front door of his house. Beyond the screen door there was that red-gray mass of leftover human. Ellen Fremont. Didn't even have much to do with the cult, except she'd married into it. Still, if you touched Cthonos, you were part of it.

He put the matchbook in his pants pocket and went out to his Bronco. He thought about checking up on Fletcher, in the small guesthouse, but decided against it. Didn't need to see old friends or family in that state.

"You were right, old buddy," Kermit whispered. "It is the end of the world."

Kermit knew of only one place left to go: his office. He could hide there, he figured, until someone, or something, came and got him.

Bram Boatwright was running. Just running as fast as he could, which wasn't terribly fast, since he was painfully aware, and had been all his life, of how physically uncoordinated he was. Never made the teams—not basketball, not baseball, not track, but, Jesus, if the coach had seen him run on this day, he would've surely been amazed. Bram had forgotten how to breathe, even, and still he was running, leaping over curbs and across mud puddles. It was difficult to run when he wasn't sure where he was running *to*, but Bram knew he just had to get the hell out of this town. In all his fourteen years he had never been so terrified.

It wasn't just his mom and how she had died that morning, or the fact that before she'd died, she'd said, "It's 'cause I was one of them. Once. My sins," she'd said, her features sliding right down the side of her face, her eyes suddenly flushing like a toilet, until there was nothing in the sockets. He'd watched enough monster movies to have seen disgusting things. He's seen all the Hellraiser movies three times over, and *The Laughing Dead* twice, so he knew about gross-outs and blood, but the movies had never been like this. The only word that came to mind was the one he'd heard people talk about when they mentioned health food or farming: *organic*. His mother's body, as it sloughed its outer layers off, was so damned *organic*. It was real skin and real blood and real goddamned organic organs! His mom would've hollered if she'd known he used the Lord's name in vain, although this time it was sort of in *vein*. He chuckled insanely to himself.

But Bram knew he was not insane, not completely.

Sure, he thought as he ran, keeping the monologue in his head running, too, *sure, I'm on the outer rim of insanity, sure. I'm dancing with the Looney Toons in the disco of the demented, but I'm not giving up my mind yet, no bitchin' way, not till I'm outta this—this—* another word came to him—*this accursed spot, this place where the sun don't shine, only maybe it's shining a little now, but I'm thinking the whole place is plunged into darkness just like Mom said when she talked about the Apocalypse, only I don't see the Four Horsemen, and where the hell is the Rapture? Take me up, Big Guy. Take me up right now, I haven't sinned much—if you don't count taking your name in vein, heh-heh. . . .*

Bram had tried the next-door neighbors' house, but he had found Mrs. Potter out at her car, already wriggling the wormy dance of the soon-to-be-dead, and her daughters in the backseat of the station wagon screaming and wailing and not wanting to move, no matter how he tried to drag them out of that car, so he had left them there and rationalized:

I'll get help, and then I'll get somebody to come back for those two little girls. They'll be okay, I just know it, but I got to get outta here or I'm gonna crawl right outta my skin just like Mom and Mrs. Potter and old man Swanson.

He had passed Swanson's Market and had forced his way through the door. Old Man Swanson had always told him, after his father died, that if he needed anything, advice or understanding, to just come on over for a man-to-man talk. But when Bram had opened the door . . . *Don't think about it. It's a slip-sliding nightmare, and if you keep running, eventually you're gonna get somewhere, but damn it, the monsters aren't supposed to get you in the daylight. They're supposed to wait until night.*

So he ran, and he ran, not really sure where he was headed, or to what.

Another area of activity in a dead town: someone had parked a car in the back parking lot of the Greenwater Motor Lodge.

60

KATE AWOKE SLOWLY, NOT KNOWING THAT SHE HAD BEEN asleep only a short while. She felt as if she'd gotten a good ten hours of sleep, and she could, as she passed from sleeping into a luxuriant wakefulness, recall a sweet dream. It took her back all those years to a happier time, when she and Ben had truly fallen in love. In the dream, they were just sitting in the cottage by the sea; she was reading, and he was making soup in the kitchenette. It was nothing more, but it left her, as she opened her eyes, with a feeling of completeness she had never felt since.

And then she felt something in her arm.

A sharp prick.

She thought she'd been stung by some insect, and when she brought her head up from the pillow, she saw a nightmare standing before her.

Robert sat on the edge of the bed with her and had thrust a hypodermic needle into her arm just above the elbow.

"Shh," he cautioned, "it's only so you'll sleep."

She twisted her arm, hard and fast, trying to get away from him. The needle broke, and its tip remained embedded in her skin. The pain was searing there. She turned to call out to Ben.

And there he lay.

"Ben!" she cried out, pushing him with her hand.

Ben lay still, face down in the pillow.

"He's out. He already took his shot, Katy, a stronger dose; he'll be out for a while. As you will be in a few minutes." Robert spoke like one of those doctors who believed that all patients were of low-normal intelligence so that everything had to be explained twice over.

"You killed him," Kate said. She reached beneath her pillow, bringing out the Smith & Wesson. She pointed it at Robert's face.

"Kate. Katy," he said soothingly, aggravatingly, "if you want to see Hope again, you'll drop that gun. Now, you're behaving like a spoiled child."

"You did all this, you bastard. You fucked my life up, you raped my daughter. You—"

Robert held his hand up to silence her. "Ever the victim, Kate. I have never touched Hope—not in that way. That was something you needed to think in order to get Hope away from the hospital. I needed you. I still need you. You are her mother. You are my wife. I know it's hard for you to understand, but all of this has been done for the greater good, as old-fashioned as that sounds. What Hope has in her, what *I* have given her, is the ability to become the prototype for a new kind of human. She is indestructible. She will never die. She has more power in her little finger than you and I have in our entire bodies. She can heal the sick, and she can cast out the sinner. She is a christ. She is a god. She is the beginning of the race of supermen. She will usher in the age of miracles."

"Jesus," Kate said, not lowering the gun, "Robert, you're talking about my baby. You wouldn't hurt her, would you? You wouldn't experiment on her like a guinea pig?"

Robert huffed, "You have always had such a small mind. Small and weak. You're addicted to your prescriptions, to your *feelings,* to your spineless, useless self. This is a step forward in evolution, Katy. Why can't you see that?" Swiftly he reached over and took the gun from her hands as if she were a small child. "I doubt you'd even know how to use this."

Kate's head began to swim, and she knew that if she didn't do something in the next few seconds, she would never get away from Robert alive. She swung out at him, pushing him down on the bed, using the leverage to get up and run for the door.

She opened it, and whether from the drug he'd given her or from her own loose grip on sanity, she saw: *her father in his wide-brimmed straw hat, his red coal eyes crisping the tips of his wiry eyebrows, his face stern and cold, a thin smile of yellow corn teeth sprouting above his chin.*

"You're nothing, you're nothing." She smashed her fists through the image, and it dissipated like fog all around her.

And then what stood beyond this vision made her sink to her knees.

"Oh, my God," she gasped, beating her fists onto the pavement, feeling the fear and guilt and anger of years explode through her very being. "Oh, my God, what have you done, Robert? You monster. You monster, Robert, what have you done with my baby?"

Standing before her, *above* her now as she had sunk down, feeling weak and enfeebled and angry beyond human rage, was a boy whose face was half melted across itself, but otherwise still resembled that of the child who (she thought) had died because of her neglect.

"Denny." Kate Stewart wept, holding her hands up and out for him, and he stepped into her embrace. "My baby."

In his hand was a small silver scythe, a shiny half-moon, which he pressed against her heart while she tasted the razor sting of death in his touch.

61

Ben Farrell awoke, thinking he'd heard something, then closed his eyes. He was so tired. He patted the bed and said, " 'S all right, Katy. Don't be afraid," and then stepped into a dream of family and friends.

He awoke once again, several minutes later, but could not sustain wakefulness.

The third time was a charm.

"Kate," he said, groggily, turning over in bed.

62

HOPE PULLED ONE HAND OUT OF THE WIRE LOOPS. SHE WAS soaked with sweat. Had been trying to free her hands for what seemed like forever, before that little boy came back. Before *anyone* came back. She had felt the warmth of her own blood as she sawed against the wires that bound her wrists, so much warmth that she didn't mind the pain of hacking into her skin. But now one hand was free.

She drew it out, and looked at her arm. Streaks of blood, but at some point the bleeding had stopped. She raised it to her mouth, and pressed her lips against the soreness. It was just like a big paper cut. Not too bad. She was able to swivel around until she was turned toward her right wrist, and this she pulled free fairly easily by lifting that wire with the fingers of her free hand.

She leaned over and undid her feet, also.

Okay, so now what, genius? She looked to the right, down the corridor, but it was not well lit. *What's down there?* she wondered. *More dead kids? No, thank you.*

The room, to the left, with its door still open.

The shaft of white light across her feet.

The boy had come out of there.

It was a chance, but where else was she supposed to head?

It's gonna be all right. Like Ben says, "Don't be afraid of the dark."

But it isn't the dark, it's what's in the dark. The nasties. The boogeyman. The maniacs who cut off each other's heads and skin each other alive.

273

She took a tentative step toward the light. She wanted to just slide into the shadows and curl up, but where had that ever gotten her? Nowhere.

I want my mother.

I want my father.

Anybody.

She felt a throbbing in her right eye socket and remembered that she had neither the patch nor the glass eye. *I must be a lovely sight—but who cares? I don't have to look at myself,* and she almost laughed to herself, but was afraid that if she did, it would mean that she was losing it.

Curiouser and curiouser, she wanted to say, because she realized that she, Hope Stewart, was Alice in Wonderland right now, having fallen down the rabbit hole. It was one of her favorite books, which she reread every year, and Hope took note that she was now playing her favorite character. Like Alice, she would get out of this tunnel and away from these crazy adventures, and then, maybe it would all turn out to have been a dream on a golden afternoon.

Yeah, right.

She stepped around Monkey's body, not looking down except to make sure she didn't put her foot smack dab into him, and then took three more giant steps toward the room with the light.

And then she heard something.

Footsteps.

Coming from the room.

A great shadow eclipsing the light.

Hope leaned into the catacomb wall—there were recesses in the wall where bones lay scattered.

Footsteps coming closer.

She pressed herself against the depression in the rock and earth. Her hands touched bone. Something else, too, something soft and cold at the same time. She prayed it wasn't a corpse.

She held her breath as the footsteps came near.

Let me blend into this wall. Let me dissolve. Let me not be seen.

She shut her good eye.

The person walking had stopped near her.

Probably seeing Monkey's corpse.

It was a man; she heard him mutter under his breath.

Hope opened her eye for a second. She thought she recognized that voice.

"Damn it, Lex, is this *your* work?"

Daddy? Hope thought, and then realized that she had actually said this aloud.

A flashlight flicked on in her direction.

She was blinded by the light.

"Hope?" her father asked. "Baby? Ah, *there* you are." He opened his arms, lowering the flashlight, and came toward her.

Hope Stewart screamed until she thought she had no voice left.

63

BEN FARRELL SAT HALFWAY UP IN THE MOTEL BED. "KATE?" He wiped sleep from his eyes. He had *really* been tired, and still felt as if a hammer had hit him over the head. *She's in the bathroom,* he told himself, wondering why the hell he didn't just go back to sleep.

But the motel room door was open.

Again, *Kate.* Went outside for something. *Too tired to worry about it.* A slight chill from the open door.

And then it hit him: he remembered hearing the door open as he fell asleep, but thinking it was a dream.

He sat straight up in bed, and as he did, he felt dizzy and nauseated. He got to his feet and slogged into the bathroom, feeling like he was running in slow motion as his stomach heaved. He lifted the toilet seat up and vomited.

"Jesus," he gasped, when he was through, but he felt a little better. He wiped his face off with a towel and then washed off under the faucet. His stomach and his arm were still sore. He had a flash of a memory: turning in bed, someone gripping his arm and stabbing him, right at the sore part of his arm. He glanced down at his arm and noticed the small red swelling. A tiny needle prick.

He'd been drugged.

Ben felt as if a truck had hit him going a hundred and ten. They had Kate.

They came and got her.

He felt sick again, and clutched the edge of the sink.

"Come on, old boy, got to help her," he muttered to his bloodshot reflection in the mirror. The bathroom began to spin as if it were on a lazy Susan, and the mirror seemed to become elongated until it looked like something out of a fun house. He reached for the doorknob, to steady himself. *Doorknob, door, wall, just hang on to where reality hits, Benjy. Slide along the wall. That's it, old boy. Make it to the bed. Good, good, sit for a second and roll across it to the other side. Now head for the outer door. You can do it. Just reach out, reach out for the knob, that shiny knob. Got it!* He held tight to the door of the motel room. The morning light broke through the clouds in jagged lightning streaks, brighter than the sunlight had ever seemed before to him, and there were liquid purples and greens from the field across the parking lot.

"Tripping," he muttered, half smiling. "I'm on a fucking trip. I can't believe it. You sons of bitches of Cthonos. Now, Benjy, don't you dare jump off a building thinking you can fly, 'kay? 'Kay?" He saw his car, parked just in front of him. The sky colors were turning, as if in a kaleidoscope, and he had to squint to see the car clearly because it disappeared every time the sun came out from behind a cloud. It looked like a housefly, his car, an orange housefly, although its wings weren't completely developed, and Ben began to laugh as he leaned against the hood.

"In-fucking-crediblicious." He giggled.

He reached into his pockets and found that his keys wriggled in his hand like bloodworms on a fishhook.

* * *

Once Ben was behind the wheel of the orange housefly and had managed to get the hooked bloodworms into the ignition, he realized he didn't know where the hell he was going.

"Fact," he said, "Kate is gone. Fact: Hope is gone. Fact: Cthonos has them. Maybe Robert, too. Fact: I need to go to the police. Where the hell are the police? Fact: I am on some drug right now, and no cop is gonna believe any of this. Especially when he sees me driving a fly." But he turned the worm-keys, and the fly buzzed to life.

On his windshield was a dead bird, or so he thought, for it looked something like a bird, but with a few minor alterations: it had been plucked and skinned.

"What a trip." He shook his head, backing out of the parking place.

Bram Boatwright stopped running when he got to AttaBurger. He was winded, and collapsed by the side of the road, not knowing whether to laugh or cry. The wind actually smelled clean as it shifted, and dabs of rain fell on his head from a willow. He was about to laugh, because as he sat there, he saw an orange Volkswagen bug swerving toward him, and Bram half expected a dead man to be driving it. To make sure he didn't get hit, Bram leaped up and stood back near the low brick wall in front of AttaBurger so that if the driver crashed into something, it would be the wall.

But the Volkswagen slowed down, and the man, his dark hair all wet and curly with sweat, his eyes wild to the point of being bug-eyed, leaned out the window and was about to say something, but barfed instead.

"Oh, gross." Bram gagged, turning away. For some reason, puking seemed worse than what he'd been stepping around all morning.

He heard the man say, "Sorry, kid, but somebody drugged me. You know how to get to the cops?"

Bram ran around and got into the passenger's seat. "Go," he said.

The man looked at him strangely.

"You really *are* drugged."

"Coming out of it fast, though, kid, with all this vomiting. I don't even think I'm driving a fly anymore. Which way?"

"I doubt there's much the sheriff can do. Just drive, drive

out of this town, mister. Let's go, let's go! Can't you see what's happening? Jesus, look around!" Bram pointed to the road ahead.

The town was quiet.

"Look, kid," Ben said, "you're gonna have to tell me where to find this sheriff."

"You look," Bram yelled, and then calmed. "My mom was right, it's Judgment Day. Jesus, I thought she was a lunatic about it, but, man, get me out of this place, 'cause judgment's gonna come down hardest here!"

"I'm not driving until you calm down."

Bram said, "You're probably one of them."

"One of who? Cthonos?"

Bram was silent for a moment. There were no tears in his eyes. "It's quiet right now, mister, because just about everybody's dead. I bet Sheriff Stone's dead, too. This ain't a ride at Disneyland. Look, mister, all I know's this: my mother used to be a hippie, and then she was born again, and she always told me she was gonna burn for the sins she committed, and how what my father did—he's dead now—makes me the mark of that sin. But you don't have to be a genius to know about this town. What it used to be. Jesus, you can figure it out by reading the brochures they give out at the Chamber of Commerce. Before *they* came, this town was just a bunch of old farts dying. The religion may have ended, but they're all still here. I could never figure that part out—how my mother hated them but how she wouldn't leave, either. And now. Now it's happening. Exactly what she said would. How God would destroy this town and all its creatures."

And then the boy began to cry.

After a minute Ben said, "They took my ... daughter. And my best friend. I have to find them. Where's the police station?"

Bram almost laughed. "You won't like what you're gonna find there."

"Just show me where it is."

"It's not much of a station. Just a little office. But, okay. And then get me out of this place before it starts to cave in. You sure you can drive?"

Ben said, "I'm sobering up *real* fast."

64

FLETCHER MCBRIDE DID NOT SLEEP AT ALL, KNOWING THE end was near. He sneaked out of his bed after Kermit Stone had worked so hard to get him there the previous night, and he went up to one of the highest points in town. He had to climb up the side of one of the oil pumps to get there, and he sat and watched the spectacle of the destruction of Empire's residents from that perch.

In his right hand he held the small hand ax that had carried him through so much in life.

He sniffed the air for a scent of that child, the one that Monkey had brought.

Her scent, which was strange and wonderful, came at him strong, like the smell of fear.

65

Poppy Freek knew she couldn't do it all by herself. She held the bones of her lost children in her arms, and shivered. *Seen the paingod too many times. I know what he can do.* The not-dead man named Stephen Grace was already awake again after having rested briefly.

"Can't sleep yet, can I?" he said.

Dead men don't need much, I reckon, Poppy said inside him.

"I need to get this girl. There's going to be an epidemic, if—"

Already is.

When this thought cut through his brain, Grace swore, and pounded the dirt around him. All those tapes. The great experiment of Dr. Robert Stewart. And Nathan Fucking Holder. He remembered the voice on the tapes saying, over and over, "We must expand into each other. The line between life and death will be taken to one remove." It was all there. And Holder hadn't even needed to get the tapes in his hand, that son of a bitch. All he needed to do was let Stewart do his thing, get his daughter to this town, this town that no one in Special Projects had seemed to have any prior knowledge of. Not even on the damn computer, Holder had said. Just a small town on the edge of the California nightmare.

"Look, Poppy, I have to get out there now." Grace began moving toward the tunnel that would take him up and above ground.

No. She touched his shoulder. *While you slept, I went outside. There are soldiers everywhere on the outskirts of town.* As she touched him, he saw the moving pictures in his head, the devastation of three square miles of a small town, the dead and dying, and in the distance on the crest of a ridge, the dark green trucks and the men in white uniforms wearing masks, all seen in a single moment.

"Sons of bitches," he muttered.

Poppy pointed down farther through her tunnel. *It becomes rock walls soon, and then the catacombs begin. We must go there. To the room beneath the mission house. The Pain Room.*

66

IN THE CATACOMBS, AFTER HOPE STOPPED SCREAMING, HER father lifted her up.

"Hope, I love you more than anything in the world." Robert Stewart hugged his daughter against him as he carried her toward the lighted room, and he felt it, too, in his deepest being, a love for this girl in his arms. She was not even his flesh and blood, like Lex, but something more. He remembered changing her diapers, holding her as a six-month-old, helping Kate give her a bath for the first time. He remembered how proud he was when she took her first step, and how shocked he was to feel fatherhood hit him squarely when she first called him "Dada." And then, as she grew, even when she looked like her natural father, how he had loved her and hugged her just so when Denny had been taken away. How he had helped her memorize her multiplication tables not so long ago, and how thrilled he was when she showed an interest in science. He remembered when she was seven and held her hands out wide on Father's Day and said, "I love you *this* much!"

Even the day he had operated on her to remove her right eye, the day that the Special Projects assassin had taken her out to kill her, and had failed, as Robert had known he would, because she could not be killed, not this one, not his girl. He recalled the sweet smell of her face as he bent over her in the lab. While she was out with morphine, he had just popped the diseased eye out from its socket. Even then, as painful as his job was, he knew that he loved her in a way that beyond any kind of love he had felt before.

He was only human, after all.

He smelled her dark hair as if it were perfumed, and he pressed his lips against her forehead. "My little girl, I am so proud of you, how you've come through all this."

She glanced up at him, opening and closing her mouth to cry out, but nothing came from her throat. She looked like a baby bird, opening and closing its beak for its mother or father to feed it.

A child's mind is less delicate than most grown-ups think, and often the traumas of childhood are stored away for an older self to handle. The child just observes and records and does what she can to survive.

Hope said several prayers under her breath, mainly the Lord's Prayer, since she knew it by heart, and also the Pledge of Allegiance, although her mind was racing so quickly that she just had to think the first two words of each and the rest would be spelled out in her head so that they overlapped each other. Part of her mind acknowledged that this was her father, who had finally come to rescue her.

Another part sensed that a monster was holding her, pressing his face against hers, a monster who was dressed up just like her father, in a dark suit, with a gold tie clip and a dark green tie. Even the monster's face looked like Daddy.

And it was Daddy.

She knew it.

But it was something else, too.

She felt a throbbing in her right eye socket.

Something was wrong with him. Some kind of sickness.

Why hadn't she felt that before?

But it was faint, the throbbing, and it seemed to be going away.

She would have to force it.

They were almost to the room; she heard other people in it.

Power.

She tightened the muscles around the empty socket.

Start up. What is it? Inside him.

"Pigeon." Her father called her by her pet name and kissed her brow just above the empty socket, above the dark of the eye.

And Hope Stewart felt as if she'd been thrown down a flight of stairs, as his lips met the socket.

The face of the razor man, like in her dreams, like when she knew she hadn't cured anyone. It was in her father. It was part of him—shiny razor smile, the blood on his teeth like a man who had just eaten an animal raw, the gnashing razor teeth, the skull head flashing with a brown-yellow fire at the back of its throat, the spinal cord slashing like a live electrical wire, spitting sparks ...

And then her father's lips slipped from her brow, down her nose, to her mouth, and he pressed them against hers and she smelled his cologne and his breath, and she pulled back from his kiss because it was making her sick.

"Pigeon," he said, "come to Daddy," and he pressed his lips to hers again, but she pushed him away and reached up to scratch at his face with all her might.

Lex stepped out from the room. "She ain't so special."

Behind him stood Loretta Swink, her hand on his shoulder. "Hush, now, Lex. She's your sister."

"Why's he love her more than me?" Lex said.

"Fathers and daughters are different from fathers and sons. It's a special bond. Like me and you, sweetie."

"She's not really his daughter, anyway," Lex pouted. "I'm his son. Why does he love her more?"

"Oh, just shut up, you," Loretta said more gruffly. "After what you did to my Monkey ..."

"His time had come," Lex said defiantly. "He's on the other side now, where he belongs."

Robert slapped Hope hard across the face. She stopped scratching him; she cowered. "You're going to have to do a little growing up right now, pigeon. You have in you a special gift. You are no longer merely human. Your blood has changed. Even your brain has changed to some extent. You are a carrier of a most rare and wonderful miracle. But you need to accept it, and to use it wisely."

The smell was the strongest here, as Hope was carried into the room, passing by the old woman and the boy named Lex. It smelled like rubbing alcohol and formaldehyde, and something else, too. Some kind of decay, sort of like the way Monkey smelled after Lex took off his skin.

The Pain Room was beneath the wine cellar of the mission house. It was a long rectangular room and had been used in centuries past as a place to store the older wines that the Spanish monks had pressed. Later, when the plague had come upon the locals, it was used as a storage room for the newly dead, before they were taken into the catacombs. But in the past twenty years, it had been remodeled. Fluorescent lights shone from its plastered ceiling, and its original bricks were covered with drywall. There was a long sink on one side of the room, and above the sink, shelf upon shelf of jars, large and small, containing bits of flesh suspended in solution. A long metal table stood in the center of the room; another table nearby, this one with drawers. A file cabinet, a computer terminal, and a boxlike walk-in refrigerator. The room was not much different from the laboratory Robert had built in his house in Devon so that he could take work home with him. Other lights, brighter than the fluorescents, hung suspended over the medical examining table, and there was another entrance to the pain room, an ordinary door, but with a small square window, as if it belonged in a classroom.

And then something else, too, something unusual: near this door was a small altar of sorts, a concession to some religion.

On the altar was a photograph of an old man with a flowing white beard.

Garlands of dried wildflowers lay across the altar, which had been constructed of human skulls, with a plank laid across them and a red cloth spread over the top.

Above this, on the wall, was a symbol, with dark brown letters beneath it. It had been painted by a true artist, for there was shading and contrast and crosshatching to create an illusion of depth. The symbol resembled an eye.

But the most remarkable thing about the room was the series of grease marks on the walls, the handprints and stains where the scalps had been rubbed against the walls.

The imprints of children's flesh as they tried to get away from whoever, or whatever, was in the room with them.

Monkey's word in Hope's mind: *paingod.*

Something wrapped in a sheet lay beside the examining table. She knew it was a corpse. She knew that her death would come here.

She thought to herself: *Hope Stewart is going to die in the Pain Room. Just make it quick. Make me go fast. Please God, please God, if they kill me, let me not feel it.*

She watched as Lex went over to the sheet-shrouded body, untangling it. The sheet was white, but a splotch of blood stained each layer. First she saw a woman's hand, its palm outstretched, and then the woman's arm, leading up to the silky edge of a slip, leading up to a shoulder, leading up to golden blond hair.

Her father whispered in her ear, "Pidge? It's Mommy, see? She's dead. But you—you and Lex—can bring her back. You want that, don't you, pigeon? It's the reason why you have your gift. So you can do more than just heal people, sweetie. You can conquer death."

Lex said, "Hey, you," and Hope glanced over at him and behind him, at the old woman with the poofy blue hair and the big round glasses, and then back to the boy. "Watch this," he said. He had some kind of curved knife in his hand, and he reached down to her mother's body and sliced across her shoulder. "She don't feel nothin'." Lex giggled. "It's what happens when you go over to our god. No pain at all, but you know, it takes pain to get you there."

The old woman came around and pulled Lex up by the scruff of his neck just like he was a puppy. He dropped the blade; it clattered on the floor. "You can't run things the way you like, Lex. Lord, you're just like your grandfather, and you're the spit'n' image of your pa." She let go of him and nudged him toward his sister.

Hope's father set her down on the floor. She was barefoot, and the floor was freezing. She shivered, and wasn't sure if it was from cold or terror. But she felt a weird calm, and an expression that Ben had used came into her head: *All bets are off.*

"My name's Loretta, angel," the old woman said, and Hope noticed that she had three big hairy moles to the left of her nose, and her eyes, through the glasses, were enormous, with slit-shaped pupils, like a cat's. She bent down near Hope, placing her hands on Hope's shoulders, steadying her. "This is all sudden," Loretta said, "but we are your family. I am your grandma, and Lex here, he's your brother."

"No, you're not," Hope whispered, and then repeated herself louder.

Loretta didn't smile kindly the way a grandma might, but she did smile, a sort of wild, nasty grin, like she had just eaten a canary. She gestured toward Lex, and he came to her side. She wrapped one arm around him, keeping her other hand on Hope. "Look into his eyes, angel. Look into Lex's eyes." She stroked Hope's hair, and as much as Hope wanted to pull away, she could not.

Lex didn't grin; he scowled. He opened up his hand to her, and Hope saw, within the palm of his hand, a human eye. "Look into my eyes," he echoed.

She saw a crib. A mobile swinging above the crib. A mobile of the silver crescent moon and three stars twinkling. Goodnight, Moon, *she read to the baby in the crib. A pale blue blanket with lace trim. And her doll, Nina, which she'd put into bed with the baby to keep him company.*

She looked at the baby's peach face, his eyes sparkling like it was Christmas morning.

"Puh," he said, which was his way of saying her name.

"Hope," she said, pointing to her chest. Then, reaching down to touch his hand, "Denny. Deh-nee."

She giggled, and he smiled like he was opening the best present under the tree.

"I love you, Denny, I love you, love you, love you. When

*you get older, I'll take you to the park for walks. And I'll
teach you how to read* Winnie-the-Pooh. *We'll make puppets
and stuff. I can't wait. You're the most beautiful baby in the
whole entire world. I love you," she said, and then turned
around.*

*Her mother was in the doorway, looking exhausted as
usual. She had tears in her eyes and a glass of water in her
hand, which usually meant she'd just taken another pill.
"Hope, it's time for bed. Leave the baby, okay? Mommy's
tired."*

*"Okay," Hope said, and felt the squeeze of Denny's small
fingers on her thumb. . . .*

Like a rock breaking through a glass window, Lex's hand,
with its unblinking eye at the center of the palm, broke
through this vision. He held it up in front of Hope's face.
"We are children of Cthonos, all of us, the all-seeing even
in darkness."

Loretta said, "Lex is your brother. Denny was his human
name. But Lex is the name of his destiny."

"No," Hope said, "you're not Denny. Denny had pretty
hair. He had normal eyes. He was *normal*. He looked like
Mom. He didn't have all that—"

Her father said, "I know he looks different now. Even his
eyes. Your right eye would be like that, pigeon. I hope you
can forgive Daddy. But the virus shows up in the eyes, if
your body doesn't fight it off well. It showed up only in one
or yours, and to be safe, I had to remove it. But you didn't
feel any pain, sweetheart, because I put you to sleep for a
while. You handled r-seven better than your brother. Or
perhaps I should say, in a different way. Your body fought
off infection, and it took. It took with you. You know how
you can heal people, sweetheart? You can do other things,
too. And now that Lex is here, the two of you together can
do so much."

"You killed Mommy."

"We've stopped Mommy's heart, pigeon, that's all. There
is no death. Not really. You can bring her back. You want
to try, pigeon? It's just like healing someone, only different.
You and Lex, both. The two of you together, the power you
both have now. It can work miracles. Come around. Put all

your energies together. It's all right, pigeon, you want to bring Mommy back, don't you? You wouldn't let Mommy die, would you?"

Loretta Swink backed away, as if she had more important things to do. She waddled over to where Kate lay, and she squatted down and hefted the corpse up into her arms.

"Lex, honey," she said, "come help Grandma get the lady up on the table."

67

ABOVE THE SURFACE OF TOWN, WHERE THE STREETS WERE quiet and empty, an orange VW Beetle chugged and sputtered as it drove halfway across the park, skidding on the wet grass, and then over the curb.

Ben parked the Volkswagen up on the curb. His dizziness and nausea had subsided, although he was still having trouble with depth perception. The sky continued to look like a kaleidoscope of blues and yellows and purples, with the sunlight white jagged lightning bolts; he could, if he thought about it, still see the multiple eyes and translucent wings of the orange housefly that the car had become; and he heard distant voices, as if he'd become a receiver for a radio station. He wasn't completely sure that the teenage boy sitting next to him—clinging to the dashboard for dear life while Ben had taken his zigzag route through Empire—was for real, but he thought, *Hey, go with it.*

As Bram unbuckled his seat belt, he said, "I can't believe I lived through that." He pointed to a small building made of sandstone-colored brick. The window sign read: Empire County Sheriff. "If the sheriff's around, he's in there."

"Okay, then," Ben said, breathing the cold air in deep. It was a little like drinking a cup of strong coffee, and the air seemed to revive him.

Ben managed to get out of his side of the car without too much difficulty, although Bram had to run around to the side and prop him up a bit because his legs felt wobbly. But it was coming back to him, his sense of reality. The colors of existence began fading to their normal hues, and he no longer thought he'd been driving a housefly. Maybe all that retching had sobered him up. The two of them hobbled up to the door to the building like drunks suffering from delirium tremens.

Ben tried the door, but it was locked.

"Dang," Bram said, shaking his head. "Even *he's* not here. Dead or gone. If he's lucky." The teenager had cooled down a bit, and Ben wondered if his serenity wasn't some kind of delayed shock at the morning's events. How many kids would so quickly get over what this kid had seen? Ben himself had experienced delayed shock back when he had walked into the old Victorian in San Francisco and had found the dead children. The horror of that scene hadn't really hit him for three days, but when it did hit, it was like a jackhammer coming down on his life, his beliefs, his understanding of the world, everything. He had ended up in therapy for nine years, and had only gotten out because he hadn't been able to afford it anymore. But those three days before the shock hit: he remembered them well, because it was as if he were pretending that what he had seen—the pools of blood, the children's hands and heads, the words and symbols carved into their bodies—was perfectly natural. He had seen human action as merely stimulus and response. He had even excused the murderers, temporarily, by thinking about what a wild animal man could be. He had been a camera, too, just taking pictures in his mind of the event, not really trying to comprehend it.

I'm doing it now, and so's he. He put his hand on Bram's shoulder just so the kid could feel another human being somewhere down deep inside there. *We'll break down on our own time. When this is over.*

They were about to turn away from the door when the knob turned, and there were two clicks.

The door opened.

A man stood there.

He had wise old eyes sunken into a forty-year-old face. His hair was short and slicked back with sweat. His face was dry, though, and his lips were white and cracked, as if he'd tasted the stress of the world. Ben looked from the face to the small badge: Sheriff Kermit Stone, Empire, California.

He looked back to the face, to the eyes.

Some have said the eyes were the windows to the soul, but with this man, it was not true. His eyes were pale green flecked with brown in the iris, bloodshot along the whites.

Ben saw there was no soul. He said, "You goddamn son of a whore." Ben said this with as much anger as was in him, but also with defeat.

Bram looked from one man to the other, scrunching up his eyebrows in confusion.

"Hello, Ben," the sheriff said.

"Siggie." Ben registered no surprise. This had all been so dreamlike and so nightmarish. He tasted something bitter in the back of his throat. If he had been under the influence of some powerful drug, its spell was broken in that moment. "Well, Siggie. Amazing. Really fucking amazing. I thought you went to Ecuador or Tierra del Fuego. I thought you and your rooster stepped off the face of the earth. How stupid of me."

Kermit Stone's voice was equally devoid of emotion. "Ben. How many years? So many. You remember my rooster. He was a good bird. They killed him. They killed everything I loved. I just wish to hell they'd killed me." A slow flow of blood dripped from Kermit's right nostril; his forehead wrinkled, as if he were experiencing some kind of migraine. "It's okay. It's okay. You know I can't tell."

Of course Ben knew. He remembered how the police had rounded up some of the members, and how they preferred to go to jail for life rather than say anything, for fear that they would die of a brain hemorrhage or something. Part of the "justice of Cthonos."

"Siggie. You motherfucker."

The sheriff shook his head, glanced from Ben to Bram. A tear of blood appeared in the corner of Kermit's left eye. "The name's Kermit now. Renamed for a little green frog who had more guts than I'll ever have. Last name is Stone, because of my heart. I even raised one of theirs as my son, Ben. I think he's probably dead now. Nice boy, too. It's been a nice charade. For a few years, anyway."

"You've got to tell me, Siggie—Kermit—whatever the hell your name is. I have a little girl. They have her and her mother. Cthonos has them. Who is Cthonos? Where are they?"

Bram spoke up, "My mother's dead. Sort of. My cat. My mother. Her birds. She looks like a skeleton, with all the—the—" The boy looked like he was about to start crying, but he bucked up. "Like a skeleton with all the organs, like the visible man, but her legs melted or something. I don't know."

Kermit Stone kept his eyes on Ben. "If I tell you, I'll be dead in five minutes flat."

"How do you know that?" Ben felt his blood racing and his heart beating like it was trying to get out. *Have to save Hope and Kate. Have to—*

"I've seen what they can do," Kermit said, with some difficulty. He pressed his hands to his forehead. The single blood tear slid down the side of his face. "I don't want to die, see, Ben. I know what comes after. I know who my judge will be."

"How do you know that? How do you even know for sure you'll die if you tell me anything? God, the few members that the cops rounded up back then—after they told, they committed suicide. They didn't die. It was all in their heads; it wasn't anything *real.*"

"I just know."

"Look, if you don't tell me, Siggie—Kermit—I'm going to fucking rip your heart out in ten seconds. Ten, nine, eight—"

But Ben stopped counting.

"Forget it," he said, "what's a couple more deaths on your head after all those children you helped kill?"

Kermit glowered at this. "I didn't kill them, Ben. You were my friend. You *knew* me. I couldn't have killed them. I didn't know until after . . . and then it was too late."

"Siggie." Ben shook his head, about to turn around and walk out the door.

"Wait," Kermit Stone said. He closed his eyes, as if saying a prayer. "All right, I'll tell you. But I will be dead. I guess I don't care. Cthonos owns the mission house. Justice Swink's widow, Loretta, lives across the road from it. They do their business in the catacombs underground. For what it's worth, I've never been down there. I never helped kill anyone. But, Ben, they own Empire. Hell, they *are* Empire—Loretta and her son Birdy."

"Birdy?"

"Her only natural son. She always had other children. Most disappeared as time went by. Birdy doesn't live there with her, but he comes back every so often. And now, with this happening, this end-of-the-world shit, I know he's here. That man had a *presence*. Birdy was his nickname; he used to keep pigeons when he was a kid. Killed 'em all one day. Hated birds. Experimented on 'em all the time. Went on to become some kind of doctor, but that nickname stuck. Birdy. Short for Robert." Then, almost as an afterthought, Kermit said, "Well, I guess I didn't die from the telling of that tale, did I?"

"You've been afraid of nothing all your life," Ben said. "They brainwashed you and you took it. Jesus."

Bram said, "I know where the Swinks live."

"All right," Ben said. "You take me there, and then we'll get out of Empire."

Kermit, head in hands, said, "There's no way out. There're roadblocks on every side of town. Must be because we're contaminated. You see the bodies yet, or are you blind? Whatever they released, it's hit every living thing."

"Not you," Ben said, "and not me. Not this boy."

"It's only a matter of time." Kermit slammed his fist against the wall.

Ben heard footsteps—someone running, heading toward them. He turned, and as he did, Bram cried out, "It's the psycho!"

Kermit said, "That's no psycho. It's just Fletcher. Ye gods and fishes, Fletcher McBride, how the hell did you survive through all this?"

The man coming up behind Ben was swinging a hand ax like it was a toy. It whiffled through the air. Fletcher McBride's nostrils were flared, and his expression was one of intensity. "It's my wild-animal nature, Kermit, you know that. Now, all of you, get it in gear. We've got to go get the Beast of the Apocalypse and fight the good fight."

68

THE CATACOMBS SEEMED ENDLESS, BUT POPPY WAS GUIDED by a fierce internal light. Stephen Grace could practically feel it emanating from her like an aura. If someone had told him twenty-four hours before that he would believe in anything like this, he would've laughed. But when a man comes back from the dead, he cannot afford disbelief. He was overwhelmed by the raw power of life, of *feeling* alive, as if he had truly been reborn, carrying none of the internal baggage he had lugged around with him all those years. Life seemed sacred to him, for he now understood its fragility. He had lost it and had been given a second chance. Now he was immortal perhaps. Undying. Not a zombie but a breathing human.

Poppy held his hand to guide him along as they walked, and as they turned corners or headed upward along a rough-hewn quarter, he caught glimpses of images from her mind, and he saw the faces of the children who had died, mangled and tortured until the end of their young lives. He felt a compassion he hadn't known before. Even in his love for Anne he'd felt nothing like this, this feeling of being connected to all that lived and breathed, as if their lives and his were intertwined, one and the same. The men he had killed—each of them was *him* also; he and they were one and the same. There was no separation except through the false gods of the senses. All humans came from the source of life itself, the fountain of eternity pouring forth. The reverie was brief, and later Grace might forget how all-encompassing it had seemed, might even consider it a brief madness on his part, given the journey he had taken through this underworld.

Brilliant red flares lit the way through a long corridor that grew wider; Grace no longer had to hunch over beneath low ceilings.

Poppy gripped his hand tighter.

The Pain Room. This is the place.

Ahead was a closed door with a small square window set a quarter of the way down from the top.

Grace dropped Poppy's hand, and it was as if an electric current had died. He reached into his pocket to feel for the Uni. It was there.

How can I kill, knowing what I do about life? he thought.

And yet he knew he must.

Still.

The girl was still a bomb.

She would destroy other lives, as would the followers of Cthonos.

As would Special Projects.

All of it had to be stopped.

Stephen Grace knew his destiny had not altered.

Assassin, the voice in his head whispered.

69

KATE STEWART LAY DEAD UPON THE MEDICAL EXAMINING table in the pain room. Her face still had some color in it, and her eyes, mercifully, had been closed.

Loretta said warmly, "She's at peace, child. Don't fear for her. Her pain was brief."

Lex grinned.

Robert Stewart led Hope over to the table.

Lex went around to the other side.

"I want you to touch her, pigeon. There, over her heart."

"Daddy," Hope began to protest.

"Pigeon," her father said, "this is serious business. You are very special. Remember in the hospital? All those tests? And how you healed that little boy? It's because you've taken a kind of vaccine. Just like your polio vaccination and the measles shot. But this one went into you, and your body began to manufacture it. You can give it to other people. It's a good thing. No one ever needs to be sick again or to die."

Hope looked from her mother's calm face to her father. *Mom was right. Dad's crazy. All these people are crazy. He's a psycho. No way out.* But her father's words seemed to have some truth to them. As frightening as her healing power was, she knew that it could mean good things for other people. She sensed that her brother—if Lex really *was* her brother—couldn't do it right, not like she could. *Maybe I inherited what Granny Weeks had, and this vaccine they used on me made it stronger.*

"Touch Mommy's heart," her father said, lifting Hope's

limp hand and guiding it to the place where her mother's slip was torn and blotched with blood. "Heal her, Hope. I love you; I want you to believe that."

Hope began crying without realizing it, until her good eye got all blurry.

Loretta snapped, "He won't want this body if it's started rotting."

Hope looked up at her father. His face was a blur, just like everything else in the room. "Who?"

Robert Stewart glanced at Loretta, shaking his head. Then he stroked Hope's hair. "Bring Mommy back," he whispered.

Lex reached across the corpse and put his hand over Hope's, pressing Hope's fingers into her mother's wound.

Hope felt her skin get warm, and then very hot, until she felt like she was made of wax and was melting. She looked over at Lex, and he was squishing his face all up like he wanted to force his brains out his ears.

She heard what sounded like car tires screeching.

And then she heard the voice that she always heard in that small dark room in her head, the soft lullaby voice that whispered to her, *"Perfect."*

She saw *the butterflies, all orange and yellow and blue, their wings moving slowly back and forth, back and forth, like kites being buffeted by a March wind. Then they blew apart, as if the wind was too strong. Hope was standing alone on a hillside with endless yellow fields stretching out before her, and behind her, a dark night.*

"Perfect," the voice said, and she recognized it.

"Mom." She looked down the hill, and there in the tall yellow grass her mother stood, wearing her slip, only there was no blood. No rips. No pain in her eyes.

Her mother waved to her and then began walking farther into the field. Hope tried to run toward her, but she couldn't move her legs. When she looked down to see what was wrong with her legs, she realized that she wasn't there at all. She had consciousness of being there, but she had no physical body.

She could no longer distinguish her mother from the lazily waving grasses with the butterflies flying north toward the horizon.

But something was behind her in the dark night.

And then she knew where she was.

She was in the realm of death. At the crossroads.

She looked into the darkness and saw nothing, but she heard this thing coming toward her, like a horse, its hooves pounding across an echoing sea.

And then the face, the eyes of burning coal, the razor-shiny grin, the human-skull necklace beneath its bony chin.

Paingod.

Cthonos.

The burning face of pain.

It moved toward her swiftly, and she tried to move from the spot, but the more she wanted to, the more she seemed to be drawn to the paingod....

Hope came back to full consciousness. She was in the Pain Room again, and she pulled her hand away from her mother's heart. Her fingers were coated with blood. She pushed Lex's hand away.

Her mother's eyes opened, and she smiled.

Eyes like burning coals.

70

THEY HAD TAKEN KERMIT STONE'S PATROL CAR, BECAUSE IT seated everyone more comfortably and because Ben insisted someone else do the driving. Bram sat in back with Fletcher McBride, eyeing the hand ax as if at any moment the madman might lift it up and slice it through Bram's neck. No one spoke on the way to the mission house, and were you to climb inside their minds, you would have found a blank screen, as if what they were about to face was beyond imagination.

Except for Fletcher, who imagined himself a berserker, ready to go hog-wild in battle against the Prince of the World, the Lord of the Flies, the Whore of Babylon, and the Beast, for he was, after all, insane by anyone's standards.

Ben was out of the car first, and Kermit said, "Ben." The sheriff made no move to get out of the black-and-white police car. "Ben," he repeated, not looking him in the face. He stared directly ahead, out the windshield. "I can no more go down there than I could walk into fire."

"I know," Ben said.

"I wish I could."

"But you can't. I understand."

Fletcher got out from the backseat and said, "I know how to find them. I can smell it. Strong smell."

"Smell what?"

Fletcher said, "The Beast. The girl. She stinks of the Day of Judgment."

Ben looked at Kermit.

Kermit finally nodded to him. "I've known Fletcher long enough. You can trust that he'll do the right thing, Ben. Believe me."

"I wish I could."

Bram said, "I just want to get out of town."

Kermit looked at him in the rearview mirror. "We all do."

Fletcher howled.

Ben said, "Wait here, at least for twenty minutes. If we're not back, take off, do whatever. But if we come back, we may need your help still. I remember that in the olden days, Siggie, you had quite a reputation as an arsonist. I think we're going to have to burn this place to the ground. Leave nothing for those Company goons to get their hands on."

"Well," Kermit Stone said, "to be honest, Ben, I still like a good fire now and then."

71

POPPY DID NOT HESITATE. WHEN SHE REACHED THE DOOR SHE flung it open. Grace was behind her, drawing his Uni. He felt something, like an invisible wind, when the door opened, an electric current emanating from the room, and for a moment he thought he saw a boy of about seven, and a girl of nine, and then several other children, behind them, all standing in the room, their eyes sunken, their skin pale, their hair greasy and matted as if they'd been living in dirt.

The dead. I'm one of them, too.

But the vision exploded before him, and instead he was looking at a medical workshop. He could well imagine that once upon a time, in a simpler form, it had been the torture chamber where Poppy had undergone radical surgery.

Poppy, ahead of him, froze in her tracks as soon as she set foot in the room.

It was warm there, and it seemed to have a different atmosphere from the rest of the catacombs.

There were five people.

Hope was standing just a few steps ahead of Poppy. She had not even turned around to see the intruders.

Kate Stewart was lying on the table, although she began to sit up, rising.

A deformed boy and a woman of sixty or so. Grace assumed they were the boy Lex and his grandmother, Loretta Swink, the widow of the founder of Cthonos. Poppy had told him of the power that Lex had; Grace wondered what it would be like when combined with Hope's own erratic talent.

And then, Dr. Robert Stewart.

Birdy.

Stephen Grace knew him from his pictures. Dark-haired and handsome, but with something in the eyes, those cold gray eyes, as if somewhere, down there, he was dead.

Given the way things are, maybe he is.

Dr. Stewart said, "Come in, sister. You're just in time for a miracle."

Just then Kate Stewart put her arms out for her daughter.

It's not Mommy. Not anymore, Hope told herself as she backed away. She heard the door behind her open, but she didn't look to see what other terrible people were coming. *Mommy died. That's what that vision meant. She went across the fields to heaven or someplace. Maybe she'll be reincarnated. This is that thing—the paingod, the razor man, the bad thing that eats away at people's insides. Don't let it be Mommy. Let Mommy feel no pain. Let her be somewhere safe, with God, or being born into some baby, or even sleeping somewhere peaceful and cool. Don't let her be in that body with that thing.*

Loretta Swink raised her ham-hock hands in the air, her breasts heaving like melons falling off a fruit cart, and cried out, "It's him. It's God!"

Hope could smell that bad thing, too. Its breath was like rotting flesh.

Robert Stewart held his hand up to warn off the intruders. "Poppy," he said, "stay back."

"Paingod," Lex said, as he, too, backed away from the dead woman as she stepped down from the examining table.

"Incarnate," Robert agreed.

Hope took another step backward, but could not take her eyes off her mother. Her hair was radiant, sparkling blond, and seemed to move in a slow-motion wind. Her skin was white, with a faint bluish undertone; her eyes burned in their sockets. Her lips were a moist red, and when she parted them, she revealed the silvery teeth of the bad thing from Hope's visions. The wound around her heart began bleeding, as if the sudden movements the corpse was making had reopened the wound that Hope and her brother had just healed.

Kate held her hand out to her daughter. Her voice was guttural, and only faintly her mother's. "Hope. Come to me. I love you."

"No," Hope gasped, backing away from her mother's arms.

Lex hugged Loretta around the waist as she continued to shout "Amen!" to her beloved god incarnate. Lex whispered, "Is it really?"

Loretta, tears in her eyes, said, "Alleluia. From the dark sea, the tide arises."

Kate Stewart, her voice garbled as if a tape were being mangled in playback, said, "All my children."

Stephen Grace pressed the button on the Uni, and a thin line of pure red light shot from it across the room, burning into Robert Stewart's arm.

Stewart was so transfixed, watching the creature that had once been his wife turn from Hope toward Loretta Swink, that he barely acknowledged the burn of his right forearm. He gripped it with his left hand.

Jesus, Grace thought, *the pain in his arm must be unbearable! But look at him: it's as if it were a slight bruise!*

The paingod opened its mouth as if to speak, but there was only a sound like rushing wind from the back of the dead woman's throat.

"It ain't taking, damn it, Birdy," Loretta said. "It ain't taking. We're gonna lose Cthonos, damn it all."

Grace grabbed Hope, holding her tight by the wrist. Hope offered no resistance. She had not stopped watching this thing in her mother, the demon that she had put there.

"You must be the assassin I've spoken with," Robert said, his face still registering the awe of what his two offspring had done. "There's no need to shoot. You will harm only the children."

Fletcher McBride led Ben Farrell around to the Swinks' back porch. "Lotsa ways into the 'combs, but this is the easiest. Don't want to go through the mission house. Never know how that's booby-trapped."

"What's to keep *this* place from being booby-trapped,

too?" Ben asked nervously as he pressed the screen door open. Apparently people didn't lock their doors in Empire, no matter what.

Fletcher pressed the blunt side of his hand ax against his forehead in thought. He shrugged his shoulders. "Never thought of that." He led Ben into the house. It smelled of flour and cooling berry pies, not of the blood and carnage that Ben had half expected.

Cthonos is just plain folks.

Just inside the kitchen Fletcher whistled for Ben to follow. "Down there." Fletcher pointed to the Dutch door to the root cellar.

Ben switched the gun Kermit had given him from one hand to the other. He glanced at the small ax in Fletcher's hand. Would these weapons be enough?

"In the olden days," Fletcher said, "men would go into battle like wild animals on a kill." He made an after-you gesture, but Ben shook his head.

Ben said, "Berserkers first."

What happened next went slowly in the minds of those in the Pain Room, but it was all over in a matter of seconds.

We shall all be changed in a moment.

In the twinkling of an eye.

Poppy tried to move from the spot she felt rooted in, but a terrible dread had overtaken her, like the memory of her childhood. She gazed at the creature that had once been Kate Stewart, and felt a river of ice flow through her veins. She didn't even see the dead woman's body. Instead, she saw the god Cthonos for what it was, the paingod who had been there when she was sliced open as a young girl on that very table. The god had appeared, with its glowing eyes, dribbling saliva from its mouth across Poppy's face as her brother tore her tongue out.

She had hoped that she would never see those eyes again.

"Gaa," she moaned, reaching a hand out as if to touch the dead woman from across the room.

"Risen," Loretta said, one hand stroking Lex's sparse hair, the other on her heart as if taking the Pledge of Allegiance, "as Justice predicted. 'Suffer the children to come to me,' said the tormented one as he suffered in the darkness of the cave of death, 'and there, in the purity of their torture, shall be my release from the abyss.' It's written, inspired by divinity in the Book of Cthonos."

The dead woman turned toward Loretta, as if understanding the words she said.

"Mama?" It was the boy's voice.

Poppy knew that voice, too.

A boy long dead, his hands hacked off.

"Harly?" Loretta said, "is that you, Harly?"

"Mama?" Kate's corpse moved slowly, deliberately, as if just learning how to walk. "Mama? Why'd you cut 'em off? My hands, Mama? Why'd you do it?"

"Harly? My baby? I knew you were on the other side. I knew it. Oh, Harly, my perfect little boy." Loretta spread her arms wide to welcome the dead woman to her bosom. Lex moved away from his grandmother and stood back near the door opposite Stephen Grace. He was shivering; his skin took on a molten quality, and the skin that had melted partway over his left eye seemed to melt farther down the side of his cheek.

Kate fell against Loretta, who let out a scream of absolute pain.

"Paingod," Lex said, his eyes opening wide in terror.

Kate bit into Loretta's neck, tearing at the flesh. Her teeth flashed silver and red as whatever occupied her body continued squeezing Loretta's head. Loretta tried fighting, but the creature was too strong, and the older woman's arms were snapped in two like twigs. Blood poured from Loretta's eyes, ears, nose, and mouth—and then the screaming stopped.

Then the creature dropped Loretta's dead body to the floor.

It flashed its grin to Lex. "Come to me, child," it said.

Lex turned and fled down through the catacombs.

The corpse of Hope's mother followed the boy, calling out now in Loretta Swink's voice, "Lexy? Angel? Wait for Grandma! Grandma's coming for you, angel!"

Robert said to Poppy, "Even you. You've seen the radiance of Cthonos before. It was all leading toward this, sister. Life and death, conquered. Religion and science, together, bringing life where there was death. Light where there was darkness."

Poppy shook her head, tears in her eyes. "Buhh," she muttered.

"That's right. I'm your brother Birdy. I've missed you, sister. All the games we used to play together, all of us— you, me, Monkey, Harly. The love we shared." Robert watched his mother's body continue to writhe, even though she could not have survived the attack. "Cthonos does not kill, you see, sister. There is no death in the realm of pain. Only redemptive suffering. You remember, Poppy, how you crossed the threshold of pain, into the divine light of the mysteries."

Poppy wrinkled her face up, about to cry, but then the sorrow turned to anger, as if she felt the pain anew as she stood before him. She darted across the room, more agile than she had ever felt, as if this were a moment in time at which she would not have a second chance. She reached for Robert's arm, where he was burned, and twisted it hard. He watched her with a bemused expression.

"I don't feel physical pain," he said. "It has been my abnormality since birth. A miracle in itself. You knew that, surely."

Grace said, "So you tortured others. A voyeur."

Dr. Stewart glanced from Poppy to Grace.

Poppy dug her mangled fingers into her brother's flesh.

Robert felt her voice inside him.

Birdy, what you did to us, what you and your mother did, you will pay, you will pay!

"You stupid cunt," Robert snarled. "Do you really think that you can come up against any of us?" He pushed her back against the examining table. With his free hand, he slapped her so hard across the face that his hand seemed to sink into her skin.

Hope wriggled out of Grace's grasp; he felt a shock in his hand where he had held her. He looked at his hand—there were blisters as if from a burn. He experienced a momentary confusion, as if his brains were, briefly, scrambled and his thoughts could not connect with each other in any coherent way.

Hope ran to her father and stood between him and Poppy. "You killed Mommy. You did that to Denny. You made him like that. And you did this to me." She felt something in the dark of her eye, and rather than resist it the way she normally would, she let it ride. It grew rapidly, the electric current running somewhere at the front of her head, and she could see from that empty socket; she could see her father for what he really was: *disease, all disease. Deathgiver*.

"Pigeon," her father said, bending down on one knee, "you have a gift. It's wonderful. It's beyond mortality."

Disease. Her mind twisted like a tornado, and she blotted out all other thoughts as she remembered her mother's dead body, and what he had just made her do, bringing it back with that evil inside it. She recalled what he had done to her mother all those years—the drugs, the dependency, the lies, and what he had done to Denny who had been such a beautiful, loving baby, how her father had warped him with his experiments, and how she too was warped and cursed and partially blinded because of his madness. *Disease—all disease.* She felt the diseases coursing through her bloodstream, cancer, leukemia, diabetes, the flu, the illnesses of the world. She remembered the story of Pandora, and she felt that she was opening the box, her gift from the gods, unleashing it all, taking aim for one target and one alone, the man she had spent her life calling Daddy but who she knew was never her father, not if he could do to his family what he had done.

Disease, all disease—sickness, imperfection, living death.

And then she felt an enormous pain in her empty socket, and she smelled something burning.

Robert Stewart felt the first of it as if he was beginning to run a temperature, and it rose rapidly until he was sweating. He loosened his collar, still not sure what was happening.

It occurred to him that this was Hope's work only when he felt the swelling in his lymphatic system, first along his neck. *Hope* ... She was using her power in a way he hadn't imagined, and if it hadn't been directed at him, it might have made him proud.

Then his throat became dry, and he could feel a rash breaking out along his stomach and chest; growths emerged under his arms, and he felt a pain in his head, just as if a tumor were growing so fast that it would cause his skull to explode.

He looked at his hands: they were swelling up to twice their normal size, and row upon row of blisters rippled up from his skin, bursting with pus and blood.

"Pigeon," he said, but he felt his blood change, and searing pain cut through his nervous system as his spine curved, and he hunched over as if an enormous weight had been dropped on his shoulders.

Robert began clawing at his throat with his swollen fingers, as if there were something caught in it. His entire body was covered with open, dripping sores that steamed.

And then his eyes bled across his face like two large round perfect tears.

Hope stood triumphant, as she watched her father melt into steamy flesh and bone.

Poppy reached forward and touched Hope's shoulder.

Hope heard her say, *You have done right. I must go and find the boy, Lex. For none must be allowed to escape.*

Poppy crossed over the still twisting body of her brother, and headed off into the catacombs.

Farther back in the dark passage, Fletcher said, "Wait, wait." He reached back and grabbed Ben, pulling him by the shoulder into one of the chambers.

Ben was about to speak when something rushed past them in the darkness.

"What?"

Fletcher waited a few seconds, then drew Ben back out onto the path that was lit with flares. "It was a devil," he said. He pointed down one of the corridors with his ax. "This way."

Stephen Grace grabbed Hope's arm again. "We have to get out of here, kid."

"Who're you?"

He could tell she was the bravest human being in the world, to have seen all this and to still remain sane. Only a child could have done it.

"Just call me Shadow."

"Are you death?"

Stephen Grace said nothing.

The girl said, "I want to die. I saw you fire that thing in your hand. I want you to kill me."

Stephen Grace felt it, that same wind of inspiration he'd felt when he was reborn, just hours ago. Something about life, how precious it could be. And then he remembered, looking at the girl—the car wreck, dying, her breath on his cheek.

She had crawled over to him in the wreckage, her breath on his cheek, breathing life into him.

She had brought him back from death then, when he was on a mission to kill her. And in doing so, she had made him immortal, perhaps.

She had given life to the one who would have taken it away from her.

"I can't kill you," he said.

"Please," she said. "Kill me."

"No," he said, "never."

Stephen Grace lifted Hope up into his arms, hugging her tight, as he carried her through the doorway of the Pain Room, into darkness, away from that well-lighted place.

Ben Farrell heard a noise down one of the corridors. He turned to Fletcher. "Is that them?"

Fletcher sniffed the air and cocked his head to the side, as if listening carefully. "Nope. It's the wrong them. If we're looking for the Beast girl, she's there, to the right. See that light? She's there."

Ben went ahead of Fletcher, brandishing his gun as he headed toward the white light of a room up ahead.

Someone blocked his way, enshrouded in darkness.

Then, as his eyes adjusted, Ben saw who it was.

"You're dead," he said, feeling an overwhelming mental confusion.

But there he stood, the man whom Kate had shot full of holes just before sunrise.

The man whose breathing he had checked.

"Hey," Stephen Grace joked, "anything can happen."

Clinging to Grace's arm: Hope.

"Let her go," Ben said, pointing the sheriff's gun at Grace, "or I'll kill you. I mean, *really* kill you."

Stephen Grace stood his ground. "Two things, Farrell. First off, I have no intention of hurting this child again. And second, you can't kill me. I'm already dead. She brought me back. Her mother tried to kill me a second time, but it didn't actually work. Now there's no time. What I know is this: Special Projects will be in this town shortly, either to dispose of the bodies or to kill us, I don't know which. But we have to get Hope as far away from here as possible or they will put her back into a living hell. You choose."

Ben lowered the gun. "Where's Kate?"

"Dead," Hope said, "and he's telling the truth, Ben." She let go of Stephen Grace's hand and went to Ben.

But Ben Farrell had slipped off somewhere inside his own head, taking a vacation from reality. His eyes blankly stared at Hope, as if the shock had finally hit and his mind had shut down.

Fletcher McBride said, "Aw, man, I didn't even get to use my ax. Well, come on, folks, nothing to gawk at. Let's get this fool up and out. We got the sheriff waiting and some crazed teen-ager, and a heap of dead bodies out in the light of day."

As they followed Fletcher through the flare-lit catacombs, Stephen Grace said a prayer for Poppy, wherever she was down here, chasing whatever phantom or whatever child eluded her.

She had never left the dark closet of her childhood.

When they emerged into daylight, from the root cellar in Loretta Swink's house, Grace heaved a sigh of relief as if it were something he'd forgotten how to do.

"It's a room," Hope said, clutching Ben's hand as they walked out onto the lawn alongside the house.

'What's that?' Grace asked.

"Death is a room. And it's dark. And there's a light switch somewhere, but it takes you a while to find it. Maybe some people never find it. Maybe everyone finds it. I kinda don't know. I hope my mom found it."

"I bet she did," Grace said.

Hope shook her head. "Nope. She isn't out there. She's here." Hope softly patted the palm of her hand against her chest. "She's in this room."

Ben Farrell's face was stone, but tears had welled up in his eyes. "Wind's blowing strong," he said.

It was, and Stephen Grace looked away from his companions, across the vineyard. The wind brought the sweet smell of things growing, growing, even with winter coming on. Small miracles. From this girl to the grasses turning with the wind, to the thought of immortality. If that was what this was. Maybe it was something worse, something that could use a great deal of study.

Grace glanced back to Ben. He was numb; Grace could tell. He'd seen it in soldiers in the jungle battlefield and in women on the streets of Bangkok; he'd seen it in his reflection in a silver pond in his late teens when he'd decided to desert his battalion and live in the mud and green confusion of Vietnam. That was the dark room of death: that numb feeling, those cold invisible arms that entwined about your shoulders and snaked into your mouth. That was the real experiment of terror, facing the stark reality of human brutality. The monkey in us, the screaming monkey with a face so familiar we dare not even name it.

But the name of the monkey is man. All of evolution, a reaching upward, forward, and yet we are still of the dirt from which we came. We still mindlessly pursue pain and cruelty in exchange for the abstract notion of progress.

"When they try to sell you a war," Grace said, "make sure you don't buy it, Hope. The idea of a war sounds fine, even noble. But the reality is this town, and every town. The end of things. The dark room. The pain room, sometimes."

Hope said, "A war?"

"It's coming," Stephen Grace said.

"But, Shadow . . . why?"

He couldn't tell her. How was he to tell this little girl that it was her, and whatever was out there, still. Whatever madness, named Lex, that still breathed beneath the ground, exhaling the fumes of r-7 synthesis, turning whatever was in his path into the living death, the future plague of mankind, would not be stopped with burial. Or death.

And yet it had to be stopped.

There's got to be a way.

There's got to be.

"Your name," he said.

"Hope?"

"That's what there is. And always there is some of it, so long as you and I and Ben are up and breathing."

"Well, then, we're safe. Because you won't ever die and leave me."

Stephen Grace studied her face: dirty, beaten, her hair greasy and matted wildly, her skin sallow, her eye twitching from nerves and stress.

I am no better than Cthonos, Grace thought, *no better than the mad doctor or my buddies at Projects.*

Because he knew that he would have to stop her, somehow. Maybe not through death. But what was in her had to be changed. Altered. She was too dangerous.

This girl who had saved him.

This girl who had been so brave and kind.

But she still had the bomb inside her, ticking.

Ticking.

If he could not get the brother, he would have to get her. He wasn't sure how. He didn't have the tools, at least not in his pockets. It would not be death that would stop this, but it would have to be something. "Don't ever let them sell you a war," he repeated, saddened.

Her face was not sad, in spite of her great loss. But she looked at him with curiosity, as if she detected something like a shift in the wind's direction.

He attempted a smile.

"I won't," she said. "But don't let it start, Shadow, not again. Do what you need to do to not let it start up." She looked wise beyond her years as she said this, and he wondered if she knew what effect her words had on him.

She knows, he thought.

We are enemies and friends, Hope. We know the way, the narrow path, don't we? And we go off the path sometimes, because we're weak and we don't always see straight, but here and now you and I will acknowledge that path, and it is the right path. It is the path that requires sacrifice, but it is still the path that is headed toward that light switch in the dark room.

"I won't hurt you, ever," he promised.

She said nothing.

Ben Farrell was still watching the western horizon, feeling the damp wind and the first raindrops. He was a child now, and Hope was all grown up; now she would need to take care of him.

"Where do you think he is?" Stephen Grace asked her.

She grasped Ben's hand and squeezed it carefully, as if making sure that he still had the pulse of life in him. Ben smiled at her, tears still in his eyes. "Somewhere safe. He needs to rest. Maybe he'll be fine then."

Grace nodded. "The Corvette," he suggested. "It's not the most comfortable place, but . . ."

She said, "No. Ben needs a bed. He needs some care."

"You don't want to stay here."

"It doesn't matter what I want sometimes. Ben needs rest."

"The wind," Ben said.

"He needs rest," she repeated.

They went back to the Greenwater Motor Lodge. It was 11:20 A.M. Shadow checked the rooms to make sure the motel really was vacant, but Hope knew it was. There was a body in one of the rooms, but Shadow told her it wasn't moving at all, and he locked that room up, just so, he told her, he didn't have to think about it.

She knew what he meant. The face. What happened to the face was sometimes worse than what happened to the body, the way the skin split around the nose and the mouth and the eyes, like tiny hooks were pulling it apart. She shuddered, but the crawling fear passed. She had to think about Ben now, not about herself. He would tell her to not be afraid of the dark, that's what he would do, and now she would have to listen to that advice. She would have to keep the lights on, though, because it was hard, sometimes, not to fear the dark.

The motel room, like the one she and her mother had stayed in just two days earlier, was green and gray, and the water ran brown from the tap. She sat Ben down on one of the double beds. She helped him take his shoes off.

He said, "I'm not really tired. I could drive all night."

She brought the roll of toilet paper out from the bathroom and tore off a section. She held the tissue to his eyes and dabbed at his cheeks and at the tears that had fallen from the corners of his eyes.

"He's a strong man," Shadow told her from the open doorway, "Remember that. This means he is a strong man."

"I know," she said. "Will you guard the door for me?"

"All right," he told her, "but only for a half hour."

"I'm going to heal him," Hope said, with conviction in her voice.

Ben crawled under the covers, muttering about having to find his beeper because someone important might call. Hope placed her hand against his forehead while he rested.

Stephen Grace stood in the doorway.

The wind blew stronger, and light rain came down.

Blessed rain.

Sheriff Kermit Stone found Grace. The motel's light was the only light left on in Empire. Kermit was driving a truck he'd borrowed. "I got it from the Eaton family," he said. "I suppose they won't be needing it."

"They're still out there," Stephen Grace said. They shared a cigarette.

"Who?"

"The 'us' part of 'them.' Special Projects. The roads'll still be cut off on every side."

"We could just stay here till we starve."

"It won't be that long. They've got their engines idling. My guess is they'll hunt us down any minute. I know. I've done it myself."

"Why haven't they come down yet?"

"There must be a signal. You got to figure that those kids out there, with their Jeeps and trucks and guns and army surplus uniforms, must be shitting bricks, wondering what the hell is happening. My guess is, like all good Special Projects operations, Holder gave them a freeze. Either they get this signal or they drop their bombs within an hour or two."

"I still don't see how they can do this. I mean Caliente and Perdito both's gonna know about it. Hell, they may know already."

Stephen Grace shook his head, dropping the last of the cigarette on the asphalt, stubbing it out with his shoe. "They don't know. It's only been a few hours since the roadblocks went up, and given the weather and the power outages, I have no doubt this went down easy with a word or two to the local politicians. Projects is like another word for pathological lying. They hired me, and I got to tell you, Kermit, I got a history of insanity that dates back to 1967. They do things their own way. Holder's probably got some kind of rumor out about radiation by now. Who knows? The asshole thinks on his feet. I wish I had those brains. Between my fists."

"Here's one man who's happy you don't."

Then Grace grew a little serious. "Any sign of the others?"

Kermit shrugged. "No. None. Bram told me he saw some children, but when I searched, I only found dead ones. Maybe there are some folks hiding out. More power to 'em. I say we get out while we can. We can take a four-wheel-drive—I think there's a Bronco up at the Hawkins place—and just go through the fields and stay off the roads."

"They'll be looking for us to do that. Their orders will be to shoot anyone resisting arrest. Shoot to kill."

After a moment Kermit said, "we are the lucky ones."

"How's that?"

"Immortality—maybe. We're intact. No spine thrashing. We're either infected or immune from that godawful sickness, right?"

"Maybe. The survival instinct seems to get stronger, too, have you noticed? Like, for all the shit that comes down, life still seems sacred. Maybe even *more* sacred."

Kermit leaned against the wall and let out what he would have called a "big ol' sigh."

"There's one other way to go," he said, as if admitting defeat.

"I figured there was," Grace said.

"I just hate the idea of it. If anything's still there ..."

"Well, we'll take some fire and some axes, and we'll pretend we're leaving East Berlin for West Berlin, like in the olden days, before we were our own enemy."

"Ah," Kermit said, "the olden days, when day was day and night was night."

"How far do they go?"

"The 'combs? Well, back when I ran, in 1970, I got almost nine miles out of town before I came up out of them. Ended up near the sewage treatment plant about ten miles outside Paso Caliente. But it's like a maze down there; I s'pose Fletcher McBride'll know the way—he used to jump the fence at Empire State and hide out down there when he got hungry for chickens."

Stephen Grace looked at his watch. It was almost noon. One thing was still bothering him about Special Projects. It was the signal that the mad doctor was supposed to use to bring the reinforcements in when the experiment was over.

What if the signal had already been given?

12:00 noon

Five miles outside town, a man in an olive drab uniform turned to his superior and said, "The signal just came in, sir."

"Green or red?"

"Green, sir."

Silence.

"Green is for go, boys," the other man said. "Give the order for the men to put on their space suits and mow this sucker down."

Hope awoke suddenly. She'd fallen asleep for a few minutes without realizing it. Shadow stood over her, and his eyes were wide. He seemed frantic. Ben was just waking up, too, and Shadow said to her, "We don't have any time. They're coming out of the fucking hills, Patch, out of the fucking hills."

Ben said, "I still don't trust him," and Hope knew that he was better if he could say that aloud.

Shadow glanced back at Ben. "I don't give a fuck who you trust. Just get up and let's get on the road."

Kermit pulled the Bronco up to the door of the room. In the back was Bram; next to the teenager sat Fletcher McBride, looking as wild-eyed as ever. Ben and Hope piled in back with them, and Stephen Grace got up front. Rain was coming down, and Grace took this as a good omen. It was cold rain. He thought for a moment, in spite of all this, *It's good to be alive.*

"Gonna rain fire," Fletcher said.

Bram groaned, already tired of Fletch's comments.

"It already did," Hope said, matter-of-factly.

"Then the Beast, whose number is—"

"Will you shut up, Fletch?" Kermit Stone snapped.

They were all silent as they drove out of the motel parking lot and up the road, then turned off onto the dirt road to the mission house. The rain came down harder; the sound was deafening; the sky was a dark blue-gray; there was no sign of life beyond them.

And then Grace said, "Wait."

Kermit brought the Bronco to a stop.

They heard the Jeeps and trucks rumbling down the Sand Canyon Road.

And then Ben pointed toward the mission house.

And the road beyond.

"They'll get there faster than we will," Ben said.

"Aw, man," Bram muttered, "just get me out of this town."

Fletch began misquoting the Bible to him.

Grace said, "Okay, Kermit, two things we can do. We can give ourselves up, or we can try to get into that house."

Kermit Stone shook his head as if he thought they were all idiots. He struck a match on the dashboard and lit a cigarette. "Or we can detonate a bomb."

Stephen Grace didn't have much time to think; he looked at Hope. She had told him, while they came up through the catacombs, that when she was with Lex and her father, she had felt as if she were being raped. She didn't know what rape was, not yet, but it felt all bad to her the way she thought it might be. How could he put her through that intentionally?

She looked so small, so tired. So much like a little girl then, not like the threat that she could be.

As if reading his thoughts, she said, "I won't do it, anyway. I have control now. No one can make me. You said no wars, right?"

Grace sighed. He looked out across the vineyard.

The trucks were coming up the road slowly. The Special Projects military unit was still checking out the streets.

"They're going to have to have some kind of contamination-resistant suits on," Grace said. "They think this is a plague. Some of those boys are only twenty, twenty-one. They'll be more scared of us than we are of them—if we play our cards right. Maybe we can run for it—not all of us, but Ben and Hope and Bram. You'll need Fletch, too, 'cause he's the only one who knows the way out."

Fletcher McBride giggled almost childishly.

Grace looked at the four in the back of the Bronco and said, "Get out now and get down to that house. We'll run interference."

After the others had gotten out of the car and started running, Grace said, "And you and me, Sheriff."

Kermit Stone grinned. He'd been grinning a lot since he'd come back from his fear of death at the hands of Cthonos, and Grace figured maybe it was because he'd lived in some kind of fear all his life, and now, in his second chance, he'd decided to let the world do its worst; he was going to enjoy the rest of his days. *Eternity.*

Kermit said, "Just like an Old West shoot-out."

"Well," Grace said, "I was thinking more along the lines of a good football game. You be the quarterback, and I'll play receiver."

"How's that?"

Grace brought the Uni out from his coat pocket. "You ever use one of these?"

"Only in my dreams."

"Well, it's easier than programming a VCR, I'll tell you that. What I want you to do is aim this at me and kill me as soon as these boys get close."

"And then what?"

Stephen Grace shrugged. "We'll wing it. They'll open fire on you, and you may get some lead in you. Who knows? Maybe they'll give you a fucking medal for killing me. Whichever happens, we'll get them to take us in."

"I don't want to get dissected."

"But we're vampires now, Kermit, only we don't even have to play by the vampire rules. They can't kill us—we've been exposed and we've survived. They don't know that yet. I doubt Stewart told Projects much of his real intention for his experiments. Hell, Stewart may not even have been aware of the results. And once we get inside Special Projects, let me tell you, I am going to take care of the man responsible."

The trucks came up on either side of the road. Grace

noted that they hadn't spotted the three men and the girl moving low to the ground, toward the mission house.

You're almost there, Patch. I'll say good-bye now, finally. If we both get through this, you and I may have business together again someday. Both you and I know it's got to be done. But I will make sure no harm comes to you until then.

He could see the faces of the boys driving the truck up from the end of the road; they wore head coverings and masks, but their eyes were sharp, and they had their weapons out.

He and Kermit got out of the Bronco, in the rain. He showed Kermit which button to push on the Uni.

"Other way, Kermit," he said. "You're gonna knock your socks off if you do it like that."

"You sure this won't hurt, Grace?"

Stephen Grace felt the beating rain upon his scalp and took a deep breath. He could hear the shouts of the men as they unloaded from the truck ahead of them. He heard the men behind them, too, but he looked up to the sky and thanked the Creator for such an interesting life, one that might go on as far as the sky. *Or who knows? It might end right here. What the hell.*

"It'll hurt," Stephen Grace told Kermit Stone, "but not as bad as the first time."

Kermit looked at him hesitantly.

The Special Projects boys were getting closer.

Stephen Grace said, *"Now!"*

He saw the sky change colors, from the darkness to a pale blue light, and then he thought he saw a rainbow. He heard gunfire and shouts from all around him, but it became the voice of a child telling him not to be afraid of the dark, and a door of wonder opening onto orange and yellow butterflies.

His thought: *Let her be safe.*

"This side," Ben said as he guided the others around to the side door of the mission house. Bram walked with Hope into the front room; they could clearly see the trucks parked out on the road, and when the gunfire erupted, Hope cried out.

"They haven't seen us yet," Bram told her. She could tell that he was fighting off tears, just as she was.

Fletcher McBride pointed down a hallway. "We can take the stairs down below."

When they were down in the underground, Hope saw the three paths that were still lit with the flares that had been set out. She wondered which one *they* were still in—her brother and the paingod that had stolen her mother's body.

Fletcher McBride sniffed the air. He took a few steps down each path. Then he returned to where the three others stood. "This one." He pointed to the path in the middle. There were bodies and bones lying at its entrance. Children. Sacrifices to Cthonos.

As she stepped over them, Hope tried to pretend they were just stones and rocks in a stream. Ben took up all the flares as they went.

"Use this as a torch," he told her, handing her one. "Be careful, it can burn, but not if you hold it out like this." He demonstrated for her. She held it in front of her with both hands.

"Let's go," she said, and looked ahead, through the dark tunnels, wondering which path would take them to the right place, and away from this tomb.

Beneath the ground in what had once been the Pain Room, a man named Birdy felt his flesh melting further, and he remembered being a boy, when his mother would fix him a grilled cheese sandwich, and how she sometimes burned his hand with the hot slices of Kraft American cheese, and how this was so much like that, only he knew it would never end, that he would never really die because he had exposed himself to his own creation, and he would live out eternity in a bubbling mass of sores and never-ending disease while his spine battered the stone floor.

Others, there beneath the earth, died with him, endlessly.

"Don't hurt the boy named Lex," Nathan Holder spoke into the mouthpiece of the radio. The helicopter flew above the burning wreck of Empire, although the rain had stemmed the spread of the fire through most of the town. He could not see much for the billowing smoke. "I want to meet with him. I want to talk with him. If any of your men harm so much as a hair on his head, it will be a long time in hell for all concerned."

EPILOGUE

In Winter

From Holder's taped interview with Lex Talionis

"Are you happy here, Lex?"

"Not really."

"What can I do to make you happier?"

"I don't know."

"You know, Lex, we are a kind of corporation, but even so, we care about you. The way corporations show they care is to jump through hoops. What hoops do you want me to jump through?"

"Hoops?"

"Special things you like. In particular."

"I want my father."

"I'm your father now, Lex. You'll see. In time."

"You're ... my father?"

"I've adopted you. I have a big farm back in Maryland, with lots of horses and dogs. You'll like it."

"Can we leave this place?"

"After a few more tests."

"I want one other thing."

"Anything."

"I want to make her hurt real bad."

"Who?"

"My sister. It was all her fault. She did it."

"Do you know where she is?"

"No. But I'm gonna find her someday. And make her hurt. Real bad. I'm gonna put her someplace where she ain't gonna get out of, and then I'm gonna make her hurt like I hurt! Like she hurt my grandma and my daddy!"

Ben would need to work soon, Hope realized. They were running out of money, and he couldn't contact his newspaper in San Francisco, because he was afraid the Company would be breathing down the necks of the editors at the *Trib*. She had a great-aunt in Kentucky, and she had memorized her address because Aunt Janie had sent postcards and gifts ever since Hope could remember, and she'd had to write so many thank-you cards back. So, while Ben went down to the beach one morning to fish for breakfast, she sat in the motel room and wrote her aunt a brief note asking for some money.

At the end of it, she added, "Please don't tell anyone where we are. I know there was a story in the papers and on TV, but it was not true. Maybe the part about the contamination is sort of true, but I was there, and the rest is phony. I know you understand because Dr. Stewart used to call you the radical nut from the hills, and you had different ideas about things than the rest of my family. I will write again when I can. We will probably be here another two weeks, so I hope you respond quickly. Thank you, and love from your niece, Hope."

Hope and Ben had been in Baja since early December, and she enjoyed the weather and the rest. She felt as if she were waiting for something to happen, and the weird thing was, nothing had occurred. No one had come for them, and she wondered if perhaps they'd been written off. Ben wasn't so sure, and told her that until they could figure out who to trust back in the States, they were better off staying put and enjoying the ocean.

But she sensed that something was wrong and that Ben wasn't quite seeing it. She had learned to control the power inside her. She knew now that it was some kind of mutation of a bacteria from space—not from heaven, like Dr. Stewart had said, but from someplace where, maybe, it was good for that place, but it didn't belong here on earth.

She mailed the letter in town and walked over to a cart to get a churro. She hated spending the money, but she was hungry, and the churros looked so good that she couldn't resist. She looked at the man in the straw hat, and he seemed friendly. Hope had a hard time not looking into him to see if he had some sickness to be healed. She hated not being able to, but knew that her cures didn't always work out for the best for people. But as she stood there eating her churro, she felt something.

Something beyond the man, and she looked around him and saw a crowd of people gathered in the *zócalo*. It was a market day, and they would be selling their crafts and foods. Usually she and Ben would wander through the square and see what wonderful things were available.

But she sensed something.

Somewhere, among that crowd, a wild animal.

Hope Stewart turned away quickly, almost dropping her churro, and hurried back to the motel room.

She found Ben on the beach, already cooking the shark he had caught in a skillet over a small fire.

"Someone's here," she said.

He glanced up from the fire, catching her meaning. "You're sure?"

"I don't know. I got that feeling. But I didn't see anybody. Nobody I recognized, anyway."

Neither of them could say it: *Cthonos*.

Ben said, "Of course they're in a lot of places. And some of them know. I just didn't think we'd run into them so soon. I thought we'd meet another Special Projects guy first."

"I won't use it, not even on them. I made a vow. Even if I get hurt."

"You're gonna find, Hope, that sometimes people break vows for good reasons. It won't be you they hurt. It'll be someone else. Someone you care about. Who knows? They may have caught Fletcher or Bram by now."

Hope went around and sat next to him. He put his arm around her. They watched the skillet and the fire.

"I want to just rest," she said.

"I know."

"Shadow promised me he would watch out for me. Sorta like my guardian angel."

"Don't be afraid, Hope."

She sighed. "I guess I'm not. Not really. I miss Mom."

"So do I. So do I."

"I wish I could change everything. I wish I could make it different."

He hugged her tight, and she looked across the beach to the seagulls as they dived straight down into the glassy sea, and then, even farther out, she watched a fishing boat as it gently rocked back and forth on the water.

She wondered if Shadow was somewhere nearby, watching over her like he'd promised.

Leaning against the bow of the small boat, the gringo in shorts turned to the fisherman and said, "I think I found what I wanted."

He set the binoculars down.

The fisherman, named Gabriel Aguirre, shook his head. "No, señor, this isn't good fishing. Up near the rocks we'll find better."

The gringo smiled; he was already sunburned, and Gabriel wondered about this man with lots of money but not much common sense. What kind of fish was this tourist after? The gringo said, "Not today. Not for me. I don't want to catch anything."

The tourist was paying for the boat that day, and paying quite a bit, more than Gabriel had wanted to charge, so he just shrugged and sat down and lit a cigarette. Let the man do what he wanted with his money, his time.

"You've been in a war?" Gabriel asked.

The tourist glanced down at the scars. "A few of them."

"You must be indestructible."

"Yes." The other man laughed, still watching the shoreline. "You could say that."

Gabriel looked in the direction of the man's gaze, but saw nothing on the beach before them but a few scattered people and gulls. "Me, I'm not much for war," he said. "In war, I think, you die a little yourself. I've seen it in some men."

"Do you see that in me?"

"Yes. Only . . ." Gabriel hesitated.

"Only?"

"Only you've come back. You've returned from that death. You found something to live for."

"Yes, yes, I have. It's here. On that beach."

"So your interest was never fishing. That's good. A man must have something to live for." He said this casually, as if just thinking it for the first time.

The tourist with the battle scars looked carefully at Gabriel, and said, "Yes, he must. Something to live for."

The man with the scars watched the shore until the sun grew too bright; the sand and the sea were one in the brilliant radiance of the day. It was not possible to see anything at a distance for the blinding light, but the man kept watch as if he could see all, clearly, with perfect sight.